DARK MAFIA BRIDE

AN ARRANGED MARRIAGE, SECRET BABY ROMANCE

MAFIA VOWS
BOOK 2

KAYLA MASON

Copyright © 2024 by Kayla Mason

All rights reserved.

No part of this book may be reproduced in any form or by any electronic or mechanical means, including information storage and retrieval systems, without written permission from the author, except for the use of brief quotations in a book review.

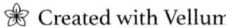 Created with Vellum

1

MIRABELLA

The rain pours down in thick, relentless sheets, drenching me as I trudge along the cracked sidewalk. I yank my jacket collar higher, but it's pointless—I'm already soaked to the bone, down to my underwear.

My feet squish with each step inside my everyday shoes —my suede flats— which are slowly being ruined by the downpour. *Just great*, I think. The last thing I need right now is the extra expense of replacing them, even though they're long past their prime.

A shiver rips through me, and I mutter a bitter curse under my breath. I've been forced to smile all night at this awful new job. I can barely stomach it, serving drinks to drunken men, pretending to be polite even when their hands wander where they shouldn't. But I don't have the luxury of quitting. With a mountain of debt crushing me, I'll take any job no matter how degrading just to scrape together enough to pay everything off.

I tighten my grip on the strap of my bag as I approach the alley ahead. My knuckles throb from the pressure, and a flicker of unease crawls down my spine as I reach the entrance of the shortcut.

It's clearly a bad idea to do this. The alley is narrow and dark—dangerous at this hour—but I need to make it to the bus before it leaves, or I'll be stuck standing in the rain for another thirty minutes.

As I step into the alley, I glance over my shoulder, a strange prickle of anxiety gnawing at me. There's no one there—just the steady rhythm of raindrops splashing against the pavement. Still, something feels off.

I'm halfway through the narrow path when shadows shift ahead of me. My heart plummets as three figures step out of the darkness as if they've been lying in wait.

Abruzzi's men.

They move with a swagger that says they own this city, and in a way, they do. Abruzzi has eyes everywhere, and nothing happens without his knowing about it. I understand this because the few times I've met him, he always seems to be aware of even the most inconspicuous details about me—things I believe I hide very well. He knows the thoughts I'm about to voice, and at times he even articulates exactly what I'm thinking.

The three men close in on me, all clad in black, their leather coats slick with rainwater.

One of them flashes a cold, empty grin that doesn't reach his eyes. "Well, well. Look who we have here."

He's the leader of the three, tall and lanky, with a crooked grin that makes my skin crawl. I know him all too well. He's one of Abruzzi's personal righthand men and the person I'd met on the unfortunate day I foolishly stepped into their underground loan shark operation. Back then, I was naïve, clueless about the mess I was getting myself into.

I had no idea that borrowing money would mean crossing paths with a dangerous, sketchy man like Abruzzi.

My body freezes, my heart pounding in my ears. But I don't show it. "I told Abruzzi I needed more time."

"Time's up, sweetheart." His voice is as slick as oil on water, and it takes everything in me not to visibly shudder.

My pulse races, the icy rain somehow feeling even colder against my skin. I square my shoulders, forcing steel into my voice. "I told him I'm working on it. He'll get his money. When have I ever backed out on a promise?"

The leader steps closer, his shadow looming over me. "Yeah, see, that's the problem. Promises don't cut it with the boss anymore. He wants his cash. Now."

"I just need a little more time," I plead, stepping back instinctively, but the three of them fan out, blocking my exit, trapping me in the narrow alley.

"How many times does he have to tell you?" growls the second guy, a thick-necked brute. "The boss gave you a favor by extending the deadline, but that favor's worn thin."

I grit my teeth, anger mixing with fear, my heart beating louder than ever. "I wasn't talking to you."

I realize what a stupid move that is when the leader's grin widens. His sunken eyes gleaming with amusement. "Feisty. I like that."

"Bet she's a wild one in bed." The third guy speaks for the first time. He's bald, buff, and clearly a bonehead. He flexes his muscles like a predator ready to pounce, and the others snicker.

Morons.

"Look," the leader drawls, his tone oozing false sympathy. "We don't wanna make this ugly. But ugly's always an option, y'know? Boss man ain't exactly known for his patience, and you're late. $20,000 too late. You know what happens to people who keep Abruzzi waiting?"

I swallow hard, trying to keep my voice steady, though my hands are trembling.

"He gets mad."

Those words still haunt me—the same ones he said when I stood in front of his imposing mahogany desk in that dimly lit office.

"Pay up early, pretty girl. Don't let me get mad."

"Bingo," the second guy chimes in as if this is some sick game. "Give the lady a prize."

The leader steps closer, his eyes glinting with something darker. "Maybe we don't gotta take it that far," he muses, his voice low and suggestive. "Maybe there's another way. Something...a little more in my favor."

I know exactly what he means, and my stomach churns. Bile rises in my throat as I instinctively back up, only for my foot to slip in a puddle. I stumble against the cold, wet brick wall of the alley. *Trapped.*

They close in on me, their laughter low and menacing. *This is bad. Really bad.*

"I-I'll get the money. I swear..."

"Of course you will," the second guy cuts in, smirking. "We just want a little payment for making us come all the way here to look for you."

My body shakes with fear, and I hate it. I hate how helpless I feel. How a desperate move to save my mother's life has led me straight into this nightmare.

The leader steps even closer, his cronies flanking him on either side, cutting off any escape. He reaches out, his fingers grazing my cheek. "Don't you worry, it'll be quick and painless," he whispers.

I clench my jaw, summoning whatever scraps of courage I can find. "You think I'm just going to let you?"

Their cruel laughter fills the narrow alley, echoing off the walls. "What're you gonna do, princess? Take us all on?" the leader taunts. "I'd love to see you try. May even make this a little more fun."

My hand tightens around the strap of my bag like it's some kind of shield, though it feels utterly useless. My mind races, searching for a plan, anything, but all I feel is the crushing weight of fear closing in.

And then, through the relentless pounding of the rain, I hear it—the low, unmistakable hum of an engine. The three men snap their heads toward the sound, and I know this is my only chance. My only way out.

Before they can react, I slam my knee into the leader's groin with every ounce of strength I have.

A groan escapes his lips as I tear myself from the wall, sprinting toward the alley's entrance. At least, I try to. Before I can take three steps, his large hand clamps down on my arm, yanking me back.

"You fucking bitch! Now you've gone and made a real big mistake," he snarls, slamming me hard against the wet brick wall.

The force knocks the wind out of me, and panic surges through my veins. I know in this moment there's no escape. He's mad now, and I'm completely trapped.

I bite back a sob as I feel his hand tighten around my arm as the other drifts downward, grazing my thigh. I want to scream, to fight back, but all that comes is a choked gasp. His hand creeps higher, brushing the hem of my dress just as the glare of headlights slices through the darkness.

"Who the fuck is that?" the leader snaps, his eyes narrowing.

I blink, focusing on the sleek black car now parked at the alley's mouth. The door swings open, and a man steps out. He's tall, broad-shouldered, and his perfectly tailored coat is immaculate despite the rain that has soaked through everything else.

There's something almost unnatural about how untouched he looks by the weather.

I can't properly make out his face as he steps in front of the car. All I can see is the silhouette of a tall man with long, curly hair that stops at his shoulders.

His face is hidden, swallowed by the light behind him. He moves with easy confidence, not caring about the rain soaking his pristine state. Every step deliberate and unhurried, as if he owns the very ground beneath his feet.

A chill slithers down my spine as I wait, unsure of what's coming next.

The second guy's face drains of color as soon as he spots him. And I don't know if that's a good or bad thing.

"Shit, Elia," he breathes. "It's The Reaper."

The Reaper? Who the hell is that?

The leader—Elia scowls, but even he can't hide the flicker of fear in his eyes. "What the fuck is he doin' here?"

I don't know who this man is, but the way they react tells me everything I need to know. This is no rescue, no guardian angel. He's here for something else, something darker.

The Reaper—or whatever ridiculous name they've given him—stalks toward us, his footsteps echoing on the wet pavement. His eyes, dark and unreadable, flick over me for the briefest of moments, but it's enough to make my skin prickle. His attention shifts to the men surrounding me, and the air in the alley thickens.

A sick silence falls. No one moves, no one speaks, but I can feel the weight of a decision hanging in the balance.

And then, without warning, he reaches inside his coat.

The tension snaps like a wire pulled too tight.

"You've got five seconds to walk away," he says to the men, his voice steady, almost bored. "Unless you want to end up dead."

He says it like he means it. The gravity of his words wraps around me like a shroud, and I exhale shakily as Elia's hand leaves my thigh. He squares up to The Reaper, his earlier bravado flickering back to life.

"We don't take no orders from you,"

The Reaper's lips curl into a slow, dangerous smile. "No? Pity."

Then everything unfolds in a heartbeat. A glint of metal catches the light, a swift slice cuts through the air, and in an instant, Elia clutches his neck, crimson gushing over his fingers.

"Fuck," One of the men screams, lunging toward The Reaper as the leader collapses to the ground.

I watch in a mix of horror and awe. This man embodies his nickname. He moves with the grace of a predator, lethal and precise. The sound of his knife carving through flesh blends with the relentless patter of rain.

The impact of fists on skin, the sickening crack of bones, the groans and curses—it's all brutal, efficient, and terrifyingly quick. Within moments, all three of Abruzzi's men lie sprawled across the wet pavement, lifeless, just as he had promised.

I stand frozen, my heart racing, staring at the lifeless bodies of the men who'd threatened to do unspeakable things to me just minutes ago. My chest heaves, the adrenaline coursing through my veins like wildfire.

The Reaper strides over the bodies as if they're nothing more than trash. He stops in front of me, his dark eyes gleaming under the streetlight. "You're welcome."

I feel a tumult of emotions—fear, relief, guilt—welling up inside me. Swallowing hard, I straighten my back, lifting my chin in defiance. "I didn't need your help."

Although his face remains partially obscured, I can make out the sharp angles of his jaw, the dark stubble that gives him an edge, and the subtle tilt of his lips as he smiles, a blend of arrogance and amusement.

"Is that right? Because from where I was standing, you were about five seconds from being raped."

Rape.

The word strikes me like a physical blow, stealing the breath from my lungs. I swallow hard, my heartbeat thundering in my ears as the reality of what could have happened sinks in.

I try to speak, but my voice fails me. He studies me in silence, inching closer with an air of casual confidence.

"I take it you were heading home from work," he drawls in a low voice.

I hate the sound of his voice—the way it makes my heart skip a beat. For some stupid reason, my brain stubbornly bypasses the fact that he just killed three men and focuses instead on the striking features of his face.

I glare up at him, trying to suppress the flutter in my stomach as I catch the dark glint in his eyes. "Why do you care? Why are you even here?"

His gaze sweeps over me, assessing every detail of my drenched skin as if he can see right through me. "I was bored."

A disbelieving chuckle escapes my lips. Of course, he

was. Whoever this man is, he's infinitely more dangerous than Abruzzi.

Before I can muster a retort, he grabs my hand—not roughly, but with enough firmness that I don't even think about resisting—and pulls me toward his car. "Come on."

"I'm not going anywhere with you."

His smirk returns, dangerous and enticing. "You're shivering. At least let me get you out of this rain before you freeze to death."

I don't argue this time, mostly because my body betrays me with a violent shiver. I follow his lead, doing a bad job at ignoring the way his skin feels against mine.

When we reach his car, he opens the passenger door for me to slip inside.

The warmth envelops me immediately, the leather seats plush beneath me. He slides in beside me, his presence filling the small space with an intensity that makes it hard to breathe. The heavy rain drums against the roof, and our breaths mingle in the confined air.

"I'll take you somewhere to warm up," he says, starting the engine. His voice is still smooth, but there's an edge of something darker lurking beneath the surface.

He drives me to a small, intimate restaurant tucked away from the main streets—a hidden gem you only discover if you know where to look. The lights inside are dim, casting a golden glow over dark wood tables and plush leather booths. The air is rich with the aroma of spices and something mouthwatering sizzling in the kitchen.

We take a seat near the window. With him positioned opposite me, I take in his face fully for the first time. Damn. He's handsome. He resembles a fallen angel...or perhaps the devil himself. With hazel eyes narrowed into slits, sharp angles and contours defining his face, and long black curly hair cascading over his forehead, he looks almost unreal.

This entire situation feels surreal. Him arriving just in time to save me, him dispatching three men in less than a minute, and us seated here as if it's just another ordinary night.

"Are you in shock?" he asks casually.

I wrap my hands around the steaming bowl of soup the waitress sets down, allowing the heat to seep into my frozen fingers. Sitting across from me, he leans back in his seat, watching me with that same unreadable expression.

"I asked you a question."

"Do you always have to get your way in every situation?" I blurt out.

"Yes. And I think you're in shock."

I roll my eyes. "I'm not in shock. What's the big deal? I just witnessed three men get murdered right before my eyes —three men who would have raped me, as you generously pointed out. They could have killed me afterward, too. Now they're dead, and I don't know if I should feel relieved or guilty. But what can I say? I'm alive, so everything is just peachy!"

He stares at me for a beat before laughing. And god, it's such a beautiful sound. I hate it when he stops.

"What's your name?" he asks.

I sigh. "Mirabella."

"Mirabella," he repeats, testing my name on his lips. The way he says it sends a pleasant shiver down my spine.

"The men who took me were terrified when you showed up. That's before you killed them..."

I can't believe I'm talking about murder so casually.

Dark humor flickers in his eyes as he observes me carefully.

I swallow before asking, "Who exactly are you, Reaper?"

"A businessman."

"What's your real name?"

He eyes me for a few seconds, and I feel my breath hitch under his heated gaze.

"Ettore," he finally replies.

Ettore. I don't know why, but the name suits him.

"Your surname?"

He chuckles. "My first name is all you need to know, Bella."

Bella. A feeling I can't describe revels through me at the nickname.

"You're a little too vague for my liking," I muse. "I need to know more about the man who killed three men and saved my life."

His lips quirk. "And you're a little ungrateful for someone who needed saving," he counters.

I can't help the small huff that escapes me. "Touché. So do you do this often?"

"Do what often?"

"Save random girls in the rain and take them to restaurants afterward?"

His eyes glint with amusement and something else I can't quite decipher. "Just you."

"Do you flirt with them afterward?" I ask, deliberately sidestepping the fact that I'm fishing for information about whether this gorgeous man is involved with anyone.

What are you doing, Mirabella? This man is a murderer.

I shouldn't even be sitting here with him.

This man saved your life. Yes. You wouldn't be here without him.

"Just you, Mirabella," he drawls, this time putting more

weight on my name, his eyes locking onto mine with a piercing intensity.

It's too intense, too deep. I look away, reaching for a spoon and scooping some of the chicken carrot soup into my mouth.

There's something about him that draws me in. Maybe it's the way he carries himself—so calm, so in control, even in the face of danger. Perhaps it's the way his gaze lingers on me—just a little too long, intense, and focused. He makes me feel things I've never experienced before, feelings I shouldn't be having at this moment.

But then I find myself wondering, *Why not?*

Why not take a risk for once? Why not do something for myself instead of scraping by day after day struggling for everyone else? I could have died today. Hell, I almost did. And here I am, sitting across from a man who's likely the most dangerous person I've ever met, and yet I feel safe...and aroused.

I'll never see Ettore again. He seems like someone I could never stand a chance of bumping into on a normal day. After tonight, I'll return to my pathetic life moving from one dreadful work shift to the next.

Maybe it's the thrill of narrowly escaping death or the excitement of having the most gorgeous man I've ever seen staring at me in this way, but I lean forward, my voice soft as I blurt out, "I think I want to have sex with you."

2

ETTORE

Mirabella sits across from me, her damp auburn hair clinging to her face in messy waves, the rain still fresh on her. The soft light in the restaurant highlights the olive undertone of her skin, making her look even more striking. She's fucking beautiful, with eyes the deep, dark brown of rich espresso, and there's always that glint of challenge in them when she looks at me.

And damned if I can look away.

I think I want to have sex with you.

Her words keep echoing in my head, relentless, and I have to fight back a groan at the way my dick hardens. She's different—completely unlike anyone I've ever dealt with before. Bold as hell, yet there's something underneath, a hint of bashfulness that shows through her confident exterior.

Her clothes cling to her, still wet, and I can clearly see the outline of her hardened nipple through the thin fabric of her dress. But it's the fire in her eyes that keeps me locked in. She's not scared—not of me, at least—and that makes her all the more fascinating.

When she leans in closer, her lips curving into that half-smile she's been flashing at me all night, I have to remind myself why I don't get involved. Not with women like her. Not with anyone, really.

"Are you in shock?" She throws my earlier question back at me, her tone teasing.

A dark thrill snakes up my spine, mixed with something more dangerous.

I've always been the one in control. Of my body. Of my emotions. I'm not impulsive, and I definitely don't let my dick call the shots. But as the tension crackles in the air between us, I feel something dangerous pulling me in. The way she keeps looking at me, her gaze moving over me like she's daring me to do something, is pushing all the wrong—or maybe all the right—buttons.

"You think?" I finally ask, leaning in just a fraction. "Or do you *know* you want to have sex with me?"

Her full lips stretch into a knowing smile as she twirls a lock of wet auburn hair between her fingers.

"I could've died a virgin tonight. Worse, someone else could have taken that choice from me," she says, and my fists tighten at the reminder of what almost happened earlier.

"So..." she gulps. "...before I die, I want to know what an orgasm feels like. People say it's the best feeling in the world, and I want to experience that..."

Her eyes flash with heat and...fuck! I feel myself harden even more.

"...I want to see a man's body. Yours, to be exact," she says, her voice soft and teasing as she bites her lower lip, her eyes glinting with mischief. "I bet it's one hell of a sight."

Her words settle deep in my chest, her meaning clear.

"Except..." she says, her voice soft but confident, "you don't want to have sex with me. Although I think you do ..." Her dark brown eyes gleam with challenge.

I chuckle, low and rough, as the temptation travels a dark path down my spine. Raking a hand through my hair, I force myself to ignore the desire creeping into my mind. It would be wrong, so wrong, to take advantage of her right now.

"You have no clue what you're asking for."

She leans even closer, her lips just inches from mine, the tension between us stretching tighter with each passing second. "Maybe I do. And maybe I don't care. I like a little danger."

My gaze drops to her lips, and for a fleeting moment, I imagine what it would feel like to taste them, to kiss her.

"Careful what you wish for, Bella," I warn, my voice a low growl.

She swallows, her eyes flicking down to my mouth. "I'm not scared of you."

"You should be."

She nods, an unreadable expression crossing her face.

"I want you to make me yours tonight. Unless..." she trails off, and my body suddenly itches to hear the words leave her lips.

"Unless what, Bella?" I ask, my voice low.

"Just leave it..."

"Unless what?" I repeat, and something flashes in her eyes at the seriousness of my tone.

"Unless I find someone else who'll satisfy my needs... someone who will make me feel like a woman..."

I don't wait for her to continue before I toss some cash onto the table and stand, offering her my hand. She smirks, not hesitating to slip her hand into mine as we step into the cool night air. The rain has slowed to a drizzle, the droplets clinging to her skin, making her hair shimmer under the streetlights. Her dress sticks to every curve in a way that's impossible to ignore.

We walk toward the car in silence, but the tension between us is suffocating, thick with anticipation. I open the passenger door for her, my fingers grazing her arm as she slides in. She shivers, and a vivid image flashes in my mind—me pressing her against the car, taking her right here in the rain while burning from anger at the thought of her mentioning another man.

I slide into the driver's seat, the engine growling to life as I pull away from the driveway. The city blurs by in streaks of light and rain, but all I can focus on is her—Mirabella—sitting beside me, her presence undeniable.

Every time we hit a bump, her leg brushes against mine, and it takes everything in me to keep my eyes on the road. She's stealing glances at me from the corner of her eye, and the silence between us is thick with unsaid words.

She shifts in her seat, her wet dress sliding higher up her thighs, and I have to grip the steering wheel harder than necessary to stay focused.

We pull into the entrance of a luxury hotel tucked away on the city's outskirts. The rain continues its soft patter against the windshield as I kill the engine. The world feels muted, as if the downpour has stolen the night's sounds to make this moment ours.

I glance over at her, and everything I've been trying to hold back begins to unravel. She has this magnetic pull, like gravity itself bends around her. I want her—badly. And the way her smoldering gaze locks onto mine tells me she feels it too.

"This where you bring all your rescues?" she teases, her voice wavering between boldness and uncertainty as she fumbles with the seatbelt. There's a slight tremor in it, a hint of vulnerability she's trying to hide.

"Only the ones I want to see again."

Her eyes widen slightly, surprise flickering across her face. "You want to see me again?" she asks, almost disbelieving. The way she says it makes my chest tighten. It's as if she's never heard those words before—not in a way that mattered.

It makes me wonder about the kind of men she's known—the idiots, the cowards. What lies did they feed her to strip away her confidence? To make her feel like she's nothing more than a fleeting moment, a passing thought, a casual fling? Shit. Was I any different from them?

I grip the steering wheel even tighter, an ache of protectiveness settling in my chest. I'm going to erase every single one of those bastards from her memory. I'll show her what it feels like to be wanted—truly wanted—by a real man.

"Why wouldn't I want to see you again?" I ask.

She hesitates, her gaze dropping to her hands. "I just thought..." she starts, but her voice trails off.

"Well, there's the problem. Don't think, Bella. Just feel." My voice softens, but there's a command there, a promise. "When you're with me, forget about the world outside. Just be here. With me."

She looks at me for a long moment, her eyes searching mine like she's testing the weight of my words. "As long as we're just having sex," she finally says, her tone light but laced with caution. "The way you're talking, it sounds like you want more than just this hotel room. You're not a serial killer, are you?"

A laugh rumbles from my chest, low and deep. "I promise, I'm not. I love women too much for that."

"Women? So, there's been more than just me," she says, tilting her head. She's fishing, but there's no edge to her voice—only curiosity. I love that she's interested in my past, but I have to stay focused. If I let myself, I'll tell her everything, and that's dangerous territory.

"Sorry to disappoint you, Bella," I say, smirking. "With the way I fuck, I don't have room for too many women."

Her breath hitches, and the playful smile slips from her lips. Her gaze darkens, heat pooling in her eyes. Lust. Pure, unfiltered lust. It's mutual. We sit there, the tension crackling between us like a live wire. I don't know how much time passes, and I don't care.

My eyes drop to her lips again, and my body reacts before my mind can rein it in. My dick twitches, straining against my pants, and I feel the last shreds of restraint slipping.

Fuck. If we don't move now, I'll lose it. I'll tear that dress off her right here in this car and make her mine—completely, utterly mine.

I exhale sharply and push the door open, stepping out into the cool night air. The rain kisses my skin, a brief reprieve from the heat burning between us.

But it won't last. Not tonight.

I round the car and open her door, and when she steps out, her skin brushes mine, igniting a spark that's hard to ignore. I find it fucking hard to believe she's still a virgin. She's beautiful, sexy—every man's wet dream.

Without a word, I grab her hand, pulling her toward the entrance of the hotel. The lobby greets us with soft lighting illuminating from the chandeliers above. Marble floors and polished wood catch the warm light.

The middle-aged receptionist behind the desk straightens slightly as she sees us, and a welcoming smile spreads out on her lips. I handle the check-in smoothly before taking the key card and turning back to the woman in my arms.

The elevator ride to the third floor is torturous. Every stolen glance, every accidental brush of her hand against mine makes my pulse race, but I keep myself in check. This isn't about rushing—it can't be. Not with her.

For the first time in my life, I don't want to dive headfirst into desire. I want to take my time, savor every second, every breath, every touch. I want to revel in this night like it's my last night on earth. She's different, and she's making me feel things I've never felt before—things I don't know how to name yet.

When the elevator doors slide open, I step aside to let her out first, my hand hovering at the small of her back. It's a light, steadying touch, and yet it sends a wave of heat through me. As we walk down the hallway, each step toward the room feels heavier, more deliberate. My hand itches to pull her close, but I don't. Not yet.

At the door, I slide the keycard into the lock and push it open, pausing to take a deep breath before stepping inside. I glance at her, my voice low but steady.

"Last chance to back out," I murmur, meeting her eyes.

She steps closer, her confidence faltering for just a moment before her resolve shines through. Her lips are so close to mine that I can feel the warmth of her breath. "I'm not backing out."

And that's it—the last wall I've put up crumbles. My hand shoots up, grabbing her by the neck, and her eyes widen, equal parts surprise and desire flickering in their depths.

"I'm not a gentleman, kitten," I drawl, my hand circling her throat while my second thumb caresses her lower lip. "I don't do sweet words in bed, and I definitely don't cuddle afterward."

She rolls her eyes, but the heat in them never wavers.

"I'm not asking for sweet words or cuddles," she whispers as her hand slides under my coat to caress my chest. The room is cold, my wet shirt is even colder, yet her touch only leaves burning in its wake. "I just want one night where I can feel alive. Just...make me forget, Ettore."

The sound of my name on her lips sends a jolt straight to my chest, but it's not lust—it's something stronger. Something terrifyingly new. I lean in, my forehead resting gently against hers, as I let out a breath I didn't realize I was holding.

"If that's what you want," I say softly, my voice thick with emotion, "then I'll give it to you. But I promise, I'll give you more than just one night to forget—I'll make you feel like the only woman in the world."

I clench my teeth as her hand slides down to the bulge in front of my pants. She stands on her tiptoes, her lips brushing my chin, and her next words come out in a breathless whisper.

"So what are you waiting for? Take me."

The soft, sultry tone of her voice sends a shockwave through me, and in that moment, I know there's no turning back. For the first time, I'm completely okay with that.

My fingers thread through her hair, pulling it roughly back as I press my mouth firmly against hers. Her breath stutters into a gasp when my tongue swipes across her teeth, then into her mouth. Her hands slide up my chest slowly, almost as if she's not sure of what she's doing. I kiss her harder, sliding my hands down to grab her ass.

A whimper slips past her lips, and I swallow the sound greedily. She wants this, and I'll make sure every moment is worth it—for both of us. One hand travels under her dress as I continue to kiss her.

I knead the soft flesh of her ass, feeling the wet lace of her panties in my hand as I squeeze. She makes a sound of approval in her throat before sliding her hands over my neck and burying them in my hair. I groan, savoring her small sounds as my mouth devours hers.

She moans before pulling away to gasp for air. I suck on her neck, her shoulder, nipping gently with sharp teeth until she lets out another strangled moan.

The pleasure from just kissing her wracks through my entire body. My breathing becomes more erratic by the second, and it takes everything in me not to rip off her clothes and fuck her against the door.

Instead, I lift her body in my arms. She instinctively wraps her legs around my waist as I carry her to the bed, gently placing her on top of the white sheets. I stand over her at the edge, unable to tear my gaze from her as I struggle to keep my dark lust on a leash.

She blinks up at me dazedly, and her cheeks are flushed pink. A sharp breath leaves my lips when she gets on her knees and swiftly pulls her dress over her head, leaving her in a matching pair of a black lace bra and panties.

She tosses the piece of cloth aside, and just as I think I'm still in control, she reaches behind her to unclasp her bra. My mouth goes dry at the sight of her smooth, round, olive-toned breasts as they spill free. Her nipples, slightly darker than the rest of her skin, harden underneath my stare.

"You like watching me undress, don't you?" she murmurs, those deep brown eyes of hers undressing me.

I run a hand through my wild locks before stepping

toward the edge of the bed. She watches me as I sink onto my knees before pulling her legs to the edge of the bed. A gasp escapes her lips when I rip her cheap, lace panties before I pull the material down her thighs and throw them carelessly to the floor. My cock twitches at the sight of her pussy, already wet and glistening.

Her hips arch forward as I kiss her ankle.

"Have you ever been kissed here before?" I ask, flicking my tongue over her soft skin.

"No," she whispers.

My mouth trails a wet path up to her knee, and her pants become louder, faster.

"What about here?" The deep murmur echoes through the quiet room. She lets out an involuntary shudder as I bite the skin just above her knee.

"No."

My tongue circles the spot before moving torturously slow to her inner thigh. Her hands find their way to my hair and tug on it, urging me to hurry. I smile before moving to the apex of her thighs.

My tongue darts out to lick the wet folds of her pussy. A loud moan slips through her lips, and I groan in approval, sucking her even deeper.

"How many men have touched you here?" I ask.

"Zero." She throws her head back and moans as my fingers play with her entrance.

I hum softly as I continue my ministrations, alternating between licking, sucking and biting softly until her knees start to shake. I hold her hips still as I continue to lap at her wetness, relishing the sound of her wanton moans as she reaches the brink of her orgasm.

When I pull away to look at her face, satisfaction warms

my blood at the sight of her—flushed and panting, with a red blush on her cheeks.

I stand and begin to undress. She watches me raptly as I unbutton my shirt, undo my belt, and pull down my briefs until I'm naked before her.

"You like watching me undress, don't you?" I repeat the question she asked me a few minutes ago. A flash of amusement appears in her eyes, but it quickly disappears as I grab a condom from the pocket of my pants and roll the latex over my hard length.

"Spread your legs, Kitten," I murmur as I approach the bed.

She obeys, spreading herself wide for me. A groan rumbles out of my throat as I climb onto the mattress over her, my cock pulsing as it brushes against her thigh.

"Are you ready?" I ask her, pressing my dick against her wet opening.

Her hip bucks upward as she grabs my shoulder. "Yes..."

I sink in slowly, taking her inch by inch. She moans and closes her eyes, her hands gripping onto the sheets as I sink deeper inside her. Tears pool at the corners of her eyes, and I let out a curse.

"Are you okay?" I grit my teeth and halt my movements.

"Yes," she gasps, opening her eyes to look at me. "Don't stop."

I press a kiss against her neck before dragging my mouth down to take one nipple into my mouth. Her hands sink into my hair again, her nails scraping against my scalp. When I feel she's adjusted, I sink further into her, letting out a low hiss when the full weight of my cock stretches her body.

I wait for a few seconds before pulling out to thrust forward again. She whimpers loudly against my ear. The sound sends a shiver of lust racing down my spine.

"Again," she pleads as I plunge deeper into her body. "Please, Ettore."

Her voice sounds wrecked, pleading, and needy. I take her second nipple into my mouth as I slam into her. She gasps, a low whimper escaping her lips. The sound causes another wave of desire to shoot down my shaft.

"Fuck," I groan, grinding against her once more. "You like that, right?"

"Yes," she moans, her hips pushing up to meet mine as I pound into her.

Her pussy clenches around me, and I curse, digging my fingers into her sides as her pussy squeezes me and makes me lose any control left in my body. Her muscles tense as her climax rolls through her body, and I watch her buck beneath me, desperately trying to escape the waves of pleasure.

Her cries of satisfaction echo throughout the room just as I feel my own orgasm hit me. I grip the sheets beneath me and thrust one final time before collapsing beside her with a heavy thud.

Our bodies are slick with sweat by the time we finally collapse beside each other. She lays her head on my chest, and my lips unconsciously pull upward.

"I thought you didn't say sweet things during sex, or..." she yawns softly, her voice barely above a whisper, "how did you put it? Cuddle afterward?"

I chuckle, my chest vibrating beneath her. "I don't." But I leave out the part where she's different—how something about her has me breaking rules I've lived by for years all in the span of a few hours into meeting her.

She snuggles further into my body, and I realize I don't hate it. Worse, I actually like it. The feeling of her soft, sweaty skin pressing against mine. The feeling of her steady, warm breath ghosting across my skin.

This...feeling helps me understand why people cuddle after sex. It makes me wonder if I could have more of this...

As her breathing evens out, I know she's fallen asleep. My eyes grow heavy, too, and as I bury my nose into her auburn hair, inhaling the subtle scent of her, a final thought crosses my mind just before sleep claims me.

This can't end as a one-night stand.

3

MIRABELLA

I wake up with a jolt and see the sun is up.

The sun is already up!

Damn it. I never sleep in. I'm always awake before dawn, racing the sun to get to my first shift out of my three daily jobs. The early light slips through the curtains, casting a soft glow across the room.

My heart pounds as my mind scrambles to catch up. It feels as if I'm still stuck in a dream, but the memories swirling in my head aren't from a dream.

The unfamiliar softness of the mattress beneath me, the solid weight of an arm draped over my waist, the dull pulse between my legs, the slow, steady breathing near my ear...

It's real. So fucking real.

Ettore.

His name rushes back to me along with flashes of last night—the rain, the alley, the fear. And then...him. The tension between us, the dinner, the hotel, and...oh, God. My pulse quickens, but no longer from the panic.

Memories of his touch burn my skin all over again. My heart pounds as I lie there, still as a statue, afraid to even breathe. How did I let this happen? Why the hell did I have sex with a stranger? A stranger who kills people...

I turn my head, and my gaze falls on Ettore. He's still fast asleep beside me. His dark, brooding face looks softer in sleep, almost...angelic. The hard lines of his jaw and the intensity I saw in his eyes last night have completely faded. He doesn't look like the dangerous man who saved me from Abruzzi's men. He doesn't look like a killer. He looks...peaceful.

God. I don't even know this man. He only gave me his first name, and all I know is that he's dangerous enough to kill. Yet last night, I acted as if none of that mattered. I convinced him—no, I practically begged him—to sleep with me. To take my virginity because I thought I might not live to see another day.

My Nonna is going to chop off my head. Stupid, stupid, stupid.

I groan inwardly. The worst part? I wasn't even that drunk. There's no alcohol-induced haze to blame it on. I did it fully aware, fully sober, and now the guilt and shame are twisting in my stomach. I can already picture Nonna's face, that stern, disappointed glare she gives when I step out of line. She'd probably lecture me about my choices, about self-respect, about letting a man like *him* anywhere near me.

But somewhere deep inside, beneath all the shame, I know I don't regret it. Not entirely.

Because if I'm being honest with myself, last night was unforgettable. I can at least brag about that, right? About how my first time was nothing short of...amazing. Mind-blowing, even. Alessia, my best friend/professional sex-enthusiast and the thorn in my flesh, always goes on and on about how incredible it can be, but I never understood—until now.

I let out a breath I didn't realize I was holding and gently pull the sheets back, slipping out of bed as quietly as I can. I need to leave now before he wakes up.

But what if he does wake up? What do I say? What do I do? What if he treats me like one of those random hookup girls I'm sure he's used to? I've seen enough movies to know how painfully awkward that could be.

Or...what if he actually wants more? What if he asks for my number and wants to see me again?

Do you really think men like Ettore want to be seen with women like you in broad daylight?

Yup. That snaps me right out of it.

I quickly grab my clothes from the floor, my heart racing as I tug on my black dress and jacket, trying to be as quiet as possible. I steal one last glance at him—still sound asleep—before I slip out of the room, carefully closing the door behind me. The hotel hallway feels colder than the room, and guilt clings to me like a second skin.

As I step outside, the city is just beginning to wake up. The streets in this part of town are spotless and quiet. I walk past pristine buildings, shiny cars, and people who look as if they've never had to struggle a day in their lives. My world is nothing like this. The fancy part of town is somewhere I only pass through by accident, usually on my way home from jobs that pay far too little for the hell I go through.

And the farther I go, the uglier the city gets. The smooth sidewalks give way to cracked pavement, the shiny storefronts replaced by dirty glass windows and graffiti-covered walls. By the time I reach my neighborhood, it feels as if I've stepped into a completely different world. The familiar smell of damp walls and stale cooking oil hits me as I reach the door.

The small, cramped apartment I share with my grandmother, younger sister, and sick mother couldn't be more different from the luxurious room I just left behind.

The sounds of bickering greet me as I open the door. My sister Giulia sits at the table with her arms crossed and a playful scowl on her face. Nonna is at the stove, stirring something that smells suspiciously like burnt toast. My mom sits nearby, wrapped in a blanket, her face pale but her eyes bright with amusement.

"Mirabella is here!" Giulia announces as soon as she spots me. "Now, settle this—who makes the best pancakes?" she asks, hands on her hips like she's ready for battle.

"Uh..." I hesitate, sensing a trap.

"Nonna says she's the best, but let's be honest—she's great at cooking, but she can't bake to save her life."

"Pancakes aren't even baked," Nonna grumbles without looking up from the stove.

"Nonna's bad at anything involving flour," Giulia huffs.

"And who do you think makes the gnocchi and pasta you devour like there's no tomorrow?" Nonna shoots back.

I shake my head as they keep going at it, leaning down to kiss my mother's forehead.

"Did you sleep well?" I ask softly, and she nods, offering me a weak but warm smile.

"Hey, you!" Nonna calls out, waving the spoon at me now. "Don't think you can sneak in and pretend like everything is fine. Where were you all night, eh?"

My pulse quickens. I can never lie to Nonna. She's got that radar, that sixth sense that can sniff out any fib. She sees right through me no matter how hard I try to hide things. "I...had dinner with a friend," I say carefully. It's not exactly a lie, but the words feel heavy in my mouth. "We went back to a hotel room to talk afterward. Alessia joined us, too."

I know throwing in Alessia's name will make Nonna relax a bit.

Giulia looks up with a smirk. "Alessia, huh? You guys must've been up all night...talking." She wiggles her eyebrows at me.

I scowl at her. Ever since she turned thirteen and entered the dreaded teenage years, as she likes to remind me every day, she thinks every word has an innuendo or a naughty meaning behind it.

Well, in this case, she's right, which only makes it even more annoying.

"Something like that," I mutter.

"Some talk that must've been."

Nonna gives me a long look, and I hold my breath, waiting for her to dig deeper. But she just hums and turns back to the stove. *Thank God.*

My eyes flick back to my mother, who's quietly sipping her tea. My heart sinks as I notice her fingers trembling slightly around the cup. She looks more tired than usual. Every day, the pain takes a little more out of her, leaving her a shell of the woman she used to be.

It's a normal morning, or at least, as normal as it can be in our household. The laughter, the teasing, the well-made breakfast Nonna insists on making every morning. But the moment is shattered when my mom suddenly lets out a violent cough that shakes her whole body.

"Mom?" I rush over to help her, gently taking the cup from her hands. Some of the tea has already spilled onto the old, worn carpet. "Are you okay?"

She nods, but the tightness in her face tells a different story. "Just having a bad morning," she says, trying to brush it off.

"Bad morning, my foot," Nonna mutters, dropping her

spoon as she walks over. "You need to lie down, my dear. Come on, let's get you to bed."

I watch as Nonna helps my mom to the bedroom, my chest tightening with worry. Every time I see her like this, I'm reminded of how little time we have left. The medication I've managed to scrape together with the money from Abruzzi and other loan sharks barely helps at this point.

The rheumatoid arthritis is eating away at her more each day. The doctor said she needs surgery, but that's a dream I can't afford. All I have is debt, and now I owe Abruzzi twenty thousand fucking dollars. I'll have to work like a slave for years before I'm able to pay him back.

As I sit back at the table, Giulia lowers her voice. "Is she getting worse?"

I nod, swallowing the lump in my throat. "Yeah. She's trying to hide it, but the pain's getting really bad."

Giulia frowns, her shoulders slumping. "I wish there was something we could do."

Me too. I wish I could do more than work odd jobs, more than borrow money from dangerous men who can destroy everything we have with a single phone call. But I can't.

I reach out and squeeze her hand. "We'll figure it out. We always do."

Giulia looks up at me, her eyes brimming with unshed tears. I ruffle her hair, trying to lighten the mood. "Finish your breakfast. You've got school."

The rest of the day moves in a blur. Luckily, I have the day off from two of my three jobs, so my late-night escapade didn't mess me up too much this morning. The last thing I need is to lose pay because I spent the night having sex with a stranger. I push those thoughts away as I go through the motions—chores, checking on Mom, making sure Giulia has what she needs.

By evening, I'm getting ready for my shift at the bar. I slip into the simple black dress that serves as my uniform and pull my hair into a tight ponytail. As I stare at my reflection in the mirror, I feel the weight of everything press down on me.

And then, just like that, my mind drifts to Ettore. His face, his deep green eyes, the intensity in the way he looked at me, like he could see every inch of my soul. I don't know why I keep thinking about him. I have enough real-life problems to deal with—debts, my mom's illness, keeping the roof over our heads. But something about Ettore lingers. The way he appeared out of nowhere and saved my life is a memory I won't be forgetting anytime soon.

I pull on my jacket, much warmer than the flimsy one I wore last night, and Nonna's voice cuts through my thoughts.

"So, where exactly did you go last night?" she asks, standing at the door of my room, her sharp eyes narrowing at me.

I pause, slipping an old umbrella into my bag. "I told you, Nonna. I had dinner with a friend."

"And does this 'friend' have a name?" she presses, not missing a beat.

I roll my eyes, trying to brush it off. "It's not a big deal, Nonna. We just talked. I told you Alessia came by afterward."

I hate that I'm lying to her, but what am I supposed to say? That I spent the night with a dangerous man who saved me from being assaulted, then killed three people without blinking? That I saw blood and death, and I'm still thinking about a man whose last name I don't even know? I can already hear her gasp, see her clutching her rosary like it'll protect me from the world.

Nonna just hums, clearly not convinced, but she doesn't push. "Hmm. Be careful with those 'friends,' my dear. It's a wicked world out there."

"I will, Nonna," I say, forcing a smile.

I follow her out of the room, say my goodbyes to Giulia, who's curled up watching TV, and step out into the cold night. As the chill hits me, my thoughts flicker back to him again. Even the freaking biting cold seems to remind me of him, of his presence that wrapped around me like a shield in the darkest moment.

I groan under my breath, annoyed with myself. Ettore was a fleeting moment, an escape from my reality. Nothing more.

I should be focusing on my jobs, my family, and the debt hanging over my head. But no matter how hard I try to shake it, a part of me, a bigger part than I care to admit, hopes I'll see him again.

4

ETTORE

"You need a wife."

Aldo's words cut through the silence like a blade, jarring me out of my thoughts. My hand freezes midair, whiskey glass poised at my lips. I stare across the table at my lawyer-turned-friend, raising an eyebrow. "A wife?"

The corner of his mouth quirks up slightly, as if he finds my reaction amusing. "You need to project the image of a humble, loyal family man."

I let his words hang in the air between us. In the vast expanse of my luxury mansion, Aldo and I sit across from each other at the glass dining table. The walls are lined with abstract art, each piece worth hundreds of thousands. The floor beneath our feet is made of Calacatta marble, one of the rarest varieties of natural stone.

I've achieved a great deal of success in my life, yet Aldo thinks I need to create an image...for *what*, exactly?

"I didn't call you here for this," I say, leaning back in my chair. "I wanted to talk about the company's expansion."

"This is about the expansion," Aldo counters, unfazed

by the deep gruff tone of my voice. He slides a folder across the table toward me, his blue eyes sharp behind his glasses. "You want to grow your empire into a legitimate business? To expand without your reputation as The Reaper casting a shadow over you? Then you need to change your public image."

The name rolls off his tongue easily—The Reaper. I'm proud of that name. I earned it by doing what others—even those who claim to be more powerful—wouldn't dare. Competitors who threaten my empire find themselves facing PR disasters, financial ruin, or worse, they vanish completely. I excel at making sure anyone who crosses me never gets the chance to make the same mistake twice. My name evokes fear and respect. Yet here's Aldo, telling me to abandon it.

"What's wrong with the name I've built?" I ask, tapping my finger against the table.

"Your reputation precedes you, Ettore. The investors you're targeting—the ones who can take this business to new heights—don't want a man with blood on his hands."

I snort. "What billionaire doesn't have blood on his hands? Even the most polished ones..."

"Now, that's the problem, Ettore. The goal is to make you seem perfect, even if you're not," Aldo interrupts in a calm, calculated tone. He's the only one brave enough to call my bluff like that. It's why I hired him, but moments like this make me want to strangle him.

He knows his words hit hard, and I can see the glint in his eyes—he's enjoying this. He knows my views on marriage and love. "You need a softer image, something that shows stability. Reliability. A family man."

I can't help but laugh—a deep, humorless sound. "And you think a wife will fix that?"

"It's worked for centuries. I think it's a solid starting point for you," he replies, leaning forward, resting his elbows on the table. "The right woman by your side could work wonders. She'll make you look reformed, like you've changed. She'll help people forget the rumors and whispers about how you built your fortune."

I glance out the window, taking in the tall trees that line my compound. Aldo's words echo in my mind, and I hate that he's right. I am a powerful man, but if I want to expand, if I want to rise above the grime of the underworld, I need more than just power. I can't let my dark reputation get in the way of my professional image.

I need a face the public can trust and heck, even a face they can love. And right now, I don't fit either of those descriptions—unless you count gossip magazines calling me one of the hottest and richest bachelors in New York, of course.

"And where do you propose I find this woman?" I ask, turning back to Aldo. "You think respectable women are lining up to marry the devil?"

Many people know The Reaper, but they don't know who he really is. My reputation truly precedes me. I doubt any woman in her right mind would want to marry a ruthless, dangerous man she doesn't know.

Aldo smirks. "There are women who'd jump at the chance. They just need to see the man behind the name."

"Ah. So I need to be more open and raw?" I say the words mockingly. If there's one thing I hate, it's the idea of opening up to people and letting them see the real me. I much prefer the fear I evoke—it keeps people away.

Except for one person...

I showed her exactly who I am, and that only seemed to intrigue her even more.

Aldo chuckles. "What you need is a wife from a wealthy background and a reputable family."

"I don't have time to babysit some spoiled, delicate socialite." I can't help the hiss that escapes my lips.

"You won't need to," he replies smoothly. "I'll handle the details. You just need to approve the candidate."

I stare at him, my jaw tightening. "You're talking as if this is a business deal."

I may not be a fan of love and marriage, but the idea of marrying a fake wife and dealing with her sounds even worse.

"It is," he says honestly, leaning back in his chair. "She doesn't have to love you, but she must be willing to stand by your side and play the part of a loving, doting wife."

My mind drifts away from business and whatever well-bred, polished woman Aldo's describing. Instead, I see her again. Mirabella.

My Bella.

Her olive skin glimmers under the streetlights, her rain-soaked hair clinging to her neck. I remember the fire in her eyes as she tried to escape Abruzzi's men, even though she knew she didn't stand a chance.

She's real and raw. The sound of her laughter echoes in my head and tightens my chest. And her eyes—dark brown, intense, piercing. I recall the way she looked at me, not with fear but with curiosity, challenge, desire...

It's been days since I woke up to find her gone, yet she lingers in my mind like a ghost I can't shake. It's funny. I'm usually the one doing the leaving or dumping. For the first time, a woman has made me feel this way.

Pining. Wanting more...

Aldo clears his throat, snapping me out of my thoughts. "Ettore. This expansion is your chance to show the world you've evolved from whatever reputation you've built over the years. Dare I say it's an opportunity for a fresh start?"

An annoyed groan escapes my lips. I've built this empire with blood, sweat, and ruthless ambition. And now Aldo's telling me I need a woman to clean up my image? It feels ridiculous.

All the years I've endured to escape my father's shadow don't seem to matter. I've fought tooth and nail not to let his failed legacy overtake me, but it still doesn't feel like enough. I've clawed my way to the top through grit and determination, taking the less-than-honorable path when necessary. I've made tough choices, choices that weigh heavily on my conscience, yet here I am—richer, more successful, and still standing.

Yet, despite all I've achieved, the idea of becoming a mere shadow of myself for some woman feels unbearable. I've watched countless men—my father included—fall victim to love's fickle nature, losing themselves in the process.

I refuse to be another casualty in that game. Love feels like a mirage—something beautiful yet elusive, promising everything but delivering little more than heartache.

I won't allow a fleeting emotion to unravel the empire I've built. I've come too far, sacrificed too much.

But deep down, I know Aldo might be right. I can't ignore the gnawing feeling that I may need more than just power to truly succeed.

"Fine," I say finally, my voice low. "You find the right woman, and we'll talk."

Aldo nods, satisfied. "I'll start looking into suitable candidates. But Ettore..." His voice trails off, and I glance at him, raising an eyebrow.

"What?"

He shifts in his seat, choosing his words carefully. "You need to take this seriously. Your past...it shouldn't get in the way of the future you're building."

It's not really my past if I killed three men just a few days ago, but I nod.

As Aldo packs up his files and leaves, I stay seated, staring out the window. The weight of his words settles over me, but it's not the fake wife or business expansion that fills my thoughts.

It's her. Mirabella.

With a frustrated growl, I pull out my phone and dial my righthand, the same man I called to clean up the mess I'd left behind from saving Mirabella. His unwavering loyalty and willingness to get his hands dirty keeps the chaos at bay.

He picks up after the first ring. "Boss?"

I run a hand through my hair, cursing inwardly as I break another one of my rules just because of her.

"I need you to find someone for me."

5

MIRABELLA

"Are you sure this is the place?" I ask, unable to hide the confusion in my voice. This looks...well, like a regular laundromat. I didn't pay to rent a dress and four-inch heels that hurt like hell to visit a laundromat!

"Am I sure this is where I work?" Giovanni chuckles through the receiver. "Yeah, I'm sure, Mira."

I roll my eyes, even though he can't see me. I'm not in the mood for his jokes.

"I'm serious, Gio," I sigh.

When I asked for an invitation to The Temple, one of the most notorious underground poker clubs in the city, I expected glitter, glamor and opulence—not this. I've spent a lot of money and time I don't even have just to be here.

"You're in the right place, Mira. Just walk into the laundromat and head toward the inner door on the left."

I sigh again before ending the call and slipping my phone into my purse. My eyes scan the sign *Quick Cleaners* above the door as I move forward. I push the door open and step inside.

The place smells faintly of detergent. Stacks of clothes are neatly folded on counters, and old machines hum in the background. A bored-looking woman behind the counter gives me a small nod before refocusing on the computer screen in front of her. I look around until I spot a wooden door just as Giovanni described. My heels click on the tiled floor as I approach the door and slip through it.

The exit leads me into a narrow corridor. My pulse quickens. Distant music filters through the unpainted walls, accompanied by a low thumping that vibrates through me. With each step forward, my heart races in anticipation. At the end of the corridor, I stop in front of a steel door. Two massive bouncers flank the entrance, their eyes locking onto me immediately. They're dressed in black, with muscular builds and expressionless faces.

One of the bouncers scans me up and down, his gaze lingering just long enough to make me uncomfortable.

Can he tell I'm trying hard not to sweat in a dress that costs more than my annual rent? I hope not.

I square my shoulders and try to look unfazed as I hand him my pass. He spends a few seconds looking at it, but it feels like hours. Finally, he grunts something into his earpiece then steps aside, pulling the door open for me.

The first thing that hits me is the loud music. It floods my senses—thumping bass, pulsing beats, and the low murmur of voices. I walk in, trying to ignore the butterflies doing somersaults in my stomach.

The atmosphere inside is exactly what I expected when I applied for a job here months ago—the dimly lit room with streaks of red and gold casting shadows across the polished floors, poker tables scattered throughout the space, and men in expensive suits surrounded by women adorned with lavish pearls. The air is thick with the smell of cigarette smoke and cologne that costs enough to pay my mother's entire medical bill.

Glasses clink at the bar, and the soft chatter and laughter blend into the music, making it hard to focus on anything in particular. I take a deep breath and glance around, trying to soak it all in. It's both overwhelming and exhilarating, and I exhale deeply before straightening my shoulders.

I've been trying for months to get into this place. At first, I applied for a job, but they don't hire girls without a diploma or any real benefit to them. The best I could do was convince Giovanni, Alessia's boyfriend, to pull a few strings and get me an invitation for the night. He works here, so that wasn't too difficult for him. And here I am, in a rented gown that hugs my curves in all the right places.

It's ridiculous and not what I'd usually wear, but apparently, there's a dress code to which I have to adhere. It's also why I'm currently wearing high-heeled shoes I can barely walk in and a dress that shows a little too much skin for my liking.

I don't have a plan, just a vague hope that I can charm a wealthy man with my wit and intelligence—they like stuff like that, don't they?—into lending me some money or giving me a job or something.

It's worked for me before—under very different circumstances, I know—but who knows? Maybe my second chance could be the charm.

As I move through the crowd, I can feel eyes on me, appraising and measuring. I feel completely out of place. Everything reeks of power and money, neither of which I have. But it's easy to pretend, and for one night, that's what I'll do. I focus on my newfound confidence. I'm experienced now, no longer the naïve virgin I used to be. I can do this.

I reach the luxurious bar and order a drink from the dark-skinned bartender, who greets me with a flirty smile.

"Vodka tonic," I say casually, trying to play it cool, even though the words taste sour on my tongue. He raises an eyebrow, like I've just made a bold choice in spirits. That can only mean one thing—either I have excellent taste in alcohol, or the drink I just ordered is ridiculously expensive.

My broke ass is betting on the latter. Well, there goes this month's electric bill. Guess I'll be picking up more shifts to pay for this tiny act of financial self-sabotage.

The vodka hits hard and fast, calming my nerves just enough to stop my hands from shaking, and I order a second. Just then, I spot Giovanni moving through the crowd, approaching me. The tension in my stomach eases a little at the sight of a familiar face.

"Mirabella!" He beams, pulling me into a brief hug. "You look stunning."

"Thanks," I mutter.

As he leans back, his grin is a mix of amusement and curiosity. "And...you also look nervous. You okay, Mira?"

I roll my eyes, though the nickname softens me a bit. "Ugh! Why do you know me so well?"

"Because we used to be best friends, duh!"

He chuckles. Before Gio and Alessia started dating, the three of us went way back to high school.

That is, until he and Alessia started their secret friends-with-benefits thing behind my back, which eventually blossomed into love. Honestly, I wasn't mad they hid it—I knew they did it to spare my feelings. And when it all came to light, I was genuinely happy for them. Still, I was a little sad that my two favorite people found the kind of love I've always wanted but have never let myself believe I can have.

He pulls up a stool beside me. "You still haven't told me why you needed an invitation to this place."

My friends know I'm having money problems, so I'm sure he realizes I'm not here for a casual Friday night out like everyone else.

My drink arrives just then, and I take a slow sip, letting the chill drink settle my nerves before replying. "I need money, Gio. Big money. Plus I could really use your advice."

His eyebrows shoot up, surprised but not completely shocked. "You mean Abruzzi? I thought you had that handled."

I shake my head, avoiding his gaze as I trace the rim of my glass with my finger. "I thought I did, as well. He promised to be patient with me, but he seems to have run out of patience."

I lower my voice as I say, "He sent his thugs after me sometime last week."

"What?!" Gio hisses, his jaw tightening.

"Shh, relax," I say, glancing around to make sure no one's eavesdropping. "Nothing happened. It got handled. I mean, I'm standing here, aren't I?"

"Fuck, Mira. Why didn't I hear about this? Why didn't you tell me?"

I sigh, shaking my head. "What could you have done?" Before he could argue, I cut him off. "This debt...it's suffocating me, Gio. I don't need advice. I need a way out."

He lets out a low sigh, leaning back against the bar. "Damn. I don't know what to say. Alessia and I have already offered to take a loan on your behalf..."

"No." I swallow. "I told you I wonn't let you guys do that."

My friends have helped me enough, to the point where I feel guilty. I already owe them a lot, even though they've said I shouldn't worry about paying them back. I can't have them taking out loans for me on top of that. I haven't even settled the ones I owe yet. Besides, there's this optimistic part of me that thinks I'll be lucky tonight.

Gio and Alessia recently moved in together, and I'm sure Gio will pop the question any day now. It wouldn't be fair to drag them down with my problems just because I made a deal with life to be unlucky.

"You're walking on thin ice here. Abruzzi doesn't play fair. He's shown you that."

"Do you think I don't already know that?" I groan. "That's kinda why I'm here." I wince, ashamed of what I'm about to say.

He studies me for a moment, and his eyes widen as he reads meaning into my words.

"I'm not here to sell myself or anything like that," I blurt out, the words tumbling from my mouth before he can jump to conclusions. "You know Nonna would have my head if she ever found out." My voice wavers slightly, and I let out a shaky breath. "I just thought...maybe I could find someone who sees my potential and wants to help me."

He sighs. "Mira..."

I pause, the weight of my own words settling in. "I know it sounds stupid." I groan, burying my face in my hands to shield myself from his reaction.

My friends never judge me, but even I know how naive I must sound right now. It's a little humiliating, exposing this vulnerable part of myself, but the words are out there now, and there's no taking them back.

Gio chuckles lightly before pulling my hand away from my face. "I know you think Abruzzi is dangerous, but there are others here who are much worse. You don't want to get involved with them."

My heart drops at his words, and just then, I feel it—a prickling sensation at the back of my neck.

Someone is watching me.

I turn, scanning the room, but nothing seems out of the ordinary. Men are hunched over poker tables, and women are chatting and laughing. Yet, the feeling lingers, sharp and unshakeable.

Giovanni follows my gaze. "Something wrong?"

I shake my head, trying to brush off the unease. "No, it's nothing," I lie.

I seem to be doing that a lot these days. Some things are embarrassing to admit, and some...well, they shouldn't even leave my lips at all.

Like the way I've been hoping to somehow bump into Ettore again. He hasn't left my mind since I practically fled our shared hotel room that morning. I keep thinking about how he saved my life and how he took my virginity afterward.

My first time was a whirlwind of hot, sizzling, unforgettable sex.

"Mirabella?" Gio's voice filters through my thoughts. "I asked you a question."

I groan inwardly. A man like Ettore has no doubt forgotten about me by now. Yet here I am, zoning out during conversations because I can't stop thinking about our time together.

I'm turning into a sex-crazed woman, and I've only had sex once! Well, twice, if I count the second round we had in the middle of that night.

My cheeks flush as Gio shakes his head at me.

"I asked if the thugs hurt you, but clearly, your mind is somewhere else."

"They didn't hurt me. He just sent them to scare me," I

lie. They may not have physically harmed me, but they definitely planned to. I'd be dead by now if not for Ettore.

Giovanni opens his mouth to speak again, probably to lecture me about my life choices, but his eyes snap to something—or someone—behind me. His lips freeze mid-sentence, his entire demeanor stiffening. The usual bravado I always tease him for is replaced with unease.

"What is it?" I ask, a frown tugging at my brow.

His answer doesn't come in words. Instead, he jerks his chin toward a figure moving through the dimly lit bar—a man dressed in a tailored black suit, polished shoes that click against the floor, and dark sunglasses that shouldn't belong in such lighting.

The hairs on the back of my neck rise as he approaches, his movements deliberate, calculated. He stops just shy of my stool, his presence unnervingly close.

"Mirabella Ricci," he says, his voice smooth but sharp enough to cut through the hum of conversations and music.

I freeze. My name. How does he know my name?

I turn slowly, heart already racing. Standing beside me is a man who's presence is commanding. I blink, caught off guard.

"Excuse me?" I manage, my voice smaller than I'd like.

"My boss has a proposition for you," he says, voice calm, ignoring my confusion entirely like this is an everyday conversation.

"What proposition? And who—"

"I would prefer to speak with you privately," he interjects, cutting me off with the weight of authority. His head tilts toward Giovanni, who straightens in his seat as if he's ready to fight. "Without...unnecessary third parties."

Giovanni snorts. "Yeah? And I'd like a private island. Neither is happening."

The man doesn't respond. Giovanni stands abruptly, his chair screeching against the floor. "Who the fuck do you think you are, anyway?"

The stranger doesn't flinch, his head turning slowly to Giovanni. Behind the glasses, I feel the intensity of his glare. They stand there locked in a silent standoff, a battle of wills playing out before me.

"Gio," I whisper, my voice breaking the tension. "Can you give us a minute?"

"What? No!" Giovanni's disbelief is palpable. "Why the hell would you listen to him?"

Because this man knows my full name, and I have a sinking feeling he knows more than that.

"You're not seriously thinking about—"

"I just want to hear what he has to say," I insist, though my pulse pounds in warning.

"This is a private matter," the man says, his tone leaving no room for argument.

Giovanni looks at me, his protective instincts clearly warring with his common sense. I give him a small nod, placing a hand on his arm, pleading with my eyes. And with a reluctant sigh, he pushes off the stool, muttering curses under his breath, and takes a seat at a nearby booth, his gaze never leaving us.

The man steps closer, his cologne—dark, woodsy, and expensive—filling the space between us. His presence looming as he leans in just enough for only me to hear.

"A marriage deal."

I blink, taken aback by the bluntness. "Excuse me?"

"My boss has an offer," he says smoothly. "He wishes to marry you," he repeats, the words rolling off his tongue as if they're the most ordinary thing in the world. "In exchange, you'll be generously compensated."

I let out a disbelieving laugh, but his expression remains impassive.

"Is this some kind of sick joke?"

"One million dollars up front. One hundred thousand dollars each month for the year you remain married to him."

The laughter dies in my throat.

"Still think this is a joke? Well, let me tell you what isn't," he continues, his tone razor-sharp. "The twenty thousand dollars you owe Abruzzi."

My breath hitches.

I stare at him, stunned. "How do you—"

He interrupts. "My boss knows everything. And he's offering you a way out."

"You're bluffing," I whisper, though my voice lacks conviction.

"Am I?" He tilts his head slightly, studying me like a predator sizing up prey. "Do you think loan sharks care about your family's well-being? They don't. But my boss—he's offering you a solution. Money, protection, freedom from the chaos swallowing you whole."

My mind reels. "A million dollars?" I whisper, the sheer number clawing at the edges of my sanity.

He nods, his expression unchanging. "Enough to erase all your problems, isn't it?"

"That's..." I start, but my voice falters.

No. Not today, Satan.

I shake my head, trying to push through the fog of disbelief. My grandmother's voice rings in my ears, reciting that story every Sunday morning and night after mass.

"Beware the devil's deals, child," she'd say. "They always seem like salvation, but they're nothing but chains in disguise."

Well, congratulations, Nonna. Looks like I found myself smack in the middle of one of those trickery fables.

And yet, I can't shake the feeling that this is worse than some biblical parable. My brain spirals into darker territory: They're going to kidnap me, aren't they? Or worse...they want to harvest my kidneys and sell them on the black market.

I glance around the room, half-expecting a group of goons to emerge from the shadows with a chloroform-soaked rag. My breath quickens, and I force myself to lock eyes with the man in the suit, trying to mask the growing panic behind my glare.

"Who's your boss?"

"That's not important," he says, brushing off my questions. "What is important is that this deal—this marriage—is your only way out."

His words make my skin crawl, but they also strike a chord deep inside me.

"What's the catch?" I ask finally, my voice barely audible.

"No catch," he replies. "You marry him. Stay married for one year. At the end of it, you walk away with your life, your family intact, and more money than you've ever dreamed of."

I narrow my eyes. "And I don't even get to know his name?"

"You'll meet him soon enough," he says cryptically, pulling a sleek black card from his pocket. He slides it across the bar. "Think it over. You'll find all the details here."

"I don't need to think it over," I snap, pushing the card back toward him. "Tell your boss I'm not interested."

He doesn't flinch. "Abruzzi won't hesitate to make an example of you, Mirabella. And if he can't get to you...well, there's your sister. How much do you think she'll fetch if those debts remain unpaid? Or should I mention your grandmother? You know how these men operate," he adds, leaning in closer.

The room around me feels suddenly colder, the air thicker. "Stop," I hiss, my voice trembling.

He doesn't. "What about your mother's surgery and treatment? Her condition is worsening. You need two hundred thousand, at least. And what about your overdue debts to other...less patient lenders. Do you really need me to spell it out further?"

"Enough," I snap, my hands trembling against the counter. "I'll only repeat this once before I walk away. Who are you?"

"I'm simply a messenger," he replies. "But I assure you, my boss can offer you protection—freedom from these chains in which you've wrapped yourself."

The temptation of it slams into me like a tidal wave. It's impossible, absurd even, but every word he says chips away at my resistance.

"I don't even know who your boss is," I say, clutching at the one thread of logic I can still hold.

"You will," he says simply, sliding the card back across the counter. "If you reconsider."

With that, he turns and disappears into the crowd, leaving me with a heart pounding out of rhythm and more questions than answers.

I stare at the card as if it might burn me. Giovanni rushes back the moment he's gone.

"What did that snake want?" he demands, his eyes searching mine.

"He wants me to marry his boss," I reply with a hollow laugh. "For one year. And he promises to fix...everything," I say flatly, still staring at the card.

Giovanni freezes, his face draining of color. His eyes flick to the spot where the man disappeared, and then back to me, his jaw tightening.

"Do you have any idea who that man works for?"

I shake my head, swallowing hard. "Who?"

His hand clamps onto the edge of the counter so tightly I think it might crack under the pressure. "You can't trust him. Or his boss. You don't know the kind of people you'd be dealing with."

"*Who is he?*" I repeat, my frustration boiling over. "What's with everyone hiding this guy's identity? Just tell me!"

Giovanni exhales, a heavy sound like this is something he doesn't want to say. "I've only ever seen him from a distance," he begins reluctantly. "He pays for the high-end tables—cash, no questions asked. Doesn't stick around. He's in, he's out."

"So, what?" I scoff, my voice dripping with sarcasm. "He's stupidly rich and probably hides because he's ugly?"

Giovanni's face darkens, his expression shifting from concern to something more serious, more urgent. He doesn't even crack a smile. "No, Mirabella. He hides because he's dangerous. And ugly doesn't even begin to cover it. From what I've heard, he's the most dangerous man in this city. Forget Abruzzi—that guy's a small fish compared to this guy. This man...he's worse. Much worse."

A cold knot tightens in my stomach. "You're saying I shouldn't get involved?"

"I'm saying you *can't* get involved. Whatever he's offering you—it's not worth it. Not when it comes from him."

I swallow hard, the weight of Giovanni's words settling over me.

As absurd as the offer is, as horrifying as the implications are, the shiny black card sits on the counter, taunting me with its promise of salvation. The stranger's words echo in my mind, mingling with the weight of my reality.

And for the first time in years, I feel something other than despair.

I feel tempted.

6

ETTORE

I see her the moment she walks into the room.
It's like a magnetic pull, something invisible, but impossible to ignore. My eyes lock on her, and I can't look away. Mirabella moves through the crowd, turning heads without even trying. I don't blame them. She's fucking sexy—undeniably the most gorgeous woman here.

She's wearing this dress—tight in all the right places, catching the light with every step. Each movement she makes, I follow like a predator watching its prey. There's something about her, something that sets her apart from every other woman in this room.

The others are perfect, polished, and practiced in how they stand, how they smile just enough to catch attention. They work too hard at it—trying to look flawless in their posture, their designer dresses, showing off the men hanging on their arms.

But Bella...she's different. There's a wildness to her, an effortless grace. She's not trying to impress anyone; she just *is*. Every subtle move she makes pulls me in deeper. From the VIP section, hidden in the shadows, I sip my whiskey and watch her, grateful for the elevated view that lets me see everything.

Mirabella Ricci.

Did she really think she could slip away unnoticed? That she could sneak out of the hotel and disappear from my life? Did she honestly believe I wouldn't track her down? Find out who she really is and uncover every single damning detail about her?

My mind flashes back to the report Luca handed me two days ago. I'd run a background check on her and her family. What I learned explained a lot—why she got mixed up with Abruzzi in the first place. Her mother's sick, her grandmother's old, and she's got a younger sister still in high school. She's balancing multiple jobs just to make ends meet. It's no surprise she turned to that scumbag for money, especially when her mother needs expensive medication just to survive.

She's too young to be carrying all that weight on her shoulders. Yet when I look at her, she doesn't seem burdened, even though I know she is. She's bold, daring, and full of life. And it only makes me want her more.

Plus, she's so damn *fucking* sexy.

I watch the way she moves through the crowd—her steps are careful, yet full of purpose. Her silky, straight auburn hair falls past her shoulders, swishing around her with each step. When she reaches the bar, she orders a drink, and I'm fixated on the way her lips move as she talks to the bartender. An image of those lips wrapped around my dick flashes in my mind, and I shake my head, trying to clear the thought.

This is what she's done to me. Turned me into some horny teenager who can't stop thinking about sex.

I've tried to stop. I've tried convincing myself—lying to

myself—that there's nothing special about her. She's just another woman, one who happened to be an amazing fuck. Yet here I am, watching her, thinking about how she felt in my arms, how I *need* to feel her again. And it's not just about the sex. There's something more—something deeper that makes me want to claim her, to own her.

Then she hugs him.

I was so focused on her, I didn't even notice the guy walk in. I watch as she leans in and circles her arms around his neck. I watch the way her lips pull up into that beautiful smile of hers —*that* smile. The one I saw that night. And it sets something off inside me. It's uncomfortable, burning in my gut, spreading like wildfire.

Jealousy.

I hate that word. I've trained myself to ignore certain emotions, to be unaffected by them. At least, I thought I had. But now, here I am, feeling jealous. And it's because of *her*.

I clench my jaw, trying to shove the feeling down. What the hell is wrong with me? I've never been the type to get worked up over a woman. Not once. Yet seeing her with someone else, even if it's just a hug, makes me want to tear him away from her. This primal possessiveness takes over, and all I can think about is reminding her who she was with that night.

Me.

She's mine.

I know I have no right to feel this way. You can't own a person. But for those hours we spent tangled together, my dick sliding in and out of her while she moaned my name, she was mine. I touched her in ways no one else has. I made her feel things no one else ever will. And right now, all I want is to walk over there, kiss her until she can't breathe, and take her home to fuck her senseless.

Fuck this.

I stand abruptly, unable to tamp down the tension clawing at my chest. This is ridiculous. No woman has ever made me feel this...*thirsty*.

"Go," I say to Luca, who's been standing beside me the whole time.

After Luca dug up everything about Mirabella, I had the impulsive idea to propose the marriage offer to her. It's probably one of the most reckless things I've ever done, but when it comes to Bella, I've learned that I can't seem to think straight.

As Luca walks off, I head to a more private lounge. The loud music fades as I step into one of the soundproof rooms. I settle into the plush sofa and close my eyes. I usually come here on Friday nights to play poker, but tonight? Tonight I'm just hiding out after spending too much time watching her like a damned stalker.

Luca appears moments later, his shoulders tense and his jaw set. The look on his face tells me everything I need to know—the conversation didn't go well.

"She didn't take the offer, boss," he says, his tone rough, like he's been chewing on nails for the past five minutes.

I exhale, trying to mask the frustration bubbling beneath the surface, but there's a twisted sense of amusement creeping in. Of course, she didn't take it. She's scared. I get it. But fear doesn't last forever, and when she sees the bigger picture, she'll understand.

"Did you really think she would?" I ask, leaning back in my chair, playing with the edge of my glass, my voice laced with irony.

Luca shakes his head, eyes flicking away. "No, but I figured...you know, the right amount of pressure could do the trick. I told her she didn't have a choice."

I laugh bitterly, rubbing my hand over my face. "Yeah, because telling her she has no choice always makes people *really* eager to sign on the dotted line."

I stand backing him, the tension in my body obvious now. "She'll learn soon enough, when Abruzzi's men are breathing down her neck."

Luca hesitates, then speaks up, voice steady. "Are you going to interfere, sir?"

I don't need to. The debts? Her family? She's too busy protecting them to see she's walking into the fire.

I turn back to him, my eyes cold. "Don't worry. She'll come around. When things fall apart, she'll have no choice but to take what I'm offering."

Luca gives a curt nod. "You sure about that, sir?"

I fix him with a stare, my voice lethal. "She'll call," I say, taking a sip of my now-warm whiskey. I know she will. She's in deeper than she can handle. Abruzzi is relentless when it comes to collecting his money, and after I killed his men, he's even more pissed.

He'll send more guys after her, but they won't touch her. Not if they want to live. He knows I'm responsible for the deaths of his men, and while he's ruthless, he's not stupid. Unless he's ready to lose every one of his men, he got the message.

Mirabella is untouchable.

The most he can do is scare her—and when that happens, she'll come running straight to me.

"What do you think, Luca?" I ask, looking for a distraction. "Is she fit for the role?"

"She's beautiful," Luca says in that same gruff, robotic tone. "Smart, too. She's hardworking and efficient. Qualities I'd say you need in a wife, sir."

I consider his words. If—*when*—Mirabella marries me, she won't need to work. I'll take care of everything.

She may have the qualities of the perfect wife on paper, but this situation is anything but typical. I need someone who looks good next to me, someone with status and wealth, someone who can help solidify my image. Mirabella doesn't fit that mold.

So why did I send Luca after her?

"You can leave," I say, waving Luca off. I lean back into the sofa and close my eyes again, trying to ignore the mess of thoughts swirling in my head.

"Are you asleep?" I hear a soft whisper close to my ears.

The voice filters into my dream, and my eyes shoot open to see a pair of beautiful, dark brown eyes staring at me.

"Not anymore," I respond in a gruff voice.

Mirabella bites her lower lip, and the sight shoots a sensation straight to my dick. That's when I become aware of our naked bodies pressed together and the fact that her naked nipples are currently grazing my chest.

"Good," she murmurs, leaning closer. "Because I want you to fuck me again."

I grin, sliding one hand over her ass under the sheets.

"You have such a dirty mouth for someone who just lost her virginity," I tell her with a husky laugh.

Her eyes flash in amusement and something else.

"I may never see you again, and I need to make the most out of tonight."

My cock twitches in arousal, and I take a deep breath as she kisses my neck. Then I feel her hot breath on my ear as she whispers, "Fuck me, Ettore. Please..."

With a groan, I flip her over to her stomach before grabbing the complimentary condom from the bedside drawer and sliding it over my hard length. Then I lean down and gently kiss her back between her shoulder blades.

"Grab the headboard, kitten," I tease softly as I slide two fingers into her pussy from behind. She moans into the sheets, making me impossibly harder than I already am. "I'm going to be rough this time around, so brace yourself."

That seems to excite her because I feel her walls clench around my fingers. I pump her slowly, relishing the sound of her whimpers and the way she arches her ass off the mattress to meet my movements.

I slide my fingers out of her, and without warning, I position my dick at her entrance and slam into her. Her head bumps slightly into the headboard, and she lets out a muffled moan before grabbing the top of the headboard.

My fingers dig into the soft globes of her ass, holding her firmly as I thrust in and out of her. The sounds of her moans mix together with my grunts and the slap of our skin against each other.

"Fuck, you feel so good," I rasp before pulling a handful of her hair and wrapping it around my fist.

My thrusts become harder as I pull her back flush against my chest. Mirabella digs her nails into my thighs as she screams out my name. I let out a guttural groan as she grinds her ass against my pelvis, her wet pussy squeezing my cock as I stretch it.

One hand slides to the front of her neck, gripping her throat loosely, while my other hand slides to her clit.

"Oh...fuck, yes!" She gasps and squirms in my arms.

I keep up with my ministrations, feeling my balls tighten with the urgent need to cum. Her body convulses in my arms and her nails dig deeper into my thighs as she climaxes. I ride her, slamming into her just as my orgasm hits me.

My body tenses, and I let out a rough grunt, slamming into her one last time. When we finally collapse onto the bed for the second time tonight, we're completely spent, exhausted beyond words.

"I think I like sex a little too much," Mirabella drawls as I pull her close, her body melting into mine.

My eyes flutter shut, a tired smile tugging at my lips. Just before sleep claims me, I hear her mutter, "Too bad you won't see me when you wake up."

And she was right. I woke up to find her gone.

A groan escapes my lips as my eyes snap open. I'm no longer in that hotel room with her soft body against mine. Instead, I'm alone in an empty club lounge, haunted by nothing but memories of her.

But I don't plan to let it stay that way.

7

MIRABELLA

The night air bites with a chill as Giovanni and I step out of the laundromat. Ever since that strange guy left, I knew I couldn't stay in that room a second longer. He knew my name and had offered me marriage—on behalf of his boss, no less—without even revealing who this boss is. The whole thing gave me the feeling I was being watched. Giovanni must have picked up on my discomfort because he suggested I call it a night.

"You'll figure out something soon," he says as we cross the empty street. "You'll get through this phase."

"Yeah." I sigh, though I'm not so sure.

"Too bad you didn't get what you came to the club for. The night's still young, though. You maybe could've met someone if you'd stayed longer," Giovanni teases, his grin a little too smug. "Maybe a rich sugar daddy who wouldn't mind you as a sixth wife."

I laugh, shoving his shoulder. "Dick. I'll tell Alessia to let you sleep on the sofa. Don't test me."

"Yeah, like *my baby* would listen to an outsider over me."

I raise an eyebrow, hands to my chest, feigning offense

even though the term *outsider* hits a little harder than it should. "Did you just refer to me as an outsider?"

Giovanni smirks. "Oh, come on. You know I love you. You're my *favorite* outsider."

I scoff dramatically, but my lips twitch. "That's it. I'll make sure Alessia knows how you bully me at her back. She'll kick you out of bed."

"Please. You think Alessia's gonna listen to you?" He shakes his head with exaggerated disbelief. "Good luck with that. You forget I've got an edge you don't."

"Oh? And what's that?"

He gives me a cheeky, mischievous smile, then proceeds to move his tongue around in his mouth, clearly imitating some sort of *suggestive* act that immediately makes me wish I could rewind the conversation back five minutes.

"Jackass," I mutter, disgusted, though I can't hold back a laugh.

"But you love me that way, don't you?" He winks, leaning back with that self-satisfied grin only he can pull off.

I roll my eyes but can't stop smiling. Despite the chaos that is my life, these little moments of ridiculousness are oddly comforting. When the world feels as if it's always about to explode, sometimes it's the stupid jokes and silly fights that make everything feel a little more bearable.

Just then, the familiar unmistakable roar from a sputtering car pulls up—a red Honda Civic, Alessia's old car she got from her mom. The engine sputters before finally stopping. Alessia bursts out of the car, her signature bright grin already lighting up her face.

"Mira," she squeals, throwing her arms around me in a warm hug. I chuckle, hugging her back, the sweet smell of her vanilla perfume filling the air.

"I didn't know you were out tonight! I would've come," she says, pulling back to flash me a smile.

"Well, hello to you too, babe," Giovanni teases from beside me, and I laugh.

Alessia rolls her eyes. "We literally live together, Gio. I saw you before you left. Meanwhile, I haven't seen my best friend in forever!"

"We had breakfast two weeks ago," I remind her with a smirk, earning me a scowl from her.

"Two weeks is forever when it's your best friend, especially since we live in the same city!" She huffs, releasing me from the hug. "Plus, it doesn't count as breakfast if you work in said restaurant and barely spend fifteen minutes with me."

I sigh, feeling a little guilty. "You know how busy I've been, Alessia."

"Yeah, I know," she says with a small, sad smile, right before Giovanni pulls her into his arms. The sad smile disappears when he plants a kiss on her neck and grabs her ass, making her giggle.

"Oh, come on, guys," I groan, but they don't hear me since he's now kissing—no, furiously making out—with her.

"Hey," Giovanni breathes as they finally break apart.

"Hey," Alessia whispers back, biting her lower lip.

"You two are so cute it's nauseating," I say, scrunching my face.

"What can I say? He can't get enough of me," Alessia teases, giving Giovanni a playful look.

"That's true," he agrees, and the way he glances at her with that soft look in his eyes, tells me he's completely honest. It's nice seeing them like this—happy. They've been through their share of rough patches, but they've managed to always come out stronger.

"Are you coming with us?" Alessia asks as they head back to the car.

I shake my head, though it's tempting. "Nah, you two lovebirds enjoy yourselves. I'll take the bus."

"You sure?" Alessia frowns slightly.

"Yup, my place is totally out of your way, anyway."

"All right, but you have to come by soon. Promise?"

"Promise," I say, smiling. "I'll visit, don't worry."

They climb into the car and wave goodbye as it pulls away, leaving me standing under the neon glow of the laundromat sign. For a moment, I think about how easy it would have been to hop in with them, but I'd feel guilty making them drive out of their way at this hour.

I turn toward the bus stop and start walking. My feet ache from these stupidly expensive shoes, and all I want is to get home, curl up in bed, and sleep. Thankfully, it's not too late—thanks to that strange guy who made me leave the club early. I can still get enough rest before I have to wake up for my shift tomorrow.

As I approach the bus stop, I spot the sign in the distance. The occasional flicker of the nearby streetlight gives the scene an eerie feel, even though it's only 8 p.m. My heels click against the gravel road as I make my way to the stop. A gust of wind rushes past me, sending a cold shiver down my spine. It doesn't help that I'm dressed so lightly in this flimsy sequined dress.

I'm almost at the stop when I notice a shadowy figure sitting at the far end of the street on a bench under the flickering light. My pace slows as a tight knot of unease forms in my stomach. It's only when I get closer that I see the soft glow of a cigarette in the person's hand.

When the streetlight flickers back on, its light catches the edge of his sharp profile. My stomach tightens. It's him.

Ettore.

I stop for a second as my heart begins to race in my chest. I watch him bring the cigarette to his lips again. His cheeks hollow slightly as he inhales, holding it for a few moments before exhaling. I'm captivated by the way the smoke curls upward lazily before vanishing into the night air. I never knew smoking could be so... mesmerizing.

But I know it's not just the cigarette. It's him.

He's seated casually on a low concrete bench, his long legs stretched out in front of him. His long black hair is pulled back tonight, with a few wavy strands escaping and falling over his face. The short scruff lining his jaw adds a rugged edge to his appearance. He wears a black button-up shirt, the sleeves rolled up just enough to reveal his muscular forearms. A thick black coat rests on the arm of the bench, adding to his striking look.

I force my legs to move. The sound of my shoes draws his attention, and that's when he turns to look at me.

For a second, I can't breathe. His hazel eyes pierce through the dim light, locking onto mine. My stomach flutters, and warmth creeps up my neck. My mind races back to that night—the heat of his body against mine, the way his rough hands explored my skin, the way he filled me up with his—

Get a fucking grip, Mirabella.

I straighten my posture and walk toward him, trying to keep my cool even though I'm anything but calm inside.

"Are you following me?" I ask, crossing my arms to hide my nerves. I'm relieved that my voice comes out sounding steady even as my heart pounds rapidly in my chest.

He doesn't answer right away. Instead, he takes his time, trailing his eyes over me in that slow, intense way that makes my body heat up. My breathing quickens as his gaze lingers on my bare legs, and I'm flooded with memories of his face between them when he made me orgasm for the first time that night.

He clenches his jaw and flicks the cigarette onto the ground, crushing it under his boot.

"You ran off before I woke up."

His words hit me like a challenge. His tone is casual, but there's an edge to it. He leans back slightly, waiting for my response.

"I don't remember making any promises to stick around," I reply calmly, even though my nerves are anything but.

"Plus," I continue when he doesn't say anything, "you didn't answer my question."

"I'm not following you," he says, leaning forward now, his elbows resting on his knees. "But I could ask you the same thing. What were you doing at that club?"

My heart skips a beat. The club. Had he seen me there?

"I didn't realize you owned it," I reply, keeping my face as neutral as possible.

His eyes narrow. "I don't."

"Then it's none of your business."

His lips twitch into the slightest hint of a smirk, and it hits me how handsome he is. For a moment there's a thick silence between us before he speaks again.

"Is he your boyfriend?"

I blink, caught off guard. "What?"

"The man you were with at the bar," he says, his voice hardening as he waits for my response.

I snort. "Again, it's none of your business."

A flicker of something—jealousy?—crosses his face, but he masks it well. A tiny thrill runs through me at the idea that he might actually care, but I force myself to stay cool, giving him a casual shrug.

"Why do you ask, anyway? You jealous?"

There's a brief pause, and I swear I see a muscle tick in his jaw. But then he smirks, brushing it off like it's nothing. "Not at all. Just curious."

"Right."

Before I can say anything else, headlights sweep over the pavement, and a sleek black car pulls up beside us. It's different from the one he drove that night. A man like him probably has a whole fleet of cars at his disposal.

Ettore glances at it briefly before looking back at me.

"You'll see me again soon, Kitten."

That fucking nickname.

Grab the headboard, Kitten...

I groan inwardly at the intrusive memory. My thoughts scatter when he grabs his coat and stands up. My heart pounds in my chest as he approaches me, but then he just walks past. My breath hitches in my throat as his arm brushes against mine, but he slips into the backseat of his car. The vehicle drives off, leaving me standing there with a racing heart and a flutter in my stomach.

After standing motionless for a few seconds, I blink, snapping myself back to reality. I turn back to the empty street, but my heart won't stop racing. What the hell was that? I start walking toward the bus stop again, my mind spinning with thoughts of Ettore. But as I near the corner, I sense something else.

A figure shifts in the shadows, followed by another. My breath catches. Two lanky men step into the dim light, their eyes cold and calculating. Their presence hits me like a jolt to the gut, and I freeze.

"Mirabella," one of them says in a low, threatening voice. "We've been looking for you."

I take a step back as my heart pounds rapidly for an entirely different reason now. They move closer, cutting off my escape route.

"You know why we're here," the taller one drawls, his eyes sweeping over me. "Abruzzi is really mad, princess."

I assume it's because the men he sent after me are now dead.

"You've got just twenty-four hours to come up with the money."

"What?" I gasp, but before I can say another word, he pulls out a phone and shows me a picture on the screen.

It's a picture of Giulia and Nonna from earlier today when they went grocery shopping. I know it was taken today because they're wearing the same clothes. My heart stops, and cold fear crawls up my spine.

"Twenty-four hours, princess. If the money isn't ready by then..." He lets the sentence trail off, the threat clear in the silence that follows.

My throat tightens. I can't even speak. I can't beg or plead. It's useless.

Without waiting for another word, the men step back into the shadows, vanishing as quickly as they appeared.

I can't breathe. Without thinking, I turn and start running in the opposite direction, one prayer racing through my mind.

I hope the strange man from earlier is still there.

By the time I reach the familiar shop, my heart is hammering so hard it hurts. I push the door open, ignore the woman behind the counter and sprint down the corridor. I flash the bouncers my pass and see a flicker of confusion in their eyes as they let me through.

The music is even louder now as I rush inside. My head is a mess as I push my way through the crowd. I know I look like a madwoman, but I don't care. My eyes dart across the dimly lit space, but I see no sign of the guy.

"Hey," I exhale, approaching the bar.

The bartender from earlier flashes a smile at me. "It's you again..."

"Did you see the guy who approached me earlier?" I interrupt him. "He's tall, wore dark shades, and is a bit scary looking?"

"I'm sorry," he says, looking at me as if I've grown two heads. "I don't think I know whom you're describing."

A frustrated groan bubbles up my throat, but I swallow it and plaster a fake smile on my lips.

"Thanks."

I step out of the club again with only one option left. My hands shake as I pull the business card sitting in my purse. Earlier, when I grabbed it from the counter, I didn't think I'd actually use it, especially not on the same night I received that ridiculous proposition.

The black metal glimmers in my hand as I dial the number.

It rings once before the call is answered.

"I'll do it." I rush out before the other person can say anything. "I'll marry your boss."

There's a beat of silence before I hear the strange man's sharp voice.

"Meet me at The Silver Key Hotel tomorrow at noon."

I tighten my grip on my phone. "What for?"

"To sign the agreement," he says like it's obvious. "Do not be late."

And without waiting for a response, he hangs up.

8

ETTORE

Red wine slides down my throat as I take a sip from my glass. A soft clink echoes in the air when I set the cup beside my plate on the dining table and gaze ahead. My family members flank the sides of the long dining table, everyone busy with the feast before us.

The chandelier overhead casts a warm glow over the dining room in the Greco mansion. The sounds of forks and knives clinking against fine china bounce off the marble floors and high ceilings. The air is filled with delicious aromas. The table is laden with lavish dishes, from truffle-infused pasta to roasted lamb, all prepared by the estate's personal chef.

I can hardly recall the last time I participated in the tradition my father started—our family dinners every night.

I'm a busy man, and most evenings I come home to find everyone else already tucked into bed. But tonight I made an effort to be here for dinner. I returned early from the poker club just in time for the meal because of the announcement I have to make.

"I'm getting married."

My voice slices through the low clinking and chatter, and the room instantly falls silent. Forks freeze mid-air. My younger brother Vittorio looks up from his plate. My two cousins Antonio and Leonardo stop whispering and fix me with stunned expressions. Even Bianca, my eighteen-year-old cousin who is obsessed with her phone looks up with wide eyes. The seconds stretch like hours as I absorb their reactions.

Zia Camilla, my oldest aunt, sits across the table, narrowing her eyes at me. I notice her lips twitch as if she's trying to suppress a smirk. It's just family dinner, yet she's dressed in a silk blouse, pearls delicately hanging around her neck. The rings on her fingers tinkle as they tap against her wine glass.

Finally, it's my other two aunts Francesca and Marta who break the silence.

"Ettore! That's great news," Aunt Francesca exclaims, while Aunt Marta chimes in, "Finally!"

I knew they'd be pleased with my announcement. They've been pushing me to get married ever since I took over the family company right after graduating college. I'm sure this is just another chance for them to plan a party that will leave everyone talking.

"Nah, I don't believe it." Vittorio chuckles. "Did you hit your head today?"

I can hardly believe it myself. While I wasn't surprised when Luca called earlier to tell me that Bella had agreed, it still feels a bit surreal.

I'm getting married.

"Who's the lucky woman?" Antonio chimes in, leaning back in his chair. "Or should I say unlucky? You're not exactly husband material."

"You must be kidding," Leonardo replies, shooting Antonio a look. "Ettore is exactly the type of man most women would die to have..."

"Because he was named the sexiest bachelor in New York?" Antonio snorts. "He's assistant probably paid the newspaper to run that."

I can't help but chuckle.

"Because everyone wants to be a Greco," Leonardo corrects, rolling his eyes with arrogance. I feel sorry for the girls who had to deal with him at UCLA.

"That's exactly why she's unlucky," Bianca adds, surprising me. She rarely speaks at the table. "She's going to be under so much public scrutiny. People will hate her just for marrying into the Greco family, but really, they're just jealous because that's what they want."

"I'm sure this conversation is doing wonders for your ego," Vittorio mutters beside me.

Antonio huffs at his sister. "They only want Ettore because they don't really know who he is." I catch the slight edge in his voice.

Interesting.

It doesn't surprise me that I'm not my cousin's favorite person. His mother, Francesca, doesn't like me, so why would he?

Our family dynamic is...complicated. The Greco family has always been wealthy, but our fortune skyrocketed when my father took over the family business at a young age after his father died. He worked hard, reinvested his inheritance, and tripled his wealth. He became significantly wealthier than his three sisters, even though they all received the same inheritance from their father. I suspect they were a bit jealous, but my father held no ill will toward his siblings.

When he built the Greco estate, he invited them all to live with him.

Their animosity toward us began when he married my mother. To them, she didn't meet the family's standards. It worsened when my parents died, and as expected, eighty percent of my father's possessions went to my brother and me. Apparently, my father should have left more than the beach houses abroad and stocks he distributed to each sibling and their children.

But they are all good pretenders—except for the children, of course. Marta, Leonardo's mother, is more subtle, cutting into her steak with slow precision, her eyes flickering with intrigue as she listens to her children's conversation.

I almost forgot about Zia Camilla, my father's older sister and clearly the boldest among the three.

I let their comments wash over me as my gaze locks with Zia Camilla's. She remains eerily silent, but her eyes gleam with curiosity. There's also a sharp edge to her gaze, the same look she always had when questioning my late father's choices—especially marrying my mother, a woman who wasn't born into wealth like the rest of them.

"When are we going to meet her? Is she pretty?" Aunt Marta asks, a calculating smile on her lips.

Mirabella's face flashes in my mind—her long auburn hair, big brown eyes, plump lips, and perfect nose...

She's not just pretty. Her beauty is ethereal.

I've only seen her twice, yet the image of her face hasn't left my mind for even a moment.

"I'll tell you more in time," I reply, refusing to indulge their curiosity.

Vittorio shifts beside me. He's perceptive, so I know he can sense the strange energy in the air. My brother is my closest family member. We've been inseparable since he was born, despite the seven-year gap between us. At twenty-five, he already runs a significant part of the business, and I'm grateful to have someone like him by my side.

Leonardo and Antonio exchange knowing glances while Bianca returns her attention to her phone.

Finally, Zia Camilla's voice cuts through the air—soft yet laced with venom. "Well, isn't that a surprise?" Her fingers tighten around the stem of her glass. "One can only hope you've chosen someone suitable. Someone who understands our family's traditions."

Traditions. Her not-so-subtle way of saying I'd better not marry someone like my mother—someone beneath the Greco name.

"You'll meet her soon enough," I respond, my tone neutral but firm. I'm not in the mood for her thinly veiled insults tonight.

Vittorio leans over, muttering under his breath, "You're actually serious about this? When did you decide? Is she someone I've met before?"

"I wouldn't announce it if I wasn't serious," I tell him. "And like I said, you'll all meet her at the right time."

He exhales, and his silence tells me he knows not to press further. At least not in front of the others. I know he'll grill me about it later.

"Is she famous?" Bianca asks in a flat voice, still not looking up from her phone. Her fingers are furiously typing away, no doubt updating her followers with whatever meaningless gossip she's conjured up today.

She's the youngest, a high school senior who's made a name for herself as a social media influencer. Hundreds of thousands of followers engage with her, even when she's doing nothing but flaunting her wealth and pretty face. She knows not to disclose any information about our family's private life, which is why I'm not worried about her spilling my announcement to anyone willing to listen.

"Famous?" I raise an eyebrow, glancing down the table at her. "No."

"Well, she will be the moment she marries you," Bianca mutters, finally looking up with a smirk. "Maybe I should give her a shoutout. Is she a social media person? I know some people aren't really into social media."

She's right. I doubt Bella is obsessed with likes, followers, and fans. She's just trying to survive.

"For someone who just announced his marriage, you're being a bit vague with the details, Ettore," Camilla interjects, dabbing at her lips with a napkin. "Is it because you're unsure if she's the right fit? I understand. Your father was quite uncertain about marrying your mother, too, in the beginning. If only he had listened..."

I clench my fists at her comment. I don't relate to the idea of love. I refuse to surrender my entire existence to loving and committing to one person. But my parents? They were definitely in love. Even a blind man could see it.

I witnessed it when they were alive. They couldn't stand being apart for long and showered that same love on my brother and me. After my father died from a heart attack when I was young, my mother couldn't bear the loss. I saw how it changed her. She barely lasted another year before she passed away, too.

"It's not too late to reconsider," Zia Camilla's voice floats through the air. "There are plenty of fine women from the right families. Ones who would—how shall I put it?— uphold the Greco legacy." She smiles thinly. "It would be a shame for the head of the family to make the same mistake twice."

Zia Camilla has always made her opinions about my parents' love abundantly clear. It didn't conform to the expectations of the Greco family. My father, the powerful head of our clan, was supposed to marry someone from our social sphere—someone wealthy, someone who would enhance the family's status. Instead, he chose my mother—a woman from a humble background, quiet yet strong, who was never enough in their eyes.

Even now, years after their deaths, her disdain for my mother lingers. She can't hide it. On the rare occasions when she tries to feign civility, her true feelings leak through in every word, glance, and action.

I meet her gaze, and the room falls silent as everyone waits for my response. I take a bite of steak and sip my wine before speaking.

"You should remember your place, Zia, or I'll be forced to remind you," I say, my voice sharp. "I am not my father."

She stiffens but remains silent. The others around us shift uncomfortably. They all know I'm the one in charge here. I paid for her two daughters' tuition at a private university in England before they eventually married influential men—again, thanks to me. She enjoys a free roof over her head and has maids at her beck and call. I provide her with a monthly allowance, just like I do for the rest of my aunts and all my cousins.

She could lose all of that in the blink of an eye. While my father was loving and kind to his family despite their ungratefulness, I won't hesitate to cut off anyone who constantly tries to hurt me. Sure, she wouldn't suffer in the same way if she lost everything I offer her, but she wouldn't be able to afford her monthly vacations, her ridiculously expensive jewelry, or her membership in the elite social clubs she frequents. And if there's one thing

Zia Camilla loves more than anything, it's her public image.

They all know this, which is why the rest have to pretend and be more subtle with their jabs. But Zia Camilla likes to push her luck, using her seniority as leverage. Yes, Italian tradition demands respect for elders, but there's only so much I'm willing to tolerate.

"Of course," she says, clearing her throat and swirling her wine glass. "I'm sure she's lovely. I can't wait to meet her."

Leonardo lets out a snort before quickly covering it with a cough.

Dry amusement bubbles up inside me, but I keep my face impassive.

"You'll all get to meet her soon."

My mind flashes back to Mirabella, and a strange feeling ignites in my chest. She'll be meeting Luca tomorrow to sign the agreement.

And then, she becomes mine.

9

MIRABELLA

My legs feel like jelly the moment I step through the doors of The Silver Key Hotel. This place is known as the most expensive hotel in New York, and I can see why. Everything around me exudes luxury, from the sparkling chandeliers above to the glossy marble floors reflecting the soft, golden light.

Never in my life did I think I would be in a place like this. My world and this world don't mix. At all. A part of me thinks this is some sort of power move from my strange husband-to-be. He wants to show me just how wealthy he is, make me swoon, and then seal the deal once the contract is signed.

But that's just delusional. A wealthy man like he is doesn't have to prove anything to someone like me.

I catch a glimpse of myself in the automatic glass doors just as they slide shut behind me. I look ridiculous compared to the usual guests who frequent this place, even though I'm wearing my best black dress, a new pair of flats, and a matching black purse.

This is annoying. I'm dressed in my Sunday best, for God's sake.

As if on cue, a middle-aged woman in a thick fur coat walks past me. She gives me a quick once-over, her eyes flicking over my frame. She's probably wondering if I've lost my way. Her gaze narrows slightly, and I snort inwardly. Yup. She definitely thinks I don't belong here.

Too bad I have bigger problems to worry about. Like, I don't know, the marriage contract I'll be signing before I leave this place.

Straightening my shoulders, I take a deep breath and head toward the elevator across the lobby. I received a brief text from the number I called telling me to meet him in a restaurant on the fifth floor of the hotel.

The elevator ride feels like it stretches on forever. As I stare at my reflection in the mirrored walls, I try to ignore the gnawing feeling in my gut. I literally have no idea what I'm about to walk into. I don't even know the names of the men I'm dealing with. This is definitely creepy, but what choice do I have? By tonight, the twenty-four hours Abruzzi gave me will be up. I have to take whatever chances I can, no matter how dangerous or sketchy it may seem.

The soft chime of the elevator pulls me out of my thoughts. The doors slide open to reveal a sleek, dimly lit hallway. A gentle melody drifts through the air, mixed with the rich aroma wafting from the restaurant nearby. My heart races in my chest as I step out of the elevator and head toward the door. I'm about to sign away a part of my life. Heck, my whole life. But I can't back down now.

I push the door open and enter the small, lavish restaurant. I don't have to scan the space for long before I spot him —the guy from the club—at the far end. He's not wearing dark shades today, and somehow that makes him even scarier. His eyes lock onto mine, and I swallow hard before making my way toward him.

"You're on time," he says in his usual calm and measured tone. "That's a good start."

"A good start would be you telling me your name," I blurt out.

Shit. That sounded sharper than I intended. I'm on edge. I hate feeling this way.

I bite back the apology that's on the tip of my tongue. He's asking me to sign something that could change my entire life. Demanding his name is the least I can ask for.

"Luca," he says, his eyes never leaving mine, unreadable. There's no flicker of annoyance at my sharpness, nothing to show he cares.

That's even worse.

"Sit," he commands, his voice cold as steel.

I shoot him a glare but sit, my movements stiff, betraying my discomfort.

He slides a black folder and a sleek ballpoint pen across the table toward me.

"Open it."

I snort under my breath. "You really love telling people what to do, don't you?"

But even as the words leave my mouth, I'm reaching for the folder, flipping it open. My eyes scan the first page, where dense legal jargon sprawls across the page.

"This is...a lot," I mutter, my voice shaky. The numbers, the clauses—it's overwhelming.

"There's a nondisclosure agreement on the first page. Nothing about this arrangement leaves this room. You don't tell anyone. Your silence is legally binding."

"Yeah, yeah, I get it," I mutter, rolling my eyes, trying to brush it off. I flip to the next page, my heart pounding louder with every word.

His voice, smooth and detached, drifts over me as he continues outlining the terms. "You and your family will relocate to his estate. You'll be under constant surveillance at all times." He lets the weight of that statement sink in before adding, "You'll make required appearances. No media. No questions."

My heart is hammering in my chest. I don't even know who these people are, but the threat is as tangible as the air between us.

"And the money," he continues, eyes cold and assessing. "One million dollars will be wired into your bank account the day after the wedding. Another $100,000 every month for the duration of the contract."

I can feel my stomach twist. This is real.

"And your mother," he goes on, his tone clinical, "will be admitted to the city's best hospital immediately after the wedding. She'll have a private room with full-time nurses." He lists the details as if he's reading a grocery list, each word landing harder than the last.

It's too much, too fast. My head spins.

"Who exactly is your boss?" I interrupt, unable to keep the edge out of my voice. "This feels like...I don't know. It's too much. Everything is happening too fast."

Luca's eyes narrow slightly, the only sign that he's actually listening. His gaze doesn't soften. It's sharp, predatory.

"You'll find out in due time," he says, his voice laced with finality.

I feel my frustration grow, something bitter bubbling up inside. "Just tell me who he is. Give me a name. Even a first name, like you did with yours."

For a brief moment, his eyes flash with something—anger, maybe?—but it's gone before I can pinpoint it.

His voice drops, and he repeats himself. "You'll find out in due time."

I grind my teeth together, the tension in my body coiling tighter. I stare him down, trying to cut through his calm with my gaze, but he's unflinching. Not an ounce of fear in him. Not even the slightest sign of intimidation.

A heavy sigh escapes me as I stand up, grabbing my bag from the chair beside me. I'm done. I shouldn't have come here.

"I'm sorry... This was a mistake," I mutter, my voice suddenly small. "I-I shouldn't have come."

As I try to stand, he slips one hand into his suit coat, and I instantly tense. This is the part in movies where the mysterious guy pulls out a gun and places it on the table, forcing the other person to sign their life away. My heart jumps into my throat as I see something black peek out from beneath the jacket.

Shit. He's going to kill me. And with how things have gone so far, I think he might actually get away with it.

Except when he drops something on the table, it's not a black gun but a black envelope.

"Ten thousand," he says. "In cash."

I don't move. I can't move. My body's locked in place, my breath caught in my throat. My eyes fixate on the sleek black envelope. It's glossy, menacing—an offer or a threat. I can't tell which.

"The rest will come three days from now."

"Wait...but you said after the wedding,"

He leans back in his seat, the faintest twitch of his lips, almost a smile, as if he's amused by my confusion. "Exactly."

"The wedding is in three days?!"

Luca's expression remains neutral, but I catch the smallest upward tug of his lips. He is giving me a smile now, and it's actually scary. "Your whole life is about to change, Mirabella. Beyond what you could have ever imagined. Even after you both walk away next year, you'll never know what it feels like to be destitute again."

I keep staring at the envelope for what feels like forever. It's the down payment on my freedom—or my imprisonment. A shaky exhale escapes my lips as I take the pen and flip to the last page of the folder. As I stare at the blank space where my signature should be, the image of Giulia, Nonna, and Abruzzi's men from last night flashes through my mind. I think of my mother and how she couldn't get out of bed this morning. I remember the old, disgusting men who try to grope me at my job at the bar.

Before I realize what I'm doing, I scrawl my signature on the paper. I feel the weight of Luca's gaze on me as he watches closely. When I'm done, I close the folder and slide it back to him before grabbing the thick envelope. It's heavy—heavier than I expected.

"What now?" I mutter as a strange mix of relief and dread wash over me.

"Your wedding is in three days. Prepare yourself and your family for the upcoming changes in your life."

I nod, biting the inside of my cheek as I slip the envelope into my bag. I stand on shaky feet and give him one last nod before walking out of the room.

The hot afternoon sun hits me as I step outside the hotel. A headache begins to pound at my temples, and I try to push it aside, but I know that's impossible. My shoulders ache from the weight of what I've just done.

But, hey! On the bright side. I am halfway free from Abruzzi and his constant harassment. I'll pay him back once

I get the rest of the money, and then he'll be out of my hair for good. The money I owe the other loan sharks doesn't even come to $1,000. I can easily pay them back after my first monthly paycheck from my *husband.*

"God, this is unreal," I groan as the throbbing in my head intensifies. Everything is happening too fast, and I can barely keep up. I can't handle the whiplash of emotions I feel or figure out the next steps I should take.

Just then, I'm reminded of the envelope, which feels like a weight burning a hole in my bag.

You should settle Abruzzi first, my inner voice reminds me.

Instead of taking a bus, I decide to walk the long route to my neighborhood. Walking has always helped me clear my head, after all. As my legs carry me from the upscale neighborhood to the rundown streets I know so well, the hot sun gives way to the crisp evening air.

By the time I arrive at the familiar large but dilapidated building that I've seen in my nightmares for months, I feel a newfound boldness.

I step into the building and take the stairs to the second floor, where Abruzzi's office resides. Upon arriving, I push the door open without knocking.

The thick smell of tobacco and expensive cologne hits me as I enter the spacious room. Two men are smoking by the window, and as I walk farther inside, their eyes drink me in. Yet, my glare is only focused on the man seated behind the large desk at the far end of the room.

His usual smirk widens into a smug grin as I approach him, fueling the anger in my veins.

"Well, well, if it isn't my favorite debtor," Abruzzi drawls, leaning back in his chair. "To what do I owe the pleasure?"

I slip the envelope out of my bag and toss it onto his desk. "Half of what I owe you."

"Oh, baby," he chuckles. "I only asked my men to rattle you a bit. You didn't have to go to such extreme lengths to get this money."

His mocking tone stings, and I clench my fists to contain my anger. Men like Abruzzi love the control they wield over poor helpless people who depend on them. It's why, even though he's loaded, he established his loan shark business here in the slums.

Dirty bastard.

"You could have come to me personally," he continued in that annoying drawl of his. "Maybe I could have come up with an agreement that would benefit the both of us."

The other men in the room laugh, and I feel disgust crawl up my spine.

"I would rather die," I bite out, and I mean it.

"Really, darling?" He smiles, and the gesture makes him look a bit younger.

Abruzzi isn't unpleasant to look at. In fact, some might consider him attractive and would jump at the opportunity to be with a man like him. But I despise him. I know he's involved in dark, shady dealings. Heck, this establishment and the men who hang around him are proof that he could be part of some criminal gang.

"You'll have your full payment by next week," I say firmly, ignoring his taunts.

"I like this newfound courage of yours," he chuckles before grabbing the envelope and flipping it open.

His eyebrows shoot up, and I see something flicker in his eyes as he scans the bills inside.

"Impressive." He closes the envelope and pins me with a stare. "Tell me, sweetheart, where did you get this kind of money?"

"You have your money. How I got it is none of your business," I snap before turning to walk away.

"Oh, but it is. My men saw you talking to Luca. Do you know who he works for?"

That makes me halt in my steps. When I turn to look at him, the smugness in his smile makes my skin crawl. He knows more than he's letting on.

I keep my face blank. "I don't care."

Abruzzi chuckles, leaning back. "You should. You think you're free? Think again. You just signed a deal with the devil."

His words send a shiver down my spine, but I refuse to let him see how deeply they cut.

"I don't give a fuck. And again, it's none of your business," I snap before turning and continuing my journey to the door.

"You'll be back, baby," he calls after me. "When you realize the mess you've gotten yourself into, you'll come running back to me."

I step out of the office and slam the door shut, blocking off the laughter echoing behind me. Even as I leave the cursed building, his words cling to me like smoke.

Abruzzi might be a sick bastard, but I can't ignore the nagging feeling in my stomach that there's truth in his words.

In my desperate need to be free from him, have I just sold my life to a greater devil?

10

ETTORE

The house buzzes with quiet activity as I stride into the drawing room where every member of this household has gathered. Twenty of my staff stand in a neat row, eyes alert and shoulders stiff. Leonardo and Antonio are bickering about something, but their voices fall silent the moment they spot me.

"My fiancée will arrive in a few days," I state firmly.

I notice the shocked expressions on my staff's faces, despite their efforts to conceal it.

"C-congratulations, sir." Paula, the head maid, manages a small smile.

"Who gave you permission to speak?" Zia Camilla snaps.

"A-Apologies ma'am," Paula stammers, fidgeting with her hands and casting her eyes to the floor.

I glance over at Zia Camilla. She sits primly with her hands folded in her lap, dressed in luxurious silk pajamas. It's just minutes before her bedtime—I know because she adheres to a strict routine—yet she wears pearls around her neck and matching earrings dangling from her lobes.

My gaze sweeps across the rest of the family scattered

on the sofa beside her. Vittorio slouches on a single couch, casually flipping through a random magazine. Aunt Francesca and Aunt Marta huddle together as usual. With only a year between them, they could easily be mistaken for twins given how they always stick together. As a child, I actually thought they were twins until my father pointed out that Aunt Marta is a year older than Aunt Francesca.

Leonardo, Antonio, and Bianca sit on another sofa to my left. I'm surprised not to see Bianca's phone anywhere in sight. However, her boredom is clear as she flicks her dark hair behind her shoulder and stifles a yawn.

"I expect this household to be ready to welcome her when she arrives," I continue, directing a pointed look at my aunts. "That includes ensuring the wedding preparations are in order."

"Wedding preparations?" Aunt Francesca frowns. "Isn't she supposed to be introduced to the family first?"

"The wedding is in three days."

Murmurs ripple through the room. Zia Camilla sits up even straighter, if that's possible, fixing me with a sharp look.

"Three days?" Aunt Marta asks, incredulously.

I raise an eyebrow. "Did I stutter?"

"Of course not. But isn't that a bit too soon?"

"You can plan a stellar wedding in three days. Or is that too much for you to handle?"

"Of course not." She looks almost insulted by my question. Her lips curl into a smile that doesn't quite reach her eyes. "It will be the wedding of the year. Everything will be perfect."

"That's what I want to hear."

I turn to the staff. "You will double your efforts around

the house. Everything has to be flawless to welcome my bride. I want no mistakes."

Murmurs of "Yes, sir," echo around the room.

I inhale before slipping my hands in my pockets. "You are dismissed."

As the staff rushes out of the room, I turn to face my family. I know the conversation isn't over yet, and out of courtesy, I'm giving them one last chance to express their opinions, no matter how annoying they might be, before Mirabella arrives.

"What's with the rush, Ettore?" Zia Camilla asks, feigning concern. Something glimmers in her eyes as she adds, "Did you get her pregnant? Is that why this marriage discussion suddenly came out of nowhere?"

At the tightening of my jaw, she hastily explains, "It's just that you've always been so against marriage in the past..."

"You mean when you tried to set me up with the women you handpicked for me to marry?" I reply.

"I was only trying to help." She glances at her sisters before continuing, "We all were. But once we realized you didn't want to get married, we backed off. So now this...I can only assume something serious prompted you to make this decision."

"And you jumped to the conclusion of pregnancy?" Leonardo chuckles. "What if our dear cousin fell in love?"

That earns a laugh from my brother and the rest of my cousins, but Zia Camilla doesn't find it amusing. Her eyes narrow as she snaps, "It wouldn't be the first time someone got pregnant out of wedlock in this family, would it? At least Ettore is being honorable about it, unlike your father..."

Leonardo's smile disappears just as Aunt Marta sits up straight.

"Why would you say that to my son's face?" she demands.

Zia Camilla chuckles, undeterred by Aunt Marta's anger. "Because it's the truth. You should be grateful our brother didn't throw you out into the streets after your attempt to tarnish our family's name..."

A tension-filled silence follows her words. Antonio shifts in his chair while Bianca leans her head on her brother's shoulder, hiding her face in her hair. Vittorio glances up from his magazine, briefly looking at me as if questioning why I'm not stopping the argument. When I return his gaze with a blank expression, he sighs and goes back to the page in front of him.

Meanwhile, Aunt Marta's knees bounce uncontrollably as Aunt Francesca pats her shoulders in an attempt to calm her down.

"Camilla...you should let this go. It's been ages," she says softly, trying to soothe her.

"If anyone hasn't let it go, it's Marta." Zia Camilla shrugs. "I'm not the one boiling with anger. I just answered a question the boy asked..."

Leonardo's sharp chuckle cuts through her sentence.

"You're just a sick, bitter widow."

The look on Zia Camilla's face is almost comical. Her eyes widen in shock as she sputters, "Excuse me?"

"Even before your husband died, he hated your guts. He only married you for your money and status, and even that wasn't enough to keep him. He wanted a divorce, and when you wouldn't grant him one out of shame for what people would say, he cheated on you with a younger woman, had kids with her, and brought them to your matrimonial home..."

"You little—"

"Your husband's family accepted them because they hate you, too," Leonardo continues with a dark chuckle. "Even your children never call or visit. I'm guessing they don't want your poisonous attitude rubbing off on their kids. You should be grateful that your brother took you in after your terrible marriage nearly tarnished the Greco name..."

"You bastard..."

"Enough." My sharp voice booms across the room.

Zia Camilla's face flushes with rage, while Leonardo wears a look of satisfaction. I still have work to do tonight, so I don't have time for this argument to drag on.

"No one is pregnant, this wedding will proceed exactly as planned, and there will be no more discussion on the matter."

As I turn to leave, the argument erupts behind me, louder than before. I retreat to my office in the west wing of the mansion, far from the noise, and close the heavy oak doors behind me.

I barely have time to sit before my phone buzzes, and the name on the screen sends a wave of memories crashing over me.

"Word in the air is that you're getting hitched." Dario's voice floats through my ear the moment I answer the call.

I chuckle despite myself. "Is that why you called at this hour?"

"Hey! I just got the invitation from your assistant. I wanted to make sure it wasn't a prank." He laughs over the line.

"The same way I was shocked when you married Ginevra. How is she, by the way?" I ask.

Ginevra is the woman who managed to bring my old friend, a ruthless businessman with underground ties like mine, to his knees.

"She's fine, and don't try to change the subject. We're talking about you here. Don't get me wrong; I'm happy for you. Being married is great..."

I roll my eyes.

"...but I can't believe you want to become a family man. You were the one who reminded me how dangerous it is to raise a family in a world like ours, and I'm not even as deep as you are. You basically run the underworld. Heck! You're even more powerful than I am, and I'm the reason you're alive today."

"You always have to remind me, don't you?" I chuckle, though the sound is humorless.

His words pull me back to years ago, before I took control of the Greco empire, before I became The Reaper. My father had just died, and at just eighteen, I became a target for the mafia bosses and gang leaders with whom my father had dealt. They wanted me gone. They wanted to take over the Greco empire.

I'd been invited to a bar to meet my father's friends, who claimed they wanted to help me out. They knew I didn't have much experience in the business world, and they'd offered their assistance. When I arrived at the location, Dario, a street thug at the time, pulled me back just before I entered the bar. He revealed that he'd overheard some men's conversation as they entered the bar. They'd planned to kill me—powerful men lying in wait for an eighteen-year-old boy.

Dario saved me that night and taught me how to survive in the darkest corners of our world. We became close, but as we grow older, our paths diverged. I became The Reaper, the king of the underworld, while Dario immersed himself in various businesses and the corporate world. Yet, despite our differences, we've remained bound by loyalty and the friendship we still share.

"Having a family means you now have a weakness, Ettore," Dario says, his tone darkening. "You may not be as involved as you used to be, but these rivals won't rest until they take you down. To them, you're still The Reaper—their biggest threat."

"I'll be fine, Dario," I reply with a chuckle, even though it feels hollow. "Being a family man sure has made you worry too much. You know who I am. I never let my guard down."

He chuckles before offering his parting words and hanging up.

I stare at the wall opposite me as his words echo in my mind. It feels like no matter how hard I try—getting married to clean up my image, limiting my involvement in mafia affairs to strictly underground dealings—I can't change who I am.

The Reaper.

I'm still staring at the wall when Luca walks in, his face set in its usual blank expression.

"Everything is in place, sir," he says, closing the door behind him. "I've sent men to watch over Mirabella's house. They'll bring her family to the estate tomorrow."

"Good." I sigh and lean back against my seat.

As Luca turns to leave, my mind fills with images and memories of Mirabella. For some reason, picturing her distracts me from Dario's nagging voice. The sound of her laughter and the memory of her smile bring a much-needed calm to my chest.

I close my eyes with only one thought in mind: I can't wait for my bride to come home.

11

MIRABELLA

The low rumble of a car engine outside my bedroom window pulls me from sleep. I groan, sitting up in bed, still foggy and tired. Why are nights so short? Why can't I just sleep as long as I want? I rub my eyes, adjusting to the soft morning light filtering through the curtains. Peeling back the worn fabric, I frown as I spot a sleek black sedan parked right outside my house.

What in the fuck is a black sedan doing in front of my house?

Cars like that don't belong in this neighborhood, so it can only mean a few things, none of them good. Has Abruzzi sent his men here? It's his style to play dirty, especially now that he's realized his hold on me is slipping, all thanks to my supposedly invincible and terrifying husband-to-be.

The second thought that hits me—they're here for me.

My throat tightens as two men step out of the car dressed in black suits, looking as rigid as stone. They step away from the car and head toward my front door, and that's when I recognize Luca trailing behind them, walking with his usual measured steps.

Why the hell are they here so early? I glance at the clock on my wall—6:14 am. My heart pounds as I push off the blanket, scrambling out of my room just as the first heavy knock shakes the front door. Panic surges through me, knotting in my throat.

They've come to take us—me and my family—and I haven't told anyone a thing. How am I supposed to explain that I'm getting married to a man I don't even know? I knew I'd have to do it eventually, but not today. When Luca mentioned we'd need to move into my "husband's" house, I didn't expect them to show up at 6:14 in the *freaking* morning.

Taking a shaky breath, I reach the door and crack it open. Two men in black suits stare back at me, tall and as stiff as soldiers. The one with dark hair and a thick beard speaks first.

"Miss Ricci?"

I clear my throat. "Yes?"

"We're here to escort you and your family to your new home," he says simply.

My throat goes dry. I'd hoped to have more time to break this insane news to my family. There's no way I'm dragging them out to some unknown place with these three intimidating men without even a warning. I slip outside, carefully closing the door behind me.

"I...I haven't told my family yet," I stammer, my voice shaky. "You'll need to leave. I'll...uh...get them ready, and we'll come later."

Luca, who has been standing back, steps forward. "We have strict instructions to bring you and your family with us. Today," he says in that familiar monotone voice.

I scoff, crossing my arms over my chest. "Tell your boss

he can't just expect me to uproot my family in a flash." My voice is firm, but inside I'm panicking.

Luca doesn't even blink. I let out a soft groan, glancing back inside to make sure everyone's still asleep.

"Look," I sigh, "I know I signed the contract and all, but I need a little more time to explain this...situation to them."

"We have orders not to return without you and your family," Luca repeats, sounding like a broken record.

I'm about to throw another snappy response his way when I hear soft footsteps behind me.

"Mirabella? Who are you talking to?" Giulia's sleepy voice floats down the hall. I turn just in time to see her standing there, rubbing her eyes and looking annoyed, like she's mad her sleep got cut short. Nonna isn't far behind her, tightening her robe as she watches the scene with growing curiosity in her eyes as she pulls her robe tighter around herself.

Dammit.

I don't have a choice now.

I shoot Luca and his men a quick glare before muttering, "Wait here." My heart races as I close the door and turn to face my family.

"Who were those men? Mira, I hope you haven't gotten yourself into trouble," Nonna says, eyeing me with suspicion.

"I...need to talk to you both," I mutter, leading them into the small living room. I catch Nonna sneaking a glance at the men through the window.

"Is Mom awake? She should probably hear this, too," I sigh, bracing myself as they settle around the kitchen table.

"She's still asleep. Should I wake her?" Giulia asks.

I shake my head, remembering how hard it was for her to drift off even with all the pain meds last night. Nonna and

Giulia sit at the tiny kitchen table, their eyes wide with worry and anticipation. My heart feels like it's going to beat out of my chest as I search for the right words.

"So...I'm getting married," I finally blurt out. Nonna's eyebrows shoot up while Giulia just blinks with her mouth open, too shocked to say anything.

The longer they stay without saying anything, the more scared I get.

An exhale leaves my lips. "Please say something."

"*Madonna mia,* Mirabella Ricci." Nonna calls my full name softly. "Tell me this is some kind of joke."

"It's not, Nonna."

Her eyes search mine for any sign that I'm playing, but there's nothing there. The pause that follows feels like an eternity. She lets out a heavy sigh, crossing her arms over her chest. "Marriage, *bambina,* it is not like picking out a dress or a flavor of gelato. It is for life, eh? How do you decide something like this so...so fast?"

"I thought about it, Nonna. It wasn't something I did on a whim."

"Oh, really?" Her eyes narrow, suspicious. "And this man, who is he?"

I hesitate, and the words catch in my throat. "I...haven't met him yet."

Nonna's mouth parts in shock. Giulia looks at me as if I've completely lost it.

"It's a...beneficial arrangement," I mutter, twisting my hands together nervously. I can barely bring myself to meet their eyes. "He'll help us with the debt... and pay for Mom's treatments and surgery. And in return, I have to marry him."

Giulia's head drops, and Nonna's eyes glisten as tears well up. Quickly, I reach over and take her hand.

"What about Giulia?" My voice cracks as I look at my

sister. "Very soon you'll be applying to different universities. The fact that it's still a couple of years away doesn't mean we shouldn't prepare. I'll have more than enough to send you anywhere you want—abroad even. You can be anyone you want to be."

Giulia lifts her gaze to me, a small frown tugging at her lips. "But I don't want any of that at the expense of your happiness, Mirabella. I won't be happy if you're miserable."

I clench my jaw, trying to keep the tears at bay. "You'll be even more unhappy if you don't get to live the life I never had. I'll be damned before I let you drop out like I did."

I glance back at Nonna, my hand trembling as I gently rub the side of her face. Her tears have already begun to fall, and I can't stand seeing her like this.

"It's okay, Nonna. He's...he's a good man." I try to sound convincing, though I'm not even sure myself. I've heard enough from Gio and Abruzzi about my fiancé to know he's nothing like the *nice guy* I'm pretending he is.

Giulia scrunches up her nose as she speaks. "So...he's like, what, *vecchio*? Like in those movies where the old guys marry young girls for some crazy reason?"

I wince, half wondering the same thing. Before I can answer, Nonna's face darkens, her eyes flashing.

"*Non ti lascerò fare una cosa del genere!* I will not let you do this!" she snaps, folding her arms tightly across her chest.

"Nonna..." I sigh, trying to explain. "I already signed a contract..."

She raises her hand to stop me. "Then unsign it! It's not a do-or-die situation, is it?"

I fall silent, and her expression softens. She places a hand on my cheek, her voice trembling. "I hate that you felt you had to do this for us, *piccola mia*."

"Don't, Nonna. It is not your fault." I hold her hand to

my cheek, feeling the warmth and strength in her touch. "I didn't sell my soul or anything…it's just marriage. So what if he's…older?" I grimace, feeling my face heat up. "Women marry older men all the time, right? And he's…he's rich. He'll help us. That's the important thing, right?"

Nonna studies me, her face a mix of worry and resignation. "Are you really sure, Mirabella?"

I let out a long sigh, nodding. "Yes. I am."

Nonna nods slowly, as if trying to convince herself. Giulia just looks at me with wide eyes, half bewildered, half amused, like she's caught in the middle of some absurd dream. If I were her, I'd probably be laughing, too—her sister announcing her engagement to a stranger at the crack of dawn.

Nonna clears her throat, her tone sharpening slightly. "I'm still not giving my consent to this, but I understand that you're an adult capable of making her own decisions."

"Thank you, Nonna," I say, my voice thick with emotion.

"Ah, don't thank me. I still wish I could smack your head right now for even considering this!" She huffs, but there's a hint of affection in her exasperation.

"And the men outside, they are…?" Guilia asks.

My stomach drops. I'd almost forgotten about them.

I glance between my grandmother and sister. I can't tell them that they have to move in with us today, not after I just broke the news of my strange marriage to them. I expect them to get used to the idea first before anything else happens.

"They're…here to take me," I admit, keeping my voice soft. "The wedding is in three days…"

"Three days?" Giulia's voice is a mix of disbelief and panic, while Nonna just stares at me, her eyes glassy, searching my face.

I exhale, trying to keep my voice steady. "There's no time to explain everything right now, but I'll see you both at the wedding—and after that, we'll all be together again."

Giulia shakes her head, her eyes darting between me and Nonna. "This is absolute bonkers! I must have fallen asleep on the couch watching those ridiculous rom coms again," she mutters. "Someone pinch me so I can wake up and pretend this isn't happening!"

Before I can say anything, a firm knock echoes from the front door, the sound pressing down on us like a weight.

"Please don't worry." I give them a reassuring smile. "I'll make sure everything's ready for you when it's time for you to join me. This...it's all going to work out."

But as I hug them goodbye, I can see the doubt and fear in their eyes. The image stays with me even as I walk out the door, past the waiting men, and into a life I can only hope I'll survive.

"I'll go with you now," I say, lifting my chin, "but my family stays here. I just told them, and they need some time to adjust. They'll come after the wedding."

They exchange glances, Luca's jaw tightening briefly before he gives a small nod. "Fine."

With a stiff nod of my own, I head back inside to pack a few essentials. My mom is still sleeping peacefully, and I ask Nonna to break the news gently once she wakes up. After hugging Giulia and Nonna goodbye, I steel myself and step out the door.

My heart pounds as Luca and his men guide me to the sleek BMW parked opposite our small house. The plush leather scent fills the car as I slide into the back seat, and I clutch my hands together, my palms sweating as I stare at the back of the driver's head, wondering how my life had spiraled into this.

The silence in the car feels oppressive, as if I'm being driven into a beautiful prison. Luxury or not, this feels like a cage made of golden bars.

The drive is eerily quiet, and by the time we reach the estate, a tight knot of anxiety has settled in my chest. The place is like something out of a fairy tale—massive, with perfectly trimmed lawns and stone walls that tower over everything. The car glides up a winding drive, finally stopping before a mansion that's more like a palace. I spot uniformed staff bustling about, their movements precise and efficient.

Luca opens the door, and I step out, my legs slightly unsteady. Two men, likely butlers, approach the car's trunk, their faces briefly puzzled when they notice the only luggage I have is the small leather shoulder bag clutched in my hands.

The large doors open, and the grandeur of the place takes my breath away. Marble floors gleam under the light from an enormous chandelier, and I have to stop myself from gawking at the intricate artwork on the walls. Everything looks pristine, like a place untouched by real life.

Two maids approach me, one of them an older woman who wears a soft smile that reminds me of my mother. My chest tightens, and a wave of homesickness hits me—it hasn't even been an hour, and I miss them already.

"Welcome, ma'am. It's lovely to have you here," the older woman says gently. "I'm Paula, and this is Clara. She'll help you settle in."

"Nice to meet you," I reply, my smile polite but uncertain.

Clara reaches for my bag, and I follow them as they lead me through the house. We end up in what looks like the living room, except it's larger than my entire house. The furniture looks expensive, the artwork on the walls likely priceless. It's a far cry from my reality, yet something about it stirs a bittersweet feeling in me.

As a kid, this was what I imagined heaven to look like.

Whoever my husband is, he's fucking *loaded*.

"We'll take you to your room, then give you a tour if you'd like…" Paula's voice filters through as I gawk at the opulent surroundings. Damn. The ceiling alone is a work of art, towering and intricately designed.

Through an open door across the room, I look into what seems to be a smaller visitors room. However, what catches my eyes are the two middle-aged women I see there. They're beautiful, dressed in tailored designer outfits, directing the staff as they arrange a lavish floral display. My heart skips when one of them looks my way, her gaze sharp as she takes me in from across the room.

"Paula, come here," she calls, her tone commanding.

I notice the way Paula stiffens slightly before turning, and I immediately realize that the women must be part of my husband's family—my soon-to-be family.

"Take her upstairs," she murmurs before heading toward the women, and I don't miss the way they watch me with a hint of…disdain. They don't like me.

"Right this way, ma'am," Clara mutters, guiding me to a grand staircase.

I shake off the nerves and follow her to the second floor, where she leads me into what I realize is *my* room. My breath catches as I step inside. A massive queen-sized bed covered in plush velvet sits in the center, while floor-to-ceiling windows overlook a garden that stretches into the distance. The en suite bathroom looks like something out of a magazine, practically a spa in itself, complete with a marble tub and I imagine taking a long, hot bath here.

When I return from gawking at the bathroom, Clara smiles warmly. "I'm here to help with anything you need, ma'am. Your bridal treatments will begin at noon," she says.

Bridal treatments. *That's* why they hauled me here so early.

"Sure." I nod absently, barely absorbing the details as she outlines the schedule of spa treatments, fittings, and other rituals planned to turn me into someone worthy of... well, whomever this man is.

Once Clara leaves, I sink onto the bed, catching my reflection in the floor-length mirror across the room. The girl staring back looks like a stranger, lost, adrift in a world that doesn't feel real.

But there's no time to settle in. I'm whisked away to the mansion's private spa—yes, they have one *inside the house*— where I'm pampered, steamed, and scrubbed until my skin practically glows. By the time I return to my room, I'm thoroughly exhausted.

Clara offers to bring dinner up, and I'm more than happy to accept. The food she serves isn't like anything I've ever eaten before—a banquet of steak, baked pasta, and perfectly seasoned vegetables that make me wonder if I've been eating veggies wrong my whole life.

When I finally slip into bed later that night, the soft sheets practically swallow me, but sleep doesn't come easily. I'm craving an escape from this new life. I let my mind wander and take me somewhere else.

Ettore.

His hands, his lips, the way he touched me, claimed me, made me feel...

I close my eyes and let the memory take me, desperate for a taste of the familiar in this strange, gilded cage.

My fingers trail down my stomach, a warmth spreading

through my body as they reach my already wet folds. I let out a soft moan, slipping two fingers in, imagining it's his thick fingers filling me up. My pussy clenches in need. I've been craving to feel something like this ever since that night.

I moan more fervently as my thumb circles my clit, flicking over the sensitive bud. I hear the sound of his grunts in my ear, feel the warmth and weight of his body pressed on me, hear his guttural voice as he calls me his Kitten.

An orgasm hits me hard and fast, shocking me. I've never been able to bring myself to such pleasure with my fingers before. I'm panting by the time I come down from my high. And when everything slows down together with my raging heartbeat, I'm left with a nagging feeling that grips me even worse than it did before.

I'm in a strange room, in the mansion of a stranger, feeling the walls close in around me. Every polished surface, every gleaming fixture in this house of unimaginable wealth is a reminder of what I've committed to, and how trapped I already feel. I can't do this.

It feels ridiculous to be having second thoughts when I only signed the contract yesterday. But there's this heavy knot in my stomach that I can't ignore, a voice urging me to run. It's telling me that staying here will only pull me further into something from which I may not be able to escape. I can't shake the thought: If this feeling doesn't go away, I may have to do something drastic. Escape. Even if it means running away on the morning of my own wedding.

I close my eyes, trying to will myself into sleep, hoping that some rest will quiet the storm in my mind. But then, like a dark whisper in the silence, Abruzzi's words echo in my head.

I've signed a deal with the devil.

12

ETTORE

"Your wife is all settled in, sir," Luca announces the moment he steps into my office.

My wife. The phrase stirs something inside me, something I've been trying to keep down since the moment I made this decision. She isn't my wife...yet, but I nod, keeping my face unreadable while my mind races.

She's here. In my house.

When I got home less than an hour ago, I could feel a difference in the atmosphere. I'd told my men earlier today to bring Mirabella and her family here, so I knew she was here. Maybe that's why I felt the shift in the air the moment I walked in. Her presence—it's like it changes everything around me.

I was tempted to head straight to her room just to see her. I haven't been able to get her out of my mind since our last encounter. The dress she wore, the way she looked me right in the eyes and told me to mind my business.

I smirk at the memory. No woman—especially one as small and inexperienced as Mirabella—has ever talked to me like that before. That spark in her, the way she challenged me...it was intriguing.

The idea of barging into her room just to see the shock on her face when she realizes I'm the man she's marrying gives me a dark sense of satisfaction.

"Boss?" Luca's voice snaps me back to the present.

I glance up at him and notice a flicker of hesitation in his eyes. "We brought her in this morning, as you requested, but...we couldn't bring her family."

I narrow my eyes. "And why is that?"

Luca shifts slightly, which is unusual for him. He's typically unreadable, always calm. "She didn't want us to bring her family just yet. She told them about the marriage only this morning and argued that she couldn't just uproot them into this situation so suddenly."

I almost chuckle. I can hear her words in his explanation. "So, she convinced you to go against my orders?" I scoff, but there's a smirk playing on my lips.

She's not even my wife yet, and already she's managed to make Luca disobey me for the first time. I should be annoyed by it—the influence she has, the power she doesn't even realize she holds—but instead, I find it thrilling. *It's a damned turn-on.*

Think straight, I remind myself. This marriage is for business, nothing more. That's how I should think of her—nothing but a strategic partner. But her attitude, her fire, her ability to command...I used to wonder if choosing her was the right move. She didn't check any of the boxes Aldo had set for the woman I was supposed to marry. But I chose her for my own selfish reasons.

Now I see she didn't need to fit any criteria. She's exactly the kind of woman I need. One who can make men—and eventually the world—fall to their knees. All without even trying.

"It won't happen again, sir," Luca says, bowing his head slightly.

Luca has never failed me before, and knowing how loyal he is, I can tell he regrets disappointing me.

But he didn't disappoint me. In fact, he's just shown me that my choice, selfish as it was, might've been perfect.

"Make sure she has everything she needs," I say, leaning back in my chair. "I want her comfortable."

Luca looks up, a hint of surprise in his eyes that I'm not angry. Then he nods. "I'll take care of it," he assures me before turning to leave.

As the door closes, I'm left alone again, thoughts of the woman upstairs filling my mind.

I know she's probably dying to see who she's being forced to marry. I can picture her pacing, losing her mind at the thought of tying herself to a stranger. I shouldn't enjoy the idea, but I do—and I feel no shame in it. I've never claimed to be a good man. Yet, despite everything, I can't shake a flicker of guilt.

I don't know how she's coping with all this, being thrust into my world, separated from her family. I planned for them to join her for the wedding and then arranged another house for them afterward. I know her family is her foundation, that they've never been apart. But it's too late for second thoughts.

She signed the contract. That's what matters. I don't need to love her or pretend we're a regular family—except in public. As long as we both hold up our end of the bargain, this will work out for both of us.

Besides, this arrangement isn't forever. We aren't committing to a lifetime together. This isn't *for better or for worse, till death do us part*. Though, for some reason, that thought leaves an odd feeling in my chest.

The door swings open abruptly, pulling me from my thoughts. Zia Camilla strides in, her sharp heels clicking against the marble floor. Behind her are Aunt Francesca and Marta, both looking critical, though their expressions lack the hostility in Camilla's.

They've seen Mirabella. And they're clearly not pleased.

"Ettore," Camilla's voice is laced with barely suppressed anger. "You must be joking. A woman like *that*? A nobody? In this house?"

"Watch yourself," I warn, running a hand along my jaw.

"*Watch myself*?" she mocks, glancing back at Francesca and Marta as if to confirm if they're watching what's happening.

"I had to do a double take when I first saw her, Ettore. I thought she was lost, a wayward soul who somehow stumbled into our lives. I honestly wondered how the guards could let someone like her cross our threshold." She pauses, a smirk forming. "But then I saw Paula and another maid trailing her, and I was struck by the irony. Surely, you wouldn't..." Her laughter is bitter, cutting. "Imagine my surprise when I inquired with Paula and learned that she is indeed the woman you've chosen to marry."

Camilla's breathing grows heavier, while I'm desperate for a smoke or a whiskey—anything to help me keep my temper in check.

"Mirabella will be my wife in three days. Two days, technically, since today's almost over," I say calmly, even though every part of me wants to throw them out of my office. "You will treat her with the respect she deserves."

"Respect?" Camilla scoffs, folding her arms. "Ettore, after I got her name from the maid, I looked her up. And I was appalled. She doesn't even have a degree. No respectable job—unless you consider waiting tables, cleaning rooms in a seedy motel, and cashiering at a mall *real* work," she hisses. When I remain silent, she presses on.

"She lives in the slums with her family. She comes from nothing, so she has nothing of value to bring into this family."

I clench my jaw as Aunt Francesca nods, her voice softer but no less pointed. "What Camilla is trying to say, Ettore, is that...Mirabella doesn't belong here. She's not...one of us."

"One of us?" I let the bitterness slip into my tone. "Like my mother, you mean?" I watch as Camilla visibly flinches at the mention of my mother.

"Your mother, God rest her soul, was different," she retorts, her gaze flitting away like a guilty child. "We accepted her because your father was obstinate in his affections. But this girl?" She shakes her head, her disdain palpable. "Do you even love her? Could you ever lower yourself to love someone like her?"

I rise to my feet, my chair scraping harshly against the floor. They all flinch at the sudden movement.

"You've always resented my mother because she wasn't born into wealth. The whispers, the scornful looks...I grew up watching all of it." I step closer, eyes fixed on Camilla. "But let's make something clear. I don't need your approval. Mirabella is going to be my wife, and the first person who disrespects her will regret it."

"I will not tolerate any more of this. You can't stand here in my office in my *house* and insult both my mother and the woman I'm about to marry."

Camilla's lips press into a thin, disapproving line, momentarily silent. Aunt Marta seizes the pause to speak up for the first time.

. . .

"Some people may be here to insult your mother, dear nephew," she says, a sneer curling her lips, while I catch Camilla rolling her eyes. "But I'm here to bring you back to reality. Dragging a girl like her into our family would be seamless. You can't expect us to embrace her with open arms."

"We are merely protecting the family's reputation," Aunt Francesca adds, her tone suggesting that family honor trumps all. "People will start to talk."

"The public will tear us apart," Camilla cuts in, shaking her head as if the opinion of strangers is the ultimate tragedy.

"Mirabella is to be my wife," I bite out, my voice echoing through the office. "You don't have to accept her, and I don't care if you don't like her. But you *will* respect her, and that is final."

Just before I finally tell them to leave, Vittorio strides in through the open door, taking one look at the scene and sighing.

"I could hear the raised voices from the hallway. What's going on here?"

"Ask your brother," Camilla huffs, still avoiding my eyes. "Have you even *seen* the woman he plans to marry?"

"No, I haven't," Vittorio replies, a lazy smile spreading across his face. "But I'm sure she's delightful."

Camilla shoots him a glare, but before she can protest, he places his hands firmly on her shoulders.

"I think it's time for a break. You've been working tirelessly on this wedding, and I assure you, it's happening whether you approve or not."

"Vittorio..."

"It wasn't a suggestion, Aunt Camilla," he counters, his tone dropping an octave as he surveys the others. "And I wasn't just addressing her."

Tension thickens the air, words left hanging as Camilla narrows her eyes, but Vittorio's unwavering gaze silences her. With a final look of distaste, she turns on her heel and storms out, Francesca and Marta trailing close behind.

"I was seconds away from tossing her and her cohorts out," I mutter as soon as they're gone.

"Out of your office or out of the house?" Vittorio smirks, stepping closer.

"Both. The only thing that stayed my hand was Papa's dying wish..."

Our father's last request—that the family remain united. Vittorio nods, as though recalling the same words.

"So, is this really what you want, Ettore? Our family already has divisions from the fallout of our parents' marriage. Do you really want to go down this path?"

His tone isn't judgmental, just curious.

I rake a hand through my hair, feeling the weight of our father's wish. It's the only reason I haven't shown my aunts the door, despite their constant meddling. But this—I won't sacrifice my own life to keep together a family that's already fractured.

"I'm seeing the wedding through," I say, holding his gaze.

Vittorio nods slowly, understanding. "Then you'd better brace yourself for whatever comes next."

13

MIRABELLA

It's the morning of my wedding—the morning that ties me to a man I don't know, the morning of a wedding I will not attend.

I stand in the center of my bedroom, wearing nothing but a bra and panties. I gaze at the woman in the tall mirror, barely recognizing the reflection.

The stranger staring back at me has sleek waves in her hair, bold red lipstick on her lips, and long fake lashes framing her eyes. Delicate diamond earrings dangle from her ears, and beside her on the bed lies a wedding gown designed by the best fashion designer in the city, waiting for her to wear it. The woman looks more beautiful than she's ever been in her life, but beneath all that glamor, I sense sadness, fear, and panic. She is set to marry in less than an hour, and the only thought in her mind is escape.

"Do you need help getting into your dress, ma'am?" Clara asks gently, breaking my thoughts.

She came in early this morning with a makeup artist, a hair stylist, and a fashion designer. I smiled politely as they painted my face, adorned me with jewelry, and styled my hair. But during those three long hours, my mind raced.

Two days—two days of frantic planning have led to this moment. The time to act is now or never.

"No, I'm fine," I mutter, forcing a smile.

I see Clara smile back, her eyes sparkling. "You look beautiful, ma'am. I totally get it if you feel jittery. It's your wedding, after all! It's normal to feel cold feet when things get real."

I turn to her, and she glances down, a blush creeping up her cheeks under my gaze.

"S-sorry if I overstepped," she stammers, nervously laughing. "It's not like I've been married before or anything."

I manage a smile, even though my heart aches. "It's okay. Could you clean up this mess?" I gesture to the powder palettes, makeup brushes, and combs scattered across the dressing table.

"Of course," she replies, her smile polite as she moves to tidy up on the other side of the room.

I let out a shaky breath, my heart racing in my chest. I'm not sure my plan will work. Too many things could go wrong. I might get caught. I could be fined for breaking a signed contract. Or worse, I could get hurt.

I still don't know who my husband is, but I know one thing: he's ruthless.

Reality hits hard. If I don't escape now, I'll be walking down that aisle in just a few minutes, sealing my fate with the devil himself.

I glance over my shoulder at Clara, who is now busy organizing the makeup brushes on the vanity. Her back is turned, and my pulse quickens. This is my moment.

Before I can think twice, my feet move, quietly padding

across the cold floor. Clara doesn't hear me coming. I remember what Nonna taught me once—a self-defense trick from her younger days, a way to disarm someone without hurting them, but not without risk. She'd used it herself, back when danger was real and survival meant outsmarting those who threatened her. Nonna made me practice until my fingers knew the movements by memory, just in case.

My fingers tremble slightly, but I block out the fear, forcing myself to focus on Nonna's words, her steady voice in my mind: *"The carotid artery, just below the ear...apply just enough pressure, and they'll drop like a stone."*

In one swift motion, I clamp my hand onto Clara's shoulder, my fingers finding that throbbing spot by her neck. I feel her heartbeat racing beneath my fingers as I locate that pulsing spot by her neck. Her eyes fly open, widening in shock. She gasps, a flash of panic in her gaze as she starts to twist away.

For a brief moment, doubt strikes me, and my grip falters.

What if I mess this up? What if I hurt her?

But I push down those thoughts, refocusing, and apply a firm, precise pressure. Slowly, the resistance drains from her body, her knees giving way as she goes limp against me. A shiver runs through me as I catch her, lowering her as gently as I can to the floor.

"I'm so sorry," I whisper, my voice shaky, almost breaking. I arrange her carefully, making sure she's comfortable, trying to ignore the rising panic that claws at my throat as I stare down at her still form.

She's just unconscious—Nonna said that's all it would do. Right?

My heart hammers, thoughts colliding.

What the hell am I doing?

But I snap out of it when I glance at the clock and realize I only have thirty minutes to leave this house. Thirty minutes until Luca arrives to drive me to the cathedral, where I will be wed.

My hands move frantically, pulling Clara out of her maid's uniform and slip it over my body. It's a bit tight—she's smaller than I am—but it will have to do. I grab a blanket from the bed and cover her, as she's only wearing a sports bra and shorts.

As I look back at the mirror, my breath catches when I see the diamonds dangling from my ears. Quickly, I remove all the jewelry and drop it onto the vanity. Then, I bundle my silky, styled hair into the maid's bonnet, rip off the false lashes from my eyes, and put on a face mask I grabbed from Clara's cleaning supplies. I take my phone from my bag in the closet and slip it into the uniform pocket.

With one last look at Clara, I'm out the door. My hands shake, but I push the panic down. I can do this. I just have to blend in. Keep my head low. Act like I belong here.

The hallways buzz with activity as I descend the stairs. My eyes dart around to make sure no one is watching me, and I'm relieved to see everyone busy with their tasks to make the wedding a success.

When I near the front door of the lobby, one of the maids—thankfully not Paula, who I think would recognize I'm not Clara—spots me.

"Where are you going? There's a lot of work to be done," she exclaims, hands on her hips.

"Errand for the bride," I mutter, mimicking Clara's soft yet hurried tone.

With a huff, she walks away, and my heart pounds in my ears as I step out of the house and into the compound. The fresh air hits my face, making me giddy. I've almost made it out. I'm not successful yet, though—I still have to navigate the large grounds, but I'm halfway there.

The estate looks even more intimidating under the morning light. Perfectly trimmed hedges, towering fountains, and endless rows of trees stretch out before me. Not to mention the high fences that surround the space, reminding me that I might never escape.

But I will.

I speed through the stone pathways, hearing the soft crunch of gravel beneath Clara's flat shoes—thank God we wear the same size. Every step echoes my racing heart. The gate is still far ahead, and I struggle to breathe under the face mask, but I push forward.

As I approach the front gates, the two security guards on duty eye me with confusion. I swallow hard as I near them.

"Where are you headed?" one of them asks, his sharp eyes scanning my uniform.

"There was a last-minute change in the flower arrangement," I say, trying to keep my breath steady. "I've been sent to pick up the peonies that will be added to the flowers." The words tumble out, and I hope I don't stumble.

"Why did they send you?" the bald-headed guard asks, skepticism in his tone.

I bite my lip, tempted to ask, *'Should they have sent you instead?'* until I remember I'm not Mirabella. I'm Clara.

"I'm on bridal duty," I explain quickly, "and everyone else in the house is busy, including Mrs. Camilla, Francesca, and Marta."

I give myself a mental high-five for remembering the names Clara casually mentioned yesterday during her chat with Paula. Just a tiny victory, but I cling to it—one piece of control in this whole twisted arrangement. Clara had been talking about Ettore's aunts, gossiping over wedding details and family quirks, giving me the clues I needed to connect faces to names.

The memory of those two women from my first day here flashes through my mind. One with a hard stare, the other with a warm smile that didn't quite reach her eyes. Ettore's family isn't just a name on paper anymore—they're real people, allies or enemies, and I'm marrying into the whole tangled web.

"They want it picked up from Fior di Luna," I add, naming an exclusive flower store in the city that only caters to the wealthy. It's a good enough excuse, believable for a family like this.

The guards exchange glances, but I keep my head down, trying my best to mimic Clara's gentle, polite manner. "I really need to hurry back," I add softly, letting a hint of nervousness show in my voice. "They told me to be back before the ceremony starts."

"I'll have a driver take you," the first guard says, reaching for his walkie-talkie.

Crap. I didn't think of that.

"Oh, no need!" I blurt out quickly. "They already sent a driver." I say it with just enough urgency that he pauses. Seriously, though? Is it really necessary to call for a driver that fast?

As the guards look at me, my mind races. What if they ask why a driver would come without the flowers if I'm supposed to be picking them up? What if they ask me any other insider questions I can't answer?

He studies me a second longer, then mutters something under his breath and pushes open the small side gate. "Fine," he says.

Holy crap. It actually worked.

"Be back soon," he warns, sounding a little skeptical. "I don't know what's going on in that house, but I know the boss is gonna flip if this wedding has any hiccups."

Behind him, the bald guard chuckles. "Yeah, still can't believe the boss is getting married. Pedro said he saw her when she arrived—said she's real pretty, too..."

"Wait!" the first guard calls out again just as I turn to leave.

What now?

"Yes..." I drag it out, trying to add a bit of playfulness to my voice.

"What's with the face mask, by the way?" he asks, narrowing his eyes. Shit. Shit. Shit. This is it. This is the end.

"Oh, you know, allergies," I reply quickly, trying to sound casual. "Terrible this time of year." He studies me a little longer, then steps closer, giving a subtle nod for me to take the mask off.

Crap. What am I supposed to do now? My genius plan to break out of here like some knock-off Michael Scofield is turning into a disaster.

He takes another step forward, motioning for me to remove the mask again. I'm about to start panicking when, suddenly, his phone rings. He steps back to answer it.

Thank you, Jesus! I've never been religious—not that it stopped my grandmother from trying to "save my soul" every Sunday. Right now, though? I could march up to the pearly gates and give the big guy a kiss myself for this save.

The bald-headed guard, who seems friendlier than, gives me a reassuring smile. "Don't worry. Just be on your way. He's been a big grump ever since his wife got pregnant. Probably terrified of those new daddy duties."

"Really?" I reply, trying to sound genuinely interested. "Didn't know he was about to be a dad."

"Oh yeah! He's been reading all the parenting books," the guard chuckles. "Swears he's going to be the best dad on the planet. You should see him, it's hilarious watching him try to hide the panic behind that tough-guy act."

I nod along, pretending to relate, even though parenting feels like a world away from my reality. "Sounds like a huge change for him," I say, edging closer to the gate.

"Big changes can be scary, but he'll figure it out," the guard says, his smile lingering as I slip through the gate.

As their voices fade behind me, my heart pounds like a drum. The instant my feet hit the pavement outside, I let out a shaky exhale.

I did it. I'd fucking escaped.

But there's no time to celebrate. My legs are trembling as I hurry down the street, clutching my phone in one sweaty hand. Sweat drips down my temple, and it takes three tries before my shaky fingers manage to dial Nonna's number.

She answers on the second ring.

"Nonna, listen to me carefully," I whisper, my voice hoarse as I glance over my shoulder. The street is alive with morning commuters, but every shadow feels like a threat. "You have to take Mamma and Giulia to Auntie's place in Hunter. Don't ask questions. Just go. I'll meet you there."

"Mira, what's—"

"Nonna, *please.*" My voice cracks, and I hate it. "Just trust me. Go now. I'll explain everything later."

There's a pause on the other end, the kind that speaks volumes. I know my Nonna—she's holding back, biting her tongue like she always does when she wants to scold me but knows the timing isn't right. I can almost hear the words forming on the tip of her tongue, the "I told you so" she's surely dying to say.

No doubt, she's already preparing to remind me how I've

gotten myself into this mess by chasing the vanities of the world. How she warned me, time and again, that a life spent grasping at shiny, hollow things would only lead to trouble. But there's no time for her lessons now, and I pray she saves her lectures for later—when we're all safe, when this impending nightmare is over.

"Pack light," I add quickly. "Only take what you absolutely need. No statues, no rosaries, no holy books—nothing extra. Just your IDs, some clothes, and enough food for the road. Leave anything that'll make anyone notice you're leaving."

"Not even my rosary?" she whispers, her voice breaking with disbelief.

I press my lips together, forcing myself to stay firm. "Just one, Nonna. Take the one you pray with. Leave the others behind. I need you to be quick, and I don't want anyone noticing anything unusual."

"But Mira—"

"Promise me, Nonna," I cut her off. "Promise me you'll keep your head down. Don't talk to anyone. Don't answer any calls. Just go straight to Auntie's. Take the bus. If you don't have enough for tickets, tell Auntie to send someone to meet you halfway. I'll explain everything when I get there. But you have to *move* now."

She takes a shaky breath, her voice fragile but resolute. "Okay, Mira. I promise. We'll go."

I exhale a long, trembling breath, relief and fear twisting together in my chest. "Good. I'll see you soon. I love you, Nonna."

"I love you too, *cara mia*. Be safe."

I hang up, my breath ragged, as I shove the phone into my pocket and start heading down the end of the street.

I did it. I'm free—at least for now. But I know they'll come after me. I can feel it. And my plan is to have disappeared from the face of the earth before they do.

I keep moving, my eyes flicking behind me every few seconds. The pristine lawns and gated mansions blur as the landscape shifts to city storefronts and chaotic sidewalks. The air smells like coffee, exhaust fumes, and freshly baked bread. Main Street hums with life—office workers hustle with briefcases and coffee cups, street vendors shout about their wares, and laughter spills from open cafes.

I weave through the crowd, keeping my head low. Each step feels heavier, each glance over my shoulder more desperate. For a moment, I almost believe I've outrun them —until I see it.

A black sedan turns the corner across the road, its polished surface gleaming like an oil slick. My breath catches, and my heart plunges into my stomach.

I know that car. Ettore's fleet.

The back door swings open, and three scary-looking men step out, their movements precise and purposeful. They wear dark suits, their expressions cold and predatory. My stomach churns as I realize they're scanning the crowd.

They're looking for me.

And that's when it happens. One of them spots me. My eyes meet the eyes of one of the men. Time seems to freeze. I don't hear the traffic anymore, don't see the bustling crowd. It's just him and the subtle hand signal he gives the others, and the way they all begin marching toward me.

Run.

The command explodes in my mind, and I obey. My legs move before I fully register what's happening. The ground feels like quicksand beneath me, but I push forward, darting through the crowd.

Heavy footsteps thunder behind me, cutting through the chaotic symphony of the street.

God, please.

It's the second time today I've prayed to a God I don't believe in, clinging to the hope of a miracle.

I veer into a narrow alley, heart pounding as I gulp in air, yanking the suffocating mask off my face. The alley smells like damp concrete and stale beer, but it's empty. For a brief moment, I think I've gained the upper hand.

Then another sedan screeches to a halt at the alley's end, blocking my escape.

"Fuck, there she is. Get her!" The man steps out, his sharp gaze locking onto me.

I spin around and sprint back the way I came, only to see two of the original men closing in fast.

No time to think. No time to breathe. I lunge left into a crowded flea market by the left, my feet pounding against the pavement as I dodge around people, ignoring the strange looks and yelps. The maze of stalls is chaotic, bursting with people and bright, mismatched colors. Vendors shout over each other, peddling trinkets and clothes. I shove through, ignoring the angry protests of those I bump into.

Behind me, their shouts grow louder. They're relentless, like wolves closing in on their prey. My legs feel like lead, and a sob threatens to escape as I realize I can't keep this up.

Then I spot it—a small boutique tucked between two larger stores.

This is it. My only chance.

With a desperate haste, I run towards the store and push my way through the doors. The bell jingling faintly overhead. The store inside is lined with mannequins dressed in bright colors, racks full of blouses, skirts, and coats create a maze inside. The smell of leather and cheap perfume fills the air as I slip past the racks, trying to steady my breathing.

The shopkeeper, a middle-aged woman with tired eyes, looks up, startled. I grab the first items I see—a navy sweater and a pair of jeans—and murmur, "Excuse me," before darting into the dressing room.

I still have makeup on my face, but it's melting off my skin now, running down my chin in rivulets mixed with foundation and sweat.

When I glance at myself in the mirror, I notice why the storekeeper had looked at me weirdly earlier. My hands tremble as I strip off the maid uniform and pull on the new clothes. My hair, damp with sweat, clings to my face until I tuck it beneath a baseball cap from a nearby display.

My makeup is still a mess— I wipe at it with trembling hands, but it only smears further. I finally settle with using the maid clothes to wipe of the remnants completely.

When I step out, I hand the shopkeeper a crumpled wad of cash without counting it. I usually tuck a few bills inside my phone case for emergencies—just enough to get by if I need to pay for something in a hurry. This moment, with my heart pounding and my hands trembling, definitely qualifies as one of those emergencies.

Her eyes linger on me, curiosity flickering, but she says nothing.

I hurry toward the door, casting a glance outside. I spot the men lurking around a nearby store, searching for me with their eyes. The street outside feels more hostile than ever. I glance toward the sedan. The men are questioning a shop owner now, their frustration palpable.

I slip out and head in the opposite direction, keeping to the edge of the sidewalk and disappearing into the moving crowd. When I glance back, I see the confused and frustrated looks on their faces as they talk to a shop owner, showing the elderly woman what I would assume is my picture.

I turn and pick up my pace, feeling the weight of each step lighten as I move further and further away from them, melting into the busy city.

When I look back one more time, they're still searching, their heads swiveling as they scan faces.

I disappear into the city, one step at a time, until their figures fade into the distance.

For now, I'm free.

Now to get to my family.

14

ETTORE

Ettore Greco is getting married.

If someone had told me this just a few months ago, I would have laughed in their face, thinking how ridiculous it sounded. But here I am, adjusting the cuff links on my sleeve, making sure the silver glints just right against the dark fabric of my suit. I look at my reflection in the mirror, and I look...clean.

My long hair is pulled back into a neat, low bun. My freshly shaved face shows off the sharp cut of my jaw. Damn, the last time I was clean-shaven was probably back in college. I usually like to leave my hair out, but Aldo insisted that I shave my beard and look as professional as possible—not my words—for my wedding ceremony.

So here I am, ready to be married. My tailored designer suit fits my lean muscles perfectly. My shoes are polished so well that they shine, reflecting the soft morning light coming through the windows.

I look like a perfect businessman. I don't look like the ruthless mafia boss who runs the underworld. I don't look like The Reaper.

Yet, that perfect appearance clashes with the storm brewing in my stomach. No matter how fake this marriage might feel, the truth is, I will be married to Mirabella by the end of the day. That thought is very real.

A knock at the door pulls me from my thoughts.

"Come in," I call out, adjusting my tie.

I expect it to be Luca telling me the car is ready, and when the door swings open, it's him. But his eyes are wide with panic, and his breathless announcement catches me off guard.

"She's gone," he blurts out.

I freeze, my fingers pausing mid-adjustment. "What do you mean, she's gone?"

"We waited for her to come out, but when she didn't, I sent Paula to check on her. She found Clara unconscious in the room," Luca says thickly.

I clench my fists as my anger simmers just beneath the surface. I want to lash out at Luca and anyone else whose negligence allowed this to happen, but I force myself to stay calm. I knew this could happen—part of me expected it. She was never going to make this easy.

The woman I know—the bold, courageous woman who fought off three men even when she knew she stood no chance, the woman who told me she wanted to sleep with me even though she was a virgin, the woman who challenges me at every turn—wouldn't just marry a man she didn't know without putting up a fight. She wouldn't tie herself down to a stranger, even if her life depended on it.

"Find her," I growl. "And send men to her family house immediately."

"Yes, boss," Luca replies, his voice steady.

I'm already storming out of the room as he makes calls and sends men to carry out my orders.

"Where's Clara now?" I ask, my voice dangerously controlled. "Is she...?"

"She's alive," Luca answers quickly. "And there are no physical injuries."

I exhale sharply. The thought of Mirabella hurting someone to escape...I don't believe she's that kind of person. She may be desperate, but she's not cruel. She can't be a murderer. She can't be like me.

"She's in the living room, still shaken," Luca continues. "I revived her, but she's terrified. She can't stop crying, and I think she's worried about losing her job."

I stride down the stairs, my anger a controlled flame as I head to the living room. Luca's steps are quick and steady as he follows me down the hall. When I step into the living room, I spot Clara in a corner, her face pale and streaked with tears.

Paula has her arm around her shoulders, trying to comfort her. Clara is wrapped in a blanket, trembling, as she holds her head in her hands.

"Clara," I say softly, trying to sound reassuring. "What happened?"

The moment she spots me, her eyes widen, and she begins to babble apologies, her voice high-pitched with fear.

"I'm sorry, sir. I didn't know...I didn't—she just touched my neck, and then everything went black. Please don't fire me. I swear, I didn't mean..."

"Enough." My voice is firm, cutting through her rambling like a knife. I crouch in front of her, and I see her shrink backward in fear.

I keep my tone low and calm as I speak to her. "I'm not going to fire you, Clara. Just tell me exactly what happened."

Her eyes widen in surprise as her bottom lip quivers, but then she takes a breath.

"Sh-she told me to clean up the vanity, and that was what I was doing when she came up behind me. She...she touched my neck, and then I...I don't remember. When Paula woke me up, I was on the floor wrapped in a blanket. I don't know what happened, I swear!" Tears pour down her cheeks as she speaks.

"I know what happened," I explain, my jaw tightening. "She knocked you out by blocking your carotid artery." I glance at Luca, who nods as the whole thing begins to click into place. Mirabella used the maid's uniform as a disguise to escape. She's clever, but not clever enough to think she stands a chance against me.

"Take her to rest," I instruct Paula. "Make sure she's okay."

Once Paula helps Clara up and leaves the room, I storm toward the security room with Luca on my heels. My anger builds with every step, and the fire inside me threatens to burn out of control.

She tried to escape me? She really tried to back out of the contract she signed? She's gone off God knows where, when she should be walking down the aisle to meet me right now!

I stand behind a chair as Luca works on the computers for a few minutes before pulling up the footage. The tension in the air thickens by the second, enough to suffocate anyone in the room. I watch her on the numerous display screens as she slips through different parts of the house and compound in a maid's uniform, her head down as she moves through the estate unnoticed. I clench my teeth as I watch her walk right out the gate.

"She left minutes ago," Luca says. "We've already got men on her trail, and they'll catch her in no time."

I run a hand through my hair, pulling it out of its ties.

"Good. I want her found, Luca. And I want her brought straight to me."

Luca nods before heading out to relay the information. I spend the next few minutes watching the footage over and over again, my anger rising each second.

When Luca returns to the security room, he's with Manuel, one of my men.

"Boss." He bends his head down in greeting.

"Any news?"

"We found her family packing their bags, but they've been moved to another location."

"Where?" I demand.

"They're still being held at their house."

"Bring them to the chapel, and don't hurt them," I snap.

Even though I'm furious, the thought of hurting her or anyone she loves makes me feel like a monster.

You are a monster, a voice whispers in my head.

I shake the thought away as I head out of the security room. The wedding is in about thirty minutes, and I have two plans set in motion. No matter what happens, I know I'll have Mirabella right where I want her before the ceremony starts.

Luca drives me to the chapel, and throughout the ride, my stomach twists in knots. When we arrive at the cathedral compound, the car pulls to a stop in front of a small prayer chapel. It's located right beside the main cathedral where our wedding will take place.

I step out of the car, the gravel crunching beneath my feet as I make my way toward the building. I order Luca and Manuel to stay outside before walking in.

When I push open the door, the cool air and calm atmosphere of the chapel greet me. But there's nothing cool and calm about how I feel inside, especially when my eyes meet the family of my soon-to-be bride.

"Get out," I order the two men watching them. They nod and quickly leave the chapel, leaving me alone with my future in-laws.

Giulia, Mirabella's teenage sister, looks a bit scared as I approach. But she's staring right into my eyes, and I see the resemblance between her and her sister.

I pull my gaze away from her and glance at a middle-aged woman who looks like an older version of Mirabella.

Isabella. Mirabella's mother. She's sitting upright, and from what my men have told me, she's been receiving treatment at the hospital. Although she appears stronger than before, I still see the weakness that clings to her body.

Beside her is Mirabella's Nonna, much older and scowling as she eyes me carefully. They all have one thing in common: they're glaring at me.

"I am Ettore Greco, your future son-in-law," I announce into the room.

"You're not old," Giulia blurts out.

I frown as I watch her mother pinch her arm lightly.

"Mirabella tried to escape me today, and I'll bet you all knew it since you were packing your bags and were ready to run," I say calmly.

But her grandmother steps forward, anger flashing in her eyes. "If a woman tries to run away from you on her wedding day, it means she no longer wants to get married," she spits. "So why are we here?"

I step closer, noticing her gulp as I place a hand on her shoulder. "Simple. I want her back," I tell her.

When she cowers slightly, I pull my hand away and slip it into my pocket. "I don't want to hurt you. You already know that my union with your granddaughter isn't...typical.

Mirabella signed a contract and accepted money, money that has been used to pay for your daughter's debts."

"We appreciate that," Isabella speaks up, her voice weary. "But my daughter doesn't want to marry you."

A part of me feels bad that she's been dragged into this mess. But they were all complicit in Mirabella's plan. Did they try to trick me after I helped settle their debt?

I shake my head, pushing those thoughts aside. Despite my annoyance, I know this family is genuine. They're dressed up, ready for a wedding, which means they were preparing long before Mirabella probably alerted them about her escape.

"You understand what she agreed to when she signed that contract, right?" I say, my voice low but pointed. "The terms were clear—she promised to uphold her side, and if she breaks it, she owes ten times what I gave her. That's $100,000 she'll need to repay immediately."

Isabella's face pales, and I can see her calculating the impossibility of it. "A hundred thousand? How could she—"

"She can't," I interrupt. "And if she can't pay, she'll face legal consequences. Do you think the courts will look kindly on someone who takes money, spends it, and then refuses to fulfill their obligations? They'll chew her up." I let the silence hang for a moment, the weight of my words sinking in. "And that's before Abruzzi gets involved."

"I don't...who is Abruzzi?" Isabella asks, genuinely confused.

Now, I feel conflicted and even more annoyed. Mirabella is so selfless. She's been harassed by loan sharks, dangerous ones like Abruzzi, and her family doesn't even know about it.

"Well, if she didn't tell you," I say, the edge in my tone unmistakable. "Then it's not my place to. My concern here is simple. Your granddaughter made a choice, and that choice has a price. One hundred thousand dollars, to be precise. If she thought she could play smart and trick me, it's time for her to learn what it means to cross me."

Nonna, frail but fierce, narrows her eyes at me, her voice shaking with anger. She shouts in Italian, "*You're a devil. You tricked my granddaughter with this dirty contract!*"

I smirk at her audacity, the nerve of speaking to me like that. Few have gotten away with addressing me so curtly, let alone more than once in a conversation. I should be reveling in this moment, enjoying the fear in their eyes as they realize how easily I could dismantle them. I should lock them up, make sure Mirabella spends a significant part of her life paying me back every damned cent she owes.

But...there's something different today. Maybe it's the fact that it's my wedding day, and for once, I'm feeling...magnanimous. Generous, even. I'll let it slide—this time. They are my in-laws, after all. And when was the last time you heard of a groom who'd imprison his in-laws over a little misunderstanding like this?

But I don't intend to let them mistake my generosity for weakness. They'll learn that soon enough.

"Devil? Perhaps," I reply, my voice calm but laced with menace. "But your granddaughter wasn't forced to sign anything. If she didn't understand the terms, that's her problem, not mine. I'm far too busy to teach grown women why you don't sign documents without reading the fine print— or without a lawyer present."

Nonna takes a step forward, her frail frame trembling with rage, as if she might strike me. But Isabella grabs her arm, holding her back. The tension is palpable, thick in the air. I glance at Mirabella's younger sister, silent and tearful in the corner, her small frame shaking. If I were a better man, maybe that sight would move me. But I'm not.

I check the time on my *Patek Philippe* watch, the glint of its polished face catching the light. My patience is wearing thin. "The clock is ticking. You have until the end of the day to get me $100,000 in cash, or Mirabella goes to prison for breaking our agreement. That's the deal. Do you really want to see her thrown in a cell after everything she sacrificed to save you?"

Isabella's face crumples, her silence speaking volumes. I turn my attention back to Nonna. Her shoulders are slumping now, her earlier fire dimmed.

"What do you want from us?"

I step closer, my presence looming over them, and lower my voice. "Call Mirabella. Tell her to come back willingly. She'll listen to you."

"Nothing about this is willing," she bites back, and despite my anger, I resist the urge to smile. I see where Mirabella gets her sass and courage.

Her bloodline runs fiery and strong.

But fire alone won't save her now.

"You can have any woman you want without lifting a finger. I knew your father. He owned one of the biggest hotels in New York. Why not marry a rich socialite from your circle? Spare my granddaughter," she continues, her tone desperate.

"You're right. I could have anyone, but I want your daughter," I reply firmly.

"Do you even care that she doesn't love you? How can you live with someone who will no doubt despise you after all of this?" she asks, raising an eyebrow skeptically.

I lean in slightly, my eyes locking with hers. "Love is just a fickle emotion forced on us. It's not a requirement for life,"

I reply coolly. "What I *can* give her is stability, security, and the freedom to live without worry. I'll provide for her, her family...all of you. No more debts. No more struggles. She won't have to bear the weight of supporting you all alone."

"You don't have to force her into this arrangement. You could date her the right way. Fall for her, like I know you will when you truly get to know her," Isabella counters.

"I didn't force her. I merely proposed this arrangement, and she came to me on her own."

I can see Nonna's not too happy about the situation, but I also notice I've slowly begun to chip away at her resolve. I have one more trick up my sleeve, and this will seal the deal. It may not be a conventional family blessing, but it'll have to do.

"You said you didn't know who Abruzzi was. Well, he's a notorious loan shark. Your precious Mirabella owes him a large amount of money. He sent his men to hunt her down like animals when she defaulted on her payments. They were going to..." I pause, recalling how cornered and defenseless she looked that night. "Anyway, I saved her, and now we're here."

"I need a wife. She's perfect for my social standing. That's all you need to know. I'm a man of *business*, not emotions," I say, keeping my voice steady.

"I will not—"

I raise a hand, cutting her off. "I think I've been more than patient. I owe you no further explanations. This isn't your concern. It's between Mirabella and me. Now," I say, my voice colder still, "call her."

Nonna stares at me for a few moments before reluctantly nodding. She pulls out a small phone from her pocket, her hands shaking as she scrolls through her recent calls.

"Put the call on speaker," I instruct.

She complies, the phone crackling to life, and I watch her closely, noting every twitch of her fingers, every breath she takes.

"You'll tell her exactly what I say," I continue, leaning in, my words deliberate. "Tell her I've taken you and your family. That she has no choice. Then, tell her to come to the chapel before the wedding, which is…" I glance at my watch, letting the moment drag. "In less than two hours. After that, you hang up. No questions. Don't say anything else."

She nods, and a flicker of guilt pinches my chest as I see the pain in her eyes. But I'm not here to hurt them. I just need Mirabella to come back.

Nonna swallows, her face drawn, before she presses the phone to her ear, her voice shaking as she begins to speak. "Mirabella…I…I have to tell you something."

The woman says softly into the phone when the call connects. "We couldn't make it to your Auntie's place. We are at the chapel for your wedding. Your…husband is here. He wants you to come back, or else…you could go to jail…"

"What?" I hear Mirabella's panicked voice through the speaker. "Where's momma and Guilia?"

I stay quiet, watching her press her eyes shut, then open them again, filled with worry.

"Mirabella please just listen. Apparently, there was a clause in the contract your husband had you sign. Did you know about that when you agreed?"

There's a long pause before Mirabella's confused and panicked voice crackles through the speaker. "What clause? No, I didn't…what are you talking about?"

Nonna's eyes flick to me before she sighs heavily. "He tricked you, Mira. He knew you didn't understand what you were signing. He's got you cornered."

I stay silent, my gaze fixed on Nonna. This isn't how I intended it to go down, but sometimes you need to use the cards you're dealt, even if they're less than noble.

The phone is quiet for a moment, and I hear Mirabella's frantic breathing before she speaks again. "Where are you? Are you safe? Did he hurt you?"

My eyes flicker briefly to Nonna as she listens, but I say nothing. Her panic is clear, and in that moment, I almost feel a flicker of guilt. Almost. But it's too late for that.

"Nonna—" Mirabella's voice cracks.

But before she can say more, Nonna hangs up the phone, the sharp click of the disconnect ringing in the air. Her eyes blaze with anger as she glares at me. "Are you happy now?" she spits, her words heavy with reproach.

I lean back, maintaining my composure as I watch her. "Not yet. My wife isn't here yet," I reply calmly, my voice smooth like glass. "You might want to take a seat. I don't want you getting tired."

"I'm not a weak old woman," she snaps, but despite her words, she walks over to a nearby pew and lowers herself onto it.

The silence in the room stretches, thick and uncomfortable. The clock ticks on, the time slipping away as we wait.

The wait doesn't last long because a moment later, her phone rings again. The woman looks at me, as if asking for permission. I nod, and she quickly answers the call.

"Nonna, where exactly in the chapel are you?" I hear Mirabella whisper through the speaker. "Can you find a way out? I think I can still save you guys..."

"Mira, don't do anything stupid," her grandmother chokes out. I see panic and sadness in Giulia's and Isabella's eyes.

"Are there any men with you? They can't keep you

hostage in a damned chapel," Mirabella snaps, frustration pouring from her voice. "I'm coming for you. I promise—"

She's cut off suddenly, and we hear a thump before the call ends.

"H-hello? Mirabella?" Her grandmother calls, just as Isabella and Giulia sit up, panic in their eyes.

Just then, the door bursts open, and Luca strides in.

"Mirabella has been found, sir," he announces.

"Well, what a pleasant turn of events."

"You are not a good man," the old woman says, her voice steady yet filled with disdain.

I hate that they are seeing this side of me and already think I'm a monster. What will they think when they truly know who I am?

I knew our marriage wasn't real, so I never craved the love and acceptance of her family. Yet now, having them here—every single one, down to the youngest—staring at me like I'm the devil makes my stomach churn.

"I assure you, neither you nor your daughter will be harmed. I just want her back, and I want the wedding to go as planned. Afterward, you will be moved into a nice apartment and well taken care of," I say, knowing it won't change how they see me.

They all stay silent, and I feel my heart thump in my chest as seconds tick by. After what feels like forever, Luca bursts into the room again, his usual blank expression on his face.

That means good news.

"She's here," he announces.

I hear murmurs and sighs of relief from her family.

"Bring her in."

Luca steps out, and a few seconds later, he comes back with Mirabella in his grip. I release a breath I didn't know I was holding as my eyes scan her body. Her hair is a mess, and her face is flushed from the chase. She's changed from the maid's uniform into a T-shirt and jeans.

"Let me fucking go," she yells, trying to pull her arm from Luca's tight hold.

He won't let her go—not if it means risking her slipping away again. Not unless I tell him to let her go.

"Leave her alone," I command, my voice booming across the room.

Time seems to slow as I watch her body freeze. She recognizes my voice. Her head turns slowly, scanning her family members until her gaze lands on me.

I see her expression shift from shock to confusion to disbelief, and I can't help the rush of excitement that flows through me.

"You," she whispers, her voice hoarse. She takes a step back, her body trembling as reality sinks in.

I smile, slow and dangerous, as I take a step toward her. "Surprised?"

She shakes her head, as if trying to wrap her mind around everything. "No...you can't...you're not..."

"But I am," I cut in. "I am the man you're marrying."

She steps back as I move forward.

A smirk curls my lips as I reveal her reality. "In less than one hour, you will be my wife."

15

MIRABELLA

I only had a total of thirty-seven minutes before the devil came for me.

And I was rendered speechless to find out that the devil is Ettore.

I can barely breathe as I watch him. He's wearing a sharp suit that hugs his frame perfectly. His hair looks disheveled, las if he's been running his hands through it in frustration, and my heart stumbles as I take in the hard lines of his clean-shaven jaw.

'In less than one hour, you will be my wife.'

His words echo relentlessly in my head as I stare, dazed.

This can't be real. The man I've been dreaming about—the one I couldn't shake no matter how hard I tried—is standing here, and I'm supposed to marry him?

"Mira, don't you know him?" Nonna's voice pulls me out of my thoughts, grounding me back to reality.

I blink, turning toward her, quickly scanning her and the rest of my family to make sure they're unharmed.

"I didn't hurt them," Ettore says, his voice low but tense.

My frustration breaks through, and I find myself glaring

at him. "Why didn't you tell me? Why hide who you were? Why didn't you just reveal yourself?"

Ettore's expression remains calm, but there's a flicker of something in his eyes. He calls for Luca, who enters promptly, casting a quick glance at me before focusing on his boss.

"Take Mirabella's family to the dressing room," Ettore instructs. "She'll join them once we're done talking."

"Mira..." My mother's voice is soft but filled with worry.

I nod stiffly. "It's fine. Just go with him."

There's no point resisting anyway. With Ettore, things always seem to go his way.

As Luca leads Nonna, Mamma, and Giulia out of the backroom in the chapel, anger builds in me, hot and sharp. The door barely closes behind them before Ettore speaks.

"I wanted to keep things professional, especially since things had already gotten complicated between us," he begins, his voice tight. "It was business. You read the contract, had no objections, and signed it. I didn't think it would be an issue."

I scoff, the sound humorless. "You didn't think it would be an issue? I was losing my mind trying to figure out who I was even marrying. I felt...unsafe, like I was selling my soul. Which, in a way, I am. Did any of that cross your mind?"

He doesn't answer, and suddenly, it all clicks. "Luca came to me at the club that night. I saw you later that evening. You were watching me, weren't you? You sent your lapdog after me. When I asked if you were following me, you lied. You've been playing me from the start!" My voice bounces off the empty walls, filling the room.

Ettore clenches his jaw and steps closer. "I didn't know how you'd react if I showed myself earlier. I couldn't risk it."

"Because you knew there was no way I'd agree to marry

a murderer, right?" The word slips out, and I shiver, feeling the weight of it in this place.

This whole situation feels wrong...surreal even. Us talking about murder in a church, me being minutes away from marrying the said murderer.

"Like I said," he replies, his eyes darkening. "It's just business."

Frustration knots in my throat, making it hard to breathe. I take a shaky breath, and the words come out before I can stop them.

"Do you even feel anything about this, Ettore? About us, whatever that even is?"

For a moment, he hesitates, then his expression softens ever so slightly. "Feelings aren't something I can afford, Mira. Not in my world."

"Your world," I repeat bitterly, shaking my head. "And now you're dragging me into it.

I can't do this. The lies, the secrets, the manipulation...it's too much. I take in the sight of Ettore, looking every inch the pristine businessman. But I know there's so much more beneath that polished exterior, so much he's not letting me see.

Abruzzi's warnings echo in my mind, and I hate that I'm even thinking about him now. I hate that I still remember every twisted thing he did. But as I look at Ettore, I notice the similarities. They're both liars, manipulators, murderers.

And me? I'm just a pawn in their games. I was one for Abruzzi when I owed him, and he had me under his control. Now I'm in the same situation but with a different man. Ettore will use everything he has against me. His power, his money, and now, even my own family. I used to think my husband saved me from Abruzzi's claws, but now I realize he just did exactly what Abruzzi has been doing for the past year. I was right about the contract being a power move to force me into a situation where I would have to feel powerless and indebted to him.

I don't know how I got here, how I found myself trapped between two men who thrive on my misery, two men who use my desperation to play and use me.

I take a shaky breath, my anger bubbling over. "You are a monster," I spit, barely able to keep my voice steady.

Ettore's jaw tightens, and I can see him thinking, weighing his response. Finally, he says, "I never claimed I wasn't. But I offered you a deal you couldn't resist. You had the choice to accept or refuse it. You accepted. Your signature is on that contract…"

"You fucking manipulated me!" I exhale my voice cracking as I remember how easily he had trapped me with the fine print. The clause, buried deep in that contract, was a cruel weapon—one I never saw coming.

"And you tried to escape me," he fires back, his voice sharp. "On the morning of our wedding, no less. I must admit, you did a good job slipping away." His tone lowers, taking on a dangerous edge as he steps closer. "Though if it hadn't been for the distraction of the wedding preparations, you wouldn't have made it past my gate alive."

"For someone who always boasts about keeping me safe, you sure have a funny way of showing it. Your entire staff didn't even notice the bride escaping. Is this how you protect me? By letting me slip through your fingers like that?" I sneer. "You're a joke, Ettore. A pathetic, controlling joke."

"It's unfortunate you feel that way," he snaps. "But too bad—you already signed the contract. There's no escaping this."

His words hit me like a punch to the gut, and I hate that

he's right. But it wasn't just the contract I signed—it was the life I never agreed to.

"You don't get it," I snap back, barely able to hold back the tears. "I didn't even read the damned contract! I was forced into it without a lawyer present! It's all legal jargon and clauses to which I never agreed."

A sudden realization hits me—my family wasn't even told what he was doing. He dragged them to that chapel without their consent, without their knowledge. They were worried about this whole thing at first, but they had no idea what was really happening behind the scenes.

"You—" My voice shakes as I point a finger at him, "You tricked my family. They didn't have to know about the contract, about your plans, and you didn't even care check with me first."

Ettore's expression remains cold, but there's a flicker of something—a twisted satisfaction, perhaps? He's basking in the moment, enjoying how he's managed to corner me, how everything has unfolded exactly as he planned. His eyes gleam with the quiet pride of someone who's orchestrated every detail.

"You signed, Mirabella," he repeats. "You signed, and now you live with the consequences of your decisions."

I swallow, my throat tight with rage. "I didn't know," I whisper, barely able to breathe. "I didn't know what I was getting into. I thought I was choosing the lesser evil. But you —you're a monster. A liar. You trap people with your twisted games."

His lips twitch into a mocking smile. "And yet, here you are. Still here, trying to fight your way out of it. Tell me, Mirabella, did you really think you could ever escape me? This was always going to be your fate."

"God, I hate you."

Ettore's expression remains stoic, but the glint of something darker in his eyes speaks volumes. He takes a step closer, his towering presence oppressive, suffocating. "I'm not really fond of you either, darling," he says, his tone almost mocking. "But it's far too late to cancel everything now, isn't it? So, what's it going to be? You either pay me back the hundred grand you owe, or you marry me. And I'll give you very little time to decide."

I think about the consequences, about how all of this will play out if I refuse. I already tried to run away once—where did that get me? Nowhere. Back in this cage, back under his control. Staying behind and trying to pay off the money? That's as pointless as trying to escape again. If I had only read that damned contract instead of getting caught up in the high of rubbing my victory in Abruzzi's face, I wouldn't be here. But here I am, stuck, trapped in a mess of my own making.

Still, there must be something to salvage from all this. What are the good sides? The money. The wealth. A rich, ridiculously handsome husband who could give me a life of comfort—at least until I can make my own way. Once I've weathered this storm, I'll be able to walk away with enough to set something up for myself, something real. Something that's mine.

I should be looking at the bright side. I should be planning how to turn this into my own advantage. And then, the thought hits me like a spark: *When life hands you lemons, you make fucking lemonade.*

Maybe I can't escape this now. But maybe I can twist it, shape it, use it to my advantage. *I'm not a victim. Not anymore.*

"I won't be your trophy wife, your mistress, or some obedient partner," I say firmly, flashes of that night we shared flooding my mind. I can't deny the chemistry, the pull we've had—no matter how much I despise him for trapping me.

How are we supposed to coexist under these circumstances?

He tilts his head slightly, his lips curling into a slow, almost amused smile. "Fine. State your terms here and now," he replies, crossing his arms, a challenge glimmering in his eyes. "What do you want, Mirabella?"

"I'M NOT NEGOTIATING with you, you asshole." I so am but I can't let him think for one second that I'm desperate, that I'm actually considering his terms. No. I need him to believe that I'm still the one in control, that he hasn't worn me down yet.

I straighten my back, putting on a mask of defiance, even though I'm already calculating every move in my mind. *He can't know I'm thinking about this. Not yet. I have to make him think he still holds the power.*

"I didn't sign up for this," I add, my voice biting, "and I sure as hell won't just roll over for you." I make the words sound as if they're coming from a place of pure indignation, though the truth is, I'm already weighing the options. He may have the power right now, but I won't stay trapped like this forever. Not if I can help it.

He smirks, the bastard. "I don't see how you have a choice, Kitten. As soon as we walk down that aisle, I won't be so gracious," he warns, his smirk infuriating me further.

"I am not—"

He tsk-tsks me, cutting me off. "Time is ticking."

I take a deep breath, my heart racing. "I want my own room. That's non-negotiable."

Ettore doesn't flinch. Instead, he watches me with

unnerving focus, studying my every word, my every move. "Is that really what you want? Your own room?" he asks, his voice a low rumble of curiosity, as if he's toying with me.

I nod, meeting his gaze head-on. He knows I'm thinking about that night. I can see it in the way his gaze flickers for just a moment, the darkness in his eyes deepening. But like the mischievous bastard I've come to know him for, he's not about to let me see just how affected he is by this conversation. He's turning the heat away from himself, deflecting the tension and regaining control of the moment.

"Yes."

Ettore's eyes darken with something dangerous, and for a moment, I wonder if he is actually going to acknowledge the elephant in the room. But then he simply smirks, that same cold amusement playing across his features. "Done, Mirabella," he says softly, his gaze never leaving mine.

"And I want to go back to college," I say, my voice unwavering. "I'm not going to be sidelined in this marriage, Ettore. I won't let you keep me from finishing my education, from having a life outside of this. I'll make sure of it."

He leans in closer, his expression shifting from annoyance to curiosity. "You still think this whole thing is about me somehow sidelining you? Keeping you in my shadow?"

"Yes," I insist, holding his gaze. "With the less-than-honorable way you went about this whole thing, it's pretty glaring what your intent was. You don't do something like this unless you want control."

"I see," he says, his voice oddly neutral, and for the briefest moment, I think I detect a hint of sadness in his gaze. But it's gone before it can register fully, replaced by the steely resolve I've come to expect from him.

"Yes," I repeat, my steady and firm tone, "I need my independence, even in this arrangement."

Ettore studies me for a moment, his demeanor softening just a fraction. "You're a tough one, aren't you?"

"I have to be," I reply, my voice steady. "If I'm going to survive this, I need to stand my ground. You're not the only one who gets to make demands."

"Very well. Done, too."

I take a slow breath, the weight of this arrangement sinking in deeper. If I'm going to be stuck in this life, then I'll make damned sure I have something to show for it. "And my family will be kept safe. No questions asked."

He raises an eyebrow. "Of course. Is that all?"

"For now, yes."

"Good," he says smoothly. "Now listen to my terms. You are not obligated to perform any...wifely duties outside of the public eye. Nothing will be forced upon you. But in public, you will act the part of the perfect wife. You'll be convincing."

I nod, feeling the weight of each demand settle around me.

"As outlined in the contract," Ettore continues, his voice smooth, calculated, "you'll receive one million dollars that will clear your debts, cover your mother's surgery, and give you financial freedom. But, most importantly," he adds, leaning in slightly, his eyes hardening, "you'll have my protection from Abruzzi. Make no mistake—he won't let you go easily. Even if you manage to pay off your debt, there's no escaping him. You'll always be on his radar. But with me, you're safe. For as long as you're my wife, he wouldn't dare start a war with The Reaper by touching you."

His eyes bore into mine, and I can tell he means every word.

I know Ettore is right, but a scoff escapes my lips at his calculated bluntness. There's not a drop of sincerity in him.

"Lastly, the contract lasts for a year. After that, you're free to go."

I inhale, holding the breath for a moment before releasing it. One year. One year, and this will be over.

"Fine," I murmur, resigned.

Then, laughter filters in through the chapel windows. My attention snaps to a few cars parked outside, and a handful of well-dressed guests stepping into the main cathedral. Reality crashes back into focus.

It's my wedding day.

"You need to get ready," Ettore says, his gaze sweeping over my T-shirt and jeans. "Everything's prepared for you in the dressing room."

Of course, he's arranged it all. It's almost as if he anticipated that today would unfold exactly like this, that we would be married no matter what.

As I'm ushered to a small room nearby, the weight of it all bears down. Inside, my family waits, their faces etched with worry and uncertainty.

"I'm getting married to him," I announce, attempting to plaster a smile on my face.

"Mirabella, are you sure about this?" Nonna's voice trembles.

I swallow hard, nodding with resolve. "This is my decision. I'll make it work. And it's just for a year."

Guilt tightens in my chest as I catch the worried expressions on my mother and Nonna's faces. I know they'll feel guilty, as if somehow it's their fault I've been pushed into this situation. The thought makes me ache inside. But there's no other way.

"Mom's surgery is happening," I say, trying to keep my voice steady. "He's going to pay for it, and she'll feel so much better in no time. It's strictly business. I need to pretend to be his wife for his reputation. Besides, it's only for a year. This will end soon enough. The money I'll get will pay off all our debts, and we won't have to worry about money anymore. I won't have to wait tables anymore."

Nonna's lips quiver, and Mom looks like she's about to say something, but I raise a hand to stop her. "It's okay," I insist, my voice softer now. "There's no other way to find the money for the operation. Trust me, this is for all of us."

For a long moment, the room falls silent.

"Everything will be fine," I add, my voice firmer now, as I meet each of their gazes. "Trust me."

Nonna frowns. "I'm sorry, but I'm still not okay with this."

"Nonna..." I plead, hoping for some understanding.

She glances at my mother, searching for backup. "Isabella, talk some sense into this girl. This is ridiculous."

My mother sighs, looking at me with a mixture of worry and reluctant acceptance. "She's right, Mira," she says softly.

"I'm just happy he's not old and ugly," my sister Giulia interjects with a wry smile.

"Giulia Isabella Ricci," Nonna scolds, her voice sharp. "Watch your mouth, *ragazza*!"

"What? I know we're all thinking it," Giulia defends herself. "Besides, he doesn't seem so bad. Not like Mirabella has men gunning down her door anyway. Might as well take this one while we have him."

"Oh, shut up, Giulia," I snap, my frustration bubbling over.

My mother laughs lightly, trying to ease the tension. "She does have a point. I think this is the first man, apart from Giovanni—who is taken, by the way—that I've seen you interact with like this."

"Mama," I groan, heat creeping into my cheeks.

For the first time all day, a genuine laugh escapes my family, momentarily lifting the heavy atmosphere. Nonna chuckles too, though I can still see the disappointment etched on her face. I wish there were something more I could do to ease her worries, but I'm equally as uncertain about how this will all play out.

Our moment is interrupted when the stylist rushes in ready to help me with my dress. As I steal one last glance at my family, who are huddled together in the back, I prepare for the beginning of my new life.

THE NEXT FEW minutes blur together in a whirlwind of activity. My family is ushered into the cathedral as I finish getting ready. The stylist adjusts my dress, and the makeup artist adds a final touch. When I slip into the dress, its fabric molds perfectly to my shape, but the bouquet feels almost too heavy in my hands, anchoring me to this moment.

As I'm led toward the front doors of the church, everything fades away.

I ignore everyone else in the room, my attention focused straight ahead on the man standing at the altar. Soft music fills the air as I slowly walk down the aisle decorated with colorful flowers. The hall feels suffocating despite its size and grandeur. My heart races faster in my chest the closer I get to the altar. I ignore the way the delicate lace of my dress itches against my skin and fight the urge to wipe my clammy hands on the fabric.

I keep my gaze locked straight ahead, looking at him —*Ettore*.

He stands tall and imposing in his black suit. His light brown eyes are a darker shade of hazel as he watches me approach. His gaze is intense, but his expression gives nothing away. How can he be so composed? I feel like I'm about to unravel right here in front of everyone.

As I come to stand before him, the officiant begins to speak. Everything blurs around me as my pulse thrums in my ears, drowning it all out. I want to run, but my legs stay rooted in place. This is happening. I signed the contract, and just a few minutes ago, he agreed to all the terms I laid out for him.

One year.

One year, and I'm done.

I can do this.

When the officiant nods toward Ettore, I know it's time for him to speak. His voice is deep, calm, and steady, and I sense a tinge of emotion in them.

He's a fucking good actor.

"I, Ettore Greco, take you, Mirabella, to be my wife," he says, his intense eyes never leaving mine. His words are slow and deliberate, like he means every syllable. "I promise to protect you, to stand by you, and to claim you as mine, for as long as we live."

A shiver runs down my spine at the possessiveness in his tone.

For as long as we live.

My gaze flickers to his tie as I'm unable to look into his eyes. Unease twists in my gut. I've never been religious, but lying before an altar? That's something else. I'm not sure what I expected, but his vows hit me harder than I thought they would.

The officiant turns to me now, and I realize it's my turn. My mouth feels dry, like the words the wedding planner made me repeat over and over again yesterday are stuck in my throat—the words I never thought I would be saying since I was so sure I would escape. I take a shaky breath, forcing myself to meet Ettore's gaze.

One year.

"I, Mirabella, take you, Ettore, to be my husband. I promise...to honor you, to stand by you, and...to fulfill the promises we make today." The words stumble out, far more confident than I thought I would sound.

Ettore's face remains unreadable, but his eyes stay locked on me, thick with an emotion I find hard to decipher. If I didn't already know this was fake, I would think I could read the look in his eyes as one of adoration and love.

The officiant asks for the rings. My fingers tremble as Ettore slides the cold metal band onto my finger. I look down at it. It's a beautiful ring with a golden band and an emerald stone in the middle. When I slip his ring onto his finger, my hand brushes his, and a jolt of something shoots down my spine.

The officiant's voice cuts through the haze. "By the power vested in me, I now pronounce you husband and wife. You may now kiss the bride."

Kiss. My heart races even faster as Ettore steps closer. The last time we kissed was that night—the night he saved me, the night I thought I gave a part of myself to him thinking that I would never see him again.

His hand cups my cheek, and for a moment, time slows. I catch my breath, staring up at him as he leans in. He brushes his lips against mine once, twice, until my arms move without my will, circling around his neck to pull him in. I hear him chuckle lightly before his lips consume mine.

His fingers trace the curve of my waist as we kiss hungrily, ignoring the presence of everyone in the room. My hands grip his tuxedo jacket, and I bite back a moan as one hand comes down to circle my neck while the other slides dangerously close to my hips. I hear him groan softly, the sound sending a shiver through me, a rush of heat flooding between my thighs.

Just then, applause, alongside hoots and hollers, explodes around us. I break off the kiss with an abruptness that leaves me dizzy for a few seconds. I kissed him like that...let him kiss me like that, in front of everyone!

He draws back slowly, and I feel the faintest brush of his breath against my lips before he finally releases me. My cheeks burn, and I can't bear to meet his gaze, afraid of what he might see reflected in my eyes.

"That was..." the officiator coughs. "Some kiss." He directs us through the next steps of the ceremony, but I barely register any of it. My mind swirls with questions, with doubts about whether I can really survive this marriage unscathed. But in a flash, Ettore's hand is guiding me, leading me down the aisle together as husband and wife.

I catch a glimpse of Ettore's smirk, which only deepens when he sees me glaring at him.

As we walk, he leans down to whisper, "See? You've made it through the first hurdle." His voice holds a note of satisfaction, a reminder of our deal—and his win.

I swallow, fighting the instinct to respond with something biting.

Once we're outside the cathedral, the press surges forward, their cameras flashing, voices calling our names. Ettore's arm slides around my waist, pulling me close, his hold more possessive than supportive. We're caught in this strange public performance, and I feel the weight of his grip as if it's a brand.

"Smile for the camera, wifey," he murmurs, pulling me to his side as we face the congregation. "The show must go on, especially after the wonderful kiss we just shared."

It's official. I hate him. I hate that he's enjoying this. I hate that a part of me enjoys it, too.

The applause gets louder as we walk hand-in-hand, and my heart races.

"I think you enjoyed that more than you'd like to admit," he remarks, his tone low and challenging.

I scoff. "Don't flatter yourself. I was playing my part, just like you."

A flicker of something dark passes through his gaze, gone before I can decipher it. "You're a natural, then. But don't worry, I'll make sure our all public scenes are just as convincing."

My jaw tightens, and I give him a withering look. "Don't get comfortable, Ettore. This arrangement may force me to act the part, but it doesn't mean I have to feel it."

He glances down at me with that same unreadable expression. "Ready for the rest of our show, Mrs. Greco?"

I force a tight smile, my voice low so only he can hear. "As ready as I'll ever be, Mr. Greco."

I force a smile, plastering it over the flush on my cheeks, but every nerve in my body is acutely aware of how close he is, of the lingering heat from that kiss that should've been nothing more than a show. A kiss that felt too real, too consuming.

How can I keep my promise to myself? How can I make sure that a kiss like the one we just shared, and any further entanglement, never happens again?

One year. Just one year.

I'll play my part to perfection—but never again will I let him make me forget that this is nothing but a deal.

16

ETTORE

I am a married man.

That's all I can think of as Mirabella and I walk through the large garden of the Greco estate where the wedding reception is being held. Flowers of different colors and variety line the paved path, their fragrance mingling with the cool evening breeze and the twinkling lights above.

It's been only a few minutes since our first dance, and we're now mingling with guests, greeting them as we move. They fill up the round tables in clusters, dressed impeccably and chatting animatedly with one another. Waiters in crisp uniforms glide through the crowd, balancing champagne flutes and elegant plates. The gentle hum of classical music and the soft clink of glasses float through the air, creating an atmosphere of effortless elegance.

I glance down at the woman on my arm. When I saw her walking down the aisle earlier, it felt like something out of a dream. She's changed now from the wedding gown into a simpler yet stunning dress. The soft light from the hanging lanterns dances on the satin fabric as she moves, her grace and beauty almost surreal. As we greet the guests, I keep catching myself stealing glances, wishing—no, craving—that we could slip away, just the two of us.

I've been wanting that ever since we shared that fiery kiss at the altar.

"Mr. Greco." A voice cuts through my thoughts.

I look up to see Valentina Romano, a well-known reporter with her own TV show, here to cover our wedding tonight. I suppress a sigh. I'd agreed to allow filming at the reception thanks to Aldo and Zia Camilla's urging, but the idea of cameras constantly in our faces doesn't exactly thrill me. Yet for a wedding like ours, it's inevitable.

I lean down to Mirabella. "Try not engage them for long," I murmur, brushing a strand of hair behind her ear.

She lets out a quiet huff, but as Valentina approaches with her camera crew, a dazzling smile spreads across her face, almost transforming her.

"Congratulations, Mr. and Mrs. Greco," Valentina says as she steps up to us. "The wedding is absolutely breathtaking. So, Ettore—how does it feel finally being married, especially after holding the title of most-wanted bachelor in the country?"

I chuckle softly. "It feels incredible. Nothing can compare to this," I say, turning to look at Mirabella with a gaze that's almost too easy to feign. "I've married the love of my life. There's nothing else I could possibly want."

Valentina arches an eyebrow, clearly curious. "And how did you two meet? You've kept that part a mystery."

I smile, a touch of mischief in my eyes. "It's a bit of a funny story, actually. We met through mutual friends, and I'm not one to believe in love at first sight...but with Mirabella, I was proven wrong." I shrug casually, the answer just vague enough to satisfy. "It was one of those things that just...clicked."

Valentina nods, satisfied with my answer, though I can see the curiosity still lingering in her eyes. It's clear she's trying to piece it together—how Ettore Greco, the most eligible bachelor, suddenly gets married out of the blue. But the look in my eyes, and the certainty in my voice, are enough to push any further questions aside.

Mirabella blushes, and I can't tell if it's real or part of the act. The camera zooms in on us, capturing the moment that will probably be regarded as the most romantic moment in the history of elite weddings. I can already imagine the pictures that will grace the front covers of magazines, with various headlines and comments of people calling it *The Wedding of the Year*.

Valentina's grin widens, and it's obviously she's satisfied with my answer. She turns to look at Mirabella, and her tone shifts just slightly as she directs the next question to my wife.

"And you, Mirabella? The world is *so* curious about how you and Ettore found each other. After all, it's quite a leap, from everyday life to this world of opulence."

I feel my stomach drop. Where's she going with this?

But before I can intervene, Mirabella starts. "Well, Ettore and I are really quite new at this—"

"Oh, of course," Valentina interjects with a smooth, practiced charm, her gaze lingering on Mirabella with a polite curiosity. "But I think everyone would love to hear about the journey, Mirabella—the transition from a more private life to one that's so...in the public eye. And stepping into this world of such prestige...it must feel like quite an adventure, yes?"

I know instantly that Zia Camilla's hand is all over this,

feeding Valentina the intrusive question. The insinuation hangs in the air, as sharp and as thin as a knife. I feel Mirabella's grip on my hand tighten, her body going rigid beside me, and the fury boils up in me.

Before I can respond, Mirabella lifts her chin, her voice steady and calm. "It's certainly a different world, but Ettore makes it feel like home."

Her words are simple, yet defiant. But Valentina isn't done.

"And do you worry, Mrs. Greco, about how others may perceive you?"

Mirabella's lips curve into a small, knowing smile. "Not at all," she replies, tilting her head. "What matters to me is how Ettore perceives me."

I give her hand an appreciative squeeze, feeling a surge of pride. Valentina opens her mouth to ask another question, but I cut her off smoothly.

"I think you're forgetting something," I say to Valentina. "Tonight is about celebrating our love and nothing else. If you don't have any worthwhile questions, perhaps you'd like to enjoy the party."

Valentina's surprise flickers only briefly before she regains her composure, her professional smile widening as she turns back to the camera.

"Well, there you have it, everyone—*Ettore Greco and Mirabella Ricci*, the latest couple capturing all our hearts," she says with practiced warmth. "I'm Valentina Romano here with *Inside Society* bringing you an exclusive look into tonight's glamorous celebration. Stay tuned. We'll be back with more highlights and interviews from this unforgettable evening."

As we turn away, I look down at Mirabella, who's still gripping my hand. "Are you okay?"

She glares up at me, a sarcastic smile plastered on her lips. "Why wouldn't I be? I'm marrying the man of my dreams, everyone here just adores me, and there's zero public scrutiny to worry about. It's everything I could wish for," she says, sarcasm dripping from her voice.

I open my mouth to respond, but before I can, a familiar voice booms through the crowd. "Ettore!"

I turn to see Dario approaching, a wide grin on his face, his arm slung around his wife Ginny. He claps me on the back as we exchange a quick hug. "Welcome to the marriage club, man."

"Dario." I smile, pulling back. "And as always, you look beautiful, Ginny," I say, turning to his wife, who smiles warmly at us.

I glance at Mirabella, introducing her. "This is Dario, an old friend, and his wife Ginevra."

Ginny steps forward, her warm smile extending to Mirabella as she pulls her into a hug. "Please, call me Ginny. And you look absolutely stunning."

"Thank you," Mirabella replies softly, and I notice the tension in her shoulders start to ease.

I smile at Dario. "How are the twins?"

He laughs. "Running around somewhere with their nanny, causing trouble, no doubt."

We chat briefly, catching up on family and small talk about the wedding. When they finally move along, I take Mirabella's hand again. "Now, let me formally introduce you to the rest of the gang," I say, guiding her toward the tables.

"When will this night finally end?" She groans under her breath, a polite smile still glued to her lips. She's already getting really good at this.

"Soon, I promise."

The reporters, the distant relatives, business associates,

begrudging family and those who came purely for appearances—it all feels endless, and I'm ready for it to be over, too.

As we weave through the crowd, guests turn to greet us with warm smiles and polite nods. Eventually, we approach a small group gathered around a table decorated with lavish dishes and champagne. Vittorio spots us first.

"Well, if it isn't the groom and his beautiful bride," he calls out in a teasing tone, standing up and stepping over to us. He pulls Mirabella into a hug, making her laugh. It's a genuine, unguarded laugh—the first I've seen from her all night.

"So you're the woman who managed to tame my brother," he says, clearly amused.

I watch the scene with a mix of amusement and something deeper I can't quite place. "Mirabella, meet my younger brother, Vittorio." I turn to the table. "And these are my aunts—Zia Camilla, Francesca, and Marta," I say, nodding to each of them, all watching Mirabella closely. "And my cousins Antonio, Leonardo, and Bianca."

Mirabella's voice is soft but warm as she greets them. "It's lovely to meet you all."

"It's our pleasure, Bella. I can call you Bella, can't I?" Aunt Marta asks, her gaze lingering on Mirabella with open curiosity.

Mirabella nods, her cheeks flushing slightly. "Of course. Bella's fine."

The others exchange glances, and it's clear they're sizing her up, curious but welcoming. Vittorio catches her eye, chuckling. "Trust me, you'll get used to them. They're not as scary as they look."

Mirabella laughs, relaxing even more as she looks at him. "I'm sure I will."

"Now, you've been with Ettore all night," Vittorio pulls her away from my grip. "Come dance with me. I know how overwhelming my brother can be sometimes. You won't admit it because you're his wife and it's your wedding day, but I can."

I watch as he spins her away to the dance floor. He says something to her, and she laughs again. He's always had that ability to make people love him at first glance. His easygoing nature is a stark contrast to mine, and for the first time, I find myself getting jealous.

Mirabella has never laughed that hard at my words.

My mind flashes back to the only time I've seen her laugh like that around me, uninhibited and carefree. Now, I stand here separated by more than just a few feet of dance floor.

A sudden shift in the air pulls my focus, and I spot Luca approaching, his face grim. He leans in close. "You have a phone call, sir."

I frown, waving him off. "I told you—no calls tonight."

Luca's gaze darts around us before he whispers, "It's Abruzzi."

The name alone sends a chill down my spine, and I clench my jaw as I take the phone from Luca's hand, stepping away from the crowd and into the garden. I haven't heard from Abruzzi since I took him down and took over the mafia world, and he's tried his best to stay away from me.

For him to call me now could mean only one thing—Mirabella.

I grip the phone tightly. "What do you want?"

His voice slithers through the line, dripping with mockery. "Relax. I just called to congratulate you on your marriage. Pity I didn't get an invitation. After all, you did steal my girl the same way you stole my territory."

My fist clenches, my voice sharp. "Don't ever mention Mirabella with that filthy mouth. She's mine, and you'll keep your distance from her and her family."

Abruzzi's laugh grates on my nerves. "No need to be rude. This is just a harmless call, Ettore."

My bitter laugh escapes before I can stop it. "I know you too well to believe that. I know you've been looking for an excuse to make this harmless call ever since I took out your men like rats."

His tone turns darker, his words calculated to hit where it hurts as always. "You think this marriage act fools everyone, but not me. I know Mirabella. I know she'd never marry you willingly. You're no different than me, Ettore. You can try to cover it up, but we're the same kind of man."

I grit my teeth, forcing myself to stay calm, to deny him the satisfaction of knowing he's gotten under my skin. "We are nothing alike. Don't fool yourself."

"Oh, but we are," he chuckles. "Your marriage won't last. People like us, we don't have happy ever afters—we always fuck up the good things in our lives. And when you finally do, I'll be there ready to pick up the pieces. I'll be her savior."

His words hit harder than I want them to. I clench my fist, resisting the urge to fling my phone across the garden. Instead, I inhale deeply, reminding myself that this is exactly what he wants. To have me rattled and bothered. I won't give him the satisfaction.

"Enjoy your pathetic life while you can, but stay the fuck away from Mirabella," I say coldly before hanging up.

As I return to the reception, the tension in my chest refuses to ease. Abruzzi's words echo in my mind. I can't help but wonder he's right. If men like me—men who've built their lives on blood and power—are destined to ruin anything good that comes their way.

Monster. Reaper.

That is what I am, but I find myself wondering if that is what I will always be. My eyes drift to Mirabella, who's still with Vittorio, laughing as he leans in, no doubt telling her some ridiculous story. She looks...happy.

I realize she was only able to show me that side of herself because she never thought we would be meeting again.

As I reach my family's table, Zia Camilla approaches, her voice cutting through the soft background music.

"They could have at least dressed better. If not for their daughter, then certainly for the honor of being in the same room as the Grecos," she mutters, just loud enough for me to catch.

Following her gaze, I see she's looking at Mirabella's family, her lips curling with quiet disdain. Annoyance flares up. I'm not in the mood for this tonight.

"Enough, Zia," I snap. "This is the only time I'll say it."

She huffs in irritation but knows better than to press further. I glance across the garden and find Mirabella's gaze meeting mine, a quiet intensity between us that feels like a tether, pulling us together even with the distance between us. I feel it.

Vittorio stands before her, saying something that makes him laugh, but her attention is unwavering, fixed on me.

There's something powerful there—real, undeniable. It pulses with a vividness that cuts through every barrier I've tried to build. I know better than to hope for too much tonight. She made her intentions clear, insisting on separate rooms.

And yet, every time she's near, I want her. It's a desire I can't shake, one that's only grown with every passing glance, every accidental touch.

My legs move almost on their own, carrying me toward the dance floor with a single, relentless goal—to hold her, to dance with her until the night fades away. But with each step closer, the words haunt me, slipping through my mind like a shadow. *No matter how perfect this feels, how close I am to the life I want, Abruzzi is right. I'm a monster. I can't escape what I am.*

And yet, as I approach her, I wonder if—for this one night—I can pretend otherwise.

And maybe Abruzzi wasn't right about one thing—a man like me doesn't deserve something pure, something...*real*—from a woman like Mirabella.

17

MIRABELLA

It's been exactly ten hours, thirty minutes, and twenty-seven seconds since Ettore and I were declared husband and wife in front of a crowd of family and friends.

Ten hours of pretending to be madly in love. Way too much time spent smiling and laughing, all because I know cameras are watching and people are ready to scrutinize every move I make.

Ten hours of being a Greco.

Thankfully, the party is starting to wind down. Most guests have already gone home, and those who remain are too buzzed or caught up in their own conversations to pay me any mind. After dancing with me for a bit, Ettore disappeared into the crowd, leaving me to navigate this sea of people alone.

This is the first moment I've had to breathe since this whole spectacle began. My eyes scan the expansive garden, searching for my family. I slip away from a small group of guests, feeling a twinge of anxiety as I look for familiar faces. The laughter around me fades into the background, and when I don't see Nonna, Mamma, or Giulia, I pull out my phone and send a quick message to Nonna.

"Where are you guys?"

It takes just a few seconds before her reply pings back.

"I was looking for you, too. Meet me by the fountain outside the garden."

I wind through a group of women in glittering dresses, flashing them a smile as they turn to watch me pass. The night air feels chillier as I make my way toward the fountain. When I get close, I spot Nonna standing there, arms folded across her chest, her expression filled with relief.

Her face softens at the sight of me, and I release a breath I didn't know I'd been holding as I close the gap between us. I've never been so grateful to see her.

"Mirabella, *figlia mia*," she murmurs, pulling me into a warm embrace. The familiar scent of her lavender perfume instantly soothes my nerves.

"I've missed you," I whisper, feeling the weight of everything settle as I lean into her. It's only been a few hours, but the thought of spending the next year apart from her makes my heart ache.

I've always been very close to Nonna, even before my mom got sick. After my father left us when Giulia was born, my grandmother stepped in and has taken care of us ever since.

We pull away, and she looks at me, her eyes swirling with emotions.

"I'm sorry, Mira, for how I spoke to you earlier. It sounded extremely ungrateful, and I regret it," she begins, her voice low. "I know the sacrifices you've made so that your mother can afford her treatment, we have food on the table, and Giulia can go to high school like other kids."

My heart softens at her apology.

"It's okay, Nonna. I expected you to react that way. I would be upset too if, in the near future, Giulia told me she was marrying a stranger just for money," I reply, trying to lighten the mood.

Nonna smiles, taking my hand and brushing her thumb over my knuckles. "You mentioned earlier that your husband promised to help us. Well, you were right. Ettore… he's already done so much for us in just a few hours of your marriage," she says, her tone cautious but hopeful. "New things have been delivered to the house. He even offered to move us to a better apartment, but I turned him down. You know I have an unhealthy attachment to that place." She chuckles, and I can't help but smile, too.

"Also, he's arranged a car and a driver for Giulia's school, and Isabella is starting her treatment at a private hospital tomorrow. She'll receive the intensive care she needs."

The news takes me by surprise. I knew Ettore said he would help us, but I didn't realize he would act so quickly.

"He didn't tell me," I murmur, feeling a mix of gratitude and disbelief.

"I think he's not as bad as I thought him to be," she admits, but hesitation lingers in her eyes. "But, Mirabella, I don't want you to feel obligated to him just because he's doing these things. If it means selling you off to this man, I'm ready to walk away from it all. I don't care if I have to find a job at my age. I'm still strong, and I'll figure out a way to support you. Together, we'll pay off our debts. We'll survive, just like we always have."

Her words hit me like a tidal wave, leaving me momentarily speechless. Nonna has always been the pillar of our family, but to hear her offer to work just so I can escape…it breaks my heart. I grip her hand tighter as tears threaten to spill from my eyes.

"The real reason I turned down the new apartment he offered us is so you'll have somewhere to run if things become too overwhelming," she continues, her voice steady. "We need a place that isn't tied to him. If you ever feel like you can't stay with him anymore, you can always come home. You'll always have a place with us."

Her voice trembles slightly, and I feel a lump in my throat. I blink back tears, refusing to let them fall.

"Nonna, listen," I say, my voice soft yet firm. "I'm okay. Ettore...he's not like that. This marriage is for a greater good, and I'm not being taken advantage of, I promise." I pause, searching for the right words to reassure her. "He's a man of his word. It's not as bad as it seems. I plan to enroll in college again and finish my degree. Our marriage may not be perfect or real, but something good is coming from it."

Nonna's eyes search mine, and slowly, a small smile begins to emerge. "College, eh? You've always wanted to go back to college. I'm glad you get to experience that. And as Giulia said, at least your husband isn't old or ugly."

We both laugh, and the knot in my chest loosens a little. It feels good to remind myself of the positives and why I accepted this arrangement in the first place.

"*Vai a dormire presto*," she says, patting my cheek lovingly. "You've had a long day. It's late, and I'm sure your mother is tired. We need to head home."

We walk back toward the garden, and she leads me to the corner where Giulia and my mother are seated. I escort them to meet the driver Ettore assigned for them, bidding them farewell before watching as the car drives away.

Once they're out of sight, the unease in my chest returns. I glance back at the garden, where the party continues, the low hum of voices and clinking glasses echoing in the distance. Exhaustion seeps into my bones, so I make my way back toward the garden, spotting Luca in the crowd. He stands near the edge of a table, his usual stoic expression watching over everything.

"Luca," I call softly as I approach. He turns toward me, eyebrows slightly raised when he sees me. "Can you let Ettore know I'm heading in?"

His gaze flickers over to Ettore, who is deep in conversation with some guests. His posture is tense, and a serious expression is etched on his face. They're likely discussing business, and I'm not in the mood to play the perfect wife and wait for him to finish.

"Of course," Luca replies with a nod. "I'll let him know."

As I watch him walk away, I can't help but feel a mix of anxiety and anticipation. The night may be winding down, but for me, the challenges are just beginning.

With that, I slip inside the main house, the noise of the party fading behind me. Just then, Clara passes by, and I'm hit with the memory of this morning's events.

"Clara," I call out.

She turns to look at me, and I notice her freeze for a moment before approaching.

"I'm sorry...about this morning. I wasn't...I couldn't..."

"It's fine, ma'am," she replies with an easy smile. "Like I told you, I understand how wedding mornings can be."

I exhale in relief, appreciating her understanding.

"Can you lead me to my room?" I ask, even though I know the way. I just want to ease the tension between us. After all, she's going to be my personal maid for the next year.

As she guides me up the stairs, the thought of spending the night in Ettore's room flashes through my mind, and heat rises to my cheeks. If we were a normal couple, this would be the time when I'd retire, take a shower, and prepare for a special wedding night.

As we walk down the long corridor, I suddenly realize we've passed my room and are continuing forward.

"Uh...I think we are headed the wrong way," I say, a hint of concern creeping into my voice.

Clara turns to me, confusion evident on her face. "Your things were taken to the boss's room earlier," she says carefully. "You are married to him now."

Right. We need to make everyone believe this marriage is real.

But Ettore had promised! I'd laid out my terms and told him I wouldn't be sleeping in the same room with him.

Clara's gaze remains fixed on me, expectant, perhaps questioning why I'm hesitating. If anyone might not buy our sham of a marriage, it's her. First, my escape attempt this morning, and now this?

I fumble for words, trying to explain the situation. "I...I think there's been a misunderstanding. I'm not, uh, planning to..."

Before I can finish, a voice drips with ice from behind me. "Well, well, well. Why wouldn't Ettore Greco's wife want to sleep in her husband's room?"

I freeze, slowly turning to face Zia Camila. Her lips curl into a knowing smirk, as if she's savoring the moment, and the women beside her lean in, their eyes sparkling with a mix of curiosity and malice.

I scoff inwardly, realizing they've been anticipating this since the announcement of my marriage to their beloved nephew—ready to ambush me, eager to witness my discomfort.

Too bad I'm not in the mood for their games.

As I fold my arms across my chest, preparing for a

confrontation, I can't help but wonder if this is how it's going to be for the rest of the year—enduring their condescension and judgement at every turn.

I was ready to escape into some much-needed rest, but it appears the night is far from over. In fact, this...this seems to be the opening act of what's to come.

18

ETTORE

The chatter around the room slowly fades, replaced by the soft strains of classical music drifting through the speakers.

"We've heard whispers about your plan to expand the Greco Empire," a voice cuts through the ambiance.

I take a slow sip from my whiskey glass, aware of the keen eyes on me. Somehow, between greeting guests, I've found myself knee-deep in a business conversation on my wedding day. Technically, this wedding is a strategic business move, designed to solidify alliances. I expected to connect with investors and associates today, but no man wants to debate business plans for hours on his wedding day, even if the said wedding is fake.

When I don't reply right away, Stefano Sanchez, the man who asked the question, presses further. "You've been tight-lipped about your next move, Greco. Word on the street is you're looking to expand your hotel business."

I nod, maintaining a neutral expression. "Something like that."

In my world, secrets rarely stay hidden for long. People

become curious; they can't help themselves. When they don't get confirmation, they leap to conclusions, often missing the mark but sometimes getting uncomfortably close to the truth.

Bruno Ramirez, an oil tycoon I'm interested to bring on board, raises an eyebrow, intrigue flickering in his eyes. "That's intriguing. Are you planning to acquire new hotels or invest in established ones? What's your angle here?"

I take another sip of my drink, allowing the silence to linger a moment longer. "I'm looking at acquiring some existing properties—major chains, recognized names, expanding into new states. That's the gist of my plan."

"I know you, Ettore," Bruno chuckles, leaning in. "You're aiming to own them outright, correct?"

I smirk, shaking my head. "More like strategic partnerships that benefit everyone involved."

They don't need to know every detail. In business, the art of saying less is crucial. I don't plan to partner with Stefano or Bruno on this project just yet, so the finer points remain under wraps. I want them to see me as a businessman making a power move in the hotel industry. What they don't realize is that this isn't just about acquiring properties. It's a game many play, and longevity isn't something everyone understands.

My expansion project aims to reshape the industry. I plan to buy out or invest in the best hotels nationwide, gaining control by holding the majority of stakes. The Greco Empire my father left behind won't merely be a player in hospitality and investment—it will embody luxury, exclusivity, and power.

Bruno looks skeptical, his brow furrowing. "And you really think these hotel chains will sell? Some of them are decades old, deeply rooted."

"They'll sell," I reply, my voice steady. "Everyone has a price."

What they don't know is that I've been laying the groundwork for this for years. My investments, my connections—have all been building toward this moment. Now, with the public image of a devoted family man, the kind of person investors trust, I've got the final piece in place. By the time they figure it out, I'll be steering the largest hotel empire in the country.

Stefano chuckles, shaking his head with amusement. "Always dreaming big, aren't you, Greco?"

I flash him a tight smile. "You know me."

As the conversation drifts to topics like Bruno's upcoming shipments from China and the deal Stefano wants to finalize with some Germans, my mind drifts elsewhere.

To her. My wife. Mirabella.

Just then, I spot Luca heading toward us from the crowd. From the look on his face, I can sense that something is wrong.

"I think you may want to see what's going on inside, boss," he whispers.

His words raise alarm bells in my mind, and I turn to glance at the towering building behind us.

"Sorry, gentlemen," I say, clearing my throat. "Our conversation will have to end here. I appreciate you coming to my wedding, and I'll catch up with you soon."

We exchange quick parting words and firm handshakes before I slip through the garden and head toward the main house.

The warm air envelops me the moment I step through the large doors, a welcome contrast to the slight chill outside. I scan the empty lobby, searching for any signs of activity.

Luca didn't need to elaborate. If he interrupted my conversation, it must be serious, and it likely concerns Mirabella.

"Where's my wife?" I ask a maid passing by.

Her breath hitches as she looks up at me, wide-eyed.

"Sh-she's upstairs, sir," she replies in a timid voice.

I stride toward the staircase, taking them two at a time. As I near the next hallway, I hear it—the unmistakable bite of Zia Camila's voice.

"You know, dear, in this family—I mean anywhere really, a wife usually sleeps with her husband." Her words are laced with sarcasm and venom, and my hands clench into fists.

Zia Camila continues her tirade just as I reach the top of the stairs. From my vantage point, I see how they've cornered Mirabella, all three of my aunts looming over her.

I'd given them one instruction—just one—don't disrespect my wife the moment she moves in here. But it seems my aunt is incapable of following orders.

"I don't know the kind of family you came from, seeing as your father isn't in the picture," Zia Camilla continues, "but I'll tell you how it's done here..."

I'm about to charge in and issue a final warning when Mirabella speaks up.

"You won't tell me how it's done here."

I freeze, and Zia Camila and the others exchange shocked looks.

"Excuse me?" Aunt Francesca is the one who speaks this time around.

Mirabella crosses her arms defiantly and tilts her head.

"I wasn't aware my sleeping arrangements with my husband required your approval."

A flicker of surprise flashes across my aunt's face, but she quickly recovers. "Forgive me for trying to confirm, dear," she says, her voice dripping with false sweetness. "I just thought it was strange that a bride wouldn't want to be by her husband's side on her wedding night."

Mirabella's gaze sharpens, her voice unwavering. "You thought it was strange? Or have you just been searching for a reason to put me in my place?"

Zia Camila's lips tighten into a thin smile, clearly unaccustomed to being challenged, especially by someone she considers beneath her.

"You're quite bold, aren't you? Perhaps you think that marrying into this family makes you a Greco," Zia Camila snaps.

"Actually, I think it does," Mirabella fires back. "I'm not sure where you're from but when a lady marries a man, that usually means she gets his surname. I am a Greco. I am the wife of the man who runs this household. "

I stifle a chuckle as shocked gasps and murmurs ripple through the room. A surge of pride courses through me. I'd been worried about how she would handle my aunts, but I'd nearly forgotten the fierce spirit Mirabella possesses.

My fearless Kitten.

A voice suddenly cuts in—Aunt Marta, her tone dripping with disdain.

"We may not be able to change the fact that you're married to our nephew, but the reality is that you are not fit to run this household. To even suggest otherwise is both disrespectful and insulting,"

"Why?" Mirabella shoots back, turning to face her with

fire in her eyes. "Because I didn't grow up with a silver spoon shoved up my ass?"

Shocked gasps ripple through the air again, and I struggle to suppress a laugh.

"I'm here because Ettore chose me," Mirabella continues, her tone bold. "Just as I assume your husbands chose you. And while I won't comment on the fact that you all should have your own families to run, it seems you've chosen to spend your time here trying to bully your nephew's new wife," she says, her smile sugary sweet. "I won't delve into the reasons why I think the three of you are here instead of in your own husbands' beds or homes. After all, as you kindly pointed out, I'm just a new member of the family, still learning the ropes."

As I expect, Zia Camila takes a step closer to Mirabella, her face red with anger as it always is whenever someone mentions anything about her marriage.

"You have no idea what you're talking about, little girl. You wanted to use that against me, but you've lost. My husband is dead, and it was very insensitive of you to bring him up! How will your husband react when I tell him you insulted my late husband?"

Mirabella stands her ground. "The same way he'll react when I tell him you brought up my absent father," she retorts, her voice steady. "Also I think it's really pathetic, trying to use your dead husband to score cheap points in an argument."

I know it's time to intervene when I see Zia Camila glaring at Mirabella, fists clenched at her sides.

"How dare you—"

"What's going on here?" My voice booms through the corridor, slicing through the tension like a knife.

Four heads whip around to face me, but my gaze zeroes

in on one person—my wife, who is glaring daggers in my direction.

"Nothing, my dear nephew," Zia Camila chirps, her tone overly bright. I shift my focus to her, narrowing my eyes. "We were just having a little welcome chat," she adds, forcing a smile that doesn't quite reach her eyes.

"Well, I think that's enough chatting for tonight," I say, striding over and wrapping my arm around Bella's waist. I feel her stiffen for just a moment before she relaxes against me. "My wife needs to get some rest."

Zia Camila's eyes flash with frustration, but she knows better than to challenge me.

"Of course. We'll leave you two alone." She motions for the others, and I watch as they retreat to the other wing of the house, their whispers trailing behind them.

As soon as the last of them is gone, Bella pulls away from my grip, her expression fierce.

"You said I would have my own bedroom," she snaps, shooting daggers at me with her eyes.

I take a step back, caught off guard by the heat in her gaze. "I meant it, Bella. But it's complicated—"

"Complicated?" She interrupts, her voice rising. "It's not complicated. You promised, Ettore! I thought I'd have a place of my own in this house. Instead, I walked into a lion's den!"

"I know. But my aunts can be overwhelming, and they won't stop until they feel they've asserted their dominance. I had no idea they'd confront you like that," I reply, trying to keep my tone calm.

"This isn't what I signed up for," Mirabella huffs, running a hand through her hair, frustration evident.

I stare at her face, flushed with anger, the rise and fall of her chest as she breathes heavily, and the way strands of her hair fall into her eyes before she tugs them back in frustration.

Fuck, I'm turned on.

Taking her hand, I pull her toward my bedroom. The last thing we need is to argue in the corridor on our wedding night where anyone could overhear us.

The moment we step inside, the air shifts. Every feeling I've been suppressing swells tenfold. We are alone, in my bedroom—my sanctuary—where no other woman has been, and suddenly all I want is to claim her.

"You handled that well by the way," I say, dropping her hand before running my fingers through my hair in frustration.

She exhales sharply, and I can see the tension in her body.

"I'm used to bullies like them. It's nothing new for me to defend myself against people who think the world revolves around them," she spits, venom lacing her words. A pang of guilt hits me, but I quickly shove it down.

I shouldn't let this woman make me feel even the slightest emotion toward her. That's dangerous. She's dangerous...

"Did you know your aunts were bullies?" she asks, then scoffs before I can respond. "Of course, you knew. You just didn't care because this is a business arrangement, after all," she mocks.

"They won't bother you again," I reply fiercely.

Her eyes widen slightly, surprise flickering across her features.

"I can't trust your words when you've already gone back on our agreement," she accuses, softly this time.

"That," I gesture toward the door. "What just happened a few minutes ago is why I changed the plans. There are nosy people around here, and the last thing we want is for anyone to suspect that this marriage is fake."

She huffs, and I find myself being upset at the fact that she's so insistent on not sharing a bedroom with me.

As she scans the room, I run my hands through my hair again. Her belongings are already moved in—clothes, personal items—everything arranged next to mine. It makes this whole situation feel real in a way it hadn't before.

There's a thick silence between us, and for a moment, neither of us knows what to say.

Finally, she clears her throat before turning to look at me. "I'm going to take a shower."

I nod, watching as she gathers her things and slips into the bathroom. The door clicks shut behind her, and all I can think about now is the image of her naked body under the water.

A groan escapes my lips as I sit down on the edge of the bed, my mind racing with the possibilities. But I push those thoughts away, reminding myself that our marriage is strictly business, and nothing of that sort will ever happen between us again.

After what feels like an eternity, she emerges from the bathroom, a towel wrapped around her chest, damp hair and skin flushed from the steam. I force myself to look away, keeping my eyes on the opposite wall as she moves around the room, pretending I'm not here, and for both our sakes, I do the same.

Eventually, I head to the bathroom myself. I need a cold shower—cold enough to wash away any lingering arousal. The steam from her shower still lingers in the air, and as I stand there in the fogged-up shower for a few minutes, just inhaling her scent, rich and intoxicating.

Realizing I've been standing here too long, I turn on the

shower, cranking the temperature down to the coldest setting. The ice-cold water cascades down my back, and I scrub my body with a loofah, desperately trying to erase every trace of her touch and the thoughts swirling in my mind.

But even as I scrub, I know it won't be that easy.

When I finally return to the room, I see Mirabella already tucked into bed, my covers pulled up to her chin. She's turned away from my side of the bed, her body curled into itself as if trying to create as much distance as possible. The sight tugs at something in my chest.

I change into my pajamas and slip into bed beside her, careful to keep my distance. But the mere fact that she's so close makes it impossible to relax. The tension between us is thick, heavy, like a weight pressing down on my chest. I can feel the heat radiating from her body and hear the sound of her heavy breathing.

"Pull yourself together," I whisper to myself, fighting the urge to pull her against me.

Time stretches on—seconds feel like minutes, minutes drag into hours—as I lie there in the darkness. My mind spins, replaying the very things it's not supposed to.

Finally, I begin to drift into sleep. Slowly. Torturously. It's a bittersweet reality—the only woman I've ever desired lies so close to me, yet somehow, she feels a world away.

19

MIRABELLA

Being married to a wealthy man comes with perks I never imagined. My marriage to Ettore was primarily about survival. All I initially thought I could gain from him was protection and money for my mother's treatment, to take care of my family, and to finally go back to college.

But one perk I hadn't anticipated was attending high-profile events. In the week since our marriage, I've gone with him to everything from charity galas to exclusive balls.

Today, we find ourselves at a horse racing event.

Horse racing—the kind of sport only the rich can indulge in.

The sun beats down on the arena, its heat baking the ground beneath my feet as we weave through the buzzing crowd. Laughter and low murmurs drift across the wide expanse of the racecourse. I'm struck by the opulence around me—the sharp suits and elegant dresses everywhere I look. Everyone here exudes money, power, and privilege.

Ettore tightens his grip on my hand as we navigate the

field. "You know, I attend events like this at least once a month," he tells me, a hint of pride in his voice.

I suspect it's less about the sport and more about mingling with other wealthy attendees.

I scan the vast green field, taking in the horses glistening in the sunlight. I never realized horses could be so beautiful and majestic. They look well-fed, their coats gleaming with health and strength.

I stifle a laugh at the irony of my situation. Just weeks ago, I was buried in debt, feeling hopeless. Now, here I am at a posh horse racing event, admiring the shine on the horses. It's astounding how quickly priorities shift when problems seem to disappear. Except, are all my problems actually solved?

The track stretches out, a wide expanse of reddish dirt that looks far more polished than anything I've seen on TV. But it's not the horses that capture my attention. It's the people. Wealthy investors, influential figures—this place feels like a playground for businessmen involved in dubious dealings.

Ettore looks completely at ease. Why wouldn't he? This is his turf.

He guides me to the grandstand, secures a seat with a perfect view of the field, and leans down to press a gentle kiss on my forehead before walking away. I know he's here for an important meeting, not just to watch the races, and I'm aware he has a bodyguard somewhere in the crowd keeping an eye on me.

I watch as he strides toward a group of men I vaguely recognize from other events. He's in his element. The way even older men pay rapt attention whenever he begins to speak. It does something to my insides.

Today, he's dressed casually yet classy. No suit jacket or tie; instead, he wears a crisp white T-shirt tucked into dark blue jeans. His long hair is pulled back, with a few strands artfully falling across his forehead. I catch a glint from his Rolex as he raises a champagne glass to his lips, taking a slow sip.

Across the rows of bleachers, our eyes lock. My breath catches as he looks at me as if he hadn't just left moments ago. There's something electrifying in his gaze.

But then, someone interrupts him, and I exhale the breath I didn't realize I was holding.

Moments later, the race begins. I try to focus on the field, but the atmosphere is overwhelming—the loud cheers as the horses take off, the announcer's booming voice over the loudspeaker, and the constant buzz of conversation swirl around me. It's a sensory overload. Suddenly, a wave of dizziness washes over me. Everything feels like it's spinning out of control.

And that's when I see him.

Matteo Abruzzi.

He stands in the midst of a small crowd just behind the metal track rail. Dressed in a fitted black dress shirt and sleek black pants, Abruzzi's attention is locked on the race before him. For a moment, I freeze. It's the first time I've seen him since I paid him off. My heart falters, and his warning about Ettore rushes back into my mind.

In the past seven days, no reminder of how dangerous Ettore could be has crossed my mind. He has been nothing but kind. So far, he's kept his promises to me and my family —except for the sharing a bedroom part, which I'm still a bit annoyed about. He's opened doors to a world I never thought I'd see, but just the sight of Abruzzi sends my doubts and fears bubbling back to the surface.

Suddenly, I feel a cold splash on my dress. Liquid trickles down my skin, jolting me back to reality.

"Signora, I'm so sorry!" A waiter with empty champagne glasses hovers above me, panic etched on his face as I look up at him. "Let me help you clean up."

"It's fine," I mutter, brushing him off. I need air. The dizziness is intensifying, and my head is spinning. "Just tell me there's a bathroom around here."

He gestures vaguely to an area behind the grandstand, but I'm already pushing myself to my feet and walking away as he stammers about the location. I maneuver through the crowd, ignoring the distant roar of the race behind me.

The world blurs as I stumble out onto the back of the track field, clutching the nearby wall for support. I close my eyes, trying to steady my breathing, but it doesn't help. Nausea rises in my throat, threatening to overwhelm me.

"Mirabella." A familiar voice cuts through the haze.

I open my eyes to see Abruzzi approaching, concern etched on his face as he steps closer. "You don't look well. Let me help you."

I instinctively take a step back. "Don't fucking touch me," I say, my voice barely a whisper.

"Listen, I mean no harm," he offers, his tone dripping with insincerity, "I can take care of you until you feel better. Or call someone. I have a personal doctor I trust."

"Like you took care of me last time?" I shoot back, remembering how he sent his goons to hunt me down the last time. "You think I'd trust you again after what you did?"

His eyes narrow, but a smirk creeps onto his lips. "You didn't seem to mind my help then. It's not too late to reconsider."

I scoff, trying to brush him off. "What do you want, Abruzzi?"

"Just to make sure you're safe." He steps closer, lowering his voice. "Tell me, has Ettore even bothered to look for you since you left the party?"

"Why would he?" I challenge, though a seed of doubt takes root in my mind. "He's probably busy."

"Busy? Or indifferent?" Abruzzi presses, his eyes gleaming with mischief. "It's only a matter of time before something worse happens. You should know that."

"What do you mean?"

"I saw you sitting all alone. Did he leave you, his vulnerable wife, to attend to more pressing matters?"

I want to snap back that I have a bodyguard, but that would only play into whatever twisted game he's trying to play. Instead, I cross my arms over my chest, feeling slightly better now that I've gotten some fresh air.

"Why are you really here? Why pretend to care about me? You've already shown me the monster you are."

Abruzzi's lips curl into a faint smile, a mix of amusement and something darker. "I only want to protect you, Mirabella. You deserve better than this. This man...he's only going to drag you into deeper trouble."

"And what? You're suddenly worried enough to warn me?" I hiss, my agitation rising. I'm done with the doubts, the mind games, and the lies.

"Ettore Greco is powerful," he continues, his tone lowering, almost conspiratorial. "That means he has powerful enemies. Enemies who want to strike at him by hitting him where it hurts most. What better way to bring down a man than by attacking his newlywed wife?"

"Stop it!" I snap, shaking my head. "You're trying to manipulate me, and it won't work."

"I'm not manipulating you, Mirabella. I'm trying to help you see the truth." He steps closer, his voice dropping to a more intimate level. "Open your eyes. If you stay with him, you could become collateral damage in a dangerous game. Think about that."

I hate how his words send a shiver of fear down my spine. I shouldn't believe a single word coming from Abruzzi's lips, but I'd be foolish to ignore the hint of truth in what he's saying.

"I have bodyguards," I finally say, feeling an inexplicable urge to defend my fake husband.

"Bodyguards?" Abruzzi snorts, his disdain palpable. "And where are they now?"

I fall silent, just staring at him as my mind swims with a whirlwind of thoughts. The longer I remain quiet, the more that smirk of satisfaction spreads across his face.

"You know I'm right." His voice softens, dangerously so, as he steps closer. "Ettore probably told whatever bodyguards he claims to have to keep me away. But here we are—minutes later—and no one has shown up. No one's even watching." He leans in slightly, his tone turning almost conspiratorial. "Do they even know you're gone?"

"You're wrong," I mutter, though his words gnaw at the edges of my thoughts, planting tiny seeds of doubt.

"Am I?" he asks, his eyes studying me like he's peeling away every layer. His smirk shifts, becoming something sharper, almost...interested. His fingers brush mine, a fleeting touch that sends an involuntary jolt up my arm. "You should be more careful who you trust, *tesoro*. Even the strongest men have blind spots."

His eyes flick to my lips for a moment, and I catch my breath, the air between us crackling with something I can't quite place. "You seem so sure of yourself," I say, my voice steadier than I feel.

"Confidence is earned," he replies smoothly, his lips

curving into a faint smirk. "But you...you're an enigma." He steps closer again, the space between us shrinking. "Tell me, Mirabella, do you always throw yourself into danger so recklessly? Or is it just with men like me?"

My pulse spikes at his words, and I refuse to look away. "I'm not afraid of you."

His brow arches, amusement glinting in his eyes. "No? Then why is your hand shaking?"

I glance down, realizing my fingers are trembling slightly against the edge of the railing I'm holding. I tighten my grip, heat rushing to my cheeks. "Maybe it's because you're in my personal space."

"Or maybe," he murmurs, his voice dipping lower, "you're afraid of what you *feel* in my presence."

For a moment, neither of us speaks. Then he takes a step back, deliberate and measured, his gaze lingering on mine as if committing me to memory. His eyes flick to my lips again, and a ghost of a smile crosses his face.

"You're intriguing, *tesoro*. I wonder if Ettore knows just how much."

He calls me that name again.

With that, he straightens, his smirk back in place like armor. "Enjoy the rest of the event," he adds smoothly, his tone light but laced with something darker. He turns and walks away, shoulders relaxed, leaving the weight of his presence looming long after he disappears into the crowd.

I don't move for a long moment. The nausea I felt earlier is replaced by a cold chill running down my spine. I glance around, wondering where Ettore or any of my so-called bodyguards are, and why they haven't noticed my absence yet.

Absentmindedly, I return to the grandstand, trying to

watch the rest of the race, pushing Abruzzi's words from my mind.

About thirty minutes later, Ettore sits beside me in the backseat of his car as we ride back to the hotel in the small western village we arrived at last night. I steal glances at Ettore, who scrolls mindlessly through his phone, the glow illuminating his intense features.

Abruzzi's words haunt me, twisting in my mind like a relentless current. The whiplash of emotions I feel sitting close to him is almost driving me insane.

"Why do you still let your family live with you?" I blurt out, breaking the heavy silence. It's a question I've wanted to ask for a while, a way to understand the dynamics of his family.

Ettore drops his phone into the cup holder and looks at me. "It's always been that way. My father wanted us to be united, to all live in the same house. Plus, I don't have a reason to send them away."

I nod, a breath escaping me as he continues.

"I never had a reason to send them away until you came along."

I turn to him, surprised by the seriousness in his gaze. "What do you mean?"

"I hate the way they treat you. I warned them..." His jaw clenches. "I told them I'd send them away if they ever disrespected you. If you want me to do it, I will."

I stare at him, taken aback by how readily he offers that. "No, it wouldn't be fair. They might not like me, and they have valid reasons not to, but they're still your family."

"What do you mean by that?" he asks, his tone low and edged.

"Your aunts...they're right. I don't deserve to be a Greco." I chuckle harshly, finally voicing the insecurities that have haunted me since our marriage. "I'm not even sure I deserve love. At least that's what my father thinks. Didn't even bat an eyelid before opting out of his responsibilities when my mom got diagnosed. We used to be close before he left, so for him to abandon us one day...I guess he thought I wasn't good enough to make him stay."

"Don't talk like that," Ettore interrupts sharply.

I meet his gaze, and the anger etched on his face is almost amusing, yet it surprises me. "Why do you care?" I ask, pushing back against the weight of his concern.

"Because you deserve better than this," he replies fiercely. "You deserve to be treated with respect, not like some mistake."

I feign a laugh. "You don't need to be mad on my behalf. I'm fine. His leaving made me stronger. I've always had to fight for what I have. Maybe that's why I don't think I deserve to get things easily..."

"You have a wonderful family. Do you know how much I wish I had a close-knit family like yours?" He says, his voice tinged with unexpected emotion.

"Yeah, I may live with my family, but there's no real love in that house. Everything revolves around money, fame, wealth, status. My aunts have hated my mother for as long as I can remember. Even now, years after her death, they always find a way to bring her up in conversations..."

"Ettore, I'm..." I choke, struggling to find the words.

"There's so much competition, gossip, and backstabbing. The only person I can trust in that house is my younger brother," he breathes out heavily. "You have something rare. You have genuine love and affection. You have people you can count on when things get tough. So don't ever say you don't deserve to be loved again. You have love in abundance already."

I swallow hard, unsure how to respond. A mix of emotions swirls in my throat as he squeezes my hand affectionately, then turns to face forward.

The rest of the drive is quiet, and by the time we reach the hotel, the tension between us feels thicker. We step into the elevator, and the silence stretches uncomfortably.

Once we're in our hotel room, Ettore breaks the silence. "Why did you leave that morning? Why did you run?"

His question hangs in the air like a heavy weight, and I feel my throat tighten.

"I didn't run," I reply, my voice stiff. "What we had was a one-night stand. It was supposed to end that way."

He laughs bitterly, and the sound grates on my insides.

"You're lying," he accuses, stepping closer, his eyes locked onto mine.

"I'm lying?" I scoff, crossing my arms defensively. "Why would I lie? Do all the one-night stands you have stay back and cuddle in the morning? I have a life. That night was supposed to be my escape, and after that, I had to go back to reality!"

"Again, that's not the reason you left, Bella."

"Then what the fuck do you want to hear?" I say, my voice louder than I intended.

"The truth," he insists, his eyes blazing as he closes the gap between us. "I want you to tell me the truth, Bella."

He studies me intently, and I can feel the heat creeping up my cheeks under his gaze.

I exhale slowly. "I left because…I didn't think I was good enough for you. It felt amazing, but I wasn't sure if I did anything you liked. It was my first time, okay? I was terrified of what your reaction would be the next morning. I didn't know if you'd want to see me again or if you'd just brush me off like some cheap fling…"

"Fucking hell, Bella," he murmurs, his hand finding my waist and pulling me closer.

My breath hitches as his other hand caresses my face. "I couldn't stop thinking about you, about that night. You made me feel like a starving man, like a dog craving more."

His confession hits me hard. He sounds genuine, but a part of me still feels as if something isn't right.

He watches me closely, his fingers tracing my face while I fight the rush of desire coursing through me.

After what feels like an eternity, he speaks again, his voice low and daring. "You want to learn," he tells me, not as a question but as a statement. He knows what I want, how to give it to me.

"Tell me, Bella," he whispers, brushing his finger over my lower lip. "Tell me to teach you."

20

ETTORE

The look in Mirabella's eyes as my words wash over her is... priceless. Her pupils dilate, and a soft breath escapes her lips.

"Ettore..." she whispers, her voice trembling slightly.

"You want this," I murmur, gently tracing her soft lower lip with my thumb. My other hand finds her waist, pulling her even closer. "You want to touch me, and you want me to touch you."

A breathy moan escapes her lips when I lean down to kiss her neck. My teeth graze the delicate skin at the base of her throat, and she tilts her head back, inviting me for more. I bite the spot again, firm enough to leave a mark. My mark. She trembles and arches into me, her fingers tangling in my hair, pulling me closer.

"Yes," she breathes, her voice filled with desire. "I want you. Teach me."

"Then let go, Mirabella," I urge, my lips brushing against her ear, sending shivers down her spine. "Let me show you just how much I want you, too."

Her breath catches, and I can see the fire in her eyes ignite. "I'm ready, Ettore. Just...don't stop."

With that, I pull her even tighter against me, savoring the moment, knowing we're teetering on the edge of something electrifying.

My hand clamps down on her waist as I push her backward against the closed door. The moment her back comes in contact with the door, my right hand comes down to the front of her dress, and I squeeze her breast through the silk material.

A tiny noise escapes her mouth, a sound that makes me grow hard in an instant. I never knew that it was possible to be in a perpetual state of arousal, but that's the way it's always been ever since she got into my house, into my bedroom, into my life.

Just then, I feel her pull the band off my ponytail, releasing my hair in waves. A groan slips past my lips as her hands slip into my hair. Just the feel of her nails scraping against my scalp makes me want to go crazy. She controls me, and she doesn't even know it.

I should stop this...we should stop. But I can't stop. I'm like a dog on a leash, doing only what she wants. And I know she wants this.

One hand slides between her legs, trailing upward slowly until my hand is buried under her dress. She leans back slightly, panting against my mouth, her fingers still tugging and twisting my hair. I pull her dress up farther just as my knuckles brush against her clothed pussy.

"You're wet," I whisper, running my hand along the seam of her lace panties, brushing the edges of the fabric. I press the heel of my palm against her mound. It's swollen and ready for me. It makes me ache deep in my bones just thinking about it, thinking about her wetness coating my dick as I push inside her.

But today isn't about me. It's not about what I want.

Mirabella gasps for air against my mouth as I push her panties aside and slip two fingers inside her. The sight of her flushed cheeks, her dazed eyes, her trembling body...it's more than enough for me.

"Is this what you want?" I ask her, my voice low and rough as I pump slowly. In and out. In and out. Her fingers dig into my scalp, making it hard to concentrate on anything but the sensations swirling inside of me.

"Yes," she breathes. "I want...I want to touch you...please."

"Ladies first, Bella," I say through gritted teeth as my fingers begin to move faster.

Inasmuch as I want to teach her how to please me, I can't stop touching her. I don't want to stop. I don't want the sounds of her wanton moans and whimpers to cease. I want to keep feeling her wet walls clench around my fingers.

When my thumb finds her clit and begins to draw circles on the sensitive nub, she pushes her hips downwards and begins to grind against my fingers. Her breathing quickens, and when I notice her knees giving out under her, I wrap my free arm around her waist to keep her on her feet.

"Oh...Ettore," she gasps when I add a third finger. I circle her clit faster and she lets out another moan.

"That feels good, doesn't it?" I murmur into her ear. "You want to cum, don't you?"

"Yes." Her eyes are half-lidded now. She bites her lower lip as one hand slides into my hair again.

I pump her again. Once, twice, and when I curl my index finger deep inside her, her body bucks off the door, and she shudders violently as she comes undone.

"That's it, Kitten," I murmur, pumping her slowly now as her body spasms. "Let go."

When she collapses against me, a chuckle leaves my lips, and a shocked gasp leaves hers when I lift her body in my arms and carry her to the bed.

"Get some rest," I say, pressing a kiss on her forehead. "You always get sleepy after an orgasm."

"No," she whines, and when I drop her on the bed, she quickly drops down from the bed. "You said you would teach me how to touch you. I want to touch you."

A sharp breath leaves my lips as she steps directly in front of me. "Tell me what to do, Ettore. Tell me how you would like me to touch you..."

An image of me grabbing the back of her head while I fuck her mouth flashes in my head, and I shake the thought away. I'm too aroused now, and I know that the moment she touches me, I'll lose the little control I've been trying so hard to grab onto ever since our wedding night.

But when she presses herself flush against me and begins kissing my neck like I kissed hers earlier, all rational thought flies out the window. I'm completely lost within this woman, and nothing in the world matters except for this. For her.

She reaches down and slips both her hands underneath my T-shirt. A sound between a sigh and a groan slips out of my lips as her fingers caress my abdomen up to my shirt.

"I see you want this," she murmurs. "So teach me."

A humorless chuckle leaves my lips, and the next thing I know, I'm doing exactly what she wants. She watches raptly as I undo the buckle of my belt, unzip my fly, and free my dick from my briefs.

"Take off your dress and get on your knees," I tell her, my voice thick with need.

She obeys immediately, pulling her dress over her head and tossing it to the side. When she kneels in front of me, her eyes are filled with lust. I glance down at the woman kneeling before me in nothing but a matching set of red lace lingerie. I step closer and slide my hand to the back of her head, gathering her long hair and wrapping it around my fist.

"Touch me," I say through gritted teeth.

Her hands come up to touch my hard length. I suck in a breath as she traces her fingers up and down the length as if admiring it. While I love the look on her face, the longer she does that, the more impatient I get.

"Stop teasing me, Kitten," I murmur before grabbing one of her hands and wrapping it around my dick. "Like this. Move up and down."

She nods and smiles shyly as I guide her hand up and down my shaft. Her fingers wrap around it to the best of their ability as she follows my lead. Her grip is soft and gentle, and I close my eyes for a moment to relish the feel of her warm flesh rubbing against mine. She strokes my cock gently, slowly, almost as if she's unsure. A groan slips past my lips as she continues her movements, and my grip on her hair tightens.

My reaction seems to embolden her because her grip turns firmer, and she increases the speed of her movement. My head falls back as I let out a loud groan, my grip tightening even further on her hair.

"That's it, Kitten," I growl. "Just like that."

She pumps faster now, and a low hiss leaves my lips when she brings her mouth down to suck the tip of my dick.

"Fuck, Bella," I groan as she takes me into her mouth. She hums against my dick, and the sound sends vibrations through my whole being. I can already feel myself coming close, my balls clenching painfully.

When she pulls away and glances up at me, I realize I've never seen anything sexier. Her brown eyes sparkle with hunger, and her hair cascades in waves down her shoulders. Her cheeks are flushed pink, her pouty lips shiny and glossy as she licks them before taking me into her mouth again.

I close my eyes as her tongue plays around on the tip of my cock. I resist the urge to grab her head and pump myself into her mouth, resist the urge to fuck her throat until it's sore. Instead, I focus on the sensations tingling in my balls and swirling their way down to my toes.

When I feel her teeth scape the sides of my dick lightly, I come undone, exploding inside of her mouth. My entire body shakes beneath me as hot, searing bursts spill from my cock down her throat. She swallows it all, moaning as I caress the side of her face. When she finally releases me and rises to her feet, I immediately pull her to me and press my lips against hers.

She moans, tilting her head to accommodate me better. Her tongue darts out to lick my lips, and she kisses me deeply. I taste salt on her tongue, and it excites me beyond words. Her tongue explores my mouth, and I welcome it eagerly.

This time, when we pull apart, my fingers glide along the length of her spine.

"Are you hungry? I'm starving."

A giggle slips past her lips as I pull her body to my side on the bed, sliding the sheets over our bodies. "I'll order room service."

In the next few minutes, I run my fingers through her hair while listening to the sound of her soft breathing. And by the time our food arrives, she's already fast asleep.

21

MIRABELLA

It's been two weeks since I officially became a Greco, and it's become painfully clear that my husband's family can't stand me. They make a point of reminding me I don't belong here through forced, tight-lipped smiles whenever Ettore is around, and the subtle—or not-so-subtle—remarks they drop like it's their personal mission. No matter what I do, they're determined not to accept me.

The only exception is Ettore's younger brother Vittorio. He's warm and genuinely friendly, always eager to chat when he returns from work. Sometimes, I wonder how someone so upbeat and open could come from the same family as Ettore. Now I understand why Ettore said Vittorio is the only family member he trusts.

The staff here are kind, too, though part of me thinks it's because they don't have much choice—they'd probably risk their jobs if they weren't polite. But even with Ettore's strict aunts around, they seem genuinely fond of me, especially when it's just us in the house. I can feel them relax, though they snap back to attention when any of the family appears.

As for Ettore's cousins, they couldn't care less. Bianca is either at a friend's place or holed up in her room making videos for her followers or binge-watching shows. Leonardo and Antonio have gone back to college and only visit on weekends, which is a relief.

In the beginning, it was uncomfortable being left with the people who clearly despise me every time Ettore and Vittorio went to work. But now, I just...don't care. I've got my almost-daily visits to my own family and the excitement of preparing for college to keep me busy. Those keep me from dwelling on the mansion's empty halls or the weird distance that's developed between Ettore and me since we...well, since that night.

Today, Alessia and Giovanni are coming over. I've barely opened the door before Alessia practically tackles me with a hug, squeezing me so tightly I nearly lose my breath.

"All right, spill," she demands, pulling back just enough to lock eyes with me, her face a mixture of confusion and excitement. "I get this unexpected invite to *the wedding of the year*—and the bride is my best friend, who I didn't even know was dating anyone! Mira, what's going on?"

I laugh, pulling away to catch my breath. "Nice to see you too, Alessia. Hey, Gio."

Giovanni gives me a small smile and an awkward wave as he steps inside. "Hey, Mira. You look...uh, stressed."

"That's because she's hiding something," Alessia accuses, hands on her hips. "You owe me an explanation. Who is Ettore Greco, and how the hell did you end up engaged to him? Don't tell me this was one of your whirlwind decisions!"

I wince. "It's...complicated."

"Complicated?" Alessia throws her hands up in exasperation. "Mira, the last time we talked, we were just making plans to hang out because we barely see each other anymore. Then, a few days later I'm RSVPing to your wedding? I mean, I'm happy for you, but I didn't even know you *liked* someone enough to marry them!"

"Ettore was thoughtful enough to send out invitations to you guys," I mutter, trying to deflect. "God knows how he even knows who my friends are."

Alessia narrows her eyes. "Uh-huh. That doesn't answer the question, Mira. Are you in trouble? Did he pressure you into this?"

"No! No, it's not like that." My voice is too quick, and Alessia's brows shoot up in suspicion.

Giovanni clears his throat, stepping in. "Okay, maybe we should give Mira a chance to breathe. She doesn't need an interrogation five seconds after we walk in."

"Thank you," I say with a sigh, shooting him a grateful look.

"Fine," Alessia huffs, flopping onto my couch. "But you're not getting away that easily. I want details, Mira. How did you meet him? What made you say yes? And why do I feel like there's more going on here than you're telling me?"

I glance between them, my mind racing for something to say that won't dig me into a deeper hole. Alessia crosses her arms, her skepticism written all over her face. Giovanni gives me a small nod, though his worry is just as apparent.

They step into the foyer, and I lead them down the hall toward the conservatory. The glass walls of the room bathe everything in sunlight, casting a warm, golden glow over the lush plants and cozy lounge chairs. They both look around, wide-eyed, and I motion for them to sit.

"This place is...wow," Alessia says, blinking in amazement. "Mira, this feels like a scene from a movie. Tell us everything."

Alessia and Gio missed my wedding because they were out of town visiting her sick grandmother. They only found out about the wedding when they got the invitation.

"Well," I say lightly, trying to keep things casual. "Obviously, I'm married now. That's what happened."

Alessia stares at me, unconvinced. "Just like that? Mira, I'm your best friend, and I didn't even know this guy existed. Then I get a wedding invite while I'm a hundred miles away, and I'm supposed to believe it all just happened out of nowhere?"

I can feel their suspicions rising, and it kills me not to tell them the truth. But the damned NDA I signed keeps me quiet.

"Yeah, I know it seems fast," I admit, shrugging. "But we met one night, he kind of saved my life, and we started seeing each other after that. One thing led to another...and he proposed."

"And you just...said yes?" Alessia scoffs, crossing her arms. She knows me too well. She knows there's more to this story.

I nod. "Yup. Just like that."

Gio finally speaks up, his tone laced with doubt. "See, here's the part where I start losing you, Mira. I was there that night when one of your husband's men approached you with some so-called *proposition*."

I raise my hands in mock surrender. "Okay, fine. I knew who Ettore was before that happened."

Alessia rolls her eyes. "So you're telling us you fell for this mysterious guy, got swept off your feet, and suddenly you're Mrs. Greco? Do we look like we were born yesterday?"

I sigh, trying to keep things light. "Look, I know it

sounds insane. But it's real, all right? I'm here, I'm married, and...well, this is my life now."

"Are you happy?" Gio asks quietly, his gaze steady.

I pause, caught off-guard by his question. I open my mouth, but words don't come right away. "It's...complicated," I finally manage.

Alessia gives me a sympathetic look. "You know you don't have to pretend with us, Mira. If things ever get too overwhelming, we're here."

Giovanni crosses his arms, giving me a once-over like he's trying to see past me. "If you were forced or coerced into this marriage, you can tell us."

I manage to laugh, even as my chest tightens. "It's not like that. Promise."

I'm not lying, but he's not wrong, either.

Alessia narrows her eyes. "Then what's it like? Living in this gorgeous house, married to a billionaire?"

I force a smile and hope to God it looks real. "It's...amazing. He takes care of me and my family, and he loves me." I lie through my teeth.

Alessia squeezes my hand, looking at me earnestly. "You know I won't judge you if you married him for his money, right? I mean, who wouldn't be tempted if a billionaire came along?"

A real laugh slips out. "No, it's not about the money."

It totally is.

Giovanni sighs, his voice softening. "Look, as long as you're safe, we're happy for you. But if he's forcing you into anything..."

"He's not," I assure him. "Really, I'm happy. Or don't I look it?"

"You actually do," Alessia teases, grinning. A mischievous gleam in her eyes. "You're glowing. I'm assuming you've, um, *sealed the deal...*"

"Oh my God," I groan, covering my face as Giovanni cringes. "I do not want to discuss that! Anyway, enough about me. What have you two been up to?"

Alessia rolls her eyes. "Trying to dodge, huh?"

"Yep." I smirk. "Now spill."

They finally give in, telling me all about their trip and how Alessia's grandmother bluntly told them she wants grandkids soon.

I laugh as Alessia recalls explaining to her that they're not exactly ready for marriage, only for her religious grandmother to say she didn't care as long as they had babies.

For the next hour, I joke with my friends, feeling more relaxed than I have in weeks. For a little while, I forget I'm Mrs. Greco.

MY FIRST DAY of college arrives faster than expected. Stepping onto campus feels surreal—tall buildings, the bustling energy of students, the hum of a hundred voices blending into the kind of chaos I missed. Here, I'm just Mirabella, an International Relations major.

In one of my classes, I sit next to a guy named Milo. He's American, with a crooked smile and a laid-back attitude that instantly puts me at ease.

"So, what's your story?" he asks, giving me a curious look after one of our lectures is over.

"Story?" I chuckle, raising an eyebrow.

"There's something about you," he says, grinning. "You don't seem like just any regular gal."

I laugh. "Oh, I'm as regular as it gets, Milo."

"Uh-huh." He glances at my hand. "That rock on your finger says otherwise."

I almost forgot about my wedding ring. I'd thought about leaving it at home for a 'normal' college experience but decided against it. Ettore made it clear that everyone, everywhere, should know I'm married.

"So, married girls aren't normal?" I ask, amused as I watch his cheeks turn red.

"N-no, I didn't mean it like that," he stammers, laughing. "That was sexist. Don't tell me I've already blown my chance of being your friend."

I chuckle. "You're forgiven. We're friends now, Milo."

The rest of the week is jam-packed with lectures and college events, but I finally squeeze in a visit home for the weekend to stay the night.

From the outside, our old house looks just the same, except for a few repairs—new windows, fresh light bulbs on the porch, and a fixed door handle. The moment I step inside, it feels like slipping into a favorite old sweater. Nonna's cooking fills the air, warm and familiar, and Giulia's laughter echoes from the next room.

"Mira!" Giulia bounds toward me, practically bouncing on her toes. "I have a boyfriend!"

"What?" I laugh as she grabs my hand, dragging me toward the kitchen, where Nonna's at the stove, stirring a pot of her famous tomato sauce.

"Well, okay, he isn't exactly my boyfriend yet," she corrects, a grin spreading across her face, "but I *know* he's going to ask me at the homecoming dance. He already asked me to be his date..."

"Whoa, slow down there," I chuckle as we step into the dining room. I lean over to give Mamma a kiss on the forehead, noticing the faint lines of exhaustion etched into her face. Her tired smile tugs at my heart as she sits at the head of the table.

"Don't lean on her too much," Nonna scolds from across the room, wagging a finger at me. "The doctor said no stress for her joints, and you're hovering like a bad habit."

I pull back immediately, guilt creeping in. "Sorry, Mamma," I mumble, though she waves it off with a soft laugh.

"So, who's this mystery guy we're talking about?" I ask, desperate to steer the conversation elsewhere.

"Kelvin!" Giulia exclaims, rolling her eyes as if I should've known.

"Oh, you mean *the* Kelvin?" I tease, raising an eyebrow as I settle into a seat beside Mamma. "Your forever crush?"

Giulia huffs, her cheeks turning pink, and I can't help but laugh, feeling right at home with my family's quirks and warmth surrounding me.

"Stop teasing your sister," Mamma says gently, though I notice the way her hands flex against the table, stiff and slow. The rheumatoid arthritis is always worse after a long day, and she shouldn't even be sitting here—but Mamma insists on being part of every family moment, no matter what.

"Are you staying the night? Please say yes!" Giulia pleads, her eyes wide with hope.

"Giulia," Nonna interjects with a sharp tone, "Mira has plenty to worry about already. She's got her husband now, and your mamma's surgery is only days away. The doctor said she needs rest, not late-night chatter!"

"Nonna," I protest softly, though the mention of Mamma's upcoming surgery twists my stomach. "It's okay. I'll stay after dinner and follow you guys for the surgery tomorrow."

Mamma reaches out, her hand brushing mine lightly. "I'm fine, *cara*. You don't have to worry so much."

But I *do* worry. The looming surgery, the medication schedule, the strict dietary restrictions—all of it is like a constant drumbeat in the back of my mind. No matter how much I try to pretend otherwise, it's impossible not to think about it.

Thankfully I have Guilia to always make me forget how depressing it can be to an adult sometimes.

"Yay...Now let's talk about me," she starts, clapping her hands. "You can help me pick out a dress! I've got a list of options, but I need your fashion expertise."

Dinner is a whirlwind of chatter and laughter. It's the happiest I've felt in weeks. Later that night, Giulia and I curl up in my old bed, and I exhale a breath I didn't realize I was holding. This...this is home. Not the cold, unwelcoming Greco mansion with its stony stares and harsh whispers, or the bedroom where I can never fully relax, knowing Ettore —my husband, who I'm supposed to feel nothing for—is right next to me every night.

This is peace. And right now, it's exactly what I need after the week I've had.

Eventually, I drift off to sleep. But sometime in the middle of the night, I wake up to the smell of smoke.

My heart pounds as I sit up, blinking in the darkness. I immediately shake Giulia awake.

"Wake up, Giulia!" I say, urgency in my voice. She stirs, mumbling, then her eyes snap open as she notices the thick smoke seeping in from under the door.

"Mira?" she whispers, her voice laced with fear.

"We need to get out, now." I jump out of bed, pulling her with me.

Giulia and I rush out of the room as my heart pounds, hoping Mamma and Nonna are safe.

The hallway is filled with thick, acrid smoke, and the heat hits us like a wall as we step out of the room. I'm about to head toward Nonna and Mamma's shared room when I hear a cough somewhere ahead of us. I exhale a short breath of relief when I hear Nonna's faint voice calling our names amidst fits of coughing.

"Nonna," I shout, voice breaking as I grip Giulia's hand tightly.

"Mira," Nonna's voice calls out, faint and strained with coughs. Relief floods through me, but my panic quickly returns.

We find Nonna struggling to breathe in the living room. "Come on, let's get out of here," I shout, supporting her weight. "Giulia, open the door—the fire hasn't reached there yet."

Giulia races to the door, shoving it open as I guide Nonna outside. She tries to speak, but it's lost in a series of coughs. As we step onto the porch, I see our neighbors gathering, their faces etched with concern. But then a horrible realization hits me—I haven't seen Mamma.

"Where's Mamma?" I gasp, looking back toward the smoky hallway. My stomach twists with fear.

Nonna grabs my arm, her grip tight. "She's still in her room. I tried to reach her, but the smoke...I couldn't breathe. I already called 911."

I'm zoned out as she continues to speak. My mother is inside the house!

My sick mother is inside the *burning* house.

I don't think—I just move. I'm charging back toward the house, the thick smoke stinging my eyes. But suddenly, a firm grip pulls me back.

I whip around, heart skipping, and find myself face-to-face with Abruzzi. He's here. But how...and why?

But I don't have the time for questions as he pulls me back.

"Get your sister and grandmother to safety," he says firmly, his eyes locking onto mine.

I don't have time to argue or question him. In an instant, he's moving past me, disappearing into the smoke.

I lead Nonna and Giulia farther from the house, my heart pounding. Flames have started to lick up the left side —the side where Mamma's room is. Grabbing Nonna's phone, I dial Ettore's number which I now have memorized. It rings, but he doesn't pick up.

"Come on, come on..." I whisper, my voice thick with tears. The phone rings out, and I scream in frustration, throwing it down.

Abruzzi reappears carrying Mamma, who is coughing and clinging to him as he brings her outside. Relief floods through me, and I rush to her side, taking her hand.

"Mamma, are you okay?" I whisper, holding her close.

Someone hands her a bottle of water, and she sips it slowly, regaining her breath. Behind me, I feel Abruzzi's presence again.

"It's cold," he says in a low, steady voice. "You all need to get somewhere safe."

I'm about to demand why the hell I should go with him when I glance back at the house, watching the flames consume it. My tired mother, my frail grandmother, and my anxious little sister all stand beside me, and I let out a shaky breath.

Without another word, Abruzzi helps us into his car and drives us to one of his safehouses on the quiet side of town. I have so many questions, so many things to say, but I'm exhausted. I just want my family safe.

An hour later, we're seated in a sterile, quiet room. My family is asleep in the other room, but I can't even close my eyes. My mind races with everything that's happened. Abruzzi brings over two glasses of water, sliding one toward me as he sits down.

He watches me over the rim of his glass. "I warned you, didn't I?" he says, his voice calm but edged with something darker. "Ettore's protection isn't as solid as you think."

I stiffen, his words sinking into me like ice.

"He doesn't know..."

Abruzzi snorts, his eyes narrowing. "He doesn't know? Is that a fucking excuse? He made you his wife, Mira. He's supposed to protect you and your family. Two hours have passed. Where the hell is he?"

"Ettore wouldn't just leave me for dead," I snap back, my voice trembling with a mix of anger and fear. "Maybe he's...busy. He hasn't been home for two nights. He's—"

"Busy?" Abruzzi cuts in, voice sharp. "So, his work comes before your safety?"

I hate that the doubt is creeping into my mind, wrapping around my thoughts like the smoke from the fire. Abruzzi leans back, studying my face and watching the seed of doubt he's planted grow.

"I have watched over you and your family since you got involved with that...brute," he spits.

"You've been watching me?" I choke, unable to process everything that's been happening.

"Yes." He lets out a sigh, a hint of frustration mingling with something I can't quite place. "I know you hate me, Mira—despise me, even. But I know what happens when vulnerable people like you get involved with monsters like

Ettore." His gaze drops to the floor, and he mutters, almost to himself, "You told me to stay away, and I did...at least in the ways you could see. I could've ignored what I saw tonight, could've let things take their course. But I didn't."

I want to lash out, tell him he's wrong, call him a liar and manipulator, but...deep down, I know he's right. Without him, this night might have gone horribly wrong. And he knows it.

Abruzzi stands, crossing his arms over his chest. "Think carefully, Bella. I may be a bastard, the monster you once accused me of being, but tonight, I was there, and Ettore wasn't." His voice lowers, but his words are sharp as knives. "I saved your mother's life. Maybe you hate me for it. Maybe you owe me for it. But don't forget that when it mattered, I was there."

22

ETTORE

My feet crunch against the gravel as I step out of my car onto a quiet street in the Lower East Side. A light drizzle falls from the sky, making the ground damp and creating a fog that hangs over the air. Across the road, a dim neon sign blinks red from an alleyway, flickering weakly in the darkness.

I cross the empty street, head down as I move toward the alley. When I reach the door, I pull it open and slip inside, finding myself in what looks like an old vinyl store. Without stopping, I make my way toward the back, where another door waits. I push it open and enter a narrow, dimly lit corridor that reeks of damp stone and stale smoke.

I walk down the corridor, each step echoing softly until I reach the door at the end. Swiping my card, I hear the click of the lock, and the door slides open.

Inside, the air is thick and heavy. Jazz hums low in the background, a lazy tune that winds through the haze of cigar smoke, settling into the dark wood and plush velvet sofas scattered around the room. My eyes sweep over the familiar faces, men draped in shadows, some lounging in armchairs, others perched on leather stools. Their expressions are hard. Focused.

These aren't ordinary men. They're dangerous, each one a silent enforcer in the criminal underworld, men who erase problems not with signatures but with silence—and sometimes blood. These are men like me, gathered here today for a reason none of us can ignore.

"I was starting to think you wouldn't show," sneers Riccardo De Santis, his sharp gaze cutting through the smoke. Riccardo, the man who owns half the drug factories on this side of the country, knows just how to throw a jab.

I ignore him, turning instead to Dante Russo, the head of Manhattan's largest drug cartel. He speaks first, his voice gravelly and tense. "You've all heard the news."

We lost the customs director this morning. Not lost as in dead, but worse—arrested. For men like us, that's a far bigger problem.

Abruzzi isn't here yet, but he's expected. Abruzzi, with his smug grin and his tendency to show up exactly where I don't want him to be.

"The authorities put out a public statement. They're launching a full-blown investigation." Dante's voice is low, but it cuts through the murmurs that ripple around the room.

Our man in customs, the one we placed there, has been compromised. He made things easy for us, greasing the wheels of our operations. Now he's in their custody, and it's only a matter of time before they start digging. To put it plainly, we're *fucked*.

Ricardo leans forward, his face shadowed. "Days. That's all we've got before they start tracing every shipment, every payout. They've frozen his accounts already. It won't be long before they track down the rest of us."

From across the table, Bruno Sanchez curses under his breath. "I've got a contact at Interpol. It's not just the Feds," he mutters, scowling. Bruno's been in the game since the early '90s, and he doesn't look like he's stopping anytime soon.

I glance around. Six of us should be here, but we're two short.

Abruzzi and Martelli.

I can't stand Abruzzi, but the reality is that our circles overlap, and we're in this mess together. He's not one to miss a meeting like this, though, and a bad feeling gnaws at me. Either Abruzzi's caught up in something that could drag us all down, or he's behind this trouble.

Dante's voice breaks through the haze, rougher this time. "It's worse than we thought. Someone's leaking intel. They know about our routes, our fronts—even our offshore accounts. This is going to blow up fast. They're hitting us from the bottom up, picking off our bodyguards, our men. They're squeezing them for names and leads."

The room goes quiet. No one says it out loud, but I can see it in their eyes—if we don't get ahead of this, we'll be next.

"That's not the main problem," I finally say. "We're all circling the obvious here. We have a wildfire at our doorstep." The room quiets, eyes turning to me as I let the words hang heavy. "They pulled Martelli this afternoon. In his villa in Barcelona."

I pause, watching the alarm ripple through the faces around me. "And he's talking."

"Martelli's a fucking coward," Bruno spits, anger gleaming in his eyes. We've all heard brave stories of the man. He's been arrested a couple of times, and each time he's asked to snitch, he asks them to kill him instead.

"He knows too much," Bruno continued, "and if they've really got him, they're closer to us than I'd thought. It's only a matter of time before they pick someone else, too."

"Then what do you suggest we do, Ettore?" Ricardo asks in a biting tone. "Since you know everything, and we've all been stating the obvious."

I glance at him, keeping my expression blank. Ricardo's had it out for me ever since I had a short, ill-fated fling with his sister. A couple of fucks some nights together, and she was talking about moving into the Greco estate, making plans for children. I told her straight—in more cruel words, I'll admit—I wasn't interested in marriage, family, any of it. The next day, Ricardo stormed into my office, hurling curses and fists. He's never forgiven me, and he's not about to start now.

I lean back, letting the silence build before I speak. "We all know what has to be done."

We have to kill Martelli.

No one objects. They know I'm right.

I lean forward, my voice low. "They're going after every network, every front we've built. They're going to rip through us piece by piece if we don't end this leak and shut down this investigation for good. And we need to do it fast."

Nods of agreement ripple through the room. Dante opens his mouth to say something, but just as he does, the door slides open, and I glance up—only to see Mirabella charging in, fury blazing in her eyes.

"What the—"

"You tried to have me killed," she shouts, her voice raw with anger. She's shaking, her face taut with rage. She doesn't care about the dozen pairs of eyes turning her way, doesn't hesitate in the presence of men who'd slit her throat without a second thought.

I stand, my tone low and deadly. "What are you doing here? How the hell did you get here?"

"Why didn't you answer your phone when I called?" Her voice slices through the room, sharp and loaded with anger. "You never, *ever* miss your calls, Ettore, so why now?"

"Is that what this is all about?" Ricardo's mocking voice floats from somewhere behind me. I catch a few amused glances exchanged by some men, while others just look fed up with the drama. But their expressions barely register as Abruzzi walks in, and suddenly, everything clicks.

Without a second thought, I cross the room in two strides, grab him by the collar, and shove him hard against the wall.

"What the fuck did you do?" I snarl, tightening my grip. "I told you to stay away from my wife. Why is she here? Why did you bring her here?"

He only smirks, his face an irritating picture of calm. If anything, his grin grows wider.

"Easy there, Ettore." He chuckles, clearly amused. "Your wife came to *me* asking for help. And what kind of man would I be to turn down an offer like that—"

Before he can finish, I drive my fist into his face. The satisfying crack of bone rings out, but it's not enough. I hit him again, and then again, each blow doing little to quench the fury boiling inside me.

"Ettore, stop!" Mirabella's panicked voice cuts through my rage, her soft hands gripping my arm, trying to pull me back.

I step away from Abruzzi, watching as blood pours from his nose. He coughs and spits, staining the floor with blood. Mirabella rushes toward him, but before she gets too close, I grab her arm and pull her back to me.

"Why the fuck are you defending him? And why were

you with him in the first place?" My voice is loud, almost a shout, and I can't bring myself to care.

Her eyes spark with anger, matching my own. "My house burned down today, Ettore! Did you know that?" She yells, wrenching her arm free. "My Nonna, my sister, my Mamma..." She chokes, her voice breaking, and I see the tears welling in her eyes.

"Mirabella..." I reach for her again, my tone softer, but she steps back.

"I called you. My grandmother called you, but you didn't answer. You promised to protect us, but when my mother was trapped in that burning house, Abruzzi was the one who went in and saved her," she screams, her words tearing into me.

Behind her, Abruzzi wipes the blood from his lip, a smug, blood-streaked grin spreading across his face.

"I saved your wife and her family, and this is the thanks I get?" he sneers, his voice dripping with bitterness. "Even for you, that's low."

"I told you to stay away from her," I growl, but the anger only fuels the shame, the regret, the disgust I feel for myself.

Abruzzi doesn't flinch. "If I hadn't stepped in and brought Mirabella and her family to safety, you'd be waking up to breaking news by morning. *Billionaire Ettore Greco loses his wife and her family in a tragic fire...*" His voice is smug, every word twisting the knife deeper.

Mirabella swipes at a tear on her cheek, and my chest tightens with anger—at her, at Abruzzi, but mostly at myself.

I swore to protect her. I swore to keep her safe. Yet tonight, I'd failed her, and the bitter irony that *he*—the man I warned her to stay away from—was the one who saved her digs deep, wounding my pride.

So instead of letting the jealousy, the frustration, and the self-loathing consume me, I let a bitter smile twist onto my face.

"Thanks for playing hero, Abruzzi," I sneer. "But don't get too comfortable. I'll be picking up my in-laws soon."

A few snickers break the tense silence in the room, and that's when I remember we have an audience. Clearly, they've been enjoying the drama we just performed for them.

I meet Riccardo's gaze, and something flashes in his green eyes before he takes a step forward.

"Isabella...it's Isabella, isn't it?"

"Don't speak to my wife," I snarl, just as Mirabella snaps back.

"I'm sure you're aware of my name." Her words spark a few chuckles around the room, and I can see she's too furious to appreciate me stepping in.

Riccardo's eyes narrow at her retort.

"Quite the entrance," he sneers, voice oozing with disdain. "You think you can barge in here and interrupt a meeting because—what? Your husband didn't answer your call? Oh, poor Isabella," he taunts mockingly.

"Funny," Mirabella fires back, her tone sharp. "I don't remember needing your permission to walk in. Only my husband can speak to me on such matter. So what are you going to do about it? Punish me for disturbing your oh-so-important meeting?"

His expression twists with contempt. "You're insolent and disrespectful, and I bet you've been enjoying watching these two men fight over you as if you're worth something." He glances at me with a sneer. "Tell me, Ettore—why did you marry a woman like this? Is it just the sex? Because she looks like a cheap slut. She—"

A deafening bang echoes through the room before he can finish. Another shot follows almost immediately, but it's not from my gun.

Riccardo's body collapses to the ground, a clean hole in his forehead and another in his chest. Slowly, I turn and see the faint smoke curling from Abruzzi's gun. His dark eyes bore into mine, filled with something unfathomable, something dangerous and unreadable.

My pulse pounds as I take in the sight—the man, my rival, who just killed another man...over my wife.

23

MIRABELLA

The man's body falls to the ground, crumpling with a lifelessness that chills me to the core. Blood—so much blood—pools beneath him, dark and viscous, spreading across the pristine white tiles like a grotesque painting. I can hear distant sounds in the periphery, but the thunderous echoes of the gunshots—the two deafening bangs—reverberate relentlessly through my bones.

"Mirabella." Someone calls my name.

I look up to see Ettore approaching me, his gun still in hand, his expression like stone. I take a step back, and he halts, glances down before slipping his gun into his coat. Does he always have a gun with him? Is there is there a gun somewhere in the bedroom we share together?

Behind him, I see Abruzzi's eyes narrow with annoyance as he tucks his own weapon back in the waistband of his pants.

My stomach lurches. These men...they just took a freaking life, yet their faces and expressions are devoid of remorse or empathy. It hits me all at once, heavy and suffocating—the emotions crash over me like a tidal wave. I can't shake the memories—watching my childhood home engulfed in flames, my mother teetering on the brink of death tonight, and now this bloody scene laid out before me.

Horror and disbelief churn in my stomach. I stumble backward, clutching my hand over my mouth, but it's futile. I double over and retch, the contents of my stomach spilling onto the tiled floor. The men's voices fade into the background, drowned out by the pounding in my head.

"Get away from her." Ettore's low growl slices through the haze. I feel a hand reach for my shoulder—Abruzzi's, I think—but it disappears as Ettore moves closer, his presence a looming shield.

"Everyone. Out." Ettore's voice brooks no argument. I raise my head weakly, my vision blurred, and I catch a glimpse of Abruzzi's face. A flicker of something flits across his eyes, but it's gone in an instant, replaced by a hardened mask. He nods before walking away, leaving just Ettore and me in the thick silence.

"Mirabella." Ettore's voice softens as he crouches beside me, but I can't help flinching back when he reaches for me.

It's all too much—the blood on the floor, the lifeless body on the other side of the room, and the coldness I saw in Ettore's eyes when he pulled the trigger. My thoughts are jumbled, and I struggle to breathe.

"I'm...I'm fine," I manage to say, but the words taste like brittle lies on my tongue. I attempt to stand, but my legs buckle beneath me. Before I can collapse, Ettore's arms wrap around me, pulling me close as he lifts me effortlessly off the ground.

I squirm, weakly pushing against his chest, but he doesn't let go.

"Drop me. I can walk," I mumble, but he simply tightens his grip, carrying me bridal-style out of the room.

He carries me to his car, gently placing me in the front seat. I can't help but notice he hasn't brought a driver or any of his men with him today. How important was that meeting that he came alone? How crucial was it that he didn't answer my calls the first time I reached out for help?

Ettore slides into the driver's seat beside me, and the engine rumbles to life beneath us as we pull away from the curb. We drive in tense silence for a few minutes before Ettore finally breaks it, his voice laced with a dangerous, controlled edge. "How reckless can you be, Mirabella? Storming into a room full of men who could kill you in an instant? Are you out of your mind?"

My dizziness begins to fade, replaced by a burning rage. "I wanted to see what had my husband so occupied that he couldn't answer my calls the one time I actually needed him to come save me!" I snap back, fire igniting in my voice.

"Who came up with the brilliant idea to go there? Was it you or your new boyfriend?"

"Oh, don't even go there," I retort bitterly, chuckling dryly. "Don't make this about Abruzzi when it's all on you. I have enemies now because of you! My family can't even feel safe in their own home because I'm your fucking wife," I scream, my voice thick with frustration.

His hands grip the wheel tightly, knuckles white with anger. "Why shouldn't I mention Abruzzi? Is he your knight in shining armor now because he swooped in to save you, coincidentally, the exact moment you were in danger?"

"He was watching me," I hiss, and that seems to infuriate Ettore even more.

"What? He was watching you? You knew he was watching you?" he spits, incredulity lacing his tone.

"He confessed it to me tonight," I shoot back defiantly. "And shouldn't you be the one who knows this? You claim you have bodyguards watching over me and my family. How is it that a man like Abruzzi has been tracking me, and they don't even know?"

"So, what, you're defending him? He confessed to stalking you, and you're defending him?" He scoffs, disbelief etched on his face as he takes a sharp turn, the car veering dangerously.

A ragged exhale escapes my lips. I may be furious with Ettore, but he's right. It's ridiculous that I'm defending a man like Abruzzi.

"You're no different from him," I retort, my voice cold. "You both just killed a man in cold blood."

"It wouldn't be the first time you've seen me kill a man, now would it?" he hisses, his tone sharp as we drive into the high-end neighborhood where the Greco estate looms ahead.

"This is different. You had no reason to kill that man."

"You're forgetting that your new boyfriend shot him too..."

We arrive at the towering gate of the estate, and it pulls open before he drives in.

"Enough about that," I snap, glaring at him. "I don't want to talk about you, or Abruzzi, or how you both have this sick penchant for murder. All I care about right now is keeping my family safe!"

We pull up to the main house, and before the car has fully stopped, I'm out of it, rushing toward the door. He follows closely behind, his footsteps heavy in the stillness of the night as I rush inside, up the stairs, and into our bedroom.

The silence stretches between us as we enter the house,

his presence like a heavy shadow behind me, his steps barely making a sound.

"I'll have Luca take them—" he starts, his voice steady as he follows me into the room.

"No," I cut him off before he can finish. I'm not sure I can even look at him right now.

"No?" His voice is sharp with disbelief. "So what's your plan, then? Leave them with your new boyfriend?"

I flinch at the word. "Would you stop calling him that?" I press a hand to my temple, the headache threatening to split my skull. "I just...I need to think."

"Bella..."

"Look what happened the last time you promised you would protect them," I tell him. "I can't risk that happening again."

"So, who's going to protect them, huh? Abruzzi?" His voice grows venomous. "The same man whose only goal is to keep you indebted and vulnerable to him? Who else has the power to actually keep your family safe?"

I want to fight back, but I know he's right. Dammit. That doesn't help the frustration gnawing at me.

"Luca will get them," he says, his tone final. "They'll stay here, where no one can touch them."

I exhale, silently agreeing with him. It'll be more comforting to have my family around, at least until everything is settled and there's no threat to their safety anymore.

The tension between us is suffocating as I move quickly to get ready for a shower. I don't even have the energy to make it a long one. I need to escape for just a moment. I don't know how long I'm in there, but when I step out, I find him watching me intently.

The air between us crackles as his gaze shifts over my face, his eyes dark. Before I can say a word, he steps forward, reaching out and brushing his thumb over my cheek.

"There's a cut here," he murmurs, his voice softer than usual, but it still carries an edge.

A shiver runs down my spine, and I instinctively pull away. "It's nothing. I don't need you fussing over me."

But he doesn't back off. Instead, he steps closer, the force of his presence drawing me in despite myself. "You were in a fire last night, Mirabella. I wasn't there to help you. The least you can do now is let me treat your cut."

Something inside me stirs—something deep and dangerous—and for a second, I forget why we're even arguing. His proximity messes with my head, and when his fingertips graze my skin, a wave of heat floods through me, making my knees weak. The tension between us thickens, and I can barely breathe.

"Fine," I mutter, barely able to choke out the word.

He leads me to the edge of the bed and gestures for me to sit. I comply, and he disappears into the bathroom for a few moments before returning with a first aid kit in hand.

"Is it really that serious?" I sigh, fatigue weighing on me more than I care to admit.

"Yes, it is." His voice is firm as he crouches in front of me, tilting my chin up gently before dabbing at the cut with a soft gauze. "Besides, I needed a reason to touch you without you protesting."

The silence stretches between us at his confession. I feel his thumb linger on my jaw, his breath brushing against my skin as he focuses on cleaning the small cut. He's so close that I feel his every exhale, feel the way his gaze darts over my flushed face.

"What are you thinking about, Bella?" His voice is rough, the sound of it pulling me deeper into this moment.

"I wasn't...I'm not..." My words trip over each other, but they're no match for the pull of his gaze.

A smirk tugs at the corner of his lips, and I scoff, trying to push past the heat rising in my chest.

"I wasn't thinking anything dirty if that's what you think," I snap, but I know I'm lying.

He doesn't look away, his thumb sweeping over my skin again. "I didn't accuse you of anything," he says, his voice deceptively calm. "I just asked what you were thinking about."

His thumb is dangerously close to my lip now, and my mind flashes back to that moment when he taught me how to please him. I can feel myself leaning in, just a fraction, caught by the intensity in his hazel eyes.

I don't know who moves first, but suddenly, his face is only a few inches from mine, and his fingers skim along my jaw, brushing against my cheek. It sends a shock of electricity through me, and I press my legs together, my body reacting before my mind can catch up.

His eyes follow the movement, and he clenches his jaw before pulling away from me. I can see the struggle on his face, in his eyes, even though he's trying so hard to hide it. It sends a rush of heat through my entire body, a rush that makes my heart hammer.

"I'll go take a shower," he says, rising to his feet and carrying the box with him.

As I watch him retreat into the bathroom, it dawns on me that us being this close is affecting him just as much as it's affecting me.

And it's not just sexual.

There's something else there. Something deeper...something scarier.

Something we both can't risk happening.

24

ETTORE

It's the morning after the fire that nearly claimed Mirabella and her family. The fire that has brought us back to square one—her resenting me because of Abruzzi's meddling.

I slip out of bed before dawn, take a long, hot shower, and settle into my office before anyone else stirs. Anger churns inside me—at Abruzzi for stalking my wife, at Mirabella for defending him, and at myself for failing to keep my promise to protect her.

Now, it's midday, and the phone in my hand remains stubbornly silent as I await answers. Last night, after Bella finally drifted off to sleep, I had told Luca I needed to know everything about the fire—both the official reports and the information he had to unearth from the shadows.

Minutes stretch into an eternity as I pace the length of my office, frustration building with each step. Finally, Luca's message buzzes through my phone:

. . .

Preliminary findings show the fire was caused by faulty wiring. But I'll dig deeper.

I grit my teeth, my fingers flying over the screen as I reply, instructing him to talk to the construction workers on the house across from hers, the neighbors, even down to anyone who might've wandered near recently. I don't care how long it takes. I need to know if this was truly just an accident.

A frustrated sigh escapes me as I sink back into my chair, my mind racing while I tap my fingers restlessly on the desk. Faulty wiring? A bitter scoff escapes my lips.

It may be an explanation, but I don't trust it, especially since there are countless reasons why that fire could have ignited. Maybe someone is after me, but it seems unlikely. My enemies haven't dared to come after me since the events of three years ago when I dealt with the Falcone family, another powerful mafia faction who attempted to overthrow me.

I took them down with ruthless precision. I exploited every weakness I could find, legally and illegally, leading the Falcone enterprise to bankruptcy before buying the company out of just for the fun of it. I even tipped off the authorities who raided their drug factory in Texas. Their downfall was a spectacle, broadcast for all to see. While the average person believed it was simply the end of a billionaire finally caught in a web of illicit dealings, those in the shadows knew I was the one pulling the strings.

No one messes with The Reaper.

So if someone is trying to toy with me now, it's because they think they've uncovered my weakness.

My thoughts drift to other possible culprits behind the fire: Abruzzi. I know he saved Mirabella's mother, and for that, I should be grateful. But it doesn't escape me how conveniently he appeared just in time to play the hero. Even if he didn't set the fire—though he certainly risks his life for someone as selfish as he—his obsession with my wife, his constant surveillance, it gnaws at me.

Fuck that. The thought makes my blood boil.

I drown myself in work, hoping to distract myself from the tumult of thoughts swirling in my mind. It's late evening when Luca finally calls.

"Tell me you've got something," I growl as soon as I pick up.

His voice is tense. "I've gone through everything—talked to the electricians who did the last repairs, checked the wiring history, even looked into recent disturbances in the grid. So far...it looks clean. It's just an old wire that went faulty."

I grind my teeth, irritation spiking through me. If Abruzzi didn't engineer this, then why had he been there "saving" Mirabella at the exact moment she needed help? If my enemies hadn't orchestrated this, then why had the old wire chosen that precise moment to ignite when my marriage to Mirabella had become public?

"Keep looking," I hiss.

There's a pause, then Luca's curt reply, "Understood."

During the course of the week, Luca returns every day with nothing more than the same answer.

Faulty wiring.

It still doesn't sit well with me. There's no hard proof, no clear link to anyone, but an innocent accident seems too convenient, especially given everything else that's been going on.

And even if this fire was nothing more than a mishap, that doesn't explain why Abruzzi feels so entitled to meddle in my life, my marriage. His presence, his interference, it's all too much.

I've been patient. Too patient, actually.

I summon Luca to my office, and he's there in minutes, a stoic figure in the doorway.

"Handle something for me with Abruzzi," I begin, keeping my tone neutral. "I want it to cause a stir, but nothing too obvious. Make sure it gets attention—enough that it won't be easy to ignore, but clean enough to be overlooked."

Luca doesn't miss a beat. "Something...discreet?"

I give him a sharp look. He knows what I mean.

"Exactly. You know what to do."

He stands there for a moment, that familiar glint in his eyes like he's already savoring the task. I don't have to say much else. We think alike.

"Leave it to me," he says, the words quiet but full of meaning.

He pauses at the door. I call after him, my voice colder now. "And Luca...make sure it doesn't come back to us. No loose ends."

He nods without turning, the door clicking shut behind him, leaving me with a quiet sense of satisfaction.

THE SUN STREAMS into my bedroom, bright and warm, casting a golden glow across the marble floor. The space beside me on the bed is empty. Ever since Mirabella's parents moved in, she spends most of her nights with them in the east wing of the house. It took me a few days to admit it, but I miss having her close.

Even when we don't touch, just knowing she's near is

enough to calm me. But she almost lost her family. Now, they're under the same roof, and I understand why she wants to be with them all the time. Still, it doesn't stop me from craving her presence.

I reach for my burner phone in the bedside drawer and dial the city's police department.

"There's a problem you might want to investigate," I say as soon as the line clicks. "Matteo Abruzzi. He runs illegal loan houses in the slums, exploiting innocent people with shady contracts. And that's not all. He's also hiding...well, drugs."

The voice on the other end hesitates before responding.

"How certain are you of this information?" A woman's voice asks.

"Certain enough..."

"How can we confirm this isn't just a prank?" she presses.

I exhale sharply, irritation bubbling up inside me. I could easily call one of my contacts in the department and file a formal report, but I don't want any of this mess tied back to me. I'm trying to go clean, after all.

"Because I was one of his victims. I've been to the place. You know what?" I scoff, the frustration creeping into my tone. "I've done my part by telling you. Do with it what you will."

I end the call and turn off the burner phone before tossing it back into the drawer, where it'll stay until I need it again.

The police won't ignore drug dealing, especially on that scale. I'm certain an investigation will be underway before the day's end.

With that thought, I head to the bathroom for a shower, knowing that my day's already off to a good start.

That evening, I sit in my study with a glass of whiskey in my hand, savoring the slow burn as I watch the news. The top headline confirms exactly what I already know...what I've orchestrated.

Abruzzi's empire is taking a hit.

The anchors detail the raid on several of his properties and loan houses scattered across the city.

"...connections to suspected drug activity...loan empire under investigation..."

They don't mention Abruzzi's name directly—he's probably already greased some palms to keep it quiet—but this is more than enough for me. It'll take him a while to recover from this, and that thought alone sends a surge of satisfaction through me.

And because I can't resist being petty, not when Mirabella is involved, I grab my phone and type out a quick text to Abruzzi.

This is only a mere taste of the fate that will befall you if you near my wife again. Don't dare me.

I hit send, leaning back in my chair as a satisfied calm washes over me. It's not just the fact that he knows I orchestrated this and owes me for sparing him. It's because I can now boldly refer to Mirabella as *my wife* when warning him. No matter what little games he tries to play, he can't change that.

He can't change the fact that she's mine.

25

MIRABELLA

Alessia's 2005 Malibu rattles to a stop, and I step out of the gate of the Greco Estate, feeling the eyes of the security guards on me. They're watching me warily, probably still shaken from my last escape attempt. I don't blame them—they probably don't want a repeat performance. I'd told my personal driver that a friend would be picking me up today, so he didn't need to take me to college. I'm guessing he's the one who tipped off the guards about my departure.

Alessia rolls down her window and leans her elbow out, her grin wide as ever. "Hey, girl! Ready?"

I laugh, glancing over my shoulder. The guards are still keeping a close eye on me. Ettore's been extra strict about security since my family moved in, so this is the first time in a while I've felt like I'm having a normal morning.

"Very ready," I say, matching her enthusiasm.

I slide into the passenger seat and inhale the familiar scent of air freshener mixed with Alessia's vanilla perfume. It takes me back to simpler times—back when we first started college together before Mamma got sick, before I dropped out, before everything became...complicated.

Her engine splutters to life, and I bite my lower lip to stop the laugh that threatens to slip out.

"You're free to express your feelings about my car," she huffs, and I can't hold it in anymore. I laugh.

"What feelings? I don't have any feelings..."

She rolls her eyes before quickly changing the topic.

"Jackass," she teases, then snorts. "I still can't believe it. You're living in a literal mansion, married to the mysterious billionaire Ettore Greco. No offense, Mira, but your life is like a soap opera."

Her laughter bubbles up, and she nudges me with her elbow. "Tell me, do you have a secret twin? Is there a hidden will? A long-lost relative waiting to make a dramatic entrance?"

It's my turn to roll my eyes, leaning back as she drives us through the early morning streets. "It's not as glamorous as it sounds."

Her smile fades a little, her eyes softening as she nods in understanding. I've told her bits and pieces about Ettore's family not accepting me, but I haven't gone into details. I can't.

"I get it," she says quietly. "But hey, at least you've got a personal chauffeur now. Isn't there a driver assigned to you? I'm honestly shocked they let me pick you up."

"I had to insist. Sometimes I just miss having a normal life," I admit, gazing out the window. The sunlight filters through the trees, casting shifting patterns across the dashboard.

Alessia's expression softens when she glances at me.

"Yeah, I get that," she says. "How's your family? How are they adjusting to all this?"

Alessia and Giovanni know about the fire, and they're aware my family's been living at Ettore's estate since then. 'He makes it hard for me to hate him,' Alessia had said when I told her about Ettore insisting on them moving in.

"They're doing okay. Giulia's the most excited about the whole thing." I chuckle, and she laughs along with me.

The conversation flows into her latest gossip about her remote job, her irritating boss, and her plans for a weekend getaway with Gio. I let her talk, grateful for the distraction. But eventually, she catches on to my silence. Her fingers tap lightly on the steering wheel as she glances at me, curiosity in her eyes.

"All right, Mira. What's going on? You've been weirdly quiet."

My stomach tightens, and I clutch my hands in my lap, the weight of the words I've been carrying making my chest feel heavy. I'm terrified to say them out loud.

"Okay, you're seriously freaking me out right now," she murmurs, and I feel the heat of her stare on the side of my face.

"The words spill out before I can even catch my breath. "I'm pregnant."

The car jerks suddenly as Alessia swerves, her grip tightening on the wheel, her eyes going wide with shock.

"Oh my God..." I gasp. "Are you trying to get me killed before I even get to meet my baby?"

She corrects her driving with a swift jerk, her heart racing.

"I'm sorry!" She huffs, trying to steady herself. "You just dropped that bomb on me out of nowhere. Say it again, but like...slowly, okay? I need to make sure I'm hearing this right."

I take a deep breath, my heart pounding in my chest. "I said...I'm pregnant."

Her eyes flicker to me in a way that almost feels like time is standing still. "Pregnant?" Her voice trembles with a mix of shock and disbelief. "Are you serious right now?"

"I—I haven't taken a test yet, but I—I haven't had my period, I get hit by random waves of dizziness, and I just...I feel different," I ramble, unable to stop the words from spilling out.

Alessia reaches over the middle console to squeeze my hand. "Mira, this is huge. How do you feel about it?"

"Scared," I manage to say, my voice barely a whisper, as I look down at my lap.

But it's more than just feeling scared. I'm terrified. I have no idea how Ettore will take the news, and I'm not even sure if I'm ready to be a mother.

"I'm guessing Ettore doesn't know yet." She sighs, her voice soft with concern.

I nod, biting my lip. "He doesn't. I don't know how to break it to him. W-we haven't even had sex since we got married..."

"Okay," Alessia says, letting out a nervous chuckle. "I'm confused."

I take a deep breath, gathering the courage to explain. "Before we got married, well...Ettore and I had a one-night stand," I confess, my cheeks flushing with heat.

"Oh my God!" Alessia exclaims, her eyes lighting up with surprise. "That's...that's hot. And unbelievable. You lost your virginity to a one-night stand? That's brave."

I bury my face in my hands, feeling the heat of embarrassment rising. "I didn't think I'd ever see him again, which is why I did it," I murmur, my voice muffled. I exhale, then look up at her. "We used protection, so I don't understand how this pregnancy could happen. What if I tell Ettore, and he doesn't believe me?"

"But you're married now," she points out. "That shouldn't be a problem. It's not like you're trying to trap him with a baby or something..."

But it *is* exactly like that.

My marriage to Ettore was supposed to be temporary—a year, tops—and then we'd go our separate ways. This pregnancy...it will change everything. Ettore may think I'm trying to trap him, and that terrifies me even more.

"You need to take that test, Mira. You need to be a hundred percent sure you're pregnant," Alessia says gently, her voice calming. "I understand if you're scared. Hey, you can come over to my place after class, and I'll give you the one I have."

Her offer is comforting, and for a moment, I feel a little lighter.

"I don't think I can come over to your house after today," I finally mutter, looking out the window as the words feel heavier than they should. "Maybe tomorrow, or some other day."

Alessia nods, squeezing my hand again. "Well, whatever happens, I'm here for you. We'll face it together, okay?"

I nod, the weight of her words sinking in. Just knowing someone else knows, that I'm not carrying this alone, makes a huge difference. I manage a small smile, feeling a little less suffocated. "Thanks, Alessia. I really needed to get that off my chest."

"Anytime," she replies, her voice warm. "And hey, if you need me to hold your hand while you pee and wait for the test result, I'm down."

I can't help but laugh, the tension easing just a little. "I may take you up on that."

We laugh, the tension in the car lifting slightly. By the time we reach the college parking lot, the knot in my stomach feels a bit looser. Alessia pulls up to a spot close to the large administration building before glancing over at me.

"What time do your classes end? I could come pick you up afterward..." she suggests, her voice light.

I shake my head. "Don't bother. It's a long drive for you. Besides, I have a driver assigned to take me everywhere, and he'd freak out if I ditched him twice in one day."

Alessia grins, raising an eyebrow. "Oh, Mrs. Greco has a driver, huh? Guess my poor, old car's not up to your standards now that you're married to a billionaire."

I laugh, giving her a playful nudge. "Stop it. You know I'll take your ancient car over a luxury ride any day."

"Uh-huh," she teases with a wink as I pull out my phone and text Logan, my driver, to let him know I'll need a ride after class. Alessia waits until I hit send, her expression softening when I look back at her.

"Well, if you change your mind, call me."

I lean over to give her a quick hug before climbing out of the car. "Will do. Thanks for everything, Alessia."

She waves, watching as I make my way across the parking lot. "Take care of yourself, Mira. And let me know if you need anything. Anything."

I give her a thumbs-up before watching as the red, worn-out car pulls away.

When her car gets out of sight, I release a heavy breath and pull my tote bag tighter over my shoulder before turning and heading over to my departmental block. The college grounds feel normal as usual, almost as if nothing in my life has changed. I weave through groups of students in the building hallway, their laughter and chatter filling the air as I head toward my first class.

When I reach the classroom, I pause, taking a steady breath. I scan the rows of seats before spotting Milo a few rows to the back. As I approach, I see his bag on the chair beside him, and I smile at the fact that he's saved me a spot.

"Hey, Mira," he waves when he catches my eye. His usual easygoing smile is in place on his lips as I make my way over. "I was starting to think you'd ditched lectures today."

I let out a small laugh as I slide into the seat next to him. "Never. Just running a little late."

"Well, this is a first," he muses, raising an eyebrow as he studies me. I notice the curiosity in his eyes, but thankfully, he doesn't press.

Just as the conversation dips into silence, the professor steps into the classroom. I sink further into my chair, trying to push everything from my mind and focus on the lecture.

THE REST of the day feels like it's dragging on forever. No matter how hard I try to focus on the lectures, the classwork, or even just the flow of the day, my mind keeps wandering back to that conversation in Alessia's car. The uncertainty, the fear—they swirl around in my head, making it impossible to focus. By the time the bell rings, signaling the end of the day, I realize I've barely absorbed a single word of what my professors have said.

"Hey, are you all right?" Milo nudges me with his elbow as we gather our stuff after the last class. "You've been a little off today."

I force a smile, shoving my books into my bag. "Yeah, I'm fine. Just have a lot on my mind, I guess."

He tilts his head, his eyes narrowing as he takes me in. For a second, I think he might press the issue, but instead, he breaks into one of his signature grins. "I know exactly what'll get you out of your head. How about we hit up Sweet Tooth for a snack?"

"Sweet Tooth?" I frown as we start walking toward the door.

Milo stops in his tracks, staring at me like I just told him I've never seen a dog before. "No way! You've never been to Sweet Tooth? Are you kidding me? It's this legendary breakfast café right across from campus. Best pastries you'll ever have in your life. I'm talking next-level stuff—everything else just tastes like cardboard after you've had theirs."

I can't help but laugh at his dramatic expression. "Guess I've been missing out, huh?"

"Exactly!" He claps his hands together like I've just seen the light. "Come on, let's go. Consider it a little break from whatever's going on with you. You need it."

"Milo..." I glance at my wristwatch. "I can't. My driver will be here any minute."

"We won't take long," he insists. "If your driver shows up, we'll just get it to-go. Problem solved."

The temptation to keep refusing flits across my mind, but he's persistent, and there's something about the normalcy of grabbing some snacks with a friend that makes me want to indulge. I think about how everything in my life has shifted so drastically lately. Maybe it wouldn't be the worst thing to take a small detour, even if only for a few minutes. It'll be nice to pretend, just for a while, that I'm a normal college student again.

"Fine," I finally say, a reluctant smile tugging at my lips. "Lead the way."

"That's more like it." Milo laughs, flashing me that goofy

grin as he takes my hand. As we step outside and cross the street, I can't stop thinking about the fact that Milo's holding my hand. I gently let go, pretending to fix a loose curl in my hair.

We reach a small, cream-colored building with a large pink sign above the door. *Sweet Tooth*. The name's cute, and it matches the vibe of the place perfectly.

Milo opens the door for me, and as I step inside, I feel his hand briefly brush against my waist. It's quick, casual, but...it feels intentional, like he meant to do it.

As we step inside, the rich aroma of coffee and freshly baked pastries envelops us, making my mouth water. The café is cozy and inviting, filled with warm lighting and mismatched chairs scattered around every corner. Milo approaches the counter with enthusiasm, clearly in his element, and orders like a regular. He insists I have a cappuccino and a croissant, swearing by their almond cream filling.

When our orders are ready, I reach for mine, but he beats me to it, deftly grabbing everything in his hands. I'm amazed nothing spills as he navigates the space. We find an empty booth tucked into the corner of the café, and he places our orders on the table before pulling out a chair for me.

"Thank you," I mutter, suddenly feeling a little strange about the situation. I should have insisted I didn't want to come.

Milo slides into the chair across from me, flashing that effortless smile that sets off alarm bells in my head.

"You know," he says, breaking off a piece of his croissant, "I'm honestly still shocked this is your first time here. I thought every student came here after classes for a snack with friends."

"All students?" I chuckle, trying to keep the mood light. "The café might be popular, but there are thousands of students at this college. It can't possibly be everyone's cup of tea."

"You've got a point," he muses, sipping his cappuccino. "I'll narrow it down to every student with a sweet tooth, and you, my friend, definitely fit that description."

"You don't even know me like that," I say with a smile, taking a bite of my croissant—and wow, it's incredible.

"I know that," he replies, his eyes lighting up as he watches my reaction. "From the look on your face, I can tell you love the croissant."

His expression shifts to one of genuine awe. That's the only word I can use to describe it. And before I can say anything, he reaches over the table to wipe something off the corner of my mouth.

Okay...this isn't just him being friendly. Theres a glimmer in his eyes that hints that he wants something more.

I clear my throat, sitting up a little straighter. "Milo, I just want to make sure we're on the same page here. You know I'm married, right? I'm not..." I hesitate, the words feeling awkward on my tongue. "I'm not interested in anything more than friendship."

He blinks at me, looking momentarily shocked before chuckling softly.

"Relax, Mira. I know that," he says, waving his hand as if to brush my words away. "We're just two friends grabbing coffee. Nothing more."

I give a polite smile, hoping that settles it, but as we sit there, I can't help but notice how his glances linger and how his hand keeps brushing against mine when he demonstrates something or shows me a photo. The more time we spend together, the more I feel like he's not being entirely honest. There's definitely something there—maybe a little crush, or perhaps more.

Just as I start to think of an excuse to leave, I hear a familiar voice.

"Bella."

My heart thuds heavily in my chest as I turn slowly toward the voice.

Ettore.

He strides toward our table, and even though he called my name, his eyes are locked onto Milo, a simmering rage flickering across his face that I've never seen before.

Oh shit.

26

ETTORE

A FEW HOURS EARLIER.

"Repeat yourself," I growl, glaring at the man standing before me.

Luca clenches his jaw, clearly not pleased with the situation. He repeats the words from earlier. "Logan just reported that Mirabella didn't ride with him to college today."

Why the hell would she do that? I've spent weeks trying to track down whoever's targeting her and her family. I've done everything I could to figure out if the fire at her house was an accident or planned. I moved her family in, bolstered security around the place—only for her to decide she doesn't want her assigned driver taking her to college?

"Tell me something positive," I hiss, clicking my pen nervously in my hands. "Tell me she skipped lectures or something. Maybe she just didn't feel like going, and that's why Logan didn't take her."

Luca finally looks up at me, meeting my gaze for the first time since walking in this morning.

"She did go to college."

I'm about to snap when he adds another line. "Logan

reported that a friend came to pick her up. I found out it was Alessia Conti, her best friend, who picked her up. And I've confirmed that she was dropped off on campus."

My irritation eases a little with the new information. It makes sense. Everything that's happened lately has been overwhelming for her—too much, too different from what she's used to. If she needs a little normalcy, even if it's just hanging out with an old friend, I get it. Plus, it's Alessia. Before the marriage contract was finalized, I had a background check done on everyone close to Mirabella, including her two best friends. And from what I discovered, they're both solid people.

"Tell Logan I'll be picking her up from college later today," I say gruffly. I've got other plans—one of my clients is flying in from Japan, and I need to meet with him at a hotel later. But Mirabella is way more important than any of that. As long as I know she's safe and okay, everything else can wait.

"You're dismissed."

Luca nods and turns to leave the room.

I let out a sigh and return to work. The hours slip by in a blur of meetings and phone calls. Every now and then, I glance at the time on my wristwatch. I've got her class schedule memorized, so I know her lectures end at 3:00 pm. The anticipation builds in me as I count down the seconds, thinking about the look of surprise on her face when she sees I came to pick her up instead of Logan.

At 2:30 pm, I tell my secretary to cancel all my remaining appointments before heading toward the parking lot. I slide into the front seat of my Range Rover, start the engine, and pull out of the building. In less than thirty minutes, I'm driving through the sprawling university gates.

I find a spot in the parking lot, and just as I pull in, I spot

Alessia several cars ahead. She's leaning against the trunk of her red Honda Civic, her blonde hair blowing in the breeze, arms crossed over her chest. She's staring out at the campus with a focused expression.

I step out of the car and head in her direction. I assume she's here for Mirabella, too. She notices me before I can approach her, and I see something flash in her dark eyes before her face hardens.

Alessia doesn't like me, and I can't say I blame her. My reputation precedes me, and since she's dating Giovanni Ferraro, a guy who works in the nightclub scene, I'm sure she's heard plenty of rumors about me—most of them probably true.

It doesn't help that she likely thinks I'm the source of all the chaos in Mirabella's life. After the fire, the whispers started, and people love connecting dots, even when there's no proof. Alessia's loyalty to Mirabella is clear, and I can tell she'd go to battle for her friend if she thought I was a threat.

"Alessia," I greet her, keeping my tone casual as I stop in front of her. "Didn't expect to see you here."

Her posture stiffens, though she tries to appear nonchalant. "I could say the same for you," she replies cautiously. "You're such a busy man. Didn't think picking your wife up from college would be on your list of priorities."

I smirk, ignoring the thinly veiled jab. "I heard you brought her this morning. That was thoughtful. Mirabella needs her friends around her, especially now."

Her lips press into a thin line. "I know she does," she says, her tone more measured this time. There's a hesitation in her eyes as if she's weighing how far to push.

"I mean it," I continue, softening my voice just slightly.

That seems to send a wrinkle in her brows. Almost like she doesn't believe the words coming from my mouth. Her eyes narrow, and I notice something unsettling in them. People usually measure me with their gaze, but with Alessia, it's different. It's like she's sizing me up, like she knows something I don't.

She just hates you, man, a voice whispers in my head.

When she speaks again, her voice is quieter, but steady. "I love her," she says. "And I don't want to see her hurt."

She isn't throwing accusations or raising her voice; instead, it's a cautious plea, one she seems to have chosen carefully.

"You won't," I say, meeting her eyes. "I'll take care of her."

She exhales slowly, her hands fidgeting with the strap of her bag. "I hope so." Her tone carries a hint of resignation, but I can tell she's still unsure. "For her sake."

I nod, offering a faint, almost disarming smile. "Thank you for looking out for her, Alessia. She's lucky to have a friend like you."

She blinks, caught off guard by the unexpected sincerity in my words, and I take the opportunity to end the conversation on my terms.

"I'll take her home," I add, my voice calm but firm.

Alessia hesitates again, then gives a small nod. As she turns to leave, I catch the faint murmur of her voice behind me, almost inaudible. "Don't make me regret trusting you, Ettore."

The fierceness in her voice has an edge to it that catches me off guard. She means every word she says, and I can't help but respect that.

I almost smile but stop myself. Instead, I nod, acknowledging her loyalty. She turns toward her car, slamming the door shut with a quick, sharp motion before driving off. I watch her go, and finally, a smile tugs at the corner of my lips.

Alessia and Giovanni may both hate me, but it's clear they don't take Mirabella's well-being lightly. That's something I can't help but admire. I wish I could relate.

I glance at my watch. Mirabella's last class should have ended about ten minutes ago, but something must've held her up inside. I'm about to head back to my car to wait for her when my eyes catch the café across the street. Perfect. I can keep an eye on the parking lot from there.

The smell of coffee hits me the second I walk in. I scan the small space for a good vantage point, finally finding a spot that gives me a clear view of the lot outside.

And then I see her. But she's not alone.

She's sitting with some guy—an American, by the looks of him.

He's tall, with sandy blonde hair that falls messily over his forehead, and a smile that's too easy, too familiar. His eyes are a sharp blue, and they're trained on her with an intensity that sends a jolt of irritation through me. The way he leans in—close, too close—and the way he smiles at her...it rubs me the wrong way. There's something about the casual confidence in his posture, the relaxed manner in which he occupies her space, that I don't like. It's as if he's already comfortable in a place that he has no right to be.

My feet start moving before I even think about it. The guy says something that makes her laugh, and I feel my fists clench as I tear my eyes away from him, focusing on her instead. The way her face lights up, the way she's listening to him... I know that look. She's relaxed, open—she likes this guy.

My body tenses, my jaw tightens. Before I even register what I'm doing, I'm calling her name.

"Bella."

She freezes, as if she's been caught doing something she shouldn't, and turns to look at me. As I approach, I grab her wrist, my grip firm but not rough.

"Let's go," I hiss, leaving no room for negotiation.

"Ettore, what are you—"

"Who are you?" the guy asks, and I feel a flash of anger rise in me. Who the fuck does he think he is, trying to protect her from me?

But I don't waste another second on him. I'm livid, and I know causing a scene here would only draw attention—attention I don't care about. It's Mirabella I'm worried about, because I'm sure she won't appreciate this one bit.

I don't answer his question as I pull Mirabella to her feet, leading her out of the café. She's silent, but I can feel the anger radiating off her, her body stiff with suppressed fury. I steer her across the street toward my car, the silence between us thick, almost suffocating—her anger, my barely-contained frustration.

I open the passenger door for her, and when she's inside, I slam the door a little harder than necessary. I walk around to the other side and climb into the driver's seat.

The drive back to the estate is stiff and uncomfortable. The seconds stretch on endlessly. Occasionally, I steal a glance her way. She's staring ahead, her lips pressed tight, refusing to look at me or anywhere else.

Finally, I can't take it any longer.

"Who the fuck is he?"

She doesn't answer, and I grip the wheel tighter, my jaw clenched. "I asked you a question, Mirabella. Who is he?"

Silence. She folds her arms and looks out the window, refusing to say anything. I feel the rage simmering off her body, and I'm boiling by the time my car drives into the estate and pulls over in front of the house.

Before the engine is completely cut off, Mirabella throws the door open and storms into the house. I follow her closely, hot on her heels, as she marches along the marble floors and up the stairs.

When we reach our room, the tension finally snaps. I slam the door shut behind me, and she throws her bag onto the bed.

"So, this is how it's going to be?" I demand, my voice harsh. "You're just going to go around campus with guys like that? Pretend you're not married..."

She whips around, eyes blazing with fury. "Pretend I'm not married?" She scoffs, holding up her hand to show me the diamond glinting on her ring finger. "He knows I'm married. He's a friend. Not that you'd understand the concept of friendship."

"Friend?" I let out a dry laugh, disbelieving. "It looked like more than that, Mirabella. He saw your ring, but it didn't stop him from asking you out on a date..."

"A date?" she mutters incredulously, but I don't let her get a word in.

"Is that what you do? String guys along, pretending you're not interested, just keeping them hanging until you get what you want from them..."

I watch as something flashes in her eyes—something more than anger—but I'm too pissed to stop. I'm on a roll now, unable to hold back.

"I won't say I'm shocked. After how easily you walked away from our first night together, why should I be surprised you use men to your advantage before tossing them aside?"

"How dare you?" Her voice rises as she storms toward me, arm raised as if to slap me.

I'm ready. I catch her wrist before the slap lands, pulling her arm, pulling her closer, until her body crashes into mine. She's staring at me, chest rising and falling with each harsh breath.

In the heat of our anger, there's something else—an undeniable spark, a pull between us that crackles in the air.

Slowly, my grip on her wrist loosens, and I lean in, my voice dropping low, every word a threat, a promise. "You're my wife, Mirabella. That means you are mine. And mine alone."

Without another word, I close the distance between us, pressing my mouth to hers in a kiss that's fierce, possessive, claiming her in a way that says more than words ever could.

27

MIRABELLA

A shocked exhale leaves my lips the moment Ettore's lips crash against mine. He swallows my gasp, taking advantage of that to slide his tongue inside my mouth. A groan rumbles out from deep in his throat as he kisses me eagerly...hungrily...as if he's been deprived of kissing me for months.

And I love it. Fuck, I love it far more than I'm willing to admit. The way one hand slides down to squeeze my ass through my jeans while the other grabs my neck to keep my head in place. I love the way he backs me into a nearby wall, pressing his body flush against mine. His fingers are digging into my thighs, and he's slowly grinding his hardness against me.

I moan, unable to contain the needy noise. It slips past my lips before I can think about holding it back. I'm pissed at him. I'm fucking mad. But the way he kisses me...the way his hand burns every path it touches on my body...it makes me ache for him. It makes me forget everything else except how damned good he's making me feel.

He pulls away abruptly, running his fingers over my mouth.

"Do you know how crazy you drive me, Bella?" he growls while my brain still struggles to catch up with what just happened—with how we went from me about to slap him to moaning his name in seconds.

"I drive you crazy?" I scoff, feeling my anger still simmering beneath. "You make me...insane." You are so infuriating! Ugh!" I yell in his face.

Something dangerous flashes in his eyes as he leans closer again, his face hovering over mine.

"Good."

"Good? You're—"

He kisses me again, this time slowly, deliberately. His tongue swipes over mine, and then he pulls back slightly to bite my lower lip. I gasp before sliding my hand over his shoulders and threading my fingers through his thick hair. He's back to sucking my mouth again. Tasting, savoring.

Another moan falls out of my lips as I arch into him, feeling the hard planes of his muscles against me. He tastes amazing, like an erotic mixture of whiskey and nicotine. His hand slips underneath my mesh top, skimming over my bare stomach before cupping my right breast. I gasp into his mouth as he squeezes me softly before pinching my nipple through the thin lace material of my bra.

"You don't seem so mad now, Kitten," he murmurs against my lips before dragging his mouth down the side of my neck.

I place my hand on his shoulders...to push him away...to pull him in, I don't know. But when he bites my earlobe, I roll my hips against his, wanting more of everything he's doing.

"Are you wet for me, Bella?" he asks as he tugs my nipple between two fingers.

I bite my lower lip and shut my eyes firmly. When I hear his deep chuckle, my eyes snap open to glare at him. My glare quickly melts away when his hand slides down past the waistband of my jeans into my panties.

"Ettore," I gasp as he slides his fingers into my wet folds.

"Hmm...you're soaked." His voice is husky, and I hear the restraint in his tone as he forces out the next words. "So tight, so ready."

"Oh...fuck," I moan when he slips two fingers inside me and begins to pump slowly.

"When did this happen?" he asks against my lips. "When I pulled you away from that guy? Do you like my possessive side? My rough side?"

I shake my head as I feel tears pool at the corner of my eyes. I can't say any words. I can't form any thoughts. His fingers inside me, coupled with the friction from the tightness of my jeans and the heel of his palm pressing against my clit makes me want to run mad.

"Don't stop," are the only words I manage to mumble in response, and I feel his smirk against my neck as he continues rubbing circles against me. I grind down against him, pushing myself against his growing erection.

"Oh," he chuckles darkly. "I'm going to bring you pleasure until you beg me to stop."

There's no way I would ever want him to stop. Not when I feel like I'm levitating, not when this feels so fucking good.

His fingers begin to pump faster, and that's when I feel myself starting to go over the edge. I clutch his shoulder firmly, my nails digging into the taut skin beneath his shirt.

"Cum for me, Kitten," he orders gruffly. "Cum for me now."

I whimper as the orgasm explodes through me, my entire body shaking wildly in his arms. He continues to pump slowly until I'm well spent. I collapse against him, panting heavily. He lets his hands slide out of my jeans and brings his soaked fingers to my lips.

"Open."

Another bout of pleasure shoots through me at the sound of his rough command. I open my mouth, and he slides three thick fingers in, coating my lips with my slick arousal. I moan and close my mouth around his fingers, sucking them eagerly the way I would suck his cock.

"Bella," he grunts as I scrape my teeth over his fingers before biting down.

He lets out a sound between a laugh and a hiss before pulling his fingers out of my mouth. "You'll pay for that."

A smile spreads out on my lips, but it doesn't last long because he walks over to sit on the edge of the bed.

"Take off your clothes," he says simply, his hazel eyes gleaming dangerously.

I nod wordlessly as hot, erotic pleasure dances down my spine. I don't understand what's happening to my body...what he's doing to my body. I hate being bossed around or told what to do, but for some reason, when Ettore tells me what he wants me to do, I find myself doing just that.

I pull my top over my head and toss it aside. His eyes darken as he watches me intently from across the room, taking in the way my breasts fill up my lace bra. I swallow nervously before unzipping the front of my jeans and pulling them down. I see his jaw clench as I reach behind me to unbuckle my bra before finally pulling the matching pair of panties down my legs and stepping out of them.

"Come here," he growls, and I don't hesitate to cross the room to stand between his spread legs.

He leans forward, and a hiss leaves my lips when he grabs my ass and licks my stomach. My hands slide down to his hair, and he makes a rough sound in his throat as his head comes down to kiss the top of my pussy.

"So pretty," he murmurs, spreading my legs to kiss my wet inner thigh.

"Ettore," I gasp when he scrapes his teeth over the soft flesh right at the apex of my thighs. "Please..."

The word sounds foreign and weak coming from my lips, but I don't care. I just want to feel him there.

"Please what?"

I glance down at him through hooded eyes. "Please eat my pussy."

A mixture of surprise and something else flashes in his eyes, but confusion washes over me when he slides back into the bed and lies on his back.

"Come here," he orders again.

He's still fully dressed, so I don't understand exactly what he wants me to do. Still, I climb his body, planting myself over his hard dick.

"Higher," he says simply.

A confused breath leaves my lips as I watch him watch me.

"You wanted me to eat your pussy?" He arches a perfect brow. "Then come sit on my face so I can eat your pussy."

Oh. Ohhh.

My body flushes with heat, embarrassment, and...excitement. I crawl up until my knees are spread right above his face. I feel his heavy breathing against my inner thigh, and I throw my head back.

This is the hottest, dirtiest thing I've ever done.

"Sit, Bella," Ettore mutters, reaching upward to grab my thighs. "Spread your legs even farther. Give me your pussy."

Trembling, I obey, moving until I'm basically straddling his face. A moan rips out of my throat when I feel his tongue sweep along the edge of my pussy.

"Fuck," I groan as my body bucks forward. I grab the headboard in front of me as he begins to stroke my center.

He's using his tongue, his teeth, his lips. He's fucking eating.

I lose control over the moans ripping out of my throat as he takes advantage of me. It feels too good from this angle. Too intense. Too raw. His tongue sweeps across my clit again, and my eyes fall closed.

"Open your eyes, Bella," he growls from beneath me. "Look at me."

I blink rapidly and stare down at him. He looks up at me, his cheeks flushed red and his expression fierce. He looks so hot, so sexy, and I ache all over.

His hands tighten around my thighs as he pulls my legs further apart. With support from the headboard, I roll my hips to meet the movements of his mouth.

"That's right, baby," he grunts. "Ride my face. Ride my mouth like the dirty girl you are."

It's unexpected. A strong surge of desire hits me hard and fast as my orgasm knocks me forward. My head hits the headboard with a soft thud, and I gasp as Ettore continues to suck me to insanity.

"Ettore," I moan and try to lean off him. His hand clamps down on my thighs, keeping me in position. He continues to thrust his tongue over, in and out of me, until my entire body crashes against him.

I exhale deeply when he flips me over to my back, hovering over me. A tired sigh leaves my lips as he kisses the skin underneath my breast before moving down even farther.

"Fuck," I hiss when he slips his fingers inside me again. "I can't take it anymore, Ettore..."

"Good," he moans, spreading my pussy lips with one hand while the other pumps in slowly. He alternates between licking, sucking and fingering. And I'm groaning, crying, and moaning.

It feels too good, so intense that it hurts. I want him to stop, but at the same time, I never want this feeling to end.

He fucks me hard and fast with his fingers this time around, while simultaneously licking and sucking my clit. The third orgasm that hits me nearly throws me over the edge. He holds me down, never stopping his ministrations until tears are streaming down the sides of my eyes.

When he finally stops, I can't move, can't breathe. I close my eyes, and I feel his hand caress the side of my face before wiping the tears from my eyes.

"Get some sleep," he murmurs, pressing a kiss over my forehead.

My eyes tiredly blink open, and I see him adjusting his pants before he grabs his suit jacket from the floor where it fell earlier and walks out of the room as if he didn't just fuck my brains out with just his fingers and tongue.

I'M PREGNANT.

Yesterday, it was a speculation, a suspicion, a fear. But now, as I stand in Alessia's bathroom clutching the pregnancy test she'd given me earlier, I realize that it's real.

"Mira?" Alessia calls from outside the bathroom.

I had wanted to be alone while checking the result, even

though I appreciated her offer to be by my side. My heart races as I step out, the weight of the moment heavy in the air.

The moment I push the door open, Alessia's face softens into a look of concern as she sees me. Her eyes search mine for answers, and I know that I don't need to say much.

"It's positive," I say, and a sob escapes me before I can help it.

She rushes over to me, her arms enveloping me in a protective embrace. "Hey, hey," she whispers, running her hands down my back. "Everything will be okay, Mira. I promise," she sighs, her voice soothing but tinged with uncertainty. "Everything will be just fine."

I hug her tightly as the tears continue to pour, soaking into the fabric of her shirt. But as much as I want to believe her, I know that from now on, things are far from being fine.

28

ETTORE

The space beside me is empty when I wake up. A wave of déjà vu washes over me as I slide my hand over the cold sheets where she slept last night. It transports me back to our first night together, when I woke up to find her gone in the morning. But today...today feels different.

Yesterday was intense—so intense that even as I drove back to my office, all I could think about was the taste of her lips, the way she felt in my arms, and the sound of her moaning my name as she reached her climax.

But it wasn't just that. I can't shake off the regret I felt when I saw the hurt in her eyes. I was furious, wanting to lash out and make her feel the anger that boiled within me when I saw her with another man. Yet, as my words landed, I realized how deeply I regretted them when they hit their mark.

I stayed in my office until it was late, until I was sure she must have fallen asleep. And then I came home with mixed feelings. Part of me wanted to find her in our bedroom waiting for me. Wanting me. Another part of me was terrified...at how fast my heart pounded in my chest when she was in the room, how I craved her like the air I breathe, how I can't seem to do anything else but focus on her when she's near.

I've fallen for Mirabella.

Fuck.

I've done the one thing that I swore I would never do—fall for a woman. But, oh, how stupid I was to think feelings like this could be controlled. How dumb I was to think I could resist the overwhelming force.

Love? It sounds like a strange concept, but that's the only word to describe the way she consumes my entire being, the way I want to live and exist for her.

I am in love with Mirabella.

A groan slips out of my lips as I get up from bed. It's a Saturday, so I'm sure she's at home. She's probably with her family in the east wing of the house, and all I can think of right now is finding her.

After brushing my teeth and showering, I throw on a simple shirt and a pair of casual jeans before stepping out into the hallway. My bare feet pad over the marble floors as I make my way down the stairs and through the large hallway left to the foyer.

As I approach the small living room ahead, I hear voices—laughter, arguing, and cheering. The atmosphere is completely different from the rest of the house. The scattered mugs on the side table and the throw blanket bunched up on one of the sofas add to the cozy vibe. It feels lighter, airier, and undeniably happier.

The voices grow louder, and when I walk in, I'm met with the delightful sight of the whole family—Mirabella, her sister Giulia, her mother Isabella, and her Nonna—all crammed together on the plush L-shaped couch, eyes glued to a horror movie. Isabella seems detached, alternating between sipping from her large mug and laughing at Giulia's quips.

But the others? They're completely unfazed. On the big screen, a character tiptoes down a dark hallway as eerie music swells. I can sense a jump scare coming, but instead of flinching, they sit, unblinking and entertained.

Isabella is the one who spots me first. Her eyes widen in surprise before her face splits into an easy smile.

"Ettore!"

That's when the rest of the family turns to me. My gaze locks onto Mirabella's, and I see something flicker in her eyes before a deep blush spreads across her cheeks.

"Um...what are you doing here?" Giulia is the one who blurts out first. She looks genuinely shocked, but there's a mischievous glint as she glances at her sister.

Mirabella, who notices this, nudges Giulia's waist with her elbow.

I can't help but laugh. "Should I leave or...?"

"No, no," Isabella speaks, throwing a glare her daughter's way. "She's just shocked, as am I, but Giulia here doesn't have a filter."

"There's a spot here," Giulia says excitedly, scooting to the side, closer to her Nonna, who still hasn't said anything since I stepped into the room. She taps the open cushion beside Mirabella, declaring not so subtly that I should sit beside my wife.

I walk over and sink into the seat, my shoulder brushing against Mirabella's. "Hey," I say, glancing down at her.

She turns to look at me before pulling her bottom lip between her teeth. "Hey."

A sensation travels through my entire body, instantly heating me up. I smile and turn to the TV, and that's when I notice the looks everyone in the room is giving me...well, us. Giulia wears a grin, as if the whole scene is amusing to her. Isabella looks genuinely pleased to see me here. And Nonna...well, she glares at me as if she'd prefer I vanish.

There's an awkward tension in the room, and it's completely ridiculous. We've spent nights together, done dirty things to each other, and yet sitting here surrounded by her family makes me feel like a teenager.

Giulia finally breaks the tension by nudging me with her elbow. "So, Ettore, you like scary movies?"

"Depends on the film," I reply, leaning back. I watch as a character tumbles to the ground while being chased, struggling for what feels like an eternity before finally getting up just as the monster is about to pounce. "I think this one could use some better acting."

Mirabella rolls her eyes, a small smirk playing on her lips. "So now you're an expert in movies?"

"There are a lot of things you don't know about me," I murmur, relishing the way her pupils dilate as she watches me.

Nonna, clearly unimpressed by my presence, mutters under her breath, "Oh, what a surprise."

I suppress a smile and meet her sharp gaze. "You seem to have a lot on your mind, Nonna. Care to share?"

"How long did my granddaughter know you before you dragged her into this...union?" she shoots back.

"Long enough to know I wanted her in my life," I reply easily, and she huffs in response.

"You're used to getting what you want, aren't you? Is that part of the Greco package?"

"Nonna," Mirabella sighs, shooting her a slightly pleading look. "Can we maybe save the sarcasm for another time?"

"No harm done," I say with a smile, which only seems to make her even more irate.

We settle back into the movie, and just as a suspenseful scene builds, the lights flicker off in the film. The music swells, and the character finally opens a door she was running toward to reveal...nothing. Silence envelopes the scene until, out of nowhere, a hand reaches out from the shadows to slit the girl's throat.

"She deserved that," Giulia mutters at the same time Nonna sighs. "How many of them are left now?"

Mirabella jumps slightly, and I take advantage of that to pull her into my arms. She stiffens for a split second before relaxing into my embrace.

"Scared?" I murmur in her ear, catching a whiff of her strawberry-scented shampoo.

"No. You?" She asks softly.

I slide my arm around her waist. "What do you think?"

Mirabella doesn't respond, but I feel the rise and fall of her chest as she breathes heavily.

Minutes pass and the movie concludes on an annoying note—no one survives.

The next film features a Halloween-themed party that spirals into chaos as a spirit haunting the house possesses the partygoers. Great concept, but the execution falls flat. Nonna grumbles, "Another silly ghost film where no character has a survival instinct," while Giulia leans forward, completely engrossed.

Minutes tick by, and in another infuriating note—no one survives.

At some point during the movie, I notice how at ease I feel. Mirabella's family seems relaxed and comfortable in a way I haven't witnessed in my own household. My family? We're tense in every situation, and each gathering is an exercise in business and social appearances. Even the obligatory dinners at the dining table do little to unite us. Instead, they become a battleground for sharp jabs and accusations.

But here, it's clear they love each other unconditionally. They might bicker or disagree, but they are relaxed in each other's presence. The thought stirs something deep within me—an ache for laughter and carefree moments, a longing for a warmth I've never truly known, especially since my parents passed away.

As the film plays on, Giulia can't help but interject with humorous commentary after every plot twist, while Nonna remains with her arms crossed, muttering critiques under her breath.

I feel a sudden coldness seep through my chest when Mirabella leans away from me and gets on her feet. Her phone buzzes in her hand, and she smiles as she stares down at the screen. As she walks away while tapping on the screen, I can't ignore the grin that's curling on her lips. My chest tightens with curiosity and a pang of jealousy, and before I can think it through, I stand and follow her out of the room.

She's leaning against the kitchen counter when I catch up, and before she notices my presence, I sneak up behind her and swipe the phone from her hand.

She gasps, spinning around. "Ettore..."

"Who's got you smiling like that?" I ask, flipping the phone over in my hands, pretending to read whatever's on the screen.

Her eyes widen, and a flush creeps up her cheeks. "Ettore, give that back." She glances toward the living room, her voice dropping to a hush.

I grin, slipping the phone into my back pocket and closing the space between us. She gasps again, but for a different reason now as I cage her against the counter, my hands planted on either side of her.

"Beg me," I say, my voice dipping low. Her breath hitches, and I can feel her pulse quicken as I lean in.

"Ettore..." Her voice is a whisper—part warning, part moan.

"Just say the magic words, Bella," I murmur against her lips, feeling myself harden as my hands slide along the sides of her slip dress. I trail my fingers over her waist, then down to squeeze her ass.

"Please," she breathes, her voice barely a whisper.

I steal her next breath away by lowering my mouth to meet hers. She moans the moment our lips touch and reaches for me, grabbing fistfuls of my shirt to pull me even closer. My hands tighten on her ass while her fingers dig into my shoulder before sliding up into my hair.

Our tongues fight for dominance as the kiss gets deeper, wetter, hotter...

I slide one hand between her legs, and as expected, she's already wet.

"Ettore," she gasps when I slide two fingers into her heat. "My family...they're just in the other room."

"I'll be quick," I murmur, pumping her slowly. She bites her lower lip to hold back her moans, a pained look enveloping her face. "Or I can take you somewhere more private so I can do inappropriate things to you," I say against her lips.

She grabs my arm in an attempt to stop me, but I can tell she wants this just as badly as I do. I slide my hand out of her pussy before bringing it up to cup her face.

"Say the word, and we are out of here."

Someone clears their throat loudly behind us, and we

both jump apart like guilty teenagers. Standing there, arms folded, and eyes narrowed, is Nonna.

"Mirabella, your mother needs her medication," she says, but her piercing gaze is aimed squarely at me.

Mirabella scrambles away from me, her face turning a deep shade of red. "Of course, Nonna," she mutters hastily, giving me an apologetic look before hurrying back toward the living room.

Nonna's stare doesn't waver, and I meet it with a defiant smirk. I don't know exactly what Mirabella has told her family about our arrangement, but I have a feeling Nonna would strangle me if she had the chance.

Too bad for her, I'm married to her granddaughter, and no one—least of all her—will come between us for the next year.

Amused, I tilt my head in silent acknowledgment. Nonna huffs, narrowing her eyes at me before turning and walking off. I head back to the living room, sinking into the sofa as Mirabella hands her mother a bottle of capsules.

We settle back into the next movie, but in the quiet moments between the scenes, I can't help but wish that life could stay this easy and light forever.

29

MIRABELLA

Does pregnancy make women horny?

Because honestly, that's the only explanation I can come up with for why I can't seem to keep my hands off Ettore. It doesn't help that my husband's libido is just as insatiable as mine, so I spend most nights tangled up in him, moaning and groaning his name until exhaustion finally drags me under.

The shocking thing is that we haven't done the actual sex by penetration yet, not after our first night together. Before, I used to think that sex by penetration was the only way to reach maximum pleasure, but Ettore has introduced me to a world of unimaginable orgasms, and he's so creative with it.

And it's not that I don't want him to fuck me or that we've never been tempted to go past our usual threshold. But whenever we get to that moment, whenever Ettore asks for permission to take it a step further, I always say no. He always respects my decision, and that worsens my guilt.

I have to tell him I'm pregnant. That's why I haven't been able to have sex with him. This secret that I've been keeping for over a month now is gnawing at my chest, and each day, I get increasingly anxious about how he'll react when he finds out.

I know it will change everything between us, and it will definitely be for the worse. So I want to pretend for a while and enjoy this little moment of bliss because I know that eventually I won't be able to keep it from him. I'll start showing in a few months, and the last thing I want is for him to find out before I tell him.

I'm scrubbing my body under the warm stream of water in the shower when the door opens and Ettore slips in behind me. A sharp gasp escapes my lips as I feel his hard length press against my lower back, hot against my bare skin.

"You shouldn't be in here," I giggle as he leans down to nibble on my neck.

"Why not? I am your husband," he says as his hands slide over to cup my breasts.

He just grins, unbothered. "Even better. Showering together saves time and water."

I roll my eyes, half amused, half exasperated. "As if you're ever going to be the one to worry about utility bills," I retort, pushing against his chest as if I stand a chance of getting him to stop.

He smirks, his hands not slowing down. "Hey, I'm eco-friendly. And you should be, too, considering how much *energy* we're using right now."

I huff, throwing him a playful glare. "You're impossible."

Another moan slips past my lips when his hand slides down my stomach to cup my pussy in his hands.

Before he inserts his fingers inside me, I turn to face him. "Not when you're touching me like this," I murmur, reaching for his hair and pulling his face down to kiss him.

He groans into my mouth as I kiss him, pull his lower lip between my teeth, and lick him until he's panting and completely aroused. When I break the kiss and lean back, the thick lust I see in his eyes makes my pussy throb. It's more than enough to knock the common sense out of me, which is why I'm sliding down to my knees and taking him into my mouth even though I know we'll be late for the function.

Ettore grunts as I stroke the base of his cock with one hand while taking him slowly into my mouth. His thick, hard length brushes against my walls as I take him in deeper, just the way he likes, until he hits the back of my throat. I hold him there for a few seconds before he pulls away for me to breathe.

"Fuck, Bella," he grunts, grabbing the back of my head and wrapping my wet hair around his fist. His other hand caresses my mouth as he waits for me to catch my breath. And then he's pushing his way back in and pulling out to thrust in again. He holds my head in place as he fucks my mouth, and I take all of him in while my hand slides down to massage the throbbing wetness between my legs.

"That's right, baby," he rasps as he picks up pace. "Pleasure yourself while I fuck your mouth."

I moan as he continues to slide in and out of me, his thrusts becoming faster and harder until finally, he shudders and releases his hot cum inside my mouth with a loud grunt. The salty, sweet fluid coats my tongue and slides down my throat, and I feel a shiver roll down my spine as I swallow every single drop.

When he pulls out of my mouth and brings me to my feet, I see the wanton need in his eyes as he bends down to kiss me again. I close my eyes and let him explore my mouth as his fingers spread my ass cheeks open to slide into my pussy from behind. I moan and whimper into his mouth, but then, my mind drifts.

If I don't stop him now...if I don't stop this, I know I'm going to loathe myself afterward. So even though my whole body protests against the idea, I place both hands on his chest to push him away.

"Down, boy," I say with a giggle. "We need to be downstairs in less than twenty minutes now. We can continue this later."

He groans in protest, but he pulls away from me. For the next few minutes, we both take turns washing our bodies. When we are done showering, Ettore scoops me up and carries me to the bedroom. Our dressing up is filled with laughter and giggles, but somewhere in the pit of my stomach, an uneasy feeling grows.

I'll miss this. I'll miss the ease and intimacy that we've somehow settled into these past couple of weeks. When the truth comes out, everything will change, and I dread the thought of that.

After we are done getting dressed, Ettore takes my hand in his as he leads us downstairs and to the dining room, where his family members, both nuclear and extended, are seated and waiting. Ettore informed me that this is some sort of family ritual that happens yearly, and obviously as his wife I have to be present.

My stomach twists with discomfort as we enter the room. The faces around the long table—some familiar while others are strangers—fix their eyes on me with a mix of interest and scrutiny. Ettore leads me to the head of the table, where an empty seat waits for him. The chair beside him, where I assume I'm supposed to sit, is occupied by Zia Camilla.

"Zia," Ettore calls out in a gruff tone as we approach the stern-faced woman.

I know exactly what he's about to do, and I won't let him. Not in front of all these people. Not when she already despises me, and making this gesture would only fuel her resentment.

Before Ettore can say another word, I lean up and kiss his cheek. "I'll sit beside Nonna," I whisper, keeping my voice low.

He'd invited them to this gathering, and I'm honestly grateful. Having my own family here makes it easier to bear the tension in this room.

He glances down at me, irritation flashing in his eyes. But when I flash him a smile—one that's soft but firm—he exhales and releases my hand, though I can tell he's not pleased.

I let out a quiet sigh as I make my way to the far end of the table, where Nonna and my mother sit. When I settle into the chair beside Nonna, she immediately takes my hand, giving it a reassuring squeeze.

"You did the right thing, Mira."

I nod, casting a quick glance around the room at the eyes that are all too aware of our every move. My gaze lands on Zia Camilla, and I don't miss the way her lips tighten. I saved her from embarrassment, but the anger in her eyes only seems to deepen. She looks like she's seething at the mere thought of Ettore asking her to vacate her seat for me.

This family gathering is nothing like the cozy ones I'm used to. It's tense—stiff, even—everyone on edge, measuring each other in silence. Ettore's family is here, of course, along with a few people I assume are from other Mafia families. When Ettore first told me his family is involved with the

Italian Mafia in New York, I wasn't exactly shocked. Now it makes sense. The man is fiercely protective, intensely private. A man like he is probably has more enemies than friends.

The conversation begins with small talk, the usual chatter about the weather, the food, the upcoming family events. Oil factories here, hotel chains there. A charity gala in need of donations. A foundation looking for support.

But even as the polite conversation flows, Ettore's relatives continue to fire questions my way. They seem interested in every little detail about me, and I can tell it's not out of genuine curiosity. They're sizing me up, gauging whether or not I'm worthy of Ettore.

I'm halfway through picking at my salad when Zia Camilla turns her gaze on me, her eyes a little too intense. "So, Mirabella," she begins, her voice dripping with sweetness, "I hear you're back at Cornell University."

I give her a steady nod, working hard to keep my face unreadable. "Yes."

"Hmmm. That must be nice," Zia Camilla purrs, her voice laced with sarcasm. "Using your marriage to Ettore as an excuse to go back to college."

"Back?" A woman I don't recognize asks, her curiosity piqued.

I bite my tongue, but Aunt Francesca leans in as if she's about to deliver a juicy tidbit. "Mirabella here is a dropout," she announces.

The table falls into a tense silence—well, our side of the table. I glance across the room at Ettore and the other men, who are engrossed in their conversation. His eyes flicker toward me, and I know he's aware of the shift in the atmosphere. He looks at his aunts, then back at me. I give him a reassuring smile, signaling that I'm fine. The last thing I want is to interrupt whatever important conversation he's having just to save me from his aunt's petty jabs.

Before I can respond, Nonna's voice rings out, sharp. "She *was* a dropout," she corrects, her tone stern.

"And what's the difference?" The woman from earlier asks again, her smile now replaced by something more condescending. I catch Zia Camilla's grin spreading wider.

"I'm just worried about her priorities." Zia Camilla sighs theatrically, her voice laced with a false air of concern. "She has…other things to focus on now—her real responsibilities. Her wifely duties. Don't you think those should come first?" She turns to the other women, her eyes narrowing slightly, and they exchange a subtle, knowing glance, their little alliance unmistakable.

"You're right, sister," Francesca chimes in smoothly, her voice laced with that same practiced sweetness. "The marriage was a while ago now. I think we should be expecting some good news soon, don't you? It's been…long enough, if I may say so myself. Back in my day, we moved into our husbands' homes on a Saturday and by Monday, we were already…well, I'm sure you can guess."

Another woman, whom I don't recognize but can already tell is part of their silent coalition, adds, "Well, you know how these young kids are these days. They can't seem to hurry into such things. They're so fixated on keeping their figures, they forget what it really means to be a woman."

Zia Camilla laughs lightly. "Which they do, of course, until they're too old to conceive properly."

I force a smile, trying to ignore the burning anger crawling up my throat, and my hands tense under the table, digging into my palms. I glance at Mamma, who shifts uncomfortably in her seat, clearly sensing the change in atmosphere.

The tension is thick enough to cut through.

"My granddaughter has her whole life ahead of her," Nonna interjects, her voice sharp and unwavering, slicing through their insinuations like a blade. "Education is important. People like you should know that."

There's a brief pause before Aunt Marta leans forward, her smile twisting into something that barely passes for polite. It's a smile with teeth, all edge and no warmth. "That's...admirable," she says, her voice laced with the faintest hint of mockery. "But don't you think it's more practical to focus on bearing Ettore his heirs now? Education is lovely, of course," she adds, her eyes flicking dismissively toward me, "but there's a family to think of now, isn't there?"

I force a polite smile, willing myself to remain calm. Maybe it's the hormones, or maybe I'm just plain tired of their nonsense, but their words are hitting harder today.

"My daughter can do both." Mamma suddenly speaks up. The surprising strength in her tone catches me off guard. "She doesn't have to sacrifice her future to be a good wife. You have daughters, don't you? So, this insinuation is especially disappointing coming from you."

Zia Camilla's face tightens, her pleasant demeanor replaced by a cold, hard mask. I can see a few other relatives nearby noticing the shift in the room, but none of them dare speak up.

"Well," Zia Camilla drawls, her eyes narrowing like a predator sizing up its prey. "Her *bright* future didn't get her here, now did it?" She sneers at my mother. "You're living here for free, getting treatment for your filthy disease, and it's only because your daughter got lucky enough to catch my bored nephew's fancy." Her words drip with venom. "Not because of any *bright future* she has."

"How dare you?" I leap to my feet, my voice loud, trembling with the force of my anger.

I feel Nonna's hand on mine, tugging gently, but the conversation on the other side of the table halts—everyone's attention is now on us.

"Oh, don't be dramatic now," Zia Camilla smirks, her tone dripping with false sweetness. "We were just having a friendly chat. You don't need to clamor for your husband to defend you—"

"You're too young to be this bitter," Nonna hisses from beside me. Her voice sharp and unyielding. "How old are you? Forty? Fifty? You could pass for my age because your nasty spirit is aging you out."

Gasps ripple through the room. Zia Camilla leans in, her face twisting with rage. "You want to educate me about bitterness?" she spits, her voice now low and deadly. "Look at you! Are you happy with your life? Your only daughter married a poor deadbeat who abandoned her and her two children with nothing. You should be enjoying the fruits of your children's success, but instead, you've been stuck taking care of them for years."

"I feel sorry for you," Nonna bites back, her voice cutting like steel. "Despite everything you claim to have, you don't understand unconditional love and the meaning of family."

"My family is the reason you're even sitting among powerful people like us," Zia Camilla retorts, cocking her head to the side. "I understand family just fine."

Her gaze shifts to me, and I feel a malicious glint in her eyes as she continues. "You should direct that question to your granddaughter. After all, she doesn't know what it's like to have a father figure in the home, does she?"

"Enough!" Ettore's voice booms across the table, but Nonna doesn't care.

"You're a disgrace to everyone around you," she spits at Zia Camilla. "We may be poor, according to you, but we have something you'll never have: a family that loves unconditionally, a family that would weep the day any one of us dies. A family that would go to war for each other. What do you have, Camilla?"

Her face contorts into a deep, ugly scowl.

"You old hag—" she starts, but Nonna cuts her off.

"Where are your children? I've heard one of them has a child. Have you ever held your grandchild?"

The air grows heavy. Zia Camilla's face tightens in anger, and I catch Ettore's jaw clenching as he runs a hand through his hair.

An uncomfortable chuckle breaks the tension—one of Ettore's distant cousins, a man who looks far too eager to lighten the mood. "Oh, come on." He laughs, glancing around at the growing storm. "This argument didn't need to go this far," he says, his voice condescending. "In families like ours, it's all about connections and money. You have to bring value, and if you don't, well, you're as good as useless." His eyes slide toward Zia Camilla. "Aunt Camilla has served her purpose—she raised children for her husband's family. Now, it's up to her kids to continue that cycle in their own homes."

Zia Camilla's face softens for a moment, but my stomach churns as the man continues.

"Human relationships are transactional. And you married into the Greco family." He gestures toward me. "You're not some charity case. It's a partnership. You bring value, or you don't. No offense," he adds, looking toward Ettore now, "but a girl with no father, no real connections...what does she bring to the table?"

I feel the words hit me like a slap, and that's it. I've had enough.

"Leave my house," Ettore says, his voice low and cold, but I barely hear him. The world around me spins, consumed by the suffocating weight of their words.

"W-what?" I hear the man stutter as the others around the table shoot me accusing glares.

I swallow hard, trying to keep myself composed. I'm trying to play my role as Ettore's wife, but my heart is racing, and my hands are shaking. But then the man speaks again, and it all unravels.

"You know," he chuckles darkly, "I've been wondering what happened to the brave Ettore I knew. You've let this cheap thrill slip into your house, into your bed..."

My breath catches in my throat, and before I can stop myself, I spring up from my seat.

"What, did she trap you with a baby?"

I don't hear Ettore's response, or anything that follows, as my feet move before I even think. I run. Away from the venomous words. Away from their hatred. Away from the truth I know is eating me alive.

30

ETTORE

As soon as the words leave Emilio's mouth, I lose it. I'm on him in an instant, my hands grabbing his collar with a fury I can barely control. I don't care that everyone in the room is watching. My vision goes red.

"How dare you?" I hiss, my grip tightening as I yank him off the floor. "How dare you speak to my wife like that?"

He tries to say something, but it's just a gurgle, his words swallowed by the pressure around his throat. I can hear people scrambling behind me, Zia Camilla pleading for me to let him go, but I don't care. All I see is the broken expression on Mirabella's face as she ran out of the room.

"If you don't want to kill him, I suggest you let him go now." Nonna's voice cuts through the chaos, low and commanding. "He's seconds away from passing out."

I glance down at her. For the first time, I don't see hatred in her eyes—just a calm, controlled warning.

Emilio squirms in my grip, choking and sputtering a mix of curses and half-formed words. With a forceful shove, I send him stumbling backward, his body slamming against the long mahogany dinner table. Plates, silverware, and food scatter everywhere as he crashes to the floor with a sickening thud.

"Get the fuck out," I growl, my voice eerily calm as I point toward the door. "All of you! Out of my house. Out of my life. I don't ever want to see your face again."

I turn to walk away, but Zia Camilla steps in front of me, blocking my path. Her face is twisted into a scowl, but I see the flicker of fear in her eyes as she steps closer.

"Ettore," she calls softly, reaching for me.

Before she can touch me, I grab her wrist and shove her aside, the rage still bubbling beneath the surface. My hand trembles with anger, but just as I'm about to turn on her, Mirabella's face flashes in my mind.

I can't let her sit in that pain alone. She needs me more than anyone right now.

Ignoring the murmurs and shocked looks behind me, I leave them all standing there and go after Mirabella. It doesn't take long to find her since she's in our bedroom, her back to me as she stares out the window.

"Mirabella," I say softly, closing the door behind me. She doesn't turn around, but I can see the tension in her stiff shoulders.

I want to walk over to where she is, take her in my arms, and comfort her, but I can't do that right now. Not when it's my fault all this happened in the first place.

"I'm sorry. What they said...everything they said." I grit my teeth as another wave of anger washes over me. "They hurt you, and they had no right."

She doesn't respond. She just keeps her gaze on something outside the window. I run my hands through my hair searching for the right words.

"I know it hasn't been easy. The comments my family

makes, the fact that you have to share the same roof with them...this wasn't part of our agreement."

I hear her exhale sharply, but she still doesn't turn to look at me.

"What do you want, Mirabella? Say the word and I'll do it," I grit my teeth. "I know you told me you don't want me to send them away, and the only reason they're still here is because you asked. But if you want to change your mind..."

She shakes her head, and my heart sinks even further. How selfless and kind could she be?

"Fine. Let's leave. Let's get away for a while. Just us."

She turns to face me, and I exhale in relief before continuing. "A vacation, maybe? We haven't even had a honeymoon. What do you say?"

She doesn't say anything. She just watches me with an unreadable expression on her face. Before I can ask her what she's thinking, she's striding over toward me with a determined look on her face.

When her lips collide with mine, I wrap my arms around her, diving in with fervor and passion. My tongue explores her mouth, and she meets me with the same intensity, pouring her anger and frustration into the kiss. I swallow her pain and hurt, dragging my hands over every inch of her skin, unable to get enough.

"Please," she moans between kisses. "Please make me forget."

A growl escapes my lips as I lift her body in my arms. Her legs wrap around my waist as I carry her toward the bed. As I place her body on the soft sheets, I'm already climbing over her, pulling my lips down to kiss her neck, her breasts, and her stomach. She moans when I rip her dress off her torso. I fling the flimsy material across the room to pepper kisses down her body, leaving open-mouthed hickeys everywhere I go.

Her fingers run through my hair before pulling at my scalp, tugging my mouth away from her skin to pull my T-shirt over my head. I work the rest of our clothes off quickly, eager for the feel of her soft skin against mine. When we are finally both completely naked, I kiss her again, slowly now, taking my time to worship her beautiful body as I trace my hand over every dip, every curve, every scar. Her breath shudders out of her lungs as I trail my hand down to her wet heat. Her hands wrap around my shoulders, and she pulls me closer to her.

"Make love to me, Ettore," she moans against my lips.

I let out a guttural sound from my throat before sinking down between her spread legs. I brush the tip of my cock over her wet entrance once, twice.

"Are you sure?" I murmur, and she nods eagerly.

"Yes."

I sink in slowly, savoring the sensation of her walls taking in my hard length. We both moan as I'm buried deep inside her, and after peppering kisses over her face and neck, I begin to move slowly in and out of her.

My arms are positioned on either side of her head, my face only mere inches away from hers. Our eyes are locked on each other, my heart thumping directly above hers.

I've never done this before. Making love. But fuck, it feels better than anything I've ever imagined. It feels like a fantasy, a high I don't want to come down from. Her nails trail softly over the length of my back as I roll my hips gently, steadily. Our eyes remain locked, and I see the desire...the emotion pooling in her gaze. The sunlight streaming in from the window hits her eyes, making them glitter like gems.

And because I can't resist, I lean in to kiss her again. I sink even deeper inside her before pulling out to thrust in again. She gasps into the kiss as my movement picks up pace. Her fingers digging into my back, her legs spreading even further to give me more access.

The orgasm that hits us is unlike any other I've ever felt. It starts from her toes, which curl as she wraps her legs around my waist. The second to final thrust makes her body tremble against mine, and it squeezes my dick painfully yet beautifully. When I thrust for the last time, her hands grab my face as she whispers, "Come with me, baby."

We come together, our bodies trembling with intensity as we surrender to each other completely.

31

MIRABELLA

The moment I step out of the private car, everything feels different.

Ettore kept his promise, bringing me to this tiny, tropical town on the island of Providencia, Colombia. Palm trees sway in the warm breeze, and a thrill surges through me as Ettore and I make our way to the little cabin ahead.

I glance around the beach, still in awe. It doesn't feel real that I'm here—in a place so breathtaking it seems like it only exists in movies. As we reach the cabin door, Ettore flashes me a smile, and my heart skips.

The small house is tucked away in a quiet corner of the island, with soft pastel-painted walls and a hammock on the porch just steps from the water. I close my eyes, imagining myself lying in that hammock, letting the golden sun warm my skin, inhaling the faint, sweet scent from the hibiscus bushes nearby.

Inside, the cabin is like a little paradise. Everything is crafted from rich, polished wood, from the low ceilings to the countertop in the small kitchen. It's simple, cozy, and feels like stepping into a dream. I linger in the small living room, marveling at the space around me, when Ettore comes back after dropping off our bags.

"Do you like it?" he asks, wrapping his arms around me.

"It's better than anything I could have expected," I whisper, leaning up to kiss him.

A low groan escapes him as his lips press against mine, his tongue teasing as his hands begin to wander beneath my sundress. I let out a quiet laugh, playfully slapping his hands away.

"Hey, that's not why we're here," I tease. "Take me to the beach!"

Under my sundress, I'm wearing the bikini I'd slipped on this morning back in New York. During the five-hour flight, I couldn't stop thinking about sinking into the sea, letting the ocean carry me away.

"Oh? So you're saying we're not going to have sex the whole time we're here?" he asks, grinning.

I give him a serious nod, trying to keep a straight face.

He chuckles, kissing me again, and I can't hold back my laughter. I feel like the luckiest woman in the world, wrapped in his arms in this paradise.

"You know that's impossible," he says, pulling back with a smirk. "You're on birth control, right? I have some very good ideas for wild, adventurous places we could...enjoy ourselves."

I force a laugh, nodding a bit too quickly at the mention of birth control. "Yeah, I'm on birth control," I lie, my voice smooth. "Now, come on. Take me to the ocean!"

Our days here on Providencia fall into a rhythm—swimming in the sea at sunrise, exploring hidden coves by day, and strolling along the beach in the evening as the ocean stretches endlessly around us. Each day, the locals greet us warmly, often offering us freshly caught fish or tropical fruits. Our cabin neighbors are an older Black couple from England who moved here seven years ago. They're the sweetest people.

"Providencia is a beautiful place to live," the man tells us one morning as we all walk toward the beach. "The people here are goodhearted, and the culture is lovely. It's mostly safe, though you have to keep an eye out for a few thugs who show up when tourists start pouring in over the summer."

The days slip by in a blur, each one more vibrant and carefree than the last. Ettore keeps me busy, and I can tell he's trying to keep me from overthinking. And it's working. It's working almost too well. Here, it's easy to pretend, to let myself believe we're just like any other couple. It's easy to lose myself in this tranquil paradise.

Today, we're kayaking down a slow-moving river, but my paddle keeps getting stuck in the shallow water.

"Here, let me help," Ettore says from behind me, guiding my hands on the paddle. A shiver runs through me as his arms stay around me just a moment too long.

We haven't done anything more than kiss since we got here, partly because, after each day's adventures, I'm so exhausted I fall asleep the instant we return to the cabin.

But now, with his arms around me, something inside me stirs. It's not just attraction—it's something deeper. Something unsettling. Something I'm not ready to admit to myself.

Things have changed between us, and there's no denying it.

We spend the next few hours exploring the river's coastline, weaving our way through mangroves, watching colorful fish dart and glide beneath the kayak. At some point I'm paddling along, feeling at ease, when I suddenly spot a large stone ahead—a second too late. Ettore's laughter rings in my ear as he tries to help steer us clear, but it's no use. We collide with the rock, and before I can even brace myself, the kayak tips over. With a yelp, I plunge into the cold water, and Ettore's hand grabs my waist, steadying me. When we surface, we're both laughing so hard that it quickly turns to coughing.

"Hey, are you okay?" Ettore asks between laughs, his eyes alight with mischief.

I catch my breath and look at him, drawn to the way his green and brown eyes sparkle in the sunlight. His wet hair falls just to his neck, and he looks so carefree, more than I've ever seen him.

Before I know what I'm doing, I wrap my arms around him and kiss him. It's a slow, sweet kiss, one that lets us savor the moment, savor each other. It's as if time stretches, letting us forget everything else.

By the time we return to shore, the sun is setting, casting a golden glow over the island. Ettore watches me with a relaxed, knowing smile, as if he understands he's slowly breaking down the walls I've built around myself. I want to ask him what he's thinking, to hear about his deepest fears, his greatest joys. But I can't shake the guilt.

I know I'm lying to him, that all of this is built on a lie. A lie that won't last. And I fear this will all take a different course if the truth comes out. I'm not ready for that yet.

So I stay silent, letting myself enjoy this brief, beautiful moment between us.

Later that evening, Ettore arranges a cozy, romantic dinner for us on the beach. A small table is set with an array of delicious seafood, surrounded by flickering candlelight, and beyond us, the vast stretch of ocean fades into the night.

"This is breathtaking," I gasp, glancing at Ettore as he settles into his seat across from me. He's changed into a colorful polo shirt and casual shorts, and I can't help admiring how beautiful he looks.

"Are you talking about dinner, the beach, or me?" he teases, a playful spark in his eyes.

"All of the above." I chuckle, feeling warmth in my cheeks.

Just as I'm about to dig into the mouthwatering food, I realize I left my phone in the cabin. "Shoot. I forgot my phone," I say, looking at him apologetically.

Understanding crosses his face. Nonna has called me every night since we arrived here, and she usually passes the phone around so everyone can talk. The second night, I noticed the look in Ettore's eyes as I spoke with my family—a mix of admiration and maybe longing.

Ever since we arrived till now, none of his family members have called him. I overheard him speaking to Vittorio once, and even though they laughed over the phone, the call had been work-related.

So from the third night on, whenever my family called, I put it on speaker and tried to involve Ettore in the conversation. Giulia adores my husband, my mother doesn't hold anything against him, and Nonna, well, she's beginning to warm up to him, as well.

"I'll be right back," I say, starting to get up, but Ettore raises a hand and stands.

"Stay. I'll get it," he says with a smile, and before I can argue, he's gone, leaving me alone under the moonlit sky.

I take a spoonful of the creamy crab soup and let the taste fill my mouth. "Oh, my God," I groan, unable to hold back a satisfied moan. It's too good to wait for him, and I can't resist taking another sip, even though I'd promised myself I'd save it for when Ettore comes back.

Just then, a loud commotion pulls me from my thoughts. I glance up, my spoon frozen halfway to my mouth, and I see three young men standing near a small snack shack. One of them has a firm grip on the arm of the local girl selling snacks, his face twisted in anger as he yells at her in a mix of Spanish and Creole.

A pulse of anger flares inside me as I watch the scene unfold. My eyes dart to the cabin, and I wait impatiently, hoping Ettore will come out soon. My mind races. The girl can't be more than twelve, and it's clear she's terrified. My knees bounce with agitation, the need to do something overwhelming.

Then, one of the men grips the girl's arm even tighter, trying to drag her away from the shack. That's the breaking point. Before I even think about it, my feet are moving. I stand up, my heart pounding with adrenaline, and I stride toward them, my voice sharp and commanding.

"Hey!" I shout. "Let her go."

The men turn, muttering in Spanish, their eyes narrowing, their sneers growing as they size me up. I see the fear in the girl's eyes, wide and panicked, and it ignites something deep inside me. I have to protect her.

"¿Quién diablos eres?" one of the guys growls, storming toward me.

My heart hammers in my chest, but I don't flinch. I stand my ground, taking a quick step back and crouching low. Before the man can reach me, I grab two handfuls of sand from the ground and fling it at him. The sand hits his face and his friend's, both of them recoiling in shock, curses spilling from their lips in rapid-fire Spanish.

I don't waste a second—I grab the girl and draw her close. "Come on, let's go," I say, trying to pull her away.

But before I can move us away, a rough hand clamps down on my arm, jerking me backward. A sick sense of déjà vu floods me, reminding me of the night I'd been cornered by Abruzzi's men. I react on instinct, kneeing the guy hard in the groin. He gasps and loosens his grip just long enough for me to shout.

"Help! Somebody help us!"

The shout catches the attention of a couple of locals, two fishermen and a trader who rush over. They shout at the men, waving sticks and yelling in the same rapid Spanish, and within moments, the men stumble back, cursing and retreating into the distance.

The girl clings to me, trembling. I glance down at her wrist and the red marks left behind by the man's grip, and anger surges in me again.

"You're okay now," I say softly, tucking a loose strand of hair behind her ear. My heart aches at seeing her this shaken. From the corner of my eye, I spot Ettore rushing over, worry etched on his face.

He skids to a halt beside me, his eyes darting between the retreating men and the girl still clinging to my side.

I rub my thumb over the girl's wrist, offering her the smallest smile, my heart still racing. Ettore places a hand on my shoulder, his voice low with concern. "Are you okay?" he asks, but his eyes are already flicking to the girl, assessing the situation with the precision of someone who's seen far too much violence in his life.

I glance at the girl, then turn to Ettore, my own anger still boiling beneath the surface. "Do they do this often? Do these men usually bother you?"

She shakes her head. "Sometimes they get drunk and

bother people here. Today they wanted free snacks. I said no, and they got angry." Her eyes meet mine then, still full of fear, but there's bravery there, too. "I'm sorry," she says softly, her small voice barely above a whisper. "I didn't mean to cause trouble."

My heart swells. I shake my head, my grip on her shoulder tightening in reassurance. "You didn't cause any trouble," I say, my voice firm. "They were in the wrong."

Ettore's gaze softens, but the tension in his body hasn't fully released. He looks at the girl, then back at me, his jaw tightening. The storm that's been brewing in his eyes is no longer about me—now it's about them. Those men. The ones who thought they could take whatever they wanted.

I nod to him, gesturing for him to leave us, and he turns away to talk to two fishermen who just arrived, probably about what just happened, all the while still staring at me, a tense look in his eyes.

I turn back to the girl, giving her hand a reassuring squeeze. "What's your name?"

"Maria," she says, and she gives me a shy smile that tugs at my heart. She reminds me so much of Giulia.

"There's a local hospital nearby that can check on both of you for any injuries," Ettore says, his voice laced with worry. "The fishermen just told me how to get there. I can get a cab right away. Should I grab your bag, and we can go?"

I shake my head, forcing a smile even though I feel the weight of his concern. "I'm good, Ettore. Perfectly fine. Those men didn't get the chance to do any harm. I'm tougher than I look, you know."

He doesn't seem convinced, his brow furrowing as his hand stays firmly on my back. "I know, but I'll sleep better once you're checked by a doctor. You too young lady" he adds, glancing at Maria with a stern look.

Maria shakes her head, though her words are soft. "I'm fine, sir. This happens all the time, especially when tourist visits are high. A good rub from mama's special oils, and my wrist will be just fine."

Ettore nods but still doesn't look entirely reassured. He glances at me again, as if waiting for something more. His lips part as if he's about to say something, but I can't let him go any further.

"I'm fine, Ettore," I interrupt, forcing a reassuring smile. "Really. Nothing I can't handle."

It's the truth, but it's also not.

There's something else keeping me from going to the hospital—something I'm not ready to tell you yet. Something I'm not sure how to explain without making you question everything. The last thing I want is for you to find out like this, while we're on this fake honeymoon, of all things.

I'm terrified that if I tell you, it might be the end of whatever this is between us. I can't risk you hating me or pushing me away before we even get a chance to see where this could go.

I don't say any of that out loud, though. I can't. And I pray to God that he doesn't suddenly develop the ability to read my thoughts.

He nods, still a bit tense, then looks at Maria. "I talked to the locals. Those men won't bother you or anyone else here again." His voice is calm, but there's a protective edge to it that makes my chest tighten.

Ettore steps away to call a taxi for Maria, and as he does, I feel her eyes on me. She glances between me and Ettore, then gives me a mischievous smile. "Is he your husband?" she asks, her eyes glinting with curiosity. She looks down at the ring on my finger before I can answer. "Ah I see. You're a lucky woman. He never stopped watching you."

I laugh softly. "Do you always say what's on your mind?" I ask, smiling as she nods, a little shyly.

"Not always. But I thought you deserved to know since you saved my life," she replies. "I'm glad you're with someone who looks that worried when something bad happens." She pauses, her lips curling into a small smile, a faraway look in her eyes. "My poppa used to look at my momma like that before he passed. It means he loves you."

The words hit me like a ton of bricks. I feel a wave of guilt crash over me.

I know what Maria means, but I also know the truth is more complicated. Ettore may look at me with that same intensity, but it's not love—not the way she sees it. Not the way I want it to be.

I can't exactly tell her that my marriage isn't real, that the man I'm with—the one who looks at me so fiercely, so protectively—isn't really my husband. Not in the way she imagines. I can't tell her that our marriage is a lie, that it's built on a contract and promises that mean nothing once the ink dries.

I can't tell her that it's beginning to feel real—*too* real. Even though we've only had sex once, we've shared moments, quiet and intense, that feel like they've forged something between us.

The way he holds me, the way he touches me, the way he looks at me like I'm the only person in the room. It's as if we've been together for years, not just months.

These moments, these gestures, feel more intimate than anything I've ever experienced. They're more than just physical. They reach deeper, into a place where words can't follow. And I don't know if it's the pregnancy or the time we've spent together, but everything is happening in a way I'm not ready for.

But most of all, I can't say that I'm carrying his child. With every passing day, I wish I could tell him, wish I could share this part of myself with him, but it's not that simple.

What if he doesn't want this child? What if the truth destroys everything, as fragile as it already is?

I shake off the heavy thoughts and force a chuckle, trying to sound light. "I'm glad I met you today, Maria. You remind me of one big-hearted girl I'd go to the ends of the earth for."

She smirks, a knowing glint in her eyes. "I'm sure she'll do the same for you."

"You think so?"

"I know so. People like you are rare. I know how many tourists would've just looked the other way if they saw me in that situation. You didn't even hesitate. You just stepped right in."

Her words hit me harder than I expect. She's sharp for someone her age—just like Giulia.

"Well, my Nonna taught me some self-defense when I was growing up. She always said, 'Never run from a fight.'"

Maria grins. "She sure sounds cool, just like you."

Before I can reply, Ettore pulls up with a taxi. I give Maria a quick wave, my voice struggling to stay steady. "Take care, okay?" I call, trying to sound normal. I can't let her see how much I feel like I'm on the edge of losing everything.

She waves back, and as the taxi pulls away, her words linger in my mind. *He never stopped watching you.*

Part of me wants to believe it—wants to hold on to the hope that maybe this could be real, that Ettore could love me, that this could somehow turn into something more than a contract, more than a duty. But then the other part of me

—the part that knows the truth, the part that remembers the coldness of our arrangement—reminds me of what's coming.

Soon, the contract will expire. And then what?

I feel Ettore's presence beside me as we start walking back to the cabin, and I try to smile, but it's not easy. He notices the change in me immediately, his eyes narrowing in concern. But before he can ask any questions, I pull him in for a kiss, then suggest we get some shut eye.

The moment stretches out between us before Ettore finally breaks the silence. "Are you sure everything is fine?"

"I'm okay," I say, my voice a little too quiet.

He doesn't buy it. I know he doesn't. But he doesn't push. He just walks beside me, the air between us heavy with unspoken words.

And for the first time in a long time, I wish I didn't have to keep pretending.

Ettore speaks up again. "You didn't have to get involved, you know."

"She needed help," I reply with a shrug. "I couldn't just sit there while those guys harassed her."

A shiver runs through me, and Ettore instinctively pulls me close, wrapping an arm around me. His warmth seeps into my skin, calming me more than I want to admit.

"Hey, I'm not chastising you," he murmurs, his voice gentle but firm. "Yes, it was risky." He pauses, his gaze softening. "But it was also brave. You did well, Bella."

I swallow, his words hanging in the air between us, stirring something deep inside. I'm not sure what to say, or if I even want to let myself feel what's threatening to surface.

A soft gasp escapes my lips as Ettore lifts my hand to his mouth and presses a gentle kiss to the back of my palm. My body tenses instinctively at the touch, then relaxes, drawn to the familiarity of his skin against mine. Part of me wants to pull away, to guard myself from getting too close. But another part of me aches for him to keep touching me, to keep closing the distance between us.

But the guilt gnaws at me, hollowing out any chance of truly enjoying this moment. I know I have to tell him, to face what I've been hiding.

Just...not now.

Not yet.

32

ETTORE

Something's bothering Mirabella. I can feel it.

Her shoulders are stiff when I hand her a cup of jasmine tea.

"Thank you," she mutters, her voice quieter than usual, before taking a slow sip.

I watch her, my mind racing, trying to figure out what's wrong. She's been fine since we arrived here—happy, even. Happier than I've seen her in a long time. But now, there's this sadness in her eyes. It's heavy and unsettling, and I can't just pretend I don't see it anymore.

"Let's go for a walk," I suggest, taking the cup from her gently.

She hesitates, blinking up at me. "But—"

"I'll make you another one when we get back." I reach out for her hand, and she finally stands, sighing, before placing her hand in mine and jumping down the kitchen counter.

I squeeze it gently, offering her the comfort I can give. Then I pull her toward the door, determined to get her to open up, to talk.

The sand feels warm beneath our feet as we walk along the shoreline of the private beach just outside our room. The stars shine brightly overhead, and I imagine telling her something sweet, like how she's as beautiful as the stars that fill the night sky. I'd expect her to laugh and call me corny, her eyes lighting up with mischief.

But today isn't that day. The air between us feels thick with tension, and I can't shake the feeling that something's wrong. I rack my brain for something—anything—that could chase the sadness from her eyes.

"I wish we could stay here forever," I say before I even think about it.

She glances at me, and for a moment, her lips twitch, almost like she's trying to smile.

"That'll be the day. You, Ettore Greco, wouldn't survive living on some little island in the middle of nowhere. I'd bet my left tit on it."

"Please don't. You know I'm especially fond of that one."

She smacks my arm, rolling her eyes. "Get your mind out of the gutter, silly man."

I chuckle. "Not joking. That's a serious topic."

"My body, my choice."

"Oh, now it's like that?" I tease, giving her a smirk. "Didn't seem that way when you were practically begging me to—how did you put it? 'Oh please, Ettore. Fuck me. Make me forget,'" I add, mimicking her voice with exaggerated longing.

She shoves me with a huff. "I hate you sometimes."

I laugh. "No you don't, Bella." I pull her close, and for a moment, our gazes lock, the space between us charged with an electricity that never fades. We're so close. It'd only take a slight lean to bridge the gap, to kiss her like I always want to.

Just then, some voices from farther down the beach break our trance, and we step apart.

This stretch of beach is supposed to be private, at least for us. Renting a cabin here includes a small section of beach to ourselves, but I went out of my way to reserve an extra buffer, an entire five-cabin width on each side. I wanted space—a place where we could roam freely with no interruptions. For now, we're alone, though not completely; it'd take someone at least five minutes to cross over from the nearest cabins.

She sighs, kicking some sand with her toes. "But seriously, you'd go crazy here," she says, a note of certainty in her voice. "The Wi-Fi is practically non-existent, and let's face it, Ettore—you're a workaholic."

I place a hand on my chest, feigning offense. "Me? A workaholic?" I snort, and she rolls her eyes.

"You literally brought work with you on vacation."

"It was just a couple of emails," I say, shrugging. "And I was willing to leave it all behind in New York, just like I left my private security. You're the one who said I didn't have to..."

She laughs, shaking her head. "Because I knew you wouldn't leave it all behind, obviously. I was just trying to make you happy."

As we reach the shade of a nearby palm tree, I take her hand, feeling its warmth in mine. I hesitate, the words pressing at the back of my mind, forming before I can stop them.

"There's something I've been meaning to talk to you about," I admit, reluctantly letting the words slip out.

Mirabella frowns, her eyes searching mine. "Oh? About what?"

I swallow, the bitterness sharp in my mouth. "About

what's going to happen...a few months from now." I pause, the weight of it sinking in. "It's already been a few month, you know that, right? Our contract..."

A flicker of something—hurt, maybe—crosses her face, and she looks away. "Yeah. I know."

I take a deep breath, my voice lowering. "I don't think I can go back to being the same person I was before I met you."

A tense silence settles between us, heavy and uncertain, as she turns back to meet my gaze.

"Ettore." She sighs, her expression is unreadable, and my heart twists painfully. Fear? Hurt? I haven't even thought about how relieved she might feel when this ends. She'll be free—free from my family's scrutiny, from the threats and the chaos of my life. And with the financial settlement, she'll be set up to do anything she wants.

Maybe her life would be better, easier without me.

But that look...it's still there, lingering in her eyes, and I can't bear it any longer.

"Bella," I murmur, turning to face her fully. "You know you can tell me what's on your mind. You look like you've been pondering about something since we got here. Just talk to me."

She gives me a quick, strained smile, but it fades almost instantly. She turns to look out at the waves crashing against the shoreline, as though she's waiting for them to give her the right words.

After a long moment, she exhales deeply, her voice barely above a whisper. "I don't even know where to begin."

"Try me." My hand moves up to gently cradle her cheek, my thumb brushing the soft skin there. She leans into the touch, just a little, before pulling away, creating an unbearable distance between us.

Pain explodes in my chest as she folds her arms tightly across her body, shielding herself from me like she's trying to protect her heart from something—*me*.

"This...us...it was never supposed to be real," she whispers, her eyes darting anywhere but at me. Her voice cracks, and the words pierce through me like shards of glass. "Yet somehow...I don't know when it happened, but it became real for me."

Her words drop into the space between us, and I feel the weight of them settle in my chest, suffocating me. I can't speak—not yet. Not until I understand exactly what she's trying to tell me. I wait, my heart pounding in my ears, my hands trembling at my sides.

She finally glances up at me, and the look in her eyes— raw and vulnerable, yet somehow defiant—makes my chest tighten even more.

"I tried to fight it," she continues, her voice low and broken. "I told myself this was just...pretend. But the truth is, Ettore..." She pauses, and I watch her throat bob as she swallows hard, her voice trembling now. "I've fallen in love with you."

Her confession hangs in the air like a weight I can't lift, and the blood rushes to my ears, drowning out everything but the sound of my heart hammering in my chest. For a moment, I can't breathe, can't think.

I take a step closer, reaching for her hand, and when she doesn't pull away, I lace our fingers together. "You think you're the only one?" I murmur, my voice tight with emotion. "You think I haven't been fighting this, too?"

She looks at me, her eyes wide with surprise, and I see her walls start to crack. "I thought...I thought you were just sexually attracted to me," she says, her words coming out in a rush, like she can't stop herself. "Not that it's a bad thing,

I'm sexually attracted to you, as well." She shuts her eyes, trying to steady herself. "I didn't think..."

"That I'm in love with you?" I ask softly, brushing a strand of hair away from her face, my fingers lingering on her skin. "I've wanted you...wanted *this*...from the moment I laid eyes on you that night. Why do you think I searched for you? Looked for you when my lawyer suggested I needed to get married for my company's expansion?"

Her breath catches, and I see her eyes flicker between mine and my lips, like she's struggling to catch up with what I'm saying.

"Even if it was a fake marriage, I knew I didn't want to be with anyone else. I wanted *you*. I want *you*, and I will always want you, Bella. Always."

Her eyes fill with tears, and my heart lurches as she slowly leans up toward me, her lips trembling with the words she's about to say.

"I love you too, Ettore," she whispers, and the weight of it crushes me in the best possible way. I watch the last of her defenses slip away, fall to the ground like crumbling walls, leaving her raw and vulnerable before me. I see her, all of her, unguarded, and I don't want to ever look away.

"But...what does that mean for us?" she asks, her voice small, the fear and doubt still clinging to her, despite the hope in her eyes.

I wrap my arms around her waist, pulling her close, feeling her warmth seep into me. "It means we're together now," I say softly, my voice firm. "For real this time."

A shiver runs through her, and a shaky laugh escapes her lips. "This wasn't part of the plan, Ettore."

"Screw the plan," I say, my voice low, before I lean down and capture her lips in a kiss that steals the breath from my lungs.

The moment our lips meet, everything crashes down around me. The world falls away, and all I can feel is her—her softness, her warmth, the way her body fits perfectly against mine. I pull her closer, my hands desperate to hold onto her as I pour every ounce of emotion, every beat of my heart into that kiss.

She's everything. Everything I've ever wanted and more. Every part of me belongs to her now, and every part of her belongs to me. And in that kiss, I know—this is real. This is the moment I've been waiting for, and I'm never letting go.

I hold her tightly, but with a gentleness, as if she's made of delicate glass. My hands roam over her, memorizing every contour, every curve, every inch. It all belongs to me. *She* belongs to me. She moans softly against my lips, her small hand finding the back of my neck, pulling me closer. In the distance, the waves crash against the shore, a steady rhythm to our own.

Slowly, I ease us down onto the sand, leaning back against the sturdy trunk of the palm tree. I guide Mirabella onto my lap until she's straddling me, her breath hitching as her hips press against me. I hold her waist firmly, keeping her close, and trail kisses down her neck, tasting the warmth of her skin, savoring each moment as if it's our last.

"Ettore," she gasps when, with one swift pull, I tug her sundress over her head, leaving her in the flimsy bikini from earlier.

"I've been dying to fuck you in these since we got here," I groan against her lips, running my thumbs along the sides of her breasts. Her breath hitches in her throat when I untie the strap of her bikini top, letting her breasts fall free in my arms. I grab the two globes, which look a little fuller, rolling her hardened nipples between my fingers.

She threads her fingers through my hair, grinding softly

against my clothed dick as I bend down to suck gently on one nipple.

"Ettore," she gasps again when I pull one nipple between my teeth and bite it lightly.

"Fuck, I love these tits. "Never sell them, or whatever the hell you said," I groan, my frustration to be closer bubbling.

"Oh, Ettore," she says with a playful smile, shaking her head at me.

Her hands run down my chest before pulling my polo top over my head. I see the desire flash in her eyes at the sight of my chest, and I hiss when she drags her hand over my abdomen and down to my dick.

"I want you inside me," she groans. "Right now."

My hands find their way under her ass to cup her perfect cheeks, squeezing them tight. "So fucking impatient," I mutter, kissing up her jawline before lifting her up slightly to pull my shorts down to my knees.

When my dick springs free, she slides her bikini bottom to one side before positioning her wet heat directly above me. I grab her waist and kiss her hungrily while she slides my cock deep inside her sweet pussy. She cries out the moment I'm buried deep inside her, and the sound echoes in the night.

She begins to move slowly up and down my cock, and I support her movement by guiding her with my hands. Her hands bury themselves in my hair again as her lips search for mine. I grunt as she bites my lower lip before rewarding the sting with a long, wet lick.

My hips buck upward, rubbing against her core as our bodies rock against each other. A low moan escapes her as our hips thrust frantically, meeting each other with a harsh slap that echoes in the silent night.

Our thrusts become faster, our kisses rougher, and soon

enough, we are both moaning and grunting loudly as we reach a climax together. Our bodies shudder violently, and our heavy breathing fills the air around us.

Mirabella collapses against my chest, her body trembling slightly as she struggles to catch her breath. I run my hand through her hair, enjoying the warmth of her skin as we lie there, wrapped in each other, basking in the afterglow. Our hearts beat in sync, racing in rhythm as if they're both trying to catch up with the intensity of what just passed between us.

When she finally leans up to look at me, I catch the glimmer of amusement in her eyes, and I can't help but smile.

"I can't believe I just had outdoor sex." She laughs shyly into her palms. "You bring out the dirtiest parts of me, Ettore."

A smirk tugs at my lips. "You love it," I tease. "Just as much as you love me."

She sighs, her breath warm against my skin as she gazes at me, her eyes soft and honest. "Yeah, I do."

"And I love you too, Bella." The words feel right, feel true, like they've always been there just waiting to be said.

We stay like that for a while, holding each other close as the sound of the waves whispers against the shore, a soft lullaby to our tangled bodies.

My heart is still racing, my breath still heavy, but beneath it all, a different kind of tension builds. I'm thinking about the future—what comes next for us. It feels as if we've both been walking on a tightrope, afraid to fall, afraid to give in to what we've been feeling. But now, here in this moment, we're finally letting ourselves fall.

And I realize that's exactly what we were meant to do all along.

33

MIRABELLA

The café buzzes around me, the noise of clinking cups and low conversations barely reaching my ears as I sit across from Milo. My eyes stay glued to the laptop screen, scanning my professor's comments for what feels like the hundredth time. I keep hoping they'll magically change, but the words remain just as harsh, taunting me.

"Your paper would benefit from a deeper exploration of the connections between historical tensions and current policies. Without addressing these key links, your argument comes across as incomplete and lacks the depth of analysis expected at this level of study."

The sick feeling in my stomach tightens, the words a bitter reminder that I've failed. I thought I'd nailed it. I'd poured hours into research, carefully structuring my thoughts, and had analyzed multiple perspectives with precision. But apparently, none of that mattered. It wasn't enough.

I blink hard, trying to fight back the tears that threaten to spill, but they come anyway, blurring the words on the screen. I scroll down, hoping for a hint of something that might redeem me, but it's just more of the same.

Milo must notice the look on my face because he leans forward, his voice a little deeper, laced with concern. "Hey, Mirabella, what's wrong?"

I shake my head, swallowing thickly as I try to keep myself together. "I just... I messed up the last project. I—" My voice catches in my throat, and I stop. I can't hold it in anymore. The tears come fast now, stinging the corners of my eyes. It's not just the paper. It's everything—the pregnancy, the highs and lows of my relationship with Ettore—it's all too much. I feel like I'm drowning. A tear escapes, slipping down my cheek before I can stop it.

Milo leans over, close enough for me to feel the heat of his presence, and his voice softens. "Hey, it's okay. It's just one project. You've got plenty of time to turn things around before the end of the semester."

But it doesn't feel that way. I don't even know how to explain what I'm really struggling with. I squeeze my eyes shut, hoping to hold it all together, but the tears just keep falling. I bury my face in my hands, embarrassed by the sudden outburst.

Milo doesn't hesitate. He slides in next to me, pulling me into an embrace. His warmth should be comforting, but instead, something about it feels off. I sink into the hug, hoping the closeness will provide some relief, but when his hand tightens around me, pulling me in closer, I'm hit with that unsettling feeling again—the feeling that this is more for him than just a friendly gesture.

I pull away, wiping my eyes, mortified. "I'm sorry, I didn't mean to—"

"It's okay," he interrupts, his voice soft. "Everyone has rough days." He reaches out, his fingers brushing away the tears on my cheeks. His touch lingers too long, and before I can pull back, his hand cradles my face, and his lips press against mine in a kiss that's far too sudden and far too forceful.

For a split second, I freeze, unable to process what just happened. Then, instinct takes over. I jerk back, shoving him away with both hands.

"What the hell, Milo?!" I can't contain the scream, my voice cutting through the café's noise. Heads turn, but I don't care. My heart races, a mixture of confusion, anger, and betrayal. I scoot away from him, shaking my head. "Don't ever do that again!"

"M-Mirabella, I—"

"No," I cut him off, my voice shaking with fury. I grab my things, stuffing them hastily into my bag with trembling hands. "That was completely out of line. I told you there's nothing more to this. You kissed me without my permission."

He exhales, clearly frustrated, but his apology is too little, too late.

"I'm sorry..."

But I don't want to hear it. Without another word, I storm out of the café, my face flushed with anger, my stomach in knots from the emotional chaos. I thought of Milo as a friend—hell, I trusted him. Why would he do something like that?

I can feel the heat of my fury simmering as I walk to the parking lot. Logan is waiting by my car, just as I'd told him to. I'd mentioned that I was meeting up with a friend to study, but now I wonder if Ettore insisted he wait for me. Something about it doesn't sit right, and the feeling lingers like a bad taste in my mouth.

I slip into the backseat, the familiar hum of the car

engine starting up, but instead of giving Logan the address to my place, I tell him to head to Giovanni and Alessia's house. The drive is quiet, the twenty minutes stretching out as I try to ignore the whirlwind of emotions in my head. When we finally pull up in front of their building, I don't waste any time. I climb out of the car and head for the front door.

Before I even get a chance to knock, Giovanni answers the door, his eyes immediately locking onto my flushed face and the puffiness around my eyes.

"What did he do?" His voice is low, protective—almost a growl, and it's impossible to miss.

I try to brush it off, forcing a weak laugh that escapes despite the heaviness weighing on my chest. I'm touched by his outburst, but I can't help but wonder if he really thinks he could go toe-to-toe with Ettore.

"Ettore didn't do anything to me."

Giovanni doesn't look convinced as he pulls me into the apartment, locking the door behind us as if I'm in immediate danger. "I find that hard to believe," he mutters, leading me toward the living room.

I try to muster a smile, but it fades instantly, and I let out a shaky breath. "I just had a rough day. Do you mind if I hang out here for a while?"

"Of course not." Giovanni exhales, pulling me into a warm, brotherly hug. The moment his arms wrap around me, I feel the walls I've been holding up start to crack, and I can't hold back the tears any longer. They spill down my cheeks, hot and heavy.

From the kitchen, I hear Alessia's voice. "I heard Mira's voice just now," she says, before I hear her sharp intake of breath. "What happened? I told him I'd cut off his balls if he messed with you," she says, rushing towards us with concern written all over her face.

I sniff, pulling away from Giovanni to wrap my arms around Alessia instead. "Who?"

"Ettore, of course. Isn't this because of him?"

"Oh my God, please tell me you didn't actually threaten to cut off my husband's balls to his face." I pause, half smiling. "You do realize he has men who could easily make you disappear for that, right?"

She huffs. "Of course, but I'd like to see him try. Now, don't change the subject—what happened? And since you're still referring to him as your husband, I'm guessing your sobbing has nothing to do with him?"

"Nooo." I chuckle, wiping away a tear.

"Oh, thank God," Alessia sighs in relief. "For a minute there, I thought I was gonna have to smack him in the face and then move to another country."

"Not so quick with the smart mouth, huh?" I tease.

"Have you seen the muscles on that guy?" Alessia shoots back. "One hit from him and I'd be sporting a face only a mother could love. And I can't afford plastic surgery—at least not until I get some better clients."

"I'll protect you, baby," Giovanni adds, with an exaggerated wink.

"Yeah, right. You couldn't even kill the spider we saw last week."

"Babe!"

"What? She already knows you're all talk and no action."

I burst out laughing as Giovanni smacks Alessia on the ass playfully, then pulls her into a hug from behind, shooting me a look.

"So, why did you both come to the conclusion I was crying over Ettore?" I ask, finally starting to calm down.

"What conclusion?" they both ask, looking at me like I'm speaking a different language.

"That I was crying because of Ettore. It could've been anything else. My mom, my annoying in-laws—heck, even hormones! I tear up at the slightest thing these days."

"Well, we've kind of been expecting you to burst in here any day now, singing some tragic love song with his name on your lips," Alessia says.

"Why?"

"Because he's a bad person," Giovanni spits without hesitation.

"Babe," Alessia chides, giving him a pointed look.

"What? We can't keep hiding the truth from her. She has to know."

"Know what?" I ask, feeling a knot form in my stomach.

"That Ettore Greco is as sinister as they come. At least, he used to be."

I know that. He killed three men to save my life the first time I met him. But I still haven't told my friends the whole story. I don't want to get into it right now—not until I hear what they know.

"What exactly did he do to make you hate him so much?" I ask, wiping the last of my tears as we all settle onto the sofa.

"I don't hate him," Giovanni clarifies quickly, though there's no missing the bitterness in his voice. "I just hate him for you. He's dangerous, Mira. Men like Ettore have no business being involved with a good woman like you."

"Did you know he's involved in the mafia?" Alessia asks softly, her eyes searching mine.

I nod, my throat dry. "I know he's involved in some shady dealings..."

"Some shady dealings?" Giovanni scoffs, his voice full of

disbelief. "That man is a murderer, Mira. He's killed entire families, burned down his rivals' businesses just for fun."

My stomach churns as his words sink in. I've always known Ettore was dangerous, but hearing Giovanni say it out loud in such brutal detail makes my skin crawl.

"I work in the nightclub industry," Giovanni continues, his voice dropping a notch, almost reluctant to share more. "I've seen a lot—been around a lot of powerful, wealthy men, and I've heard things. Things about how Ettore deals with anyone who crosses him..." He pauses, his eyes darkening slightly. "It's brutal. Merciless. He doesn't hesitate to kill."

I swallow hard, the weight of his words pressing down on me like a vise, but Giovanni isn't finished. "But, as much as it pains me to admit it, I think he's pulling away from that life now," he says, his voice softening as he looks at me. "And I think a big part of that is because of you."

My heart skips a beat, and I can't help the mixture of warmth that floods through me. It's like a tidal wave, building slowly in my chest.

"Yeah. Word gets around fast in these parts," Giovanni continues. "It's been said he's decided to go clean since his expansion, since he went public with your marriage. I don't like the guy, but I don't think he'd intentionally cut ties with people like he has over the past few months just to project some family image. In his world, connections are everything —even shady ones. Yes, he has to keep up a front, pretending he no longer associates with certain people. But to actually cut them off—powerful cartels, influential backers that support his empire? That's big. Means there's more to it than meets the eye."

"So you think it's because of me?" I force myself to stay calm, even as my chest tightens, anxiety swirling inside me.

Giovanni shrugs, his expression serious. "He opted out of one of the biggest society clubs in the city. And I overheard my boss saying that when they asked Ettore why, he told them to 'mind their fucking business.' Sounds like he's pussy-whipped to me."

Alessia smacks him on the shoulder, and Giovanni groans. "What? Those were your words, not mine."

"Wow," I mutter quietly, not trusting myself to say anything more. The realization stirs something inside me, a strange cocktail of emotions.

Alessia, sensing the shift in mood, leans back with a playful grin, her eyes sparkling. "Can we change the topic now?" she teases, her tone light and mischievous. "I've been dying to hear some gossip. So...how was the honeymoon?"

Her sudden shift in energy helps break the tension, though a small part of me wonders if the truth of what Giovanni said will hit me later, when I'm alone with my thoughts.

Her question catches me off guard, and I feel my cheeks heat up, the memories of our trip flooding back. "It was nice. We got to know each other better. We did a lot of fun stuff. Had dinner on the beach, bathed in the sun..."

And then, the things we don't talk about. Confessed our feelings, had amazing sex on the beach.

Alessia raises an eyebrow, clearly intrigued. "Sounds like you had a really good time, with you being vague and all." she says with a naughty smile. "Fine, don't give me details. But you look...good. You're glowing. You're happy..."

"I am happy," I exhale, and for a moment, I ignore the guilt gnawing at my chest, ignore the panicked thoughts about our future.

"I know Ettore acts tough and emotionally unavailable," I continue, "but on that island, I saw a side of him I'd never seen before. He was loving, caring, attentive..." I sigh, the words slipping out before I can stop them.

Giovanni and Alessia exchange a look, and I feel the tension shift in the room.

"Our best friend is in love," Alessia gushes, her eyes sparkling with excitement. "I'm so happy for you, girl. The man you just described—he doesn't sound like the Ettore at all. He's totally smitten."

I can't help but smile, her joy infectious. "I don't know what to say." I laugh, feeling a warmth spread through me. "It feels too good to be true sometimes."

The rest of the afternoon slips by in a blur of laughter and playful teasing. Giovanni and Alessia somehow manage to make me forget, even if just for a few, the weight of the world pressing down on me. For those precious hours, I feel lighter than I have in so long, like I'm breathing easier, free from the worries and uncertainties that have been gnawing at me.

I even tell them about Milo, and Giovanni makes a big show of wanting to follow me to the university the next day and punch his teeth in. It's ridiculous, but it makes me laugh—something I hadn't exactly been doing when I got here.

But deep down, beneath the laughter and the joking, there's a truth I've been hiding—one that's eating at me more than I care to admit. As the day fades into evening, I realize with a clarity I haven't felt in weeks that if I want to keep feeling this way, if I want to break free from the suffocating guilt that's been suffusing everything, I have to tell Ettore the truth. All of it. There's no other way.

When it's finally time to leave, Alessia and Giovanni walk me downstairs where Logan is waiting for me by the car. Before I can get inside, I grab Alessia's arm, pulling her aside.

"I'm going to tell Ettore everything. No more stalling," I whisper, the words coming out heavier than I expect.

Her eyes widen. "You mean about the baby?"

I nod solemnly. "I can't keep it from him any longer. It's not fair to either of us. If we really stand a chance together, I have to brave enough to see if he acts up when I tell him."

Alessia takes my hand and squeezes it gently. "That's the right thing to do," she says, her voice full of quiet support. "When are you going to tell him?"

I take a shaky breath, trying to steady my nerves. "Tonight," I say, the finality of the word making my heart race. I know it won't be easy, but it's the only way forward.

She nods, her eyes full of understanding. "You've got this. I'm proud of you, Mira."

I force a weak smile and finally step into the car. As Logan starts the engine and pulls away, the nervous energy begins to coil tighter inside me. Every mile that takes me closer to home feels like it's stretching out the inevitable.

Tonight, everything will change.

And all I can do is hope it changes for the better.

34

ETTORE

The office is drowned in darkness, the blinds pulled shut like a barrier between me and the sunlight I can't even bear to look at today. My head is pounding, my thoughts a muddled mess as I stare at the cluttered papers on my desk. The voices of my family, my so-called family, loop relentlessly in my mind.

"Mirabella is cheating on you."

The words feel like a punch to the gut, stealing the air from my lungs. I don't want to believe it. I can't. But the evidence is right there in front of me—those damned photos.

My aunts' cruel words haunt me, each one more biting than the last, as they play over and over in my head. Every sneer, every judgment cutting deeper than I ever thought possible.

"I told you, Ettore," Zia Camilla spits, pacing in front of me like a caged animal. *"I warned you. But you refused to listen. Did you really think someone like her could ever be the wife you needed? Did you think she'd bring any kind of stability to your life?"*

"She was raised by a single mother," Aunt Francesca adds with a sniff, her voice dripping with disdain. *"Clearly, she had no idea what a stable marriage should look like."*

"Exactly why she was never good enough for you," Aunt Marta sneers, her words sharp as a knife. *"She should never have been allowed in this family."*

"She's trash, Ettore..."

"Not just a cheat. She's a liar, a manipulator, a gold digger..."

"And you? You were so kind to her. So generous with her and her family. She repaid you by betraying you—betraying all of us."

"She didn't even have the decency to wait until your marriage had a chance to breathe before showing her true colors."

A growl escapes from deep in my chest. In one violent sweep, I send everything on my desk crashing to the floor. The sound of paper and glass shattering fills the silence like a thunderclap. My fingers dig into the bridge of my nose, trying to hold it together, but the image of Zia Camilla's smug face as she threw that damned file at me keeps flashing in my mind. The way she looked at me with satisfaction, the smugness in her tone as she told me she'd been right all alone, and the photos...

I hadn't been prepared for the photos.

Fuck.

I wish I could forget, wipe my mind clean. But the images are burned into my brain, replaying over and over again. I can feel the glossy paper still in my hand. I can still remember her smile, her laugh, the flower-patterned dress I bought her. I can't shake the memory of her lips—those lips I once worshipped—pressed against another man's.

Not just any man, either. The same American she'd sworn meant nothing. The same one I saw her with just weeks ago, the one I had no reason to suspect.

My stomach churns violently, the taste of bile rising in my throat as I remember each photo. The way his hands—filthy hands—touched her. The way he'd wiped away her tears, holding her face in his palms as if she were the most precious thing in the world. It makes me sick.

How could I have been so blind? How could I have trusted her so completely, so easily? Every time I thought I was protecting her, every time I felt guilty for not being good enough for her, I'd been the one being played.

My stomach twists again as my eyes scan the floor. I see the pregnancy test. Zia Camilla had handed it to me with such pleasure. The smirk on her face never faded as she confirmed my worst fear.

"Found it in her trash," she'd said, with a shake of her head. "Unused, but clearly a sign of her secrets."

And that's when I told them all to get out. I couldn't bear to see their satisfaction, the victory in their eyes as they watched me fall apart. But there was no denying it anymore.

Mirabella is *pregnant*...with another man's child.

Questions swarm in my head, each one more suffocating than the last, dragging me deeper into a hole I can't climb out of.

Mirabella and I have only been together for a handful of nights. Three times. The first night we fucked I'd used protection. The second and third times where I'd gone without bare only happened a week ago. If she suspected she was pregnant, it couldn't have been from those last two times. And if she didn't use the test right away, she must have already known.

That leaves only one possibility: *him*. Milo. The man in the pictures. The man who's now a part of this twisted mess.

How long had she been playing me? Had this always been her plan? To use me for my money, then run back to her lover the moment our marriage was over? Was that why she'd told me she was on birth control? Or had she planned to lie, to say that Milo's baby was mine? To trap me? To milk me dry until there was nothing left?

The questions flood in, relentless, each one more bitter and cutting than the last. I'd opened my heart to her. I'd *loved* her. I'd thought we had something real. I'd waited for her...

My phone buzzes in my pocket, snapping me out of my spiraling thoughts. I pull it out, barely able to focus as I see an incoming message from a client.

Get it together, Ettore, a harsh voice whispers in my ear.

And I try. I fucking try.

I manage to pick up the mess on the floor, pushing the scattered papers and files back onto my desk, trying to restore some sense of order. Then, I force myself into a scheduled online meeting. But my mind is elsewhere, lost in a fog of confusion and hurt. Twenty minutes of Skype, and I can barely remember a word anyone said. I sign the wrong documents, send the wrong emails.

I'm a damned mess.

A heavy knock echoes against the door a moment later, and before I can react, it swings open. Vittorio steps in, his eyes scanning the room with his usual confidence, but then they soften when he sees me.

"You look like shit. And why the fuck is it so dark in here?" He strides over, yanking the blinds open. The sudden light slices through the room, and I flinch, like it's burning my skin.

He walks back to the desk, sitting across from me, his gaze sharp. "I saw Zia Camilla, Francesca, and Marta leaving. What the hell's going on?"

I push the file across the table without a word, watching

as he flips it open, pulling the photos out and examining them. His brow furrows as confusion and sympathy cloud his expression. He lets out a heavy breath, then looks back at me, shaking his head.

"I don't buy this."

"What...?" I choke out, unable to keep the bitterness from my voice.

"And I'm shocked you're buying into this nonsense. You know Aunt Camila," he continues, his tone measured but firm. "She hates Mirabella. Hates being wrong even more. You know how she is."

He lifts one of the pictures between his fingers.

"This isn't what it looks like—"

My harsh laugh cuts him off before he can say whatever bullshit he was about to spew.

"I'll tell you exactly what it looks like." I snatch the picture from his hand, my finger stabbing at the faces in the frame. "This is my wife, Mirabella, kissing another man. The same man I saw her with a few weeks ago, all cozy with him. I asked her about him, and she lied to my face. Told me he was just a *friend*."

Vittorio leans back, his expression softening slightly, as though he's trying to calm the storm he sees brewing. "The picture could be taken out of context, Ettore. I'm just saying, you shouldn't be jumping to conclusions. Why don't you talk to her first?"

"Talk to her?" I snap, my voice sharper than I intend. "Why, Vittorio? So I can hear her tell me more lies? So she can look me in the eye and deny everything like she did before?"

"You're overreacting, brother."

"Oh, fuck you, Vittorio." I stand suddenly, pacing the office, feeling my frustration boil over. "What the hell do you even know? You're so high up in your happy little world, you don't see how shitty people really are. That's why I never let you get mixed up in family business. You're just a child."

"I'm a child?" He stands too, his voice biting. "Oh, please. Show me how to be an adult. A grown man like you gets handed pictures of his wife's infidelity from the same people who hate her guts, and instead of even giving her the benefit of the doubt, you go ahead and blindly believe them. Why? Because you're too afraid to look like some simp?"

"That's not—"

"No, tell me I'm wrong," he cuts me off. "Tell me this isn't about you being scared to love someone the way our father did. That in your twisted head, admitting you're a different person because of your feelings makes you weak."

"Just shut up, Vittorio," I mutter, my hands clenched at my sides. "Father's life and love for our mother have nothing to do with this."

He shakes his head slowly, disappointment in his eyes. "You're even weaker than I thought, brother. What would it cost you to just talk to her first? I'm sure she has a reasonable explanation."

His words hit harder than they should, and I let out a shaky breath, my chest tight with emotion I can't keep inside any longer. "I loved her, Vittorio. Hell, I *still* love her. I thought she loved me too. I should've seen the signs when she kept shutting me out. I thought she was just sad because of how the family treated her. I thought she was nervous, dealing with the pressure of being newly married, of all the scrutiny. I even killed for her..." My voice cracks, and I hate the weakness I can't hide.

I hate how desperate I sound.

Vittorio leans forward, his gaze steady and unwavering.

"I still don't think you know the full story. You need to talk to her. Don't let this turn into something worse than it is."

For a moment, I can't speak. His words linger in the air between us, heavy with a truth I don't want to face. But deep down, I know he's right.

I turn away from him, staring out the window at the hazy lights of the city. The early evening is already creeping in, and the thought of going home to see her only deepens the ache in my chest. "I don't want to talk about this anymore."

I hear him sigh heavily, his footsteps quiet as he leaves. Alone again, the silence presses in on me. Time drags by. As the darkness outside grows thicker, the thought of facing her grows more unbearable.

I can't go home. I can't. The thought of her touch, her voice, her smell—it's like poison. I can't stomach it today. I can't even look at her.

Without thinking, I grab my phone off the table, my fingers moving quickly across the screen as I send her a simple message:

I won't be home tonight.

The words sting, and yet, there's a strange kind of relief in sending them.

I make my way to a hotel in town, checking into a room that feels too sterile, too bright—too fucking empty. The walls are so white they almost hurt to look at. I thought being alone would give me peace, give me space to think, but it only amplifies the silence.

I sit there motionless, waiting for something to make sense, but nothing does. The world I thought I understood, the life I thought I was building, is falling apart piece by piece, and I don't know how to stop it.

35

MIRABELLA

I'm one unlucky bitch.

Why, of all days, did I have to choose today—the one day I finally planned to tell Ettore everything—for him to not come home at all? I was ready to get everything off my chest, but now I'm stuck with this secret lodged in my heart for another night. He doesn't know, and I feel like I'm drowning in it.

I wake up early, the tightness in my stomach gnawing at me. It's a weekend, so I know Ettore will come back. He always does. Whatever kept him late last night better be resolved because I need some time alone with my husband. Time to talk. Time to finally breathe.

The seconds tick by, slower than I can stand, each one scraping against me like a dull blade. The clock in the living room chimes loudly—noon—and already, the day feels as if it's stretched out forever.

My stomach twists tighter with nerves, excitement, and dread. I've worked up the courage to tell him everything, and it's all I can think about. I'm desperate to share it, to finally tell him the truth. He'll be angry, of course. He has every right to be. But he loves me. He'll forgive me. After the storm, we can start fresh.

Then, finally, I hear his car. It pulls up in front of the house, and my heart skips. I straighten up, smoothing my hair and glancing at my reflection in the hallway mirror. Paula's already rushing to the door. The moment he walks in, I can't wait any longer. I rush toward him.

"Why didn't you come home last night? I missed you," I say, throwing my arms around his waist. My voice is soft, but my chest is tight with hope, with need.

But instead of the warmth I'm expecting, there's nothing. Nothing at all. I wait for him to pull me in, to lift me up, to tell me how hard it was to be apart. I wait for the affection, the familiarity of his embrace. But nothing happens. When I pull away, he just dusts his hand over his suit jacket, barely glancing at me.

"Ettore?" I manage, my voice catching, the words sticking in my throat like they're too heavy to speak.

Without sparing me another glance, he brushes past me, walking down the hall like I'm not even there. I stand frozen, the world suddenly too quiet, too still. Paula stands there, too, looking between us, but I don't care. I follow him.

Something's wrong. Maybe it was a tough day at work. Maybe something with the project. He's been stressed about it, constantly on the phone with his lawyer, debating over things I don't even understand. But this...this is different. I can feel it in the air, thick and suffocating. Something's broken, and it's not the project. It's him. It's me.

He's mad at me.

"Are you okay?" I ask, my voice small as I follow him into our room. "Did something happen at work?" I keep my tone careful, hoping I don't push him further away. Whatever's wrong, I don't want to make it worse.

He doesn't answer. Doesn't even look at me. Instead, he takes off his jacket like I'm invisible and walks into the bathroom without a word. I stand there waiting. My heart pounds, my mind racing through all the possible reasons for this sudden coldness. What could have happened? Did I do something wrong? Does he still love me?

When he steps out of the bathroom, I move toward him, desperate for some connection. I reach out to touch his arm, but the moment my hand brushes his skin, he flinches. He actually pulls away. It feels like a slap on my face, sharp and cold.

The rejection stings deeper than I expected. My throat tightens, and I have to blink hard to hold back the tears. "Ettore, if I did something, just tell me...please." My voice cracks at the end, a rawness leaking through that I can't control.

Still nothing. He walks toward the closet, taking his time as if I'm not even in the room. I follow him, a hollow ache spreading through me. I feel so small, so foolish. I keep waiting for him to turn around, to say something—anything—to make sense of all this. But he doesn't. The silence grows louder, heavier. His back to me, like I don't even exist.

"Fine," I snap, the words coming out before I can stop them. "You're mad at me? Well, I'm mad at you too..." My voice wavers, but I stand my ground.

His movements stop, just for a second. A flicker of attention. I exhale, relieved for a moment that I've gotten through to him, that maybe—just maybe—he's finally going to say something.

"You left me all alone last night," I say, my voice barely a whisper, but it feels like a scream in my chest. I take a step forward, standing just behind him. "Do you know how cold and empty this room feels without you here?"

I move to wrap my arm around his waist, but before I can even touch him, his hand shoots out, grabbing my wrist and dropping it back to my side.

"Okay," I exhale, the breath shaky. "You're definitely mad at me. What did I do?"

He doesn't answer. He just pulls on a simple T-shirt and shorts. Then, without a word, he heads back to the bedroom. My eyes follow him, my heart hammering. I watch as he picks up his discarded jacket and pulls an envelope from the pocket, tossing it onto the bed like it's nothing.

I stare at the envelope, confusion churning inside me, but when I look back at him, he's already moving toward the door.

"Separate rooms have been arranged," he says, his voice cold and flat, like he's reading from some script. "Our one-year contract will soon be over, so this agreement will proceed exactly as planned for the remainder of the months."

Contract? Agreement?

The words don't make sense. They hit me like a punch to the gut, knocking the wind out of me.

"Ettore, what are you talking about? What exactly is going on?" I manage to croak, panic rising in my throat.

His hand twists the doorknob, and his words slice through the air. "It's what we should have done from the beginning. There's no need for pretense anymore." He doesn't even look at me when he says it.

I stand there, rooted to the spot, my mind racing, but I can't seem to move. I feel like I've been frozen in place, a statue of shock, as he walks out of the room and slams the door behind him.

What the hell just happened?

My hands are trembling as I walk toward the bed,

reaching for the envelope. I open it slowly, my fingers clumsy and unsure, and pull out the pictures inside. As I unfold them, the air seems to disappear from the room, from my lungs.

It's me. And Milo. In all of them.

Frozen moments of us, captured in these damning images—his arm around me, my head on his shoulder, his hands cupping my face, his lips brushing against mine...

Fuck. Fuck. Fuck.

My mind is spinning, questions flooding in, one after another. Who did this? Who sent these to Ettore?

Abruzzi? No, he'd stayed away since the fire, hadn't he? Maybe it's someone else...someone from the past? The person who'd set that fire?

Or maybe Ettore had Luca watch me?

But why?

No, he wouldn't. We've been in a good place lately. It doesn't add up.

For a long moment, I just stand there staring at the door. I should be angry. Furious. I should be burning with rage that Ettore could think so little of me, that he could believe this, but I feel nothing. Just emptiness. A hollow ache spreads through my chest, freezing me from the inside.

I don't know why, but I don't run after him to give him an explanation or shout the truth in his face. I won't beg him to listen. I promised myself a long time ago that I wouldn't break down over a man. I wouldn't let a man's actions pull me under. I watched my mother break apart piece by piece every time my father broke her heart, and I swore to never let myself become her.

I inhale deeply, and with trembling hands, I shove the photos back into the envelope, trying to ignore the weight of them. I toss the envelope onto the bed, as if discarding everything that I once thought we had. Then, without another thought, I rush downstairs and out of the house.

I don't look back.

My breath comes in shallow pants, each step heavier than the last as I head toward the estate gates. Just before I leave the compound, I glance back, almost against my will. I see a shadow shift behind the curtain of his home office. I know he's watching me, and it hurts. It stings more than I thought it would that he doesn't try to stop me.

The guards at the gate don't stop me. No one does. By the time I reach the end of the street, my heart is a battlefield—anger and heartbreak warring inside me. I reach the nearest bus stop, my hands shaking as I pull out my phone. I dial the one number I know will bring some sense of peace, even if it's temporary.

Alessia picks up on the second ring.

"Hey, baby boo. What's up?" Her voice is warm, cheerful, like nothing's wrong, and for a split second, I want to crumble into it.

I swallow hard, trying to keep my voice steady. "Alessia...I need a ride. Can you come pick me up?"

There's a pause on the other end, and then she speaks, her tone softer now. "Of course, Bella. Where are you? I'll be there in ten minutes."

I tell her where I am, giving the description of the spot before hanging up. I sink down onto the bench, my body shaking. I bite my lip, trying to hold the tears back. I won't cry. Not here. Not now.

Not for him.

36

ETTORE

The sound of laughter and soft jazz music drifts through the ballroom, blending with the delicate clink of champagne glasses. I don't want to be here—not at another soul-sucking charity gala that's more about flaunting power than promoting genuine goodwill.

Honestly, I don't want to be anywhere without Mirabella by my side. My arms feel hollow, aching for the weight of hers, her presence I haven't felt in days.

Still, I circulate around the room, shaking hands, offering up rehearsed smiles while my mind drifts elsewhere.

Mirabella and I barely speak anymore. Since that night, I can count the times I've seen her at the house. And when I do catch a glimpse of her—maybe chatting with Paula in the kitchen or doing yoga in the garden at dawn, by the time I decide to approach her, she's already disappeared, leaving behind only a faint lingering scent, a maddening reminder of her absence. It eats at me more than I'm willing to admit.

I'm heading to the champagne bar when I feel someone sidle up beside me. I already know who it is before he speaks—Abruzzi. The smug grin on his face is unmistakable. I don't have the patience for him tonight.

"Ettore," he calls, his voice louder than necessary, drawing the attention of a few nearby guests.

"Abruzzi," I ground out, my steps slowing. "Didn't expect to see you here."

"Why wouldn't I be here?" He laughs, a self-satisfied chuckle. "Life's been good to me. Just picked up a custom-built Maserati. Business is booming. Can't complain, man. I'm living large and giving back to the people."

I hum, barely listening. My glass is empty, and I could really use another drink.

"But you didn't expect me here because you still think I'm just some underground thug, huh?" He smirks. "Still stuck in your old ways, Ettore. I told you—I'm global now. Bigger than ever."

He spreads his arms wide like he's the king of the world, and I roll my eyes.

"I told you," he continues, lowering his voice as he steps closer. "We're cut from the same cloth, you and I. I guess that's why Mirabella's into both of us. Though, she'd rather die than admit it. She's got a thing for dangerous men, guys who would kill for her..."

His words hit me like a punch to the gut, and I see the ghost of that night we'd both shot Riccardo for her flash in my mind.

I clench my jaw. "What did I tell you about mentioning my wife's name?" I step closer to him, keeping my voice low and dangerous. "I see you haven't learned your lesson."

The smugness falters in his eyes for a split second, and I savor the sight, feeling the adrenaline surge through me at the remainder of what I did to him.

"That's funny," I mutter, stepping right into his space. "I

thought you'd be lying low after that whole drug scandal. Didn't expect to see you at an event like this."

His eyes darken, but he doesn't back down. "You're not the only one with connections, Ettore. It'll take more than a little setup to bring me down."

I smirk. "Of course, I knew that. Just messing with you."

"But here's the real question," he says, his voice dropping to a casual drawl as his gaze studies me. "Why isn't Mirabella on your arm tonight?"

I freeze, and I see that glint of satisfaction in his eyes, the same one I've seen a thousand times before.

"You usually bring her along to these things, Ettore. Then again, if I were married to Mirabella, I'd flaunt her everywhere too..." Abruzzi's voice slithers into my ear, venomous and low. My fingers curl into fists, the urge to shut him up scraping at my restraint.

"Watch your mouth," I warn, the words ice-coated, but he doesn't flinch. In fact, he leans closer, eyes gleaming with a sinister delight.

"Oh, hit a nerve, did I?" His voice drops to a murmur, the kind of mock sympathy that only serves to dig deeper. "She didn't want to come with you tonight, huh? Trouble in paradise? It was just a matter of time. She's a sharp woman, that Mirabella. Sooner or later, she'd have to see what you are. I'm glad she's finally woken up."

My chest tightens, and I want to shove him away, make him regret ever speaking those words. I want to scream that Mirabella hasn't left me, that she's at home—our home—but the truth hangs over everything like a dark cloud. The only thing keeping her there is the contract we're bound to until the end of this charade.

The silence between us is thick, charged with something I don't want to acknowledge. Abruzzi's smirk never fades. He knows exactly what he's doing, and that's the most dangerous part.

Satisfied that his words about Mirabella finally struck a nerve, Abruzzi slinks away, still wearing that insufferable smirk. The anger surges through me, a hot wave that fills every inch of my body. I ball my hands into fists, my knuckles cracking with the tension.

My blood hums, that dangerous anger simmering just below the surface. He thinks he's won. He has no idea. My mind has already shifted into something darker, colder. If he thinks he's bruised me, then he's about to understand the real cost.

I turn to Luca, who's been watching quietly nearby. A subtle nod is all it takes. He follows as I slip out through the back of the ballroom. Luca waits, his posture alert, and I take a moment, feeling the careful calculation settle over me.

"Abruzzi's car," I say, my voice steady and low. "I want it to send a message, Luca. Something he'll understand."

Luca's eyes gleam as he nods. "Understood, boss."

"Make sure he watches," I add. "No loose ends."

Luca vanishes into the night, as the air hits me sharply, cold enough to wake up the part of me that craves control. It always feels this way—when I'm about to take something back.

From my pocket, I retrieve a phone, dialing in instructions with practiced efficiency, watching the ballroom from the shadows.

Using a secure VoIP address, I'll place a call to him from a disguised number, knowing my call will appear as *Unknown* on his screen. Abruzzi might still be smiling in there, still smug, but he has no idea the clock has started ticking.

In the next twenty minutes, Luca will have everything in place. I glance down at my Rolex, each tick bringing me closer. The faint sound of laughter reaches me as I watch from across the compound. I watch as Abruzzi exits with his usual smile on his face.

At exactly 11:17, I make the call using the encrypted line. Abruzzi answers with an impatient, "Who the hell is this?"

The automated voice comes through loud and clear. "Check your ride."

A pause. I imagine his irritation fading, replaced by confusion. From my vantage point, I see him outside now, scanning for the caller, before he approaches his Maserati, his jaw tightening in annoyance. The night is so still, I can almost hear his footsteps.

Then, the silence is shattered. A flash of light, a thunderous roar that ripples through the compound, flames erupting in a fiery bloom as his car ignites.

Abruzzi is thrown back, landing hard, the heat licking at his face as he scrambles to his feet, coughing and stumbling. He watches, horrified, as the machine he boasted of just minutes ago crumbles into twisted metal, the acrid smoke billowing into the night air. His smirk is long gone, replaced by a look of pure terror as he stares at the wreckage.

In that moment, satisfaction rolls over me like a slow, dark wave. I don't have to touch him to make him bleed. And as Abruzzi gapes at the ashes of his arrogance, I step back into the shadows, a smirk edge on my lips for good measure.

It's brief, but damn, is it gratifying.

Once the damage is done, I leave, heading back home just in time for dinner. The thought of what the chef might serve doesn't even cross my mind. I'm not hungry, and honestly, I don't care. The only thing that matters is seeing her. I haven't seen Mirabella at dinner for days now. She's been eating with her family in their wing. I think about enforcing a rule that would require everyone to gather in the main dining room, but I'm not that cruel.

I know the tension between our families all too well. Pushing things any further would only make it worse. But the need to see her, even if it's just for a few minutes, is too strong to ignore. I'll crash if I don't.

The universe seems to be on my side tonight because, at dinner, she finally appears. Her head is held high as she positions herself beside Bianca and opposite Vittorio. In other words, the spot farthest from me on the table. She's wearing a gown that accentuates her curves and, annoyingly, the slight swell of her breasts. It catches my attention, and a thought claws its way to the surface, ugly and unwelcome—she's glowing because there's another man's baby inside of her.

Guilt explodes in my chest as Vittorio's words haunt me. I know I should just ask her instead of assuming, but I can't bring myself to do that.

The dinner proceeds with the sound of polite conversation filling the air. The food is served, and people dive in, murmuring around me. I steal glances at her, watching her every move. I can usually read her, feel what she's thinking just by looking into her eyes. But tonight, I can't read her. There's a distance in her gaze, a coldness that I can't shake off. It boils something inside of me, an anger that I try to suppress but can't.

My breath hitches when our eyes meet, but the indifference in hers nearly knocks the wind out of me. She barely acknowledges me before turning her attention back to her plate. It's as if I don't even exist to her anymore.

As dinner drags on, the tension in the room grows

thicker. My aunts, my cousins—they're all watching, flicking nervous glances between me and Mirabella. It's obvious to anyone with a pulse.

"You haven't come down to dinner in days, Mirabella," Zia Camila begins with a forced smile on her face. "Is everything okay?"

"Why wouldn't everything be okay?" Mirabella replies, her voice cool as she takes another sip of juice.

"Tell me," Aunt Camila presses, her eyes flickering between us. "Is everything all right? Are you...ill?"

Aunt Camilla is edging her on, and even though I hate it, I won't interfere. A part of me wants to see how this unfolds and if Mirabella's expression or words will give anything away. But the other part of me admires the unbothered calm she maintains.

""I'm sure nothing stays hidden for long when it comes to you, Zia," Mirabella shoots back, her smile as cold as ice. "Besides, if I were sick, your nephew would've arranged for me to see the family doctor."

Your nephew.

Not *Ettore*.

Not *my husband*.

Your nephew.

I swallow the lump in my throat, feeling my chest tighten.

"If you all would excuse me." With an exaggerated politeness, she smiles at everyone in the room *except* me before standing and gliding out without a second glance.

I grit my teeth. The tension crackles in the air. Everyone at the table knows something's wrong. But I don't care. I don't care if they're all watching.

I stand up so abruptly my chair screeches across the floor, and I storm after her, my heart pounding in my ears.

Her footsteps echo in the stillness, but mine are louder as I follow her up the stairs.

"Mirabella," I call out, my voice sharper than I intended. She's heading for the guest room—the one she stayed in when she first moved in here, the room where it all started to go wrong.

She freezes mid-step but doesn't look back. She's waiting, her back straight, shoulders tense, and I can see the way her fingers clench by her sides.

"I think we need to talk."

She turns slowly, her eyes meeting mine, but there's nothing in them. No remorse. No fear. Just that damned unreadable mask she's gotten so good at wearing.

"Do we?" she responds, her voice dripping with sarcasm. "Because, as far as I'm concerned, you made it pretty clear there's nothing left to discuss."

"That's not for you to decide," I snap, my voice low but steady. "You don't get to walk away from this. You don't get to act like the victim when *you're* the one who cheated."

Her jaw clenches, her eyes narrowing, and she shoots me a look that could kill. "I didn't cheat on you."

I let out a bitter laugh, a sound that doesn't reach my eyes. "Do you think I'm stupid, Mirabella? Do you really think I'll believe your lies anymore? Did you think I wouldn't find out?" My voice cracks, and I hate how much it betrays me, but I'm too far gone now.

"If you're so sure of what you think you know, then why are you even here?" Her voice is venom, but the cracks are there. I can hear it. She's losing control, too.

"Because I *need* to hear it from you," I say, stepping closer, my chest tightening. "I need to hear why you did it."

She presses her lips together, holding something back. "I didn't cheat—"

"So the pictures were fake, then? You didn't kiss Milo?" I spit the words at her, each one like a slap.

"Milo kissed me," she says through gritted teeth.

I feel the heat rise in my chest. "Oh, *so* that's how it was? He kissed you, but you didn't kiss him back?" I almost choke on the bitterness. "Did he *force* you to kiss him? Did he force you to cry in his arms while he wiped your tears away?"

"I didn't expect him to kiss me. I didn't want him to kiss me--"

The words come out sharper than I mean them to, but I can't stop. "Tell me, Mirabella, did you cry about how awful it is being married to me? Did you cry because you couldn't wait for it to end so you could go back to him?"

She recoils, but the damage is already done. "What the hell are you talking about?" she scoffs, her face a mixture of confusion and something darker I can't place. "You're insane."

"I guess Zia Camilla was right after all," I mutter, the words tasting like acid in my mouth. "You're nothing but a gold-digging slut."

Her eyes flash with fury. For a split second, I think she's going to strike me, her hand raised in a blur of motion. But before she can, I catch her wrist in mid-air, gripping it tight and pushing her back against the wall.

She gasps, trying to yank her arm free, but I don't let go. My heart's hammering in my chest, every muscle in my body rigid with a mix of rage and something darker.

"You haven't learned a damned thing, have you?" I growl, my voice rough, barely under control. My body presses against hers, and I can feel the heat of her skin, the rapid beat of her pulse against my fingers.

"Fuck you," she hisses through clenched teeth, her eyes blazing.

I feel a surge of something—anger, frustration, raw desire—all of it coursing through me. Without thinking, I lean down, grabbing her by the neck, and claim her lips in a kiss that burns with everything I can't say.

She doesn't kiss me back at first. Her lips are stiff, unyielding, but as the seconds stretch on, I feel her body betray her, her lips softening under mine.

And I hate myself for it. I hate that this feels like *anything* other than what it should be—a final goodbye. But I can't stop. Not now.

She groans as she slides the palm of her hands up my chest to push me away. But I deepen the kiss, grabbing her jaw while my thumb strokes the curve of her cheekbone. My other hand cups the back of her head to keep her in place while I devour her mouth. She lets out a soft moan before snaking her arms around my neck so she can pull us closer together.

"I can't believe you did this to me." My hand slips under her dress while I drag my lips to her neck. "To us."

She moans again when I bite down just below her ear and grind my erection against her stomach. She gasps when I slip my fingers inside her panties and tease the tip with my thumb.

"Did he touch you like this?" I grit my teeth as my thumb flicks over her clit. She lets out a sound between a groan and a whimper, arching her hips involuntarily towards me.

A hot, white rage sears through me at the thought of the other man even laying a finger on her, the image of her in his arms—moaning his name—enough to push me to the edge.

"I'll kill him tonight," I growl, lips tracing her neck with a hard, possessive intent.

"Ettore, please..." Her voice trembles, and I feel the

slightest tension in her body. I press myself further against her, making sure there's nowhere for her to go, no escaping my hold.

"Oh, I already have men waiting to take me straight to his door," I say, each word dripping with menace. "But first, I'll take what's mine—one last time—before I get you out of my system," I spit. "Because that's exactly what you deserve."

37

MIRABELLA

Ettore's harsh words snap me out of the haze I've been drowning in, the fog of lust and confusion that clouded my mind. My wrist jerks from his grasp, and I shove him away with every ounce of strength in me, my body trembling with rage.

"I'm done, Ettore! Do you hear me? DONE!" I scream, not caring if the whole house hears. The words explode out of me, raw and broken. "I never want to see your face again. Not you. Not your family. None of this mess. I'll get my family out of here. We are DONE!"

He steps toward me, his jaw clenched tight, eyes narrowing with something dark and unyielding. His suffocating presence looms over me.

"Oh, I'll like to see you try. You know that's not possible, Mirabella," he says coldly, his voice like steel. "You signed a contract. Legally, you belong to me. You can't leave me."

His words hit me like a punch to the gut. *Belong.* Like I'm nothing but some object he purchased. A thing he can possess.

"I don't give a damn about your fucking contract," I spit, my voice shaking with fury.

The memory of his words stabs through me. *You're nothing but a gold-digging slut!* They replay in my mind like a cruel loop, making my heart ache, my chest tightening so much it's hard to breathe.

"You can go to hell with whatever favors you think you've offered me," I shout, the bitterness rising in my throat. "Keep your protection. Keep your money. I'd rather work my ass off for every single cent than stay in this hellhole you've made. And I'll pay you back for every penny you've spent on me—so you don't have to worry."

"Bella..." His voice cracks, but I don't want to hear it.

I turn to leave, not wanting to listen to the twisted logic or manipulative tactics he'll use to reel me back in. His footsteps pound behind me, relentless, and his voice cuts through the silence like a knife.

"Mirabella, stop! You're not being reasonable. Don't do something you'll regret just because you're mad..."

"I don't give a damn!" I yell, my voice a raw scream that echoes off the walls. I don't care if anyone hears me. This is it.

"You're being selfish!" He's right behind me now, his voice gaining ground as I storm past the living room, where our families sit, watching the storm unfold. They're silent, but I can feel their eyes burning into me, their judgment weighing me down as I march into the vast, cold lobby.

"Think about your family! Think about the risk you're putting them in if you leave this house. Think about your mother—"

"You sick, manipulative bastard!" The words hiss out of me like poison, and as he reaches for me, I duck away, twisting in a blur of motion. I spin back around and hiss in his face. "Don't you *ever* try to use my family against me again."

"You are making a big mistake!" He says through gritted teeth.

His eyes are sharp, panicked, and I sense a hidden emotion beneath the green-brown orbs. His long hair looks wild from running his fingers through them in frustration. He looks.. broken and devastated, and his usual hard, mafia-like mask is gone. Not like a man who just threatened—no, promised—to kill a man just a few minutes ago. That makes my blood boil even hotter.

"The only mistake I made was marrying you in the first place," I spit through clenched teeth, holding back the tears that threaten to spill from my eyes.

"Let's talk about this..."

His voice is desperate now. But I can't listen anymore. His words blur into nothing, drowned out by the pounding of my heart, the suffocating pressure in my chest.

I can't stand this. I can't stand him.

I turn and break into a run, my footsteps loud against the marble floor, the sound echoing down the hall. A tear slips down my cheek. Then another. And another. Until I'm sobbing, unable to stop it. I don't care anymore. I just need to get out. I need to escape this cage.

"Mirabella!" His voice cracks with panic, his steps growing closer, faster. "Stop! Please, just listen..."

I don't stop. I push open the heavy door and step out into the cool night air, hoping the chill will somehow cool the fire inside me. It doesn't. My breath comes in shallow, frantic gasps, and I move faster, desperate to get away.

I hear him behind me, his footsteps closing in. He's not letting me go—not without a fight. His heavy, desperate footfalls are chasing me, echoing through the night.

I have to get to the estate gate. This thought is the only thing that matters now, the only thing driving me forward as I push through the compound. My mind is consumed with the need to escape, to break free from this nightmare. I don't hear the screeching sound, don't see the movement to my left until it's too late.

"Mirabella, watch out!" Ettore's voice rips through the air, panic-laced and urgent.

I spin around, but everything happens in an instant. A motorcycle rounds the corner, headlights blinding, too fast, too close. I freeze—caught between shock and terror, unable to move. Before I can react, the world erupts in pain. The sharp, brutal impact of thick metal slamming into my body sends a wave of searing agony through me. I'm thrown back, my body weightless for a moment before crashing to the ground.

The world tilts, spins, and the blinding pain in my head makes everything go hazy. My body crumples against the cold, unforgiving pavement. My skull aches with a sharp, pulsing throb that feels as if it's going to split me in two. I try to move, to get up, but the pain locks me in place, leaving me helpless.

My baby...

The thought pierces through the fog of pain, sharper than anything else. The fear clutches my chest.

Somewhere, distantly, I hear Ettore shouting, his voice breaking, frantic. His footsteps are heavy, pounding against the ground as he rushes toward me. When his hands finally reach me, they tremble as they cup my face, warm but shaking.

"Bella," he breathes, his voice raw with desperation. "Fuck! Stay with me. Please, stay with me."

I try to speak. I try to say something, anything, but the

words get stuck in my throat. All I can think of is the dull, gnawing fear spreading through my body like a cold weight.

My baby. Our baby.

My hand moves on its own to cradle my stomach, the small, reassuring gesture almost too much for me to manage. Through the haze, I hear his voice again—panicked, wild—giving orders, yelling for help. The commotion around me is a blur, but his voice cuts through it all, unsteady, frantic.

I hear his heartbeat, rapid and unrelenting, pounding against my ear as he lifts me, cradling me against his chest.

My head is a blur of pain, my body heavy, and my eyes, oh God, my eyes—so tired.

"Bella!" Ettore's voice hisses, fierce and broken. His grip tightens on my face, his hands almost too firm, but I can't feel anything except the agony, of everything slipping away. "Don't you fucking leave me. Stay with me...please!"

I try. I force my eyes to stay open, to stay with him, but it's too much. The pain pulls me under. The seconds stretch into eternity, each one heavier than the last. I can barely keep my eyes open now.

"Our baby," I manage to whisper, the last of my strength draining out of me.

And then, without warning, everything fades—my vision goes dark, my body still—and I let go.

Everything goes black.

38

ETTORE

Don't leave me, Mirabella. Don't you fucking leave me.

The words beat in my head, relentless, like a drum I can't escape. I run toward the waiting car, my wife unconscious in my arms. Her limp body presses against mine, and I hold her as if she's the last thing tethering me to reality, the last breath of fresh air in a world that's drowning.

My world is drowning.

Her hair brushes against my neck, soft and familiar, but it feels like a ghost against my skin. I press my lips to her temple, whispering things I don't even hear, my heart pounding too loudly to make sense of the words.

"Please," I choke out. "I'm sorry...please, Mirabella. Just stay with me."

Her lashes tremble, but her eyes stay closed. Her skin is too pale, and the bruise already forming on her jaw—so dark, so wrong—makes my stomach churn. I see her family and mine standing in the distance, their faces frozen in shock and fear. Nonna's voice rings out, frantic, echoing into the night, but I don't hear her, nr the way Isabella clutches Giulia in her arms while they both sob.

I don't hear anything except the urgent thud of my own heartbeat, the cold pressure of her body in my arms.

All I can think is *I need to get her to a hospital. I need her to wake up. I need her to live.*

I climb into the back seat, holding her tight against me, cradling her like a fragile thing. Luca slams the car into gear and speeds through the streets, weaving between traffic with a ferocity that borders on madness. The world blurs around us—lights, shadows, the low hum of the city. My pulse races, a wild, desperate thing beating against the confines of my chest.

My hands are firmly clutching Mirabella's cold ones as she lies in my arms. The way she never squeezes back when I squeeze her, the way her cold skin feels against mine, sends me into a fit of panic that I try to keep on a leash.

I've never felt anything like this before. This panic, this horror, this *fear*.

Is this what love truly feels like? How could something so sweet and wholesome, something that made my heart full in ways I'd never experienced, something that made me feel more alive than I have ever felt in my thirty-two years of living, be the same thing that digs painfully into my spine, the same thing that spreads like acid in the pit of my stomach, the same thing that makes the air thinner and thinner as I struggle to breathe?

I've faced enemies, betrayals, gunfire, but this... this feeling of complete helplessness is more terrifying than any bullet. I take lives and let people live, yet I can't do anything to save the woman I love.

Seventeen minutes, forty seconds.

That's how long we've spent so far in the literal hell that

is this drive. As every second drags on, heavy and relentless, like a countdown. I want to scream, to punch something, anything, to let out the storm raging inside me. Guilt gnaws at me, sharper than any knife, twisting in my gut.

It's all my fault.

The thought claws at me, relentless. If only...if only I'd said something else, done something different. If I hadn't let my anger make me say things that cut deeper than I realized.

You got exactly what you wanted, you monster.

I run my thumb across her cheek, a trembling gesture, desperate. I need her to open her eyes. To scream at me, to hate me. Anything.

Just don't let her slip away. Not like this. Not because of me.

I keep touching her with the same hands that have spilled blood, the hands that don't deserve to be anywhere near her tonight. But I can't stop. Maybe—maybe if I keep touching her, she'll come back to me.

"Stay with me, *amore*," I beg, my voice cracking, raw. "Don't you dare leave me. Not now. Not ever."

Nineteen minutes, two seconds.

The hospital looms ahead, its bright lights cutting through the night like a beacon. As the car screeches to a stop outside the emergency entrance, I burst through the doors, my voice raw and frantic as I shout for help.

"Please, someone! Help us!"

My words are a desperate scream, but I don't care. I can barely hear myself over the pounding of my heart. In seconds, medical staff rush forward with a stretcher, an oxygen mask, and a portable oxygen tank. For the first time in the last torturous twenty minutes, I am forced to let her go.

They take her from my arms, and I feel the cold emptiness of my hands. Her limp body is transferred to the stretcher, and they wheel her away from me, urgency in every step they take. I want to scream, to chase them, but I can't. My legs feel like lead as I stagger after them.

They push her through double doors, and I try to follow, but two nurses block my way.

"I'm sorry, sir, but you can't go in—"

"You'll be sorry if you don't let me in," I growl, the words slipping out before I can stop them. But before I can move, Luca's grip is on my shoulder, firm and unyielding.

"Boss," he says quietly, but there's an edge to his voice. For the first time since he started working for me, I hear the emotion there.

"Let me go," I snarl, struggling against his hold, my voice cracking with the weight of it all. "I need to be with her."

Just then, I hear footsteps behind me—heavy, measured steps. I turn, and my heart drops when I see Vittorio, flanked by Isabella, Giulia, Nonna, Aunt Francesca, and Zia Camilla.

Isabella crumples into sobs, her body trembling as Giulia holds her hand tightly. Nonna stands rigid, fury and pain radiating from her like heat. Her eyes lock onto me, full of accusation, and the sight of their grief twists the knife in my chest.

But none of that matters. Not right now. My entire world has narrowed down to Mirabella. She's the only thing I can think about. She's all that matters.

Three minutes and twenty seconds.

That's how long I've been pacing in this sterile, cold waiting room. The fluorescent lights buzz above, casting harsh shadows on the white tiles beneath my restless feet. I can't sit still. Every step I take is another echo of my heartbeat, and it feels like I'm suffocating in here.

The tension in the room is enough to choke on.

Isabella and Giulia have stopped crying, but their eyes are swollen, red. Nonna sits, her hands folded tightly in her lap, her gaze searing into me every time I pass by. Vittorio stands at the side, his jaw clenched, his body rigid. He hasn't said a word to me—not even a small gesture of comfort. I know he's angry, maybe even disgusted by me.

I should have listened to him. I should have talked to her, not thrown insults at her.

Please. Let her be okay. Just let her and the baby—

My fists clench at the thought, and I force my eyes shut. I can't think about that. I won't. It doesn't matter if the child is mine or not. It should matter, but right now, nothing does except Mirabella.

Then, I feel the soft scent of jasmine perfume behind me. I turn, and Zia Camilla is standing there, her expression tight, lips pressed into a firm line. She gives me that look, the one that only makes my rage boil hotter.

"Ettore," she starts, her voice too soft, too calm. "You need to calm down. Mirabella will be fine. Your pacing around here isn't helping anyone. You've done enough. Let the professionals take care of her."

My hands curl into fists at my sides. Before I realize it, I've grabbed her arm, my grip hard and unrelenting. "You either go back home and the get fuck out my face or keep your fucking mouth shut," I spit out, my voice low and dangerous.

Zia's eyes widen slightly at my tone, but she doesn't argue. She winces when I release her, running a hand through my hair in frustration.

"Mr. Greco?" A firm voice cuts through the tension.

My heart lurches in my chest. I turn to see a tall woman

in teal scrubs, her stethoscope around her neck, her expression unreadable but kind.

"How is she?" I choke out, stepping toward her, my feet moving before my mind can catch up. "How is my Mirabella?"

The doctor's professional gaze softens, just a fraction. "She's stable. A slight concussion, but nothing life-threatening. She'll need to rest and be monitored, but she's going to be fine."

Fine. The word barely registers. I stand there, frozen, as a wave of relief crashes over me, but it's still not enough to ease the tight knot in my chest. Mirabella's not out of the woods, not yet. But for the first time in hours, I can breathe again.

I try to steady myself, but the doctor adds more words that freeze me in place.

"And," she says, glancing down at her clipboard, "we'll also be keeping a close eye on her pregnancy."

A soft gasp ripples through the room, and I turn, my eyes catching Mirabella's family as their faces fall into stunned silence. They didn't know.

"Mirabella is pregnant?" Isabella's voice cracks, barely a whisper, but the weight of it lands hard in the room.

The doctor looks between us, gauging the atmosphere, and responds carefully, "Yes. She's approximately eight weeks along. The baby appears healthy, though we'll need to conduct further tests to confirm."

I pause, the shock pulsing through me. I couldn't have heard her correctly.

"I'm sorry, what did you just say?" I demand, struggling to keep my voice steady. "How far along is she?"

The doctor meets my gaze, calm and unflinching, as if she's dealt with this reaction before. "I said she's about eight weeks along. Despite her condition, she kept repeating the words 'my baby,' so we conducted a check. I'm pleased to tell you that no harm has come to the pregnancy. Once she's stabilized, we'll proceed with more tests to ensure everything is progressing well."

Eight weeks. My mind spirals, calculating the timing. Eight weeks ago... That was before everything, before the pictures, before the lies, before the betrayals. It was a time when it was just us—she and I, tangled in a storm of rain and passion, no secrets, no doubts.

Before I took her virginity. Her innocence.

Before I fucked everything up.

The world tilts, and I stagger back, my legs suddenly weak. I grab the back of a chair, trying to steady myself, but everything feels like it's slipping out of my control. *The baby is mine.* The thought hits me like a punch to the gut. I can't—*I can't*—believe it. Eight weeks, and there's no way...

"Thank you, doctor," I hear someone say—Vittorio, maybe Nonna—but their words fade into the background, a blur of sound.

As soon as the doctor leaves, Nonna is on me, her fury a blazing fire. She rushes toward me, her face twisted with disgust. "You devil," she spits, her voice trembling with righteous anger. "You knew she was carrying your child, and yet you did this to her! You and your demonic family will pay for this!"

The room goes quiet, the weight of her words sinking into my skin. My aunts look pale, guilt written across their faces, and even Vittorio stands still, stunned. But none of it registers. Not the accusations, not the looks. My mind is consumed with one, overwhelming thought.

The baby is mine.

The realization hits me like a freight train, bringing with

it a storm of emotions—relief, guilt, love, and a fear so raw it grips my heart. The anger I threw at her, the accusations I hurled without even listening—*I did this*. I refused to hear her, to trust her, and now...now the woman I love, the mother of my child, is in a hospital bed, fighting for her life because of me.

Shame and anger crash into me, suffocating, drowning me. How could I have let this happen?

I force myself to breathe, my fists clenched so tightly that my nails bite into my palms. The guilt and anger churn inside me, unbearable. But nothing is worse than the suffocating realization that I've lost control of everything.

"Once Mirabella is well, once she's out of here, I will never let her anywhere near you or your family again," Nonna spits, her words laced with venom.

Her words sting. But so do the accusing gazes of Isabella, Giulia, and Vittorio.

I don't respond. I can't. The weight of their fury, their disappointment—it's too much to bear. Without a word, I turn on my heel and storm out of the waiting room. My chest is tight, my mind a storm of guilt, confusion, and raw anger. But as I walk, a dark, violent thought rises.

Milo.

This is his fault as well as mine.

It's time to deliver punishment accordingly.

Minutes later, the chaos inside me settles into a sickening calm, the anger now cold, like a winter frost. My legs carry me through the halls, but I don't even register where I'm going until I'm standing in front of his door.

I push it open slowly, the hinges creaking in the quiet of the night. The moonlight streams through his drawn blinds, casting long shadows across his sleeping form.

In my hand, I grip the gun, knuckles white. My finger hovers over the trigger.

Rage bubbles beneath the surface. Killing him would be so easy, so satisfying—every inch of me wants it. But...

It won't bring Mirabella back to me. It won't make her forgive me. It won't change anything.

But it will ease the gnawing rage and guilt, even if it's just for a moment. I press my finger to the trigger, the gunshot ringing out, the sound shattering the quiet like a crack in the world.

39

MIRABELLA

A harsh light seeps through my eyelids, pulling me from the depths of unconsciousness.

My mind stirs, groggy, reluctant, as I hover between awareness and the lingering darkness. I want to groan, but the sound catches somewhere in my throat, refusing to rise.

I can't move.

My mind is awake, foggy and blurred, yet my body feels pinned down—heavy, sore, and unresponsive.

Eventually, my eyes peel open, squinting against the glare from a harsh overhead bulb. The blinding brightness forces me to blink rapidly until the sterile white of a hospital room sharpens into focus.

The pungent scent of antiseptic and the soft, rhythmic hum of machines press in around me, and a dull throb pulses at the back of my skull.

I slowly turn my head, muscles stiff and resistant, until my gaze lands on a familiar figure slouched in the chair beside me. Ettore. Memories start filtering back in.

Dinner, the argument that came afterward, the door slamming behind me as I stormed out.

I was leaving him.

Determined.

And yet here I am, with the very man I'd been desperate to escape, hovering like a shadow.

I guess the universe was strongly against that because why am I here with said man whose presence makes my heart clench painfully with the cutting words he'd said earlier.

The man I love.

For a long, silent moment, I just watch him. He's still wearing last night's clothes—a T-shirt and sweatpants, wrinkled and clinging to his form. His hair, long and slightly wild, falls messily over his face, covering tired, hollowed eyes. He looks as if he hasn't slept in days, his jaw shadowed with dark stubble that's grown thick. There's a weariness about him, a weight that makes his strong features look somehow...fragile. As if he's aged overnight.

With effort, I shift, inching up in bed, and the subtle rustling is enough to rouse him. His eyes snap open, instantly locking onto mine. Relief floods his expression, as if the weight of the world has been lifted from him in that single, painful moment. He straightens quickly, jerking upright in the chair. His hands twitch, reaching for me, then faltering, dropping uselessly to his sides.

"Mirabella," he whispers, his voice rough. "You're awake." His words crack around the edges, and the sound twists something deep in my chest.

He exhales sharply, and despite himself, reaches forward, his fingers brushing the edge of my cheek. "How are you feeling? Are you...in pain? The doctor said you have a concussion. Does your head hurt?"

I flinch, instinctively pulling away from his touch. His hand freezes, a flicker of hurt crossing his face, but he tries to hide it. "I'm fine," I rasp, though we both know it's far from true.

His gaze sweeps over me, lingering on my face as if he's trying to memorize every detail, every line. "You scared me," he murmurs, so softly it's almost a confession. "You have no idea how frightened I was."

His vulnerability pricks at my resolve, stirring something that wants to soften, but I shove the feeling down. His concern is touching, but it doesn't erase what's been said, what's been broken between us. "You don't have to be here," I manage, forcing my voice to stay steady, even though my heart pounds erratically.

His face falls, the color draining as if I've slapped him. He looks shattered, his mouth opening and closing as he struggles to find words.

"Bella...I'm sorry," he says, voice trembling. "I'm so sorry. I know I can't take back what I said. I know I can't fix everything with just words." He swallows hard, the rawness of his regret bleeding into his tone. "But please, just tell me what I can do to make this right."

I take a deep breath, swallowing down the ache in my chest. "Leave," I say softly, the single syllable dragging out painfully.

He doesn't flinch this time. He just stares at me, jaw tightening as though bracing for a storm. "I'm not going anywhere," he says, his voice firm, unwavering. "I'm going to fix this."

I turn my head, refusing to let him see the cracks that are starting to show. "Fix this?" I repeat, disbelief lacing my words. "Do you even realize what your actions have cost us? What they've done to us?" My voice trembles with emotions

I can't quite contain. Fear, anger, uncertainty—everything floods over me again.

Ettore's fists clench, his shoulders stiffening as he looks away. "I know I've hurt you," he admits, his voice barely a whisper. "I made a terrible mistake. But I swear, I'll make things right."

I scoff, the bitterness in my words coming out sharper than I intend. "Make it right? You think your apologies can undo everything that's happened? Can you just erase the things you said to me? Pretend none of it ever happened?"

I see the hurt flash in his eyes, but I can't bring myself to care. Not now. Not after everything.

"You wouldn't believe me when I tried to tell you the truth," I continue, the words spilling out before I can stop them. "You accused me of cheating. You called me a gold-digging whore." My chest tightens at the memory, and I clutch my hand over my heart, trying to soothe the pain inside me.

His face twists in pain, and I want to stop—want to reach out and tell him I don't mean it, that the anger is just the aftermath of everything that's broken between us. But I can't. I can't let him off the hook this time.

Ettore's eyes follow my every movement, his gaze locked on me with an intensity that feels almost suffocating. With each subtle shift, I can feel the weight of his broken heart pressing down on me.

When his eyes snap back to mine, something shifts in his expression. There's a flicker of something dark and desperate beneath the pain, and for a moment, I wonder if it's regret or anger—or maybe both. "I know I can't fix everything I've said and done," he says, his voice low, the words slow and deliberate. "But I'll do whatever it takes." His sincerity is so raw, it almost terrifies me.

I can hear the desperation in his voice, as if he's teetering on the edge of something real, and it's almost enough to pull me in. Almost.

But a part of me—maybe the part that's been hurt too many times—won't let me believe him. It won't let me trust that things could be different. I can't be the kind of woman who keeps accepting this, who keeps allowing a man to hurt her only to promise change when it's already too late.

The silence between us stretches out, until the door creaks open, breaking the tension. The doctor steps in, her face a mask of calm professionalism, clipboard in hand. She's wearing light blue scrubs, and she gives me a polite, practiced smile.

"Good morning, Mrs. Greco. I see you're awake now. How are you feeling?" Her voice is calm, almost soothing, but I can't focus on anything but the tightness in my chest.

I sit up a little straighter, suddenly aware of the exhaustion in my limbs, and the sharp ache that still lingers in my head.

"How is my baby?" I blurt, unable to stop myself. The words spill out before I even process them, and I can feel Ettore's eyes boring into me as if he's hanging on every syllable.

The doctor's smile widens, and for a moment, I think I can finally breathe. "Your baby is okay, Mrs. Greco. We still need to perform another checkup before you're discharged, but everything looks good for now."

From Ettore's expression, I know he's already been told the details of my condition. I don't know how to feel about that, and honestly, part of me doesn't want to know. If he thinks I cheated on him, then...no.

Don't think about it.

The doctor moves through her questions with a brisk

efficiency. I answer her, but my mind keeps drifting back to Ettore—the man sitting so close yet feeling like a lifetime away. He asks about how long I'll need to stay in the hospital, what I'll need for a speedy recovery, and when I'll need to come in for checkups because of the baby. The questions are well-meaning, but they make my skin crawl.

I stop myself from scoffing when he asks about the frequency of checkups. The last thing I want is for him to be involved in any of it.

When the doctor finishes, she gives me a quick nod, her expression satisfied. "Everything looks good for now," she says. "I'll check back in later." With that, she steps out, leaving the two of us alone again.

The silence returns, I can feel Ettore's gaze on me, and it burns. My hands clench around the thin hospital blanket, my chest tight, but I force myself to speak. "I'm not going back to your house," I say quietly. "When my family comes, I'm leaving with them."

Ettore's jaw clenches, his eyes darkening. "You're not leaving me," he says, his voice dangerously low. "Especially not now. You're carrying my child."

His words freeze me in place, my breath catching. "How did you know?"

"The doctor told me how far along you are. It wasn't hard to figure out," he replies, his gaze unwavering.

"I see."

He leans forward, frustration flashing across his face. "Why didn't you tell me? It's my baby too, Bella. I had a right to know."

"Like you would have listened?" I say bitterly.

"Of course, I would have," he argues, but I can't help but scoff.

"Oh, like you did the last time?"

"Bella—"

"My name is Mirabella," I snap. "And I don't want to talk about this anymore. It doesn't change anything. You didn't listen to me before, so don't pretend to now."

His shoulders sag slightly, and he rubs a hand over his face, as though he's trying to steady himself. "I didn't mean for things to get so out of control. I overreacted—I know that. But you can't shut me out now. I would have kept you safe..."

But he doesn't see it. The possessiveness in his tone, the way he's already claiming this pregnancy as if it validates every hurtful word, every dismissal. I ignore the way my heart stutters, my pulse quickening against my will. He's drawing a line, laying claim, as if it justifies everything.

"Safe?" I laugh bitterly, the sound harsh in the quiet room. "I was supposed to be safe with you, Ettore. You promised me safety but look where that got me." My throat tightens, and I fight back the tears threatening to spill. "Just another thing you've failed at. I can't...I can't do this anymore."

The guilt in his eyes is unbearable, and for a fleeting moment, I almost feel sorry for him. I can see how deeply it's eating at him. But those feelings get swallowed by the weight of what he's done. His pain doesn't erase mine.

"Please," he says, the word strangled in his throat, raw with desperation. "Don't push me away. We can work through this."

Before I can answer, the door bursts open, and my family floods in, their presence a wave of warmth and relief. I exhale, feeling the tightness in my chest loosen just a little when I see Nonna, Mamma, and Giulia rushing toward me.

I exhale deeply, the tightness in my chest loosening just a little as they surround me, their hands gently touching my shoulders, my arms, grounding me. For the first time since waking, I feel a sliver of relief, a sense of belonging that Ettore's presence can't provide.

"You're okay." Mamma sniffles, tears already in her eyes. "You're alive."

I hate seeing her like this—hating that I've put her through this, that she's had to worry like this. Nonna's eyes are red-rimmed, filled with concern as she takes both of my hands in hers, her grip tight, trembling.

"Thank God you're okay, *Mia Piccola*!" she breathes. The relief in her voice is enough to make me feel grounded for a second. But then, her gaze shifts to Ettore, and that relief turns to something much darker.

"This is all your fault," she spits, her voice shaking with fury. "And I swear to God, once we leave here, you'll never see her again." Her words hang in the air, heavy with threat, as if she could crush him with them. And maybe, just maybe, she could.

"You won't take her from me," Ettore says, his voice eerily calm but taut with an edge of something I can't quite place.

"I told you I'll be going back to my family." I cut him off, my words firm. "That's not up for negotiation."

He holds my gaze for a long beat, eyes dark and unreadable, but I don't flinch. I won't. I stare right back, daring him to challenge me, to say anything that might make me second-guess myself.

I wish things were different. I wish we could have the kind of love I've always dreamed of. But we're too broken. We come from different worlds.

Ettore doesn't argue, though. He simply stands, takes one last look at me and walks out. The door clicks softly behind him, and I let out a long, shaky breath.

I spend the next few minutes in silence with my family. Their presence is a soothing balm through everything. Mamma is quieter now, her eyes red from crying, but her fingers never leave mine. Nonna sits by my side, as though guarding me, and Giulia hovers at the edge of the bed, her gaze flicking nervously from me to the door.

When I feel exhaustion creeping back in, my family insists I rest. I let them go, sinking back into the bed, my body too tired to protest, too worn to fight.

The next morning, I open my eyes to find Ettore entering my room. It feels oddly like yesterday, only this time, his gaze is unwavering, full of an intensity that pins me in place as he sits by my bedside.

He tells me he's here to go over the results with the doctor, and despite my immediate resistance, he stands his ground, challenging me with a fierceness I haven't seen in a long time. After a short, quiet debate, I reluctantly let him stay. Silence settles between us as we wait, both bracing for what's to come.

Minutes later, the doctor walks in, her expression noticeably more serious. My pulse quickens, a cold knot of dread forming in my stomach.

"Mrs. Greco," she begins, "How are you feeling today?"

"Much better, doctor," I reply, barely keeping my voice steady. "What did the results say?"

She glances at Ettore, then back at me, her tone gentle yet firm. "I have some news. We did another ultrasound...and we found two heartbeats. It appears you're expecting twins."

The air leaves my lungs. I'm frozen, struggling to process what she just said. Ettore's hand closes over mine, and for once, I don't pull away. His grip tightens, grounding me as I try to comprehend the reality of twins—*two heartbeats*.

The word echoes in my mind, reshaping everything in a single, overwhelming moment.

I glance over at Ettore. His face has gone pale, his eyes wide with shock, but there's something else there too—a flicker of awe, of quiet, unguarded hope. For a brief moment, I want to soak it in, to let myself feel that fragile, tentative joy alongside him.

But deep down, I know the truth hasn't changed. I'm leaving him.

This miracle doesn't erase the pain, the history, or the broken pieces of us. So I hold his hand a moment longer, then gently let go, feeling the weight of the decision I've already made settle even deeper.

40

ETTORE

Four weeks. Twenty-eight days. Forty thousand, three hundred and twenty minutes.

That's how long it's been since Mirabella walked out of my life.

I miss her. Terribly. More than words can express.

Every second without her is torture. I miss the sound of her voice, the warmth of her presence, the way she laughs—so light, so easy.

I miss waking up with her beside me, feeling the soft rise and fall of her breath as she sleeps. I miss falling asleep with her in my arms, her hair tangled around my fingers.

Every moment since she left feels like it's dragging me further into this endless pit. And today, I decide I've had enough. I can't stand the emptiness anymore.

The afternoon sun is fading as I park in front of the sleek glass tower where she works. Global Hope Initiative. It's an NGO dedicated to providing educational resources and support to underprivileged helping children in war zones, disaster-stricken areas—places that would break your heart if you let them.

Mirabella's not just working here to build a resume for her future career in international relations—she's here because this is the kind of person she is—someone who wants to make the world a better place

When I heard she applied for this internship, I couldn't let it go. I pulled strings, called in favors, did whatever it took to make sure she got the job. The CEO owed me a big one—he'd taken a donation from one of my foundations—and though I promised myself I wouldn't meddle in her life again, I couldn't stop myself.

Mirabella has always been too proud to ask for help. And now, as much as she'll hate me when she finds out, I can't stand the thought of her struggling more than she needs to.

I step into the building, the cold air hitting me with a crispness that feels almost too sterile. The scent of fresh paper lingers in the air, mingling with the quiet buzz of activity around me—interns and associates rushing between meetings, phones ringing in the background. My eyes scan the room, and then they lock onto her.

She's sitting at the front desk, her fingers dancing across the keyboard with a familiar intensity I used to admire so much. She looks tired. There are faint shadows under her eyes, her complexion flushed from the exhaustion. But even in this state, she's still the most beautiful woman I've ever seen.

I can't help but watch her for a moment, taking in the subtle changes since the last time I saw her. Her clothes fit her differently now—more snugly, showing off the curves of her body and her protruding tummy. I notice it all—the way her blouse clings to her chest, the way her hips fill out her tailored trousers.

She doesn't see me yet. And for a moment, I let myself

just *see* her. Really see her, like I haven't in weeks. It's obvious that she likes her new job by the way she smiles genuinely when talking to her colleagues, but when our eyes finally meet, her face immediately hardens, that familiar coolness returning.

"Ettore," she says, her voice clipped. "What are you doing here?"

I don't answer immediately. Instead, I take a step closer, noticing her posture. Her back is straight, but she's clearly been standing for far too long.

"Do you stand all day?" I ask, trying to keep the concern out of my voice, though it's impossible.

She blinks, clearly thrown off. "What?"

"You shouldn't stand for hours like that, Mirabella. It's not good for you..."

Her eyes flash, and I can see she's already shutting me out, the walls going up.

"So, you came all the way here to tell me how to do my job?" Her voice is sharp now, defensive. "How did you even find out where I work?"

I can feel the heat rising in my chest. Her tone stings, but I force myself to stay calm.

"You're monitoring me," she accuses.

"I'm not—"

"So you're stalking me?" She cuts me off, her words like a slap to the face. "Why am I even surprised?"

I clench my teeth. "I'm not stalking you, Mirabella." The words come out slower than I expect, but they're true. I'm not, not in the way she means. But damn, I wish she could understand how much I've tried to respect her space, even if that means keeping a distance I hate.

I may have asked her boss to keep an eye on her for me, and I may have reached out to Nonna and Isabella a million times since she blocked me, but that's it. I didn't send Luca or any of my men to watch over her.

"And why should I believe you?" She crosses her arms, her eyes narrowing.

I sigh, running a hand through my hair. "I just wanted to see how you're doing, okay?"

She doesn't look at me when she replies, her fingers moving furiously over the keyboard. "As you can see, I'm fine. Busy."

Her coldness hits me harder than I expect. I *do* see how she's doing—too damned well. Too well for my own peace of mind. It infuriates me. She doesn't need to work here—hell, she doesn't need to work at all. She's juggling a full-time job, college, and the pregnancy, and she's doing it all on her own, stubbornly refusing any help.

The pay here is garbage, and the thought of her struggling like this, when I could make everything so much easier for her, drives me insane. It's maddening that she refuses to accept a single cent of what I send. Instead, she sends it all back, along with a tiny bits of what she calls her "debt owed," as if she thinks she owes me something. She doesn't.

She's trying to pay me back what she claims she owes me for the few months we stayed together while I covered her bills, and the mere thought of that is as annoying as it is funny.

She's so damned stubborn.

And yet...I can't help but admire her. Even in this moment, even when she's pushing me away, I admire her for her pride. But God, it's making this harder than I thought it would be. It's absurd, and yet I can't stop caring. I can't stop wanting to take care of her.

But I won't push it. Not now. I'll keep letting her send her so called 'debt owed,' and then I'll wait until the end of the month to return it all. And more—much more. She and her family will have everything they need. Our children will have everything they need.

I clear my throat, trying to push past the weight in my chest. "Can we talk... later?" I ask her quietly.

Her silence is an answer I know too well. The dismissal. The contempt.

"I'll be here when your shift ends," I add, but I don't expect her to respond. She doesn't.

So, I wait outside, in my car, parked across the street where I can watch the door. Time crawls by. I watch the sun dip lower, and with it, my patience thins. Conversations run through my mind, my words rehearsed and reshaped. I'm not sure how long it's been, but when she finally steps through the front doors, my heart stutters. She's holding her work bag with one arm, her eyes scanning the parking lot, and she's beautiful in the fading sunlight. The glow around her makes my chest tighten, but I push the feeling away. I can't let her go. Not like this.

I walk toward her, and she sees me before I get too close. Her expression tightens, and her lips purse as if she's trying to stop herself from saying something sharp.

"You're still here," she says, her voice laced with annoyance.

"I told you I would be," I reply, stepping closer, matching her stride as I fall into step beside her. "Let me drive you home."

She doesn't even look at me when she answers. "I already called an Uber."

"Cancel it."

She stops abruptly, turning her head to glare at me, her eyes burning with anger. "There you go again, trying to order me around," she snaps. "You don't get to tell me what to do."

I swallow hard, trying to keep my composure. "I wasn't trying to—" I sigh, running a hand through my hair. "Okay, I'm sorry. I didn't mean it to sound like that. I just...I really miss you, and I can't stand seeing you take some stupid cab when I have more than enough cars to drive you anywhere you want to go. Hell, I'll buy you one if you don't like any of mine."

She scoffs, shaking her head, her jaw tight. "This isn't about cars or money, Ettore, and you know that. If it was, we wouldn't be having this discussion."

The words hit me harder than I expect. I've been acting as if it's about luxury or convenience, but it's never been about that. "I know, I'm sorry. If that's how it came across, that's not what I meant. I just hate seeing you struggle and not let me help."

She's quiet for a moment, her chest rising and falling. "Ettore..."

"Please, Bella..." I say her name like a plea, my voice softer now, hoping she can hear the desperation underneath. "Just...let me take care of you. You don't have to do everything on your own."

There's a long silence between us. She stands still, her expression vague as if she's weighing her options.

Finally, she exhales a long, defeated sigh. "Fine," she mutters, stepping closer. "Let's go."

Her words are a like an instant joy, one that gives me the smallest of hope for the dark days I've been succumbed to since she left me. And though she hasn't fully given in, it's enough to make me feel like I've won, even if just a little.

We climb into the car, and the ride is met with silence. The only sound is the hum of the engine, the blur of the city passing by in a wash of neon lights. She's curled up in the passenger seat, her arms wrapped protectively around her abdomen, her gaze distant as she looks out the window. She's rubbing her stomach absentmindedly, as if she's trying to soothe the ache in her heart as much as the ache in her body.

I know what she's thinking about. The babies. Our future. I feel the same fear twisting in my gut. I want to be the best father to them, to help her raise them, to be everything she needs me to be, but I don't know how.

"Have you thought about how we're going to do this?" I ask carefully, breaking the silence because I know the next words won't be easy. "Raising twins won't be easy."

She straightens, her eyes narrowing. She knows exactly where I'm going with this. "I'll do everything the way I see fit," she says, her voice sharp with warning. "Don't you dare start telling me what I should and should not do. I'm not your puppet."

I feel the heat in my chest rising, frustration bubbling over. "Mirabella, I'm not trying to control you. I just want to be there for you, for our children. I want to help."

Her gaze hardens, but beneath it, I see the weariness. She's exhausted. Her voice cracks when she speaks next.

"Support?" she repeats, a bitter laugh escaping her lips. "Like you've done all along? You think I want to depend on you after everything that's happened? I want to be with my family when I give birth, not isolated in your world."

Her words cut deep, but I fight to keep my composure. "Of course you'll be with your family. With everyone you love. I'm not trying to take you away from them. You're acting like I'd lock you up somewhere. That's not what I want."

She laughs but there's no joy in it. "So, that's what this is about, right? What you want? You think because I'm carrying your children, I'll just do whatever you say?"

"Why are you so against me helping you?" My voice is louder now, too loud. I can hear my own annoyance slipping through, but I'm already past the tipping point. So to hell with it, anyway. I'm going to be there for this beautiful stubborn woman, whether she wants me to or not. The sooner she gets it the better.

"I'm the father. We don't have to agree on everything, but I'm allowed to want to be there for you, for them. I'm allowed to offer help, aren't I?"

"I don't want your help," she snaps, her words biting into me. The stubbornness in her tone makes my hands clench around the wheel.

I breathe through my teeth, forcing myself to stay calm. "I have the resources, Bella. I can make this whole journey easier for you. Smoother."

She shakes her head, her voice full of disgust. "Everything isn't about your money, Ettore," she yells. "Your world is dangerous. It swallows people whole, and I won't have my children trapped in it."

I want to argue, to tell her how much I would do to protect them—to protect her—but I can't find the words.

Anger surges inside me, but I fight to hold it back. I can't let this turn into another fight. I have to see this from her side, as hard as that is.

"I don't live that life anymore," I whisper. "I let it go for you. I'd walk away from it a million times more if it means I can have you again. I'll protect you—always. I'll make sure you're safe. All I need is for you to trust me."

She lets out a short, bitter laugh. "Like the last time?"

"I'm sorry about that," I say, my voice quiet but sincere as we wind through the busy streets. "Give me a chance to prove that I'm better now. For you. For our children."

She turns her face away, staring out the window, and a sickening fear grips my chest. The kind of fear that tells me I've lost her for good, that nothing I say or do will change anything. But then, after what feels like an eternity, she sighs. Her voice is softer when she speaks again.

"I have scheduled an appointment with the doctor next week," she says, her tone quieter, almost hesitant. "It's my first official doctor visit. We can go together if you have the—"

"I'll make the time, Bella. I promise," I interrupt. My heart leaps in my chest, relief flooding me like a wave. "Together," I repeat, the word in my mouth, like it the last two minutes might disappear if I don't. But it's something. It's hope.

The silence in the car settles again, but it's different now. It's not as suffocating.

As we pull into her neighborhood, I glance over at her, and I swear I see something shift in her eyes. It's not trust—not yet. But it's a flicker of something that may just be the beginning of what I thought was the end. Maybe it's a hint of the connection we used to have.

And for the first time in a long time, I let myself hold on to that. It's not much, but for now, it's enough.

41

MIRABELLA

The fluorescent lights hum above me, casting a harsh, sterile glow over the rows of students hunched over their notes. I sit at the back of the lecture hall, my pen tapping absently against the blank page in front of me.

My attention is less on Professor Ricci's lecture about global governance than on the empty seat beside me. The one that should be occupied by Milo. If he were here today, that spot would be his.

I haven't spoken to him since the day I walked out on him at the café. At first, he tried reaching out—calls, messages, endless attempts to apologize. I didn't respond. I couldn't. I let his messages pile up, unread. Then, one day, everything stopped. He vanished. It's been weeks now, not since I resumed classes after being discharged from the hospital.

At first, I didn't mind the silence. I almost preferred it. I didn't have to face him in class, didn't have to listen to his apologies, didn't have to be reminded of everything we'd been through. Hell, the pictures of him kissing me were used against me by my own husband. I hated how easily everything had crumbled.

Then, the absence starts to gnaw at me. It's been over a month now. I try not to care. I shouldn't care, especially not after everything he did. I know it was his fault.

So why does my chest feel so tight? Why does a part of me still want to know what happened?

But I can't control the feeling that worries me as I struggle to make out what might be wrong.

The professor drones on about 'economic diplomacy' and 'global governance.' The words bounce around the room, meaningless, while my mind races with questions I can't seem to quiet. What's going on with Milo? Is he sick? Out of town? Taking a break from college? Or worse...is he avoiding me?

I scoff at the thought. Milo wouldn't ditch classes for almost a month just because we'd fought. This is something more serious.

The lecture finally ends minutes later, and the room becomes noisy and bustling with activity as students pour out of the lecture hall in chattering groups. I sling my satchel over one shoulder and make my way towards the door.

In the hallway, the voices grow louder, and I feel a pang in my chest. It feels like I'm just going through the motions. I pull my phone out of my bag and, before I even realize what I'm doing, I've dialed his number.

It rings once. Twice. And when the third ring comes and goes, I can't stop myself. I pull up our last conversation. The last message from him was an apology—a desperate, heartfelt one. My fingers hover over the screen, guilt sinking in as I realize I've never replied to any of his messages.

I bite my lip, then type the words.

Hey. Haven't seen you in a while. Just checking to make sure you're okay. Call me if you want to talk.

I hit send before I can second-guess myself. Immediately, the guilt coils tighter in my stomach. I know Milo crossed a line, but it doesn't erase the time we spent together. The friendship, the way he made my first days here easier, the fact that he genuinely seemed to care about me...It doesn't just disappear, no matter how hard I try to ignore it.

And then there's the darker worry I can't shake.

Did Ettore do something to him? He'd threatened to kill him before, and knowing him, he isn't one to joke about certain subjects like that.

I force the thought from my mind, but it lingers. Ettore wouldn't...would he? He's always made his feelings clear about Milo, but would he go that far?

I close my eyes as flashes of the hospital flood my mind—doctors, beeping machines, the overwhelming fragility of life. It all feels so delicate, so fragile. That withing a blink of eye everything you've ever known can change quickly.

I can't shake the image of Milo fading into the background of my life just because I'd let my anger take over. If something happened to him, and I didn't know...I wouldn't forgive myself.

The heat outside hits me like a wall when I step into the faculty parking lot. The sun is blinding. And there, unmistakable, is Ettore—leaning against his black Lamborghini Urus, wearing his usual look of effortless magnetism. He stands with his arms crossed, looking every bit as dangerous as he always does. His jawline is sharp, his hair a mess of dark waves I can't seem to forget burying my hands into.

God, he looks good.

I hate the way my heart flutters at the sight of him. It's so damned stupid. After everything, why does he still have this effect on me?

He straightens as he spots me, and I feel the weight of every eye around us as he walks toward me with those long, purposeful strides. There's something magnetic about him —the way the crowd seems to part for him, as if they know exactly who he is. It doesn't help that his presence seems to fill up the space between us before he even says a word.

"Hey," he greets, and I don't know how his voice can sound so soft yet gruff.

When he takes my bag from my shoulders, his hand brushes against my arm, and the electricity between us zings through my skin. My heart skips, then stutters, then races. The tension between us vibrates like a pulled string.

"Hey," I croak, my throat suddenly feeling dry.

It's been a roller coaster of emotions ever since I left him, but I never let myself revel in the fact that I missed him terribly. Not until now.

"Ready?" he asks, taking my hand and leading me toward his car.

I nod, though my stomach is in knots. I swallow hard, trying to hold myself together, but I'm not sure how long I can keep pretending. Today is our first doctor's visit, and I'm terrified. Not just of the checkup, but of being there with him.

He opens the car door for me, and I slide inside, immediately hit by the scent of him—clean, expensive, and familiar. It wraps around me like a second skin, and for a moment, I forget the weight of everything else. The door shuts with a soft thud, and Ettore slides in on the other side, his presence suddenly filling the space.

The engine hums to life, and within seconds, we're leaving the campus grounds and merging onto the highway.

My heart hammers in my chest, a frantic rhythm I can't ignore. The nerves crawl under my skin, twisting in all sorts of directions. I'm not just nervous about the doctor's appointment. I'm nervous about the fact that I'm here with Ettore, that we're together again like this.

"How are you?" he asks, his voice low as he turns a corner, his grip on the wheel tight and steady.

I notice the way he's driving slower than usual, almost too carefully, as if every move he makes is designed to protect me. His voice is gentle, almost painfully so, and something about it makes my chest ache.

"I'm good," I answer, my words coming out too flat.

"Just good?" he presses. "That's it?"

I chuckle, trying to deflect. "What do you want me to say?"

"The truth."

I raise an eyebrow, a flash of irritation stirring. "So you think I'm lying?"

"I want you to tell me everything, Bella," he says, his voice intense, almost desperate. "I want you to tell me how you've been, how you've been managing college and work. Tell me if you really think being apart from me is working for you."

"I knew it would come to this," I mutter, folding my arms over my chest, already bracing myself for the familiar push and pull. "I'm fine, Ettore. I've got a good job, a supportive family, and my grades have never been better. Is that what you want to hear?"

I glance at him, but his face is tight, his jaw set in that way that makes me feel like he's holding something back.

He chuckles bitterly, the sound slicing through the silence. "No."

"No?" My head jerks back in surprise.

"I want you to admit that being away from me has been miserable," he says, his voice growing raw, "that you made the wrong choice when you left, and that you miss me..."

I feel the words hit me like a slap to the face, and a wave of emotion crashes over me. "Ettore," I warn softly, but I can't stop the ache that spreads through me at his words.

"Because that's how I've been, Bella," he continues. "Miserable. Missing you. Hating myself for letting you walk away."

"I'm sorry you feel that way..." I murmur, but even as I say it, I know it's not enough.

"Are you?" He shoots me a look, his eyes dark, filled with too many emotions to name. I bite my lip, trying to keep my ground.

"No," I admit sincerely, my voice softer than I want it to be. "I'm glad you regret what you did. I'm glad you see how wrong it was. But we can't keep looking back, Ettore. We have to move forward. That's why we're going to this checkup today. To make sure the babies are okay. That's all that matters now."

He hums low in his throat, clearly not convinced. "And after that? What happens then? We just go our separate ways?"

I swallow hard. "Until we have to meet again for them, yes."

"This won't work, Mirabella, and you know it, I know it. We can't do this...coparenting thing while we're apart. We just can't. We are better together as a family."

A scoff leaves my throat. "So, what, you want me to move back to the Greco Estate?"

He doesn't even flinch, his gaze locked onto mine as he drives. "I want you to move back home."

I don't know how to respond. I don't know what I want.

Home. I hear the word, and for a fleeting moment, it sounds comforting. But deep down, I know he's wrong. That place—his house—never truly felt like home. Not when our marriage was nothing more than a façade. Not when his family despised me.

"We don't have to live as a couple," he says, his voice soft but insistent. "You can stay in a different wing of the house. I just...I worry so much because you're not close to me. Do you know the torture I've been subjected to?" He says it so earnestly, and I can't ignore how his words tug painfully at my chest.

I force a smile, one that feels too thin, too brittle. "You don't have to worry about me. I'm not alone. I have my family."

His grip on the steering wheel tightens, his knuckles white. "I am your family."

I bite my lower lip to hold back the tears that are threatening to spill, and I turn to look out the window, trying to find something to focus on. Something, anything, to stop the emotions from overtaking me. I want the same things he does. I want us to be a family, but I can't keep pretending it will be simple.

Even if I do move back, even if I raise our children in his home, it won't change the fact that his aunts still hate me. Their disdain won't just disappear. I've seen how Ettore interacts with them, how there's no warmth, no love. It's cold, and it's harsh. The last thing I want is for my children to grow up feeling like they don't belong, like they're unwanted.

The streets blur past, and I focus on them, on the city's landscape outside the window as if it's the most interesting thing in the world. The silence between us is heavy, but at least it's peaceful. He doesn't push. For now, that's enough.

A few minutes later, we pull into the hospital parking lot, and Ettore opens the door for me. As I step out, I feel his presence behind me like a shadow. My breath catches when my body brushes against his.

"Come on," he says, and I follow him, though every step feels like it's taking me further from the calm I had in the car.

The walk through the hospital and to the doctor's office feels like an eternity. Finally, we're seated in a sterile, white room that feels as cold as the silence between us moments ago. But Ettore's hand still grips mine, and that warmth—his warmth—sends a shiver through me.

"Mr. and Mrs. Greco," the doctor greets, her smile kind. "It's lovely to have you both today."

The appointment begins in earnest, with Ettore asking so many questions that I can't help but chuckle at his overzealous concern.

"Are you sure she's getting the right vitamins?"

"What about the risk factors?"

"When should we schedule the next visit?"

"Do you think she should be working a job while also being a student?"

I roll my eyes at the last question.

"I have to work, doctor," I say, though I can already feel how Ettore's breathing picks up when I admit that.

"No, you don't. You just *want* to work," Ettore grumbles, turning to face the doctor again. "I'm sure you've dealt with stubborn pregnant women in your years of practice. Could you talk to her? Maybe she'll listen to you..."

The doctor clears her throat, looking slightly amused.

"Well, it depends on the kind of job. It's advisable for pregnant women to keep themselves busy, as long as it's not too physically demanding."

"See?" I shoot Ettore a smug look, but the doctor isn't done yet.

"But if those activities involve physical or mental stress, then it's not safe for the mother or the babies."

"No stress whatsoever, Doc," I quickly reply, a little defensive. "I love my job, and I'm pursuing a degree I'm passionate about."

The only thing truly stressing me out is constantly thinking about Ettore and this...situation in which we find ourselves.

The doctor smiles kindly at both of us. "It's natural for the expecting father to worry about his partner's well-being," she says.

I can hear Ettore's frustrated huff beside me, and I can't help but tease him a little. "He doesn't just worry. He acts like he's the one carrying the babies."

And even though he acts like he's upset, I see a crack of a smile on his lips.

"Can't help it," he murmurs, running a hand through his hair. "I worry."

For a moment, everything feels right. We share a small laugh as the meeting continues, and with time, the tightness in my chest eases a little bit. I know this moment will pass and we will snap back to reality when this is all over, but for now, I just want to pretend like everything is okay.

It's fleeting, I know, but for now, I'll take it.

Ettore holds my hand as we walk back to the car after the doctor appointment, his grip firm, as if we're still a normal couple, as if nothing has changed between us.

There's a silence that settles between us, not awkward or forced, but comfortable, as if we're both content to just exist in the moment. It's the kind of quiet where words feel unnecessary, where the space between us is filled with everything that doesn't need to be said.

I can feel his hand still holding mine, his presence grounding me. I just want to hold onto this. Just us, here, as if nothing has changed.

I wish it could stay that way—quiet, simple, without all the mess. But then he speaks, his voice cutting through the stillness.

"So, when's the next appointment?"

"A few weeks, I think. Wait, let me check my hospital card." I pull it up on my phone, swiping through the screen. "Okay, that would be next month, on the 23rd."

"Oh."

"What do you mean, *oh*?" I glance up at him, narrowing my eyes.

"It's nothing. I'll be there," he says, a little too quickly.

I don't buy it. "Ettore..."

He hesitates, and then there's that familiar glint in his eyes—something he's not saying. "But it might clash with a trip I've got scheduled."

"A trip?" I raise an eyebrow, crossing my arms. "What kind of trip?"

"Business," he says quickly, but I can tell there's something more. His tone is a little too casual, like he's trying to cover up a truth he doesn't want to say out loud.

"You know you don't have to come if you don't want to?"

"I don't want to miss it, Bella. But you know how things are."

I stop walking, turning to face him. "Hence, why I said you don't have to come. It's fine. You always seem to find a way to miss things that matter."

The words hit harder than I intended. I see him flinch, just for a moment, but it's enough. His jaw clenches, and I can feel the shift in the air. "What's that supposed to mean?" he asks, his voice low.

"I just—" I take a step back, frustrated. "I don't need you to be here when it's convenient, Ettore. I don't need you to show up for just the *good parts*. I've been doing this on my own, and I can keep doing it."

His eyes narrow, and there's something in the way he looks at me, a flicker of pain beneath his usual tough exterior. He takes a deep breath, his voice steady but with an edge. "I'm not asking you to do it alone. I never wanted that. I just...I don't want to lose any more of this. Of us."

He steps closer, his hand reaching for mine again. "I know I haven't been perfect. I've messed up, Bella. But I'm not going to keep making excuses. I want to be here. For everything. For *us*."

I look away, unsure of what to say, my chest tightening at the sincerity in his voice. The truth is, I've missed him, more than I want to admit. But the anger and hurt still linger.

And then, in a softer tone, he says, "I want us back, Mirabella..."

My heart stutters, but I don't answer immediately. I can't.

"Ettore..." I sigh, my voice a little more exhausted than I intend. "We've already talked about this..."

"I know," he interrupts, his tone uncharacteristically gentle, almost pleading. "But just...listen to me for once, okay?" He pauses, his voice faltering before he continues. "It's not about the maids or the money or any of that. Yes, I want you to be taken care of and not be alone through this but it's about you. I miss *you*, Bella. I miss waking up and seeing you beside me, hearing you laugh about something ridiculous I said. I miss being a part of your world, your life."

He takes a shaky breath, his usual confidence stripped

away. "We're having twins, Bella. Two little pieces of you and me, and I don't want to miss a single moment. Not their first cries, their first steps, their first days of school—I want to be there for all of it. For you. For them. I don't want to be some shadow in their lives. I need you to give me that chance."

His words hit me harder than I expect, and I swallow past the lump in my throat. "Ettore...it's not that simple. You know it's not."

"I know it's not," he agrees softly, his dark eyes locking onto mine. "But life without you? That's impossible. I'll do whatever it takes to prove it to you, Bella. Whatever you need from me, I'll give it to you. I just need you to let me in. To let me fight for us. Please."

I don't respond immediately, unsure of what to say, and he leans over, brushing a strand of hair from my face, his touch achingly tender. His voice drops to a whisper, his words laced with a bittersweet honesty that makes my heart ache.

"You're my home, Bella. You always have been. And I'll spend the rest of my life proving it, if I have to."

He opens the passenger door and waits, his expression hopeful yet braced for rejection. Slowly, I slide into the seat, my emotions in turmoil as he shuts the door and moves around to the driver's side.

As he gets in, he glances at me again, his eyes scanning my face like he's memorizing every detail. "You don't have to decide now," he says softly, his voice steady but full of longing. "Just... don't shut me out completely. That's all I'm asking."

But he doesn't start the car. Instead, we sit there in silence, a silence that feels heavy with everything unsaid. I can feel him watching me, probably hoping for a reply, but

I'm tongue-tied as usual—helpless whenever he opens that goddamned beautiful mouth.

He fiddles with the push-to-start knob, his fingers restless, while I focus on staring at anything but him. The dashboard, the rearview mirror, my own hands in my lap—anywhere but those freaking eyes.

I open my mouth to say something, anything, but he beats me to it. The quiet is clearly gnawing at him just as much as it is at me.

"Do you get backaches? Foot aches? Any kind of body aches at all?" he asks casually, but there's an underlying tension in his voice. "I give really good body rubs."

I roll my eyes, unable to stop the corner of my lips from twitching upward.

I hate that he's getting to me. His words, his presence—they've always had this way of undoing me, no matter how hard I try to keep myself together. Nothing has changed. I can feel it. The pull. The gravity of him, of *us*.

I glance at him, and there it is—the look. That look that makes my thoughts scatter and my heart stumble over itself. Before I say anything, he leans in to brush my cheek with the pad of his fingers. Then suddenly, the air feels thick, and my heart races as I stare into his eyes.

"I really miss you," he whispers, his voice raw and honest. "Tell me you miss me too."

My breathing becomes heavier as I stare into the depths of his hazel orbs. I try to fight it, try to push the flood of emotions back, but his thumb moves in slow, agonizing circles on the curve of my neck, and it's over. Every wall I've built, every ounce of resolve I've clung to—it all crumbles beneath his touch.

I'm not strong enough to resist him anymore.

"I-I...miss you too, Ettore..."

My words barely leave my lips before he leans in, closing the distance between us. His lips are on mine in an instant, fierce and hungry. It's as if the world drops away, and all I can feel is him. His warmth, his desperation, and the way my heart is beating so wildly I can barely catch my breath.

For a moment, it's just us. Nothing else matters. Not the past, not the hurt, not the future. Only this kiss. Only him.

42

ETTORE

As soon as my lips touch Mirabella's, a trembling exhale escapes me. My hands instinctively rise to cup her face as I kiss her slowly and tenderly. The warmth and softness of her lips against mine is something I savor in this moment. She tilts her head up gently, our chests brushing against each other as she fills the space between us.

Her arms wrap around my neck, pulling me closer, her touch grounding me even as I feel like I'm free-falling. My thumb brushes over her cheekbone, a small, tender motion, as if my hands are memorizing the feel of her.

"I've missed your lips," I whisper, slightly pulling away. I nuzzle my nose into her neck and inhale deeply. Her fragrance, a mix of vanilla and strawberries, fills my lungs. "I've missed your smell. I've missed your voice." I dip in to kiss her again. "Fuck...I've missed your taste."

She gasps against my lips when one hand grabs her neck possessively as I kiss her again. This time, it's harder, rougher, unrestrained. She moans when my hand lands on her exposed thigh, my fingers curling beneath the hem of her dress.

I pull the material up until it comes to rest on the tops of her thighs. Her bare skin is warm under my fingertips, and my throat bobs when I see the goosebumps that have spread along the length of her legs.

"How much did you miss me, Bella?" I murmur, dragging my kisses down to her neck. But I don't wait for her to answer. I'm too impatient to wait. I slide my hand under her dress before tugging the lacy material of her thong to the side.

"Ettore," she lets out a choked gasp as I brush a finger over her wet center. Her hand reaches over the center console to clutch my shirt collar, and before I realize what I'm doing, I'm adjusting my seat to accommodate her and pulling her body over until she's straddling my lap.

A low hiss escapes my lips when she fully lowers herself onto me before she starts rocking herself back and forth over my crotch. I'm painfully hard, and I know she can feel every inch and outline of my dick just as I feel her slick wetness through the material of my pants.

"Fuck, baby, you feel good," I breathe tensely. My hands are on her hips, squeezing tightly, and I feel her nails dig into my shoulders. I bite back a groan when she throws her head back, leaning slightly against the steering wheel as she rolls her hips over mine.

I see the arousal in her face—the way her mouth drops open in a quiet moan, the way her eyes roll up the back of her head, the whimpers and soft sounds coming out of her —and it drives me fucking mad. She's totally enjoying this, and that alone heightens the pleasure I already feel.

I bury my face into her neck, inhaling her addicting scent as I drag my nose down to her soft, full cleavage.

"Ah... oh, God," she moans when I roughly palm one breast with my free hand before dragging her neckline down to expose her matching lace bra.

Without thinking, I pull the material down before pulling her puckered nipple into my mouth. She moans again, burying her hands into my hair while her fingers scrape at my scalp.

Her breath hitches as I take my time sucking on her hard, plump nipple until it's tinged pink. A shiver runs through her body, and she grinds herself harder against my cock, pleasuring herself.

"Fuck...I missed you, Bella," I choke.

I know I've said it a million times before, but I'd gladly say it a million more if it means she knows how deeply I mean it.

She leans in and presses her lips to mine, her movements slowing, becoming deliberate—each roll of her hips more languid, more sensual. This kiss feels different. It's not just passion; it's layered. I can taste everything—her anger, her fear, her frustration, and her desire—all tangled together.

"I want—no, I need—you back, Bella," I say, cupping her face in my hands. My voice shakes, but I press on. "I can't keep going through life without you. I'm sorry for everything I've done. If it takes the rest of my life to make things right, I'll do it."

Her breath hitches, and her voice trembles as she whispers, "You broke me."

Her confession shatters me, and I press my forehead to hers. I can't bring myself to meet her eyes, not when hot tears are streaming down both our faces.

"I'm sorry, love. I'm so, so sorry," I murmur. "I was selfish, cruel, and utterly unforgivable. You deserved so much better than what I gave you. But I swear, from this day forward, I'll strive to be better—for you, for us. I'll spend every moment proving I'm worthy of your forgiveness, and I won't stop, not even in my last breath."

"Ettore..." she sighs, her hesitation evident even as her hand slides to rest on my shoulder.

Before she can say something—anything—that might destroy end this moment, I speak.

"Please, Bella. Give me another chance." I kiss her tear-streaked cheek gently. "Let me fix what I broke. Let me be there for you, for our children." My hands move to her stomach, and I let them rest there, feeling the taut muscle beneath my palms. "Let me love you."

The last words are barely a whisper, breathed into her ear as I press a soft kiss just below her earlobe. The small, involuntary whimper that escapes her lips tells me everything I need to know—how much she wants this, how much she still wants me. How much she wants us to work.

When her eyes meet mine, heavy and glazed with emotion, I can see it—the spark of hope, of longing. I know she's on the verge of giving us another chance.

But before the words can leave her lips, the shrill ring of her familiar ringtone slices through the tension in the car, dragging us both out of the heated haze.

She scrambles for her purse in the passenger seat, relief flickering across her face. It's clear she's grateful for the distraction, for the reprieve from having to answer me just yet.

That realization sends a pang of hurt slicing through my chest, but at the same time, I'm just glad to be here with her. Glad she let me kiss her again. Touch her again. Even though we're in an uncertain place, I know we've come a long way from where we were. We're bruised, but not broken. It would take more than this for either of us to simply throw in the towel and give up on us.

As she reaches for her phone, I gently help her back into her seat. When she retrieves the device from her bag and glances at the screen, her expression shifts—blank yet somehow loaded. She stares at the ringing phone for a moment that feels like an eternity.

Then she looks at me, and the steady rhythm of my heart twists into a frantic, erratic beat for an entirely different reason.

"It's Milo," she says softly.

43

MIRABELLA

The tension in the air seems to intensify, but for an entirely different reason, the moment Milo's name falls from my lips. I swallow hard and try to keep my nerves from showing as I study the unreadable expression on Ettore's face.

"There's nothing going on between us, Ettore," I blurt out, perhaps more urgently than I intend. I know I don't owe him an explanation—I've been honest this whole time, there's nothing between me and Milo. But a part of me feels like I'm not the only one who needs reassurance.

Ettore needs it too, especially after the heated moment we shared was interrupted by a man he saw kissing me.

"I just want you to know that. You believe me, right?" I ask, my voice tinged with nervousness as I brush a loose strand of hair behind my ear.

"Mirabella..." Ettore's gaze softens, the hard edges of his expression easing. "I believe you. I made a terrible mistake for not doing so before...when I should have."

I bite my lower lip and nod, a wave of relief washing over me. "I just...I called him earlier because I hadn't seen him in lectures for over a month, and I was worried. Maybe something had happened to him. But he didn't answer, so I texted hi—"

My rambling is abruptly cut off as Ettore leans in and presses his lips against mine. The kiss is warm, tender, and disarming, and in an instant, my defenses and anxieties dissolve. My breath catches as his hands cup my face, his thumb brushing my cheek with such delicate care that I almost want to believe everything will be okay.

In the distance, my phone stops ringing, but my mind is too clouded, too overwhelmed by the heat of the kiss to stop. I slide my hand over his rough stubble, savoring the way it scrapes against my palm. Ettore makes a low, rumbling sound in his throat as my fingers find the nape of his neck. One hand slides to the back of my head, holding me in place as he deepens the kiss.

I moan into him, my body responding in ways I can't control as my pulse quickens. His other hand moves dangerously close to my lap, and just as his thumb nears my center, my shrill ringtone slices through the moment again. A sharp exhale escapes me as I push Ettore away, the break more for my own sake than his.

"I need..." I gasp breathlessly, my voice shaky. "...I need to take this call."

Before he can say anything, I push the driver's side door open and stumble out of the car, my legs unsteady beneath me. The fresh air hits my skin, but it does little to calm the storm of desire and confusion raging inside me. My chest heaves, not just from the kiss but from the jumble of confusion swirling in my gut.

Ettore follows, unfolding his tall frame from the car. The way he watches me makes my heart ache. There's something tender in his eyes, but beneath that tenderness, I can sense a mixture of lust and frustration. He says nothing, crossing his arms over his broad chest, the muscles in his jaw clenched tight.

I swallow hard, glancing down at the phone still vibrating in my hand. With a deep breath, I press answer. "Milo?"

There's a brief pause on the other end before a long sigh.

"Mirabella," Milo's familiar voice fills my ear, but it's not the same. His tone is rough, drained—so different from the boyish playfulness he used to have. "I'm...sorry. For everything."

It feels as if I've been holding my breath for days, but his words don't bring the relief I expected. "Where have you been?" I manage to ask, the guilt thick in my voice. "I haven't seen you in weeks, Milo. I was worried."

He exhales shakily. "I took some time off from college. After everything...I just needed to get away. Needed space to think about what I'd done."

"I saw you a few days after...after what you..." I glance at Ettore, who's watching me closely, eyebrows raised. "...after what happened. That's not why you stopped coming, is it?"

A selfish part of me hopes that it wasn't. I would hate to think Milo skipped a month, missing important quizzes and assessments, all because I couldn't bring myself to accept his apology.

"No," Milo says quietly. "It wasn't that. Something else happened."

Even though these were the words I'd hoped for, they still send a shock through my chest, leaving my heart suspended in midair. I grip the car door for support, the metal cold beneath my fingers.

"What do you mean?" My voice comes out as a whisper,

and I can feel Ettore's gaze burning holes into me, but I can't bring myself to look at him now.

"There's something you need to know," Milo continues, his voice cracking with emotion. "A woman—she, uh...approached me. She offered me money—fifty thousand dollars—to get close to you, to make you look bad. She wanted to ruin you."

The world seems to blur around me, and I feel like I'm teetering on the edge of a cliff, ready to fall. "What?"

"I thought..." he chuckles bitterly, the sound heavy with regret. "I thought it was some kind of miracle. Here I am, stressing about student loans, and a wealthy stranger offers me more money than I've ever had just to befriend someone."

"So you...you took the money?" My voice comes out small, almost childlike, and I hate how vulnerable I sound.

"I did," Milo admits, the weight of guilt clear in his voice. "But then I met you, and everything changed. You were so real, so kind to me. I didn't expect to...to like you, let alone fall for you. But I did. And that kiss—it was real, Mirabella. I swear."

The betrayal slices through me, deeper than I ever imagined it could. Tears prick at my eyes, but I force myself to blink them away. "But you still went along with it," I whisper, my voice trembling. "You still lied to me. You still kissed me knowing I was married and that it would hurt me, that it would definitely implicate me, just like you were paid to do..."

"I'm sorry," he says, and his voice cracks. "That was selfish, and I hate that you suffered because of it. I'll never forgive myself for that."

"Is this why you called me? To tell me you've skipped

classes for so long because you feel bad?" I spit, anger surging through my veins like fire.

"I stopped attending after I heard about your accident," he admits, exhaling a shaky breath. "I felt like somehow I had a part in it."

I don't know how to process his words. He hurt me. His actions hurt me. But at the same time, it wasn't his fault that I got hit by a damned bike.

"I was going to come see you. I was going to confess what I did and ask for your forgiveness, even though I knew you'd probably send me away. But..." His voice wavers, and I hear him swallow thickly. "Your husband came to see me first."

The word *husband* crashes into me like a wave, and I feel a fresh surge of disbelief flood through me. I turn slowly to look at Ettore, his arms still crossed over his chest, his face a perfect mask of indifference.

"What did he do?" I ask, my voice low but urgent, the question hanging in the air like a ticking time bomb, waiting to explode.

Milo hesitates, then lets out a dry laugh. "He didn't kill me, if that's what you're worried about," he says, trying to lighten the mood with a joke, but it falls flat. "But I'm in the hospital..."

A sob rises in my throat, and I hang up the phone, letting it slip from my numbed fingers. My vision blurs with angry tears as I turn to face Ettore. "You put him in the hospital?" My voice shakes, a raw mix of horror and disbelief.

Ettore doesn't flinch. His expression remains unmoving, and his eyes meet mine with an unyielding indifference that makes my blood boil. "He hurt you," he says in a dangerously calm voice. "I made sure he understood the consequences."

My hands ball into fists at my sides. "You can't just put people in a damned hospital because they hurt me. That's not how the world works!"

Ettore's face darkens, and he takes a step toward me. "In my world, that's exactly how it works," he replies, his voice low and fierce. "And you should be grateful. I had Luca take him to the hospital. He could've bled to death in his own damned house."

The cruelty in his words, spoken with such ease, makes my stomach churn. "You think I should be grateful?" My voice rises, and I hate that it wavers. "You think I want this? Violence and control? This is exactly why I left you!"

He takes another step closer, and I instinctively take a step back. I see the hurt flash in his eyes before he stops, his expression hardening once more.

"Get in the car," he says, his voice harsh, carrying an unmistakable command. "We need to fix the real problem here."

I glare at him, the heat between us thick and suffocating. "Why? So you can control my life some more? Beat up—heck, hurt—people who hurt me? What exactly did you even do to him?"

"I shot at him..." he replies, his voice colder than I expect.

A sharp gasp escapes me, but he doesn't stop. "Fuck it, Mirabella, I wanted to do more than that," he growls, his tone hardening with every word. "Believe me, I was tempted —so damn tempted—to aim higher. His chest. His head. One tilt of my hand, and he'd be done." His jaw tightens, the veins in his neck visible as he fights to control his rage. "But I didn't. You know why? Because of you. I knew you'd never forgive me. I knew he was your friend, and that you still cared about him. So I held back. For you."

"Then how did he end up in the hospital?" I ask.

"The bastard panicked when he saw me," Ettore says with a sharp laugh, though there's no humor in it. "Tried to bolt like a coward. Ended up tripping over himself and tumbling down the stairs. Lucky all he broke was his damn hip and nose. He could've died." His lips curl into a cold sneer. "Would've served him right."

"Ettore," I chide softly, relieved he didn't actually shoot Milo outright, though his anger still sends a shiver through me.

Ettore's expression softens, but his intensity doesn't fade as he steps closer. He cups my face with his calloused hands, his touch surprisingly gentle. "Why do you keep fighting me, Mirabella?" he murmurs. "Everything I do—every goddamn thing—is to protect you. Don't you see that?"

His words shake something deep inside me. This is who Ettore is—violence, blood, and crime are etched into his soul. This is the world he knows, the only way he understands how to love and protect.

And I don't want to accept it. I don't want to understand him or this pull between us that never seems to fade. But I do. God, I do.

With a heavy sigh, I step back, breaking the spell between us, and slide into the passenger seat. Ettore follows, closing the door quietly before turning to me.

"Are you coming home?" he asks, his voice laced with something I can't quite place.

I let out a sharp breath, my arms crossing tightly. "No, Ettore. I'm still mad at you. You can't just go around shooting at people, no matter how justified you think it is."

His jaw tightens, and he nods, guilt flickering in his eyes.

"I told you I'd spend my whole life making up for what I've done, didn't I?"

I narrow my eyes, leaning in slightly. "Then start now. For the next two weeks, you're not coming to any of my appointments. None. You don't get to be involved in this part of my life if you can't control yourself."

His eyes widen in shock. "Mirabella, come on. That's not—"

"Fair? No, it's not. But neither is you playing judge, jury, and executioner. Actions have consequences, Ettore. You're going to sit this one out and think about that."

He looks like I've just punched him. "I can't—what if something happens? What if you need me?"

"I'll be fine," I say firmly, holding his gaze. "Logan will drive me. Alessia can come if I need her. But you? You're on timeout."

His lips part like he wants to argue, but then he sighs, his shoulders sagging in defeat. "Two weeks?"

"Two weeks," I confirm. "And don't think about showing up uninvited. If I see you at the hospital, I'll have Logan escort you out."

He groans, raking a hand through his hair. "You're killing me, Mirabella."

"Good. Maybe that'll stop you from shooting at people next time."

"Whatever you want, Kitten." I ignore how his solemn words make my heart flutter, focusing instead on the real issue at hand—the person who'd paid Milo to set me up.

But as the words form in my mind, I realize something. I don't need to search for the person anymore. I already know exactly who it is.

44

ETTORE

I've always prided myself on my self-control, but right now, every muscle in my body is wound tight, threatening to snap at any moment.

The living room of the Greco estate feels suffocating with thick, tangible tension today. Despite the sunlight streaming in through the grand windows and glinting off the polished marble floors, the air is cold, heavy, and oppressive.

I stand rigidly in the center of the room, my hands entwined with Mirabella's. She's trembling, her fingers gripping mine so tightly, as if afraid I might disappear. I can feel her pulse racing beneath her skin, a frantic rhythm that mirrors the fury burning in my veins.

Across from us, Zia Camila sits in one of the plush armchairs, her legs crossed with practiced grace, her fingers drumming absentmindedly against her knee. As always, her face is masked with a calm, rehearsed smile, but her eyes betray her—flickering with fear. She knows she's been backed into a corner, yet she's still pretending to be oblivious, and that pretense is that is slowly driving me mad.

"I asked you a question," Mirabella says, her voice shaking. "Why did you do it? Why did you pay someone to get close to me so you could set me up?"

Camila's icy gaze sweeps over her, a chilling calmness that contrasts sharply with the seething storm in Mirabella's eyes. "And I've already answered," she responds coolly. "Why do you keep asking? If you believe your husband's little confession so much, perhaps you've mistaken me for the person to whom he's referring. Go find them. Leave me out of this."

A wave of seething anger surges through me.

"Don't insult my wife, Camila," I spit, watching as her eyes widen slightly at the sheer disrespect of calling her by her guest name. "And don't insult my intelligence. We already know exactly what you did."

Her lip curls in a mocking smirk. "Do you?" Camila arches an eyebrow, her voice silky yet harsh. "Or is your wife's...condition clouding your judgment? Her pregnancy, perhaps?"

Before I can respond, she turns to Mirabella. "I think you need to rest, darling. You've been through quite a lot lately. The trauma these few weeks is certainly not good for the babies," she says with sickly sweet condescension, her voice dripping with feigned concern.

"Stop lying," Mirabella demands, her voice cracking slightly. "Just...stop. You're the only one who had the motive to do this. You've hated me since the moment you laid eyes on me. You're the only one who would go to such lengths to make sure I leave your precious mansion."

"Fine," Zia Camila snaps, her sugary smile evaporating as a cold, tight expression replaces it. "Believe what you want. I only did what I had to do to protect this family..."

"Protect?" I growl, my voice echoing throughout the

room. "Protect this family from what? From *her*? From my wife? The mother of my children?"

Camila's cool demeanor falters, if only slightly. "I didn't know she was pregnant when I started this," she stammers, the first crack in her mask. She shifts uncomfortably, uncrossing and recrossing her legs in a display of nervousness that contrasts with her earlier poise. "But let's be clear, we weren't sure *the baby* was even yours, Ettore," she adds, her tone darkening. "I couldn't risk history repeating itself. I had to protect my family. I did what I had to do."

I take a deep, controlling breath, the words cutting deeper than she intended. "I've forgiven your past transgressions, all because of Mirabella. But this?" I hiss, taking a step closer, my fists clenched. "This is crossing the line."

Panic creeps into her voice as she sits up straighter. "This is exactly what I was trying to prevent. Don't you see it? She's already turning you against me! She's trying to tear our family apart."

"The only person responsible for that," I growl, my words hardening into ice, "is you."

Her eyes flash with a toxic blend of malice and fear, and her lips twist into a bitter, defiant line. "She's a threat," she spits. "You're too blinded by your emotions to see it. But I see it. I always have. That's why I did what I did. It's my responsibility to make you see the truth. I'm not sorry for pushing a few buttons to make you open your eyes."

"Push a few buttons?!" I roar, taking a step toward her, but Mirabella's delicate grip tightens around my hand, holding me back.

Zia Camila's eyes dart to the movement. "She clearly controls you. This is what I was trying to prevent."

"As opposed to you controlling him?" Mirabella's voice

rises. "You see me as a threat because I *am* a threat—to your selfishness, your wickedness, and your cruelty!"

I hear footsteps approaching just then, and Aunt Francesca and Aunt Marta slip in, drawn by the commotion, their faces pale with shock. At the unfolding scene before them, they linger by the entrance with wide and shocked gazes, not daring to interrupt.

"You don't belong here," Zia Camila hisses. "You were never meant to be a part of this family. A threat? Don't flatter yourself. I'm trying to protect what's rightfully mine. What's ours." Her voice tightens, and her eyes glint with cold satisfaction. "Ettore was too blind to see it, but I found someone who wasn't."

My mind whirs, pieces finally clicking together. "You found someone?" I echo, my voice low but threatening. "What the fuck do you mean by that?"

For the first time, Camila's eyes widen with panic. Her control slips, a crack in the mask she's so carefully constructed. "I-I didn't—" she stammers, but I cut her off before she can regain her footing.

"No more lies, Camila," I say with razor-sharp finality. "I'll ask you one more time before I do something that will make you question whether we really are family. What the fuck do you mean by *you found someone who does*?"

Her hesitation dissolves into a sneer. "I couldn't risk handling the transaction myself," she spits. "Not when there was a chance that foolish American boy might rat me out. Someone helped me set up an offshore account for the transfer. Using my own account would've left a trail."

Her voice softens as she meets my glare. "I did this to protect the family, Ettore. Our family."

I take a slow, deliberate step closer, my gaze fixed on hers. "Who was it?" I demand.

Camila hesitates, her lips parting as if to speak, but then she closes them again, her eyes darting away for the briefest moment. The silence stretches, heavy with anticipation, and for a moment, I think I know the name she's about to say.

Then she speaks, her voice calm and almost mocking. "The person the tramp belonged to in the first place."

Her words blur in my mind, the puzzle pieces snapping together in rapid succession.

'Ettore couldn't see that, so I found someone who did...'

'Someone helped me secure an offshore account to carry out the transfer...'

Abruzzi.

This scheme reeks of him. His signature chaos, his appetite for destruction—all to maintain his leverage over others. And Camila? That she would stoop so low as to ally herself with *him*—just to torment Mirabella—is enough to make my blood boil. *Fuck!* I'm barely hanging onto my restraint.

My fists clench at my sides as I fight to maintain control. The air around me feels charged, heavy with blinding fury, but even through the haze of anger, one question still burns in my mind—a question that has haunted me, unanswered, for months.

The fire.

The fire that had destroyed Mirabella's house, upended her family's life, and set this entire nightmare into motion. No matter how hard I tried to uncover the truth, it always led back to dead ends, half-truths, and shadows. But now, standing here staring into the eyes of the woman who has confessed to orchestrating Mirabella's suffering, I know.

It's all connected.

"The fire at Mirabella's house," I say, my voice dropping

to a cold, deadly calm. "Was that part of your *master plan* to protect this family with your *helper*?"

The room seems to hold its breath.

Camila freezes, her carefully constructed composure splintering. Her eyes widen ever so slightly, and she stiffens in her chair. I catch Mirabella's confused gaze flicker toward me.

Mirabella shifts beside me, her brow furrowing in confusion. "The fire...it was an electrical issue, wasn't it?" she whispers, her voice barely audible, but I can't tear my eyes away from Camila.

She pales, her lips trembling. "I-I didn't mean for it to go that far," she stammers. "He said it was just to scare her... I didn't—"

"You do realize," I say slowly, "if the house burns down, I'll just move them into your place. Or didn't you think that far ahead?"

Camila's face drains of color. Her lips part, and she stammers, "I... I... I didn't—"

"Didn't what?" I press, leaning forward. "Didn't think about the consequences? That they could have ended up dead?"

Her voice shaking, clearly showing that she didn't think this well enough.

Mirabella lets out a strangled sob, her hands flying to her mouth as the weight of Camila's words hits her. Her anguish slicing through me, and whatever restraint I had left shatters. The betrayal, the fury, the sheer audacity—it consumes me.

In a blur, I close the distance between us, grabbing Camila by the throat and slamming her against the wall. The impact sends a framed family portrait crashing to the floor, shards of glass scattering across the marble. My grip tightens as I watch her struggle, her hands clawing at mine, her face etched with terror.

Her hands claw at mine, her nails scraping against my skin as she gasps for air. Her face contorts with terror, her composure shattered like the glass scattered at our feet.

"You nearly killed her," I snarl through clenched teeth, my voice a guttural roar. "You almost killed her entire family—for what? Your *pride*? Your fucking *greed*?"

Camila's lips part in a desperate attempt to speak, but no sound escapes. Her eyes widen, the whites showing as they roll back, and her struggles weaken.

Behind me, chaos erupts. Aunt Francesca's muffled gasp pierces the tension, and Aunt Marta's frantic cries reach me as if from a great distance. I feel their hands on me, pulling at my arms, trying to break my grip, but they are nothing.

"Ettore!" Mirabella's voice rises above the din, desperate, pleading. But I can't hear her, not really. My vision tunnels, the world shrinking until there is only Camila, gasping, trembling, breaking.

"You brought him into her life," I seethe. "You allied yourself with *Abruzzi*! Do you even realize what you've done? You handed a monster the tools to destroy her. To destroy me."

Her mouth moves again, a pathetic croak escaping her lips. A single word, barely audible. "Please."

"Please?" I echo, my laugh sharp and humorless. "You think you deserve mercy? After everything you've done? After you nearly burned Mirabella alive in her own home, with her family inside? Her sick mom—her *sister and grandmother*—could have *died* because of you!"

I tighten my grip, my body trembling with the force of my anger. "You're no better than the demons that plagued my father," I spit. "You think you're protecting this family?

You're nothing but a leech, clinging to power, destroying everything good in your path. I spent my whole life trying to escape his shadow, to be *better* than him, but here you are—proof that I let his rot linger. Proof that I let the Greco curse into my home. Not anymore."

Camila's face turns a ghastly shade of purple, her gasps growing fainter, weaker. For a fleeting moment, I want to finish it. To snap her neck and be done with her poison. To silence her forever.

But then Mirabella's voice cuts through the haze, trembling, raw. "Please, Ettore. You're scaring me."

And then I feel her throw herself against me, her arms wrapping around me tightly, her tears soaking through my shirt. "Please," she whispers again, her voice breaking, her desperation anchoring me.

The fog begins to lift. The rage, hot and all-consuming just moments ago, starts to ebb as her touch pulls me back to reality. Her warmth reminds me of what's real—what's important.

I glance down at Camila, her face pale, her chest heaving as she struggles to breathe, and the truth crashes over me like a tidal wave. I don't have to be this. I don't have to be the monster they've always whispered about—The Reaper they've called me.

I can be better.

For Mirabella. For the unborn children she carries. For the future I've sworn to protect, the life I've promised to build with her.

My grip slackens completely, and I step back, letting Camila collapse to the floor. She clutches her throat, coughing violently, but I don't look at her. I can't.

Instead, I turn to Mirabella, who clings to me with trembling hands. Her tear-streaked face tilts up, her eyes filled with fear—not of Camila, not of the situation, but of *me*. It guts me more than anything else ever could.

"I'm sorry," I whisper. "I'm so sorry."

She shakes her head, her fingers tightening against my chest, as if holding me together. "Ettore..."

I close my eyes, inhaling deeply, forcing myself to push the rage down, to lock it away. For her. For our children. Because in the end, they're all that truly matters.

My eyes scan the room when I open my eyes. It is filled by a suffocating, deathly silence. The tension is so thick it feels like it could shatter. Aunt Francesca and Aunt Marta remain frozen in place, their wide eyes brimming with shock. Mirabella stumbles back, her face ghostly pale, her cheeks glistening with tear tracks.

I glance around and catch the horrified expressions etched onto the faces of everyone present. At some point, maids and other staff had crept into the room, drawn by the chaos. Their presence only magnifies the gravity of what had just happened. Yet, even as guilt starts to gnaw at the edges of my resolve, I find not a single shred of regret within me. If Mirabella hadn't stopped me, Camila might be dead —and a part of me thinks she would've deserved it.

Now, there's no room for negotiation, no space for forgiveness. This was the final straw.

I take a step forward, my heart pounding, my voice trembling but resolute. This is long overdue.

I look at my aunt. I can tell she's trying to say something. But I don't care. I don't care about her excuses or her manipulations. She's nothing to me now.

"Get out," I rasp. "Out of this house. Out of our lives. If I ever see your face again, I won't stop."

Camila doesn't respond, still choking and gasping on the floor. At length, she finds her feet and runs out of the room.

I shift my gaze to Francesca and Marta, the anger simmering in me spilling over. "All of you," I say, my voice rising. "This place is no longer your home."

The stunned silence deepens as they exchange nervous and exit as well.

Turning my back on her, I focus solely on Mirabella, my arms wrapping around her as if shielding her from the poison that has tainted this family for far too long. Whatever monster I was called, whatever darkness they tried to pull me into, I won't let it win.

It's over.

45

MIRABELLA

The first chill of November nips at my skin as I sit on the front porch of our new house. It's a small place, but compared to where we used to live, it feels like a haven. That thought should be enough to comfort me.

After everything we've endured—the fire, moving into the Greco estate, moving out again, and finally landing a stable internship—I'm grateful to afford a place of our own.

The neighborhood is a clear improvement—quieter, safer, with tidy, modest homes lining well-kept streets instead of cracked roads and peeling paint. Our new house even has a little fenced-in yard, and although the wooden swing beneath me creaks with each gentle sway, it feels like a treasure.

I pull my oversized sweater tighter against the cold, my hands instinctively cradling my belly beneath the thick wool. I'm showing much more now, my belly is rounder, firmer, and I've become obsessed with caressing its gentle curve.

The fact that I'm pregnant— carrying not one, but two

lives within me—still fills me with a mix of disbelief and quiet joy. In just a few months, I'll be a mother. Giulia will be an aunt, Mamma a grandmother, and Nonna a great-grandmother. Nonna, in particular, I think, is the most excited about my pregnancy.

It's funny, really, considering how indifferent she was toward Ettore in the beginning. Actually, indifferent might be too generous—downright hostile feels more accurate.

After I was discharged from the hospital, Nonna declared our home a *No Ettore Zone*. She wouldn't let anyone so much as mention his name. When he came to visit, she wouldn't let him past the front door. The one time she did, she made him stand there like a deliveryman holding the flowers he'd brought me as she stared him down as if she was deciding whether to waterboard him with holy water.

But over time, I've watched their dynamic shift. His persistence—and maybe a touch of his tragic "kicked puppy" vibe—seems to have chipped away at her resolve. Her countless sharp jabs and snide comments never fazed him, and somewhere along the line, their verbal sparring turned into a strange, almost endearing routine. The insults softened, the eye rolls became less frequent, and now they actually look forward to outwitting each other.

Imagine my shock when Nonna—*Nonna!*—became his loudest advocate. She calls him constantly now, pestering him to bring over anything and everything she thinks I might need.

One time, it was pickled artichokes "to prevent cravings." Another time, an industrial fan "to keep her precious *bis-nipoti* from getting too warm in my belly."

When I finally confronted her about it, she crossed herself dramatically and went full-on spiritual deflection mode.

"Mia cara," she said with an exaggerated sigh, *"children are a gift from God. Even if their father is a control-obsessed fool with a face like a sad mouse, who am I to judge? I wouldn't be a good Christian if I didn't accept him—especially since he practically lives here now, coming over here every day like some dejected stray cat."*

Her logic was, as always, bulletproof. And now, Ettore is practically part of the family, whether she'll admit it or not.

The rest of my family has adjusted to him, too. As so have we to his.

Vittorio has made himself the self-appointed curator of our movie nights, dropping by with carefully selected films and snack suggestions. Francesca and Leonardo, meanwhile, have taken Giulia under their wing, helping her settle into her new school since the move. They've somehow turned into the older siblings I didn't realize she needed.

And me? I'm still trying to figure out how to fit into this new life. Alessia and Giovanni stop by occasionally, and their visits are a comfort, but they don't fully fill the ache I feel for what's been lost.

I sigh as I watch the neighborhood kids racing their bikes up and down the street. The crisp air carries the scent of freshly cut grass and the faint aroma of whatever masterpiece Nonna is cooking in the kitchen—something involving enough garlic to ward off a small vampire coven. Everything should feel perfect.

And, in many ways, it does.

My family is safe and healthy. The bills are paid. Mamma is recovering better than I'd ever hoped—her medications and treatments are finally within reach, and she's regaining a vitality I haven't seen in years. For the first time, we're experiencing a stability that feels almost miraculous. We're not rich, but we don't need to be. Life is finally steady.

And yet, there's a gnawing emptiness that refuses to go away.

Because he's not here.

The man I am madly, recklessly in love with.

The man I am *still* married to.

I miss him. I miss the way his presence fills a room—intense and commanding yet comforting in a way I never thought I'd crave. I miss the way his hands—rough and calloused from years of being so hardened—soften when they touch me, as if I'm the only delicate thing in his entire world.

I miss the way his voice wraps around my name, making it sound like something sacred.

I miss the way he looks at me as though I'm his light in the darkness, even when he's too proud or too stubborn to say it.

It's been over two months since everything happened.

Since I left the Greco estate—since I left Ettore. But even in his absence, his presence looms over my life. I see it in the brand-new water heater that mysteriously appeared when we moved in, the weekly deliveries of fresh produce, and how he never misses a doctor's appointment. Even in his unexpected visits, just to check in, remind me he's still here in ways I can't escape.

Ettore's attentiveness makes it even harder to emotionally stay away. I try to picture a future without him—my children growing up in a loving home, surrounded by care and security, in a neighborhood where everyone cares about the person next door. It's an idyllic vision, one I desperately want to hold onto.

But every time I imagine that perfect life, he slips into

the picture unbidden. Every fucking time, to the point where it's become frustrating. And when he's not there, the future feels hollow, incomplete.

"Mirabella, *Cara*, come inside before you catch a cold," Nonna calls from the kitchen. Through the window, I see her stirring a pot of tomato soup. The rich, savory aroma wafts out into the crisp evening air, making my stomach growl.

I rise from the swing, wrapping my arms around myself for warmth as I step inside. The small living room is cozy; Giulia is sprawled on the couch, completely engrossed in the latest Marvel movie. The kitchen is bathed in a soft yellow glow across the linoleum floor, its warmth wrapping around me like a blanket.

Nonna gestures toward the table where a steaming bowl of soup waits. "Sit. Eat," she orders in her no-nonsense tone. Since I became pregnant, she's made it her personal mission to keep me well fed, preparing three meals a day without fail and even packing lunch for me on workdays.

"*Grazie*, Nonna," I say with a smile as I sink into the chair, letting the warmth of the soup chase away the chill.

"You're always out on that damned swing," she grumbles. "It's fall now—the evenings are cold."

"I was wearing a sweater, Nonna," I reply, rolling my eyes.

Mamma shuffles into the room, draped in a shawl she recently knitted herself. She's taken up knitting as a hobby, which explains why everyone in the house now owns at least one fall-themed sweater.

She takes the seat across from me, and I can't help but smile. It still feels like a small miracle to see her upright and vibrant again.

"Someone's in a good mood," I tease as Nonna places a

bowl of soup in front of her. "Does it have anything to do with your physical therapy class?"

Mamma's cheeks flush a faint pink, confirming my suspicion. She's met someone—Cade, a widower with three grown children. She insists it's nothing serious, but her blush tells another story.

She smirks, her tone playful. "And someone's in a bad mood. Does it have anything to do with your husband?"

Her words make me pause, the warmth of the soup suddenly unable to reach the cold ache inside me.

Nonna's laughter rings through the kitchen, light and mischievous, as I release an exasperated sigh. "Why do you always get so defensive when I bring him up?" I ask, rolling my eyes.

"Because there's nothing going on between us," Mamma retorts, her voice a little flustered.

"Oh, admit it, Isi," Nonna says, her grin widening as she settles beside Mamma, clearly enjoying herself. "You are crushing that man."

"Oh my God, Nonna. It's, *'You have a crush on that man,'* not whatever you just said," Giulia pipes up from the living room, her voice dripping with teenage sass.

"Óh, *stai zitta!* What do you know about anything?" Nonna shoots back, a playful spark in her eyes.

"A crush?" My mother asks incredulously. "I'm too old for that, Mamma!"

Nonna smirks, clearly unfazed. "Too old? Nonsense! You're never too old for a little romance. Look at me—I'm ancient, and I still know how to appreciate a good looking man! And no, Ettore does not qualify."

I can't help but laugh, but I'm also secretly relieved to see Mamma's usual stoic exterior cracking just a little.

"No one is too old for crushes," I chime in with a sly

smile. "You like him. And from everything we've gathered, *he* likes you, too. So why are you pushing him away?"

She scoffs, waving me off. "You're one to talk."

My smile falters. "What's that supposed to mean?"

Mamma's eyes soften as they settle on me. "You've been pushing Ettore away for weeks now…"

"Our situations are completely different," I counter, my voice sharper than I intended.

Nonna leans forward. "Give the man a chance, Cara. He's proven himself. I almost feel bad for him now."

I gape at her in disbelief. "I can't believe you're both ganging up on me right now. I thought you hated him."

Nonna shrugs, unapologetic. "Like I said, he's proven himself. I think he really loves you, Mira. Just like I know you love him, too."

Her words strike a nerve, and I look down, tracing aimless patterns in my soup with the spoon. "It's complicated," I murmur. "Yes, Ettore has changed, but I don't know if I can trust it. Or if I can trust myself around him."

Mamma reaches across the table, her hand warm and steady as it rests over mine. "You're scared, and that's understandable," she says softly. "But love isn't always supposed to be simple. Sometimes, it's about taking risks, even when it's terrifying."

Her words hang heavy in the air, their weight pressing on my chest. Ettore is a risk—one I'm not sure I have the courage to take again no matter how much every part of me still aches for him.

∼

LONG AFTER DINNER, Mamma's words linger in my mind as I rock gently back and forth on the porch swing. The sky is a canvas of deep blues, sprinkled with stars that shimmer like tiny diamonds. The cold air bites at my cheeks, my breath forming soft white clouds in the stillness.

The quiet is broken by the low hum of an approaching car. My heart leaps when I recognize the sleek black vehicle pulling up in front of the white picket fence. Ettore steps out, his tall frame silhouetted against the headlights. He visits regularly, but it doesn't matter—his presence still always sets my heart racing.

His dark coat flows behind him as he strides into the yard, his black boots crunching softly on the stones and grass.

"Hey," I greet him softly when he gets to me.

"Hey," he replies, his voice low and warm. He leans down to press a kiss to my forehead, and his hand instinctively moves to rest on my belly. The simple gesture makes my breath hitch. His hand lingers for a moment, protective and reverent, before he pulls away and sits on the wooden porch beside me.

We've been doing this dance for weeks now, but still, I never get used to it.

"How are you? How's the morning sickness?" he asks, his gaze intense, scanning me as though looking for any signs of distress.

"It's better now," I reassure him, giving him a small smile. "I don't get it as badly as I did during the first trimester. Though, last week was rough. I think I ate something that didn't quite agree with me. But I'm okay now."

His jaw tightens slightly, the flicker of concern not escaping my notice. Last week, when he found out how sick I'd been, he'd been furious with me for not telling him sooner—even though the symptoms had only started the day before. He'd rushed me to the doctor without a second thought, his concern evident in every action.

"How was work?" I ask, shifting the focus.

"The usual," he replies. "I was driving by and thought I'd check in on you."

I raise an eyebrow, skepticism creeping into my voice. "It's Sunday and your office isn't anywhere near my neighborhood, Ettore."

"Oh really?" He grins, feigning confusion. "Swear I thought I opened a new branch just down the street."

I stare at him, the playful gleam in his eyes making my heart race. "Ettore..." I warn him, not because I think he's messing with me, but because I know him too well. He could actually do that—buy an entire freaking building and make it a subsidiary of his company, all just to be closer to me.

The thought makes my stomach flutter, but I keep my voice steady, eyeing him suspiciously. "You'd actually do that, wouldn't you?"

His smile widens, that trademark glint in his eye. "Wouldn't be the first time."

I roll my eyes, though I can't help but laugh. "You're impossible."

"Maybe," he replies, leaning closer. "But I'm *your* impossible."

His smirk widens, but then he shifts, his voice dropping into something more sincere. "Well, you're right," he says, a small, teasing smile playing on his lips. "I just wanted to see you. Had a shitty day and figured I should be around what makes me happy."

The glint in his eyes sends a shiver down my spine, and for a brief moment, I forget everything else, my breath catching in my chest.

He's always had that effect on me. The way he looks at me—as if I'm the only thing in the world that matters.

I don't say anything after that, because, well, I don't have anything to say.

His honesty—and the way his eyes glint with something gives me butterflies—leaves me momentarily breathless. We've already had the conversation about boundaries. I told him to stop confessing his feelings or asking me to come back. If I were to return, it will be on my terms, not because I feel pressured.

It will be at the right time.

An uncomfortable silence stretches between us, thick with everything we're not saying. It's one of those things I still haven't gotten used to—the awkwardness, the tension, the discomfort. But most of all, it's the undeniable clarity that we still want each other, even after everything.

I catch myself wanting to say something, anything, to fill the space between us. But the words get stuck, tangled up with all the jumbled thoughts swirling in my mind. His gaze lingers on me, and for a moment, it feels like we're on the edge of something.

Neither of us moves, but the air feels charged. There's a pull, a magnetic force we can't ignore, even if we tried. But how do we bridge the gap between us? How do we move past the mess we've made of things?

The thickness in the air crackles, feeling like an invisible thread pulling us together even as we try to resist it. Our eyes lock and I see the vulnerability he's trying to hide—the longing, the desire, the love.

Something inside me shifts in that moment, and suddenly "the right time" I'd been waiting for feels like now.

I struggle to steady my breathing as I finally find my voice. "Take me home."

Ettore freezes, the words hanging between us like a delicate thread. Then his eyes light up with understanding, followed by relief, joy, and something darker—something that sends a chill down my spine and sets a fire in my heart.

He stands up slowly and reaches out his hand towards me with a deliberate, almost reverent gesture. My throat tightens as I reach back towards him, feeling the anticipation coursing through my body like electricity.

This is it—the moment I have both dreaded and longed for.

The moment I tell this frustratingly unpredictable man that I love him.

46

ETTORE

As the car rolls down the winding driveway of the Greco estate, a current of electricity buzzes between us, igniting every nerve ending in my body. The anticipation thickens the air, and I can feel the heat of Mirabella's presence through my thick coat.

It's like a tempting flame, drawing me closer to consume me. Every stolen glance reveals the same desperate need reflected in her eyes—a longing that has been simmering, unchecked, for months.

The car comes to a stop with a loud screech in front of the house. We step outside, and the cool night air contrasts sharply with the warmth radiating from our bodies. The world around me fades into nothingness, and the only thing I can focus on is her.

Reaching for her hand, I ignore the jolt of pleasure that races through me at the simple touch. Her fingers intertwine with mine, soft and trusting, and I lead her up the familiar steps of the house and through the grand doors. The echo of our footsteps on the marble floors feels deafening in the silence, each step carrying us closer to the inevitable.

Up the staircase and down the hall, we arrive at my bedroom—our bedroom. The moment the door closes behind us, the thin thread of restraint I've clung to snaps, and I'm capturing her lips with mine. She moans at the contact, kissing me back with equal fervor.

Her arms wrap around my neck, pulling me closer until there's no space left between us. My hands find her waist, gripping her as if she might disappear if I let go. Her touch is just as desperate as her hands glide over my shoulders, pushing my coat off and letting it fall unceremoniously to the floor. The sensation of her fingers through the thin fabric of my shirt makes my pulse race, each touch unraveling me further.

As soon as the material drops to the floor, I immediately lift her up, carrying her to the bed while she wraps her legs around my waist. I lay her back against the soft mattress, my body following suit to kiss her lips and drag my mouth down her neck. I run my hands over every inch of her body, greedy for every single inch of her.

She moans as my hands skim across her breasts before slipping beneath the straps of her dress to pull it off before unclasping her bra. I pull one sensitive nipple between my lips as my fingers trail lower down her torso, brushing the sensitive skin of her inner thighs until my fingertips find their target.

"Ettore." She releases a choked gasp when I push her thong to one side to slip two fingers inside her. She arches her hips slightly, showing me just how much she wants this. I can feel her arousal pulsing against me, feel her pussy clenching around my fingers.

I drag my lips from her breasts down to the firm curve of her stomach.

"I love you, Mirabella," I whisper against her skin before pressing a long kiss on her stomach.

I hear her release a sharp exhale as one hand sinks into my hair. "I love you too, Ettore."

Her confession dissolves into a moan when I insert a third finger inside her and begin to pump. She moans loudly as her hands begin to hastily unbutton my shirt. I lean back slightly to watch her pussy while I fill her up and tease her with my fingers.

"Your pussy is as pretty as I remembered," I whisper as I stare down at her, taking in her lush curves. "So tight...so ready to take my cock..."

"Ettore," she moans, pushing my shirt over my shoulders and then tugging at my pants.

"So impatient," I growl, continuing to pump her slowly as her long fingers fumble to unbuckle my belt and undo my zipper. When she finally has my fly open, she slides her hand underneath, running her warm palm over my hard stomach muscles. As her fingers touch the head of my erection, I groan in satisfaction. She knows just what buttons to press to drive me insane.

"I want you now, Ettore," she whispers, looking up at me with pleading, needy eyes.

"Fuck," I say through gritted teeth as I hastily shove down my pants and pull her thong off completely. I shove my boxer briefs down my legs before positioning myself behind her and adjusting between her spread legs.

We are both lying on our sides, and I am being cautious not to put too much weight on her bump.

When I slide into her slick, wet heat, we both groan at the sensation. I roll my hips slowly, taking my time to savor and enjoy the moment. Mirabella leans back to kiss me again, wrapping her arms around my neck and one leg around mine to hold me close. A wave of ecstasy ripples through my chest and explodes into my brain as she starts to grind herself against me faster and harder.

My balls tighten with each stroke, and I start thrusting faster, deeper.

Her nails dig into my shoulders as she calls out my name in pleasure.

"That's it, baby," I groan, sliding one hand around her throat while I find a steady pace that hits her right where she likes.

"Oh, fuck," she chokes. "Ettore..."

The seductive sounds she makes are like music to my ears, sending shivers down my spine. I rock my hips harder, faster, and deeper until I feel her body stiffen slightly before she begins to shudder. My own orgasm hits me, and we ride out our climax together.

When we both come down from our high, I lean slightly back to take in her flushed face.

"Welcome home, Bella."

She laughs, and fuck...I've missed that sound.

"I'm happy to be home," she says dreamily, gazing at me with adoration in her eyes. "I missed you."

I lean in to kiss her again, softly, tenderly and full of the emotions words can't convey.

"I love you so much," I whisper against her lips.

She smiles back at me. "I love you, too." And minutes later, she falls asleep in my bed—our bed—a place where we can finally be together after being apart for far too long.

GOLDEN SUNLIGHT STREAMS through the curtains, painting delicate patterns across the bed and bathing the room in a soft glow. I wake slowly, cocooned in the warmth of the sheets—and the warmth of Mirabella.

She lies curled against me, her breathing steady, her dark hair spilling over the pillow like a cascade of silk. The air still carries traces of last night, a reminder of how far we've come.

I watch her for a moment, unable to tear my gaze away. From a one-night stand—a night born from a whirlwind of adrenaline and gratitude after I saved her life—to this.

Falling hard and fast, we've weathered a rollercoaster of emotions, yet every twist and turn is one I'm more than willing to go through again because it's worth it.

Carefully, I reach out and brush a strand of hair from her face. She stirs slightly but doesn't wake, her peaceful expression tugging a small smile from me. She looks so innocent, so content.

A glance at the clock on the wall tells me it's 7:36 a.m. I slip out of bed quietly, not wanting to disturb her, and head to the kitchen.

"S-sir!" Paula stammers, startled as I enter, heading straight for the coffee machine.

"You can leave, Paula," I instruct calmly. "Also, let the others on kitchen duty know that I'll handle breakfast myself today."

Her wide eyes betray her surprise, but she nods quickly and hurries off, likely wondering why I, of all people, am suddenly interested in cooking—a task I haven't taken on in years.

The answer is simple: Mirabella.

I set about preparing coffee for myself and tea for her. As the kettle comes to a boil, I crack a few eggs into a pan, the aroma of sizzling bacon soon filling the air.

Just as I flip the bacon, I hear soft footsteps behind me.

Turning, I see Mirabella standing in the doorway, her eyes adjusting to the light. Sleep still lingers in her expression, but when her gaze finds me, a slow, sweet smile spreads across her face.

"Good morning," I say, my voice warm as I focus on the pan.

"Good morning...Chef Ettore," she teases, her voice carrying a playful hum as she approaches. "I didn't know you could cook."

I chuckle, glancing at her over my shoulder. "I'm not just some spoiled rich boy, Bella."

Her laughter rings out, and she wraps her arms around me from behind, her touch sending a surge of warmth through me. In that moment, I can see our future—a life filled with laughter, quiet mornings like this, the sound of little feet running through the house.

It's a vision of perfection.

As minutes roll by, we settle into an easy rhythm, working together to finish breakfast, our lighthearted banter flowing like music. When the food is ready, I serve her a plate of fried eggs and bacon, setting it on the small round table in the kitchen.

Just as we sit down, the television in the background breaks through our quiet moment.

"We're receiving reports of a tragic accident involving the infamous mobster Matteo Abruzzi," the news anchor says, her voice heavy with feigned neutrality. *"Early details describe the scene as catastrophic. Witnesses report his car veered off a sharp cliff on the outskirts of the city, plummeting into the canyon below. Authorities state the vehicle was found mangled beyond recognition, with no chance of survival for the driver."*

Mirabella's hand freezes mid-air, the glass of water she was reaching for forgotten. Her wide eyes meet mine, searching, questioning. The silent conversation is deafening.

Was this you? Did you...?

"You know me, Bella," I say, my tone calm, deliberate. "I had to make him pay for what he did to you. To your family."

Her lips part as if to argue, but she hesitates. For once, she doesn't scold me or jump to lecture me on limits or consequences. Instead, she studies me. And maybe, just maybe, there's a part of her that understands.

"Ettore..." she begins softly, but the words trail off.

I take her hesitation as my cue, moving to kneel before her.

My hands find her face, cradling it delicately.

"You are mine, Bella. Mine to protect. To love. To cherish," I say, my voice steady, filled with an unshakable resolve. "I'd die a thousand deaths and fight a million wars before I let any harm come near you. For every battle you faced before you met me, I'll make sure to obliterate those memories alongside the bastards who caused them. You'll never have to face them again."

My thumb brushes her cheek as I hold her gaze, my words pouring out like a vow I've made a hundred times before—and will make a hundred more. "I'll always fight for you. Always. And that includes putting assholes like Abruzzi, who've already earned their spot in my black book, six feet under without a second thought. You're my world. Protecting you is my purpose, and I'll never hesitate."

My words hang in the air, charged with sincerity as I lean closer to her. I seal my promise with a kiss. A declaration of my commitment and loyalty. I pour all of my love and determination into the moment.

When we finally part, her eyes shimmer with unspoken

emotion and her breath catches ever so slightly. She gazes at me as if I've given her the entire universe, but still manages to tease me with her soft voice, saying, "You sure know how to make a girl feel like royalty, don't you?"

"Royalty? Damned right. You're my queen, Bella. And anyone who forgets that will have to deal with me."

"You're impossible."

I lean closer, my lips a breath away from hers. "Impossible? I prefer *devoted*, but I'll take it."

"Devoted? Is that what we're calling your particular brand of crazy now?"

"Call it what you want, Kitten," I reply, smirking. "But you're stuck with me. Barbarian, lunatic—whatever label you slap on me—I'm yours, Bella. Always."

"Oh, absolutely you are. And while we're at it, let's not forget to add *personal chaos magnet* to the list."

"A chaos magnet who keeps your world in order. Admit it, you'd be bored without me."

She tilts her head, pretending to consider. "Hmm...possibly. But I'd also get a lot more sleep."

I can't help but laugh at that, pulling her even closer. "Well, I'll just have to keep making it worth your while."

She shakes her head, but there's a smile on her lips. "I'm still not sure how I ended up with you."

"Fate," I say simply, my voice low. "And because no one else would dare keep up with you."

She laughs again, and I capture the sound with a kiss. Her hands slide up to rest against my chest, and I know in that moment that everything I've done—everything I'll ever do—is worth it.

For her. For us.

For our twins.

When we finally break apart, the news anchor's voice cuts through again.

"Police are continuing to investigate the circumstances surrounding the crash, but given the extensive damage and lack of evidence, it may remain a mystery."

Mirabella arches an eyebrow at me, and I shrug, entirely unapologetic. "What? Sometimes karma just needs a little...encouragement."

She swats my shoulder, but her smile betrays her. "You're lucky I love you."

"Oh yeah? Why don't you show me just how lucky *I am* to love you," I murmur, pulling her into my arms. Her laughter softens into a contented sigh as she leans into me, fitting perfectly like she always does.

In the warmth of her embrace, I know I've found my peace, no matter how many wars I've waged to get here.

I seal the moment with another kiss. It's slow and deliberate, a quiet declaration that no chaos, no fight, and no storm could ever steal this from me.

I realize I've found my peace, my home. This—her in my arms—will always be my favorite thing to come back to.

THE END

If you enjoyed *Dark Mafia Bride,* then you'll also like *Dark Mafia Vows*.

(Click Here to get Dark Mafia Vows)

Ginny is forced to marry her brother's enemy in this arranged marriage, enemies to lovers romance that will leave you yearning for more. ***Read Chapter One on the next page!***

SNEAK PEEK

Dark Mafia Vows

She's my enemy's sister, but that only makes me want her more.
Her brother sold her off, and now she belongs to me—she just doesn't know it yet.

Ginevra Bianchi is nothing like the spoiled billionaire princess and politician's fiancée I thought she'd be.
She doesn't bow, doesn't break, and that smart mouth of hers is going to get her into serious trouble—my kind of trouble.

Her family owes me, and I always collect.
An arranged marriage to the woman I can't stop thinking about? I'll take that deal.
The more she fights, the more I want to break her, make her bend to my will.

I see the fear in her gaze when I get too close, but I see the fire too.

Now, I don't just want her submission. I want all of her.

She doesn't understand—I always win.

And when it comes to her, I won't stop until she's mine in every way that matters.

She thinks she can escape me, but what she doesn't realize is, I'd burn the whole world down to keep her—and protect our unborn child at any cost.

(Click Here to get Dark Mafia Vows)

CHAPTER ONE
Ginevra

My knuckles are white as I grip my steering wheel firmly, trying to navigate the congested streets at 8:30 in the evening. The roads are packed with cars, their honking horns drowning out the music blaring from my car's Bluetooth speaker.

As I sing along to the lyrics of Pharrell Williams' "Happy," my stomach twists with nerves, trying to distract myself from the impending breakdown that's bound to occur any minute from now.

I hate being late. I hate being stuck in traffic, and most importantly, I hate it when my brother is pissed at me.

As if on cue, my music pauses abruptly, overridden by the shrill sound of my ringtone.

"Shit," I mutter under my breath as Lorenzo's name flashes on my phone screen.

I place a hand over my racing heart and clear my throat,

forcing a strained smile as I answer the call. "Hey, big brother—"

"You're this close to getting a security detail and a nanny, Ginny," Lorenzo's impatient voice booms through the speakers. "Where are you? The event started already!"

My smile wavers, and I let out a sigh. It's not the first time he's made this threat. We both know assigning a security detail would be pointless. I've managed to evade every bodyguard and infuriate every nanny since day one, much to Lorenzo's consternation.

"I know, I know! I'm on my way," I reply, trying to keep my tone light, but my frustration bubbles beneath the surface. "I've been stuck in traffic for almost thirty minutes now."

His exasperated sigh fills the car's interior. "You wouldn't have been stuck if you'd left the house earlier. Or, hell, if you'd let your fiancé pick you up."

I roll my eyes as he continues. "Rinaldo is already here, and he's getting pissed. He wanted to introduce you to some important people."

"I got held up discussing ideas for the bakery. You know how it is."

"Discussing ideas?" he scoffs. "What the hell, Ginny?"

I steal a glance at the dashboard and huff. "Relax, I'm right on time. The party doesn't really even start until eight."

"Ginny, the event started thirty minutes ago," he informs me. "I must've told you the time a hundred times, but then again, you've always had selective hearing."

I groan. "It's not my fault today."

"Hmm," Lorenzo hums sarcastically. "Where and when have I heard that before? Oh yeah— from you, every other day."

His tone makes me bristle. Lorenzo has never fancied

the idea of me starting a business of my own. He's always taken pride in taking care of me, and now that the family business is facing challenges, he's more determined than ever to keep me under his wing.

Rinaldo Sanchez, my fiancé, hails from a family of affluent politicians and is one of Lorenzo's business associates. According to my brother's grand plan, Rinaldo is supposed to ensure I'm well taken care of.

So, the idea of me starting my own bakery? It drives him up the wall.

"I've been out with the people who can help me." I try to make my tone light. "Small business owners, locals, exactly the kind of people who know what works. You know that."

"Is this really necessary, Ginny? You could just focus on socializing with Rinaldo, keeping up appearances for the company, and maybe your upcoming marriage," he huffs, and I roll my eyes again. "Why do you even need this bakery?"

I can almost hear him pacing on the other end, his over-protectiveness almost suffocating. I don't take offense, though. It comes from a good place. We've been on our own for so long, separated from the rest of our extended family, that we're all we have for each other. I'm just as protective of Lorenzo as he is of me.

Okay, maybe not as much. My brother can be a bit overbearing, but I still love him.

Lorenzo loves me too, that much I know. He's the best big brother anyone could ever ask for, and if there's a next life, I'd definitely want him right back in his role as protector, pseudo parent, and sibling. He's been my only family since our parents died, and I wouldn't trade him for anything.

If only he didn't still see me as that five-year-old with missing teeth, pigtails, and a jean romper. It's frustrating how he treats me like I'm made of glass, something fragile that needs to be handled with care.

I can't even tell the most important person in my life about my passion because he thinks I don't need to make money, that I should be devoting my time to broadening my social circle and prepping to begin my role as a trophy wife.

"It's a passion project, Enzo." I feign a chuckle, trying to lighten up his mood. "And how many times do I have to tell you I'm doing this for myself?"

"Passion project or not, you're late. You need to prioritize family over... whatever this is."

"I promise I'll be there in no time. Just give me a moment," I tell him. "The traffic is clearing up."

I hear his heavy exhale before the goes dead.

"Rude," I scoff, pressing the gas pedal as my car inches forward.

The song resumes right where it left off, and I hum along, feeling the tension in my shoulders ease just a bit. I'm finally ready to launch my bakery, and I won't let anyone—not Lorenzo, and certainly not Rinaldo—make me feel guilty about it.

I merge onto the main road, the city's tall buildings rising against the night sky, their glass shining with the city lights. Each one feels alive, showing the energy of the city, and for the first time in a long while, I feel like I'm in sync with it.

As I drive farther, the street opens up with fancy shops and nice cafes, their glowing signs lighting up the evening. I glance at the time again, and...shit, I'm running late. I hope I can still make a grand entrance with Rinaldo if I hurry.

Otherwise, he'll be pissed, too. Not that I care all that much, but having a grumpy fiancée by my side all night will definitely be my thirteenth reason.

Finally, I arrive at the luxurious hotel, its bright entrance looking inviting. The valet area is busy, and I decide not to use it. I don't want to hand over my keys in this casual outfit.

My faded blue jeans and a simple white top feel utterly inappropriate for the fancy party and the high-profile guests inside. I can already picture the glances I'll receive from the socialites if I'm caught wearing this, or worse, if any photographers or paparazzi take pictures and they end up online.

Lorenzo would be livid for sure. Rinaldo, too. I can just imagine the scandalous headlines. I shudder slightly at the thought. The last thing I want is to attract any more negative publicity to me or my brother. The best plan is to drive inside myself and change into the clothes currently sitting in the backseat of my car.

The cool air greets me as I pull into the underground parking garage. White lights flick overhead, illuminating the sea of already parked flashy cars. The concrete walls are designed with sleek artwork, and the lighting is soft, creating an inviting atmosphere. I quickly scan the space, relief washing over me when I spot an empty space near the back.

The overhead lights cast a soft glow on the polished concrete floor as I maneuver my car. I signal and steer into the spot, my eyes again glancing at the time. I exhale in relief when I realize I may not be as late as I thought.

Just as I'm about to put the car in park, a sleek, tinted sedan suddenly swerves into my lane and cuts me off. My heart races as I slam on the brakes, the tires screeching loudly against the pavement. I grip the steering wheel tighter, irritation bubbling up inside me.

"What the hell?" I hiss as my car comes to a stop.

Seriously? Who does that?

I take a moment to steady my breath, frustration coursing through me like hot embers. After everything I've gone through today, this is the last thing I need.

I throw the car into park and fling open the door, my heels clicking sharply against the concrete as I step out. The air is sharp and cool, and adrenaline courses through my veins.

The driver of the tinted car remains inside, seemingly unfazed as he scrolls through his phone, my presence not appearing to matter. My annoyance is growing.

"Excuse me!" I call out, raising my voice to cut through the low hum in the garage. "Do you mind? You just stole my spot!"

Silence. The driver doesn't even glance my way. My frustration intensifies, and I take a step closer, my heart pounding in my chest. "Hey! I'm talking to you," I shout, my hands on my hips, feeling the heat rise to my cheeks.

When he doesn't budge, I go red in anger. I raise my hand and bang the inside of my fist against his window.

That's when the driver opens the door.

"How dare you—"

My words are cut off when the culprit emerges from the car. A man steps out, tall and imposing. The familiar sharp features—high cheekbones and a strong jawline—are striking.

A deep scowl etches his handsome face, the same face gracing covers of various business magazines and news articles, giving him an air of arrogance. Dark hair frames his piercing green eyes, which seem to hold an intensity that commands attention. Dressed in a tailored suit that fits him perfectly, he exudes a stinking level of wealth.

Dario De Luca.

The name hits me like a punch to the gut, bringing back a flood of memories I'd rather forget. Me, a little girl with a silly crush, and he, my brother's former best friend, who only saw me as that and nothing more. Over the years, he has turned into the man about whom I've only heard bad things. His reputation precedes him like a storm cloud.

What is he even doing at an event like this? Last time I checked, he never socializes or attends parties like this. Lorenzo claims he sees everyone as beneath him, and now, judging from the way he's looking at me, my brother's right.

"Yes?" His tone is dismissive, as if I'm nothing more than an annoyance.

And that's when I realize that he doesn't even recognize me. I can't help but feel a mix of anger, embarrassment, and disbelief.

"Are you serious?" I reply, incredulous. "You just cut in front of me and act as if it's no big deal? I could've hit your car if I hadn't seen you in time."

He shrugs, a faint smirk tugging at the corner of his lips. "If you'd been paying attention, this wouldn't have been a problem."

I recall some of the things I've heard about him—cold, arrogant, condescending. And now, he stands before me with that smirk, proving the rumors were indeed true.

My blood boils at his words. "What?" I choke. "Are you seriously suggesting this is my fault? You're the one who—"

"It is your fault." He cuts me off sharply. "I don't insinuate."

I inhale deeply, trying to calm myself down.

"I can see that acting like an arrogant jerk comes naturally to you," I shoot back. Calm down, my ass. I'm fucking pissed.

His eyebrows raise slightly, and so does my voice. "You think you can just do whatever you want. Who the hell do you think you are?"

His green eyes harden, and I spot a hint of anger in them.

"Look," he bites out, his eyes sweeping over me dismissively. "I don't have time for this nonsense. Doesn't the staff have a different entrance?"

His voice drips with condescension, and my eyes twitch at the insult. I stand there seething, my fists clenching at my sides.

"Staff?" I splutter, staring down at my body, wincing. "I'm not the staff, I'm—"

"When I care, I'll let you know."

He turns away from me and heads to the elevator as if I'm not even worth his time. I can't believe he has the audacity to treat me like this. "You're not used to being called out, so you're walking away like the coward you are," I call after him, my voice louder and sharper than I intended.

He doesn't respond. The nerve of him!

The last time I saw Dario, he was with my brother, his aloofness and cold demeanor always getting under my skin. Memories of his dismissive remarks flood back, and I realize just how much I loathe him, especially since he doesn't even remember me.

Before I can even think it through, I find myself walking toward him, determined to catch up before he reaches the elevator.

"Hey, I'm talking to you," I call out, grabbing him by the arm to halt his movement.

He freezes, his gaze dropping to my fingers wrapped around his arm, his face twisting in disgust, as though I've just hurled a pile of excrement at him.

"Get your hands off me." His voice is cold and forbidding. If I had any brain cells in my head, I'd pretend this was an accident, laugh it off, and hurry away. But I didn't get where I am by running.

"So you're not going to apologize?" I snarl.

My heart pounds against my chest, each beat resonating like a warning bell, urging me to stop. But I ignore it.

"Apologize for what, exactly?" His tone is casual, almost bored.

I raise an eyebrow, feigning thoughtfulness. "Hmm, let's see. For starters, how about what I just told you? You clearly saw me going for that spot, and now you're playing dumb as if it never happened."

What are you doing? My inner voice screams at me, but it's too late to back down now.

On a list of stupid things to do, confronting Dario De Luca—the man who was once my childhood hero but is now a name synonymous with danger—tops them all.

Dario's eyes narrow and if possible, they get colder. I can't help the shiver that courses down my body, and I resist the urge to take a step backward. I'm not going to give him the satisfaction of showing him I'm scared of him or that he intimidates me.

"You have no idea who I am, do you, or you wouldn't make the idiotic mistake of laying your hands on me," he drawls, his voice dripping with disdain.

"I'm not by any means a professor of English, but I don't think that combination of words meant *I'm sorry*, so let's try again, shall we?" I retort with a bright, mocking smile. His jaw ticks in response.

I've seen countless photos of Dario online and in the newspapers our butler likes to read, but seeing him in person, tight-jawed, eyes narrowed, makes me pity the poor cameras that struggle to capture his true essence.

Dario is a stunning man. Even as a teenager roaming the halls of our house, he was an angel to my too-young eyes. How wrong I was. From what I've heard, beneath that perfectly sculpted face and full, red mouth, Dario is nothing but pure evil.

"You can't just treat people anyhow you want and think you can get away with it." I throw my hands into the air, releasing him. "That's an asshole move."

"And you assume I have a problem with being the asshole?" His brow arches in a way that's far too sexy for my liking. Everything about him is sexy, from the way his navy three-piece suit molds to his impressive physique to the way his dark hair falls over his forehead in messy waves.

His face remains impassive, and I wonder for the millionth time what happened to Dario that changed him so much. I don't remember a lot about him, but what I can remember is the dimple that used to peek out when he occasionally smiled. Now, he looks as if he hasn't smiled in years.

Suddenly, he reaches inside his suit jacket. I let out a startled sound and jump back, half-expecting him to pull out a gun and shoot me for bothering him. Instead, he withdraws a wad of cash and holds it up.

"You can have all of it if you get out of my way and forget this conversation ever happened."

I glance down at the money and then force a stiff smile. "You couldn't buy me if you tried."

"I'm not trying to buy you," he replies coolly. "I'm trying to get you out of my face."

I grit my teeth. "I wouldn't even be here, if you'd just say you're sorry, which, by the way, is the right thing to do. No. It's the least thing you can do, and—"

"You seem to enjoy the sound of your own voice far too much," he says, cocking his head. "But I don't. You're clearly a child, and I've had enough of you wasting my time," he bites out, tossing the wad of cash at me.

I flinch as it flies toward my face, and by the time I remember to catch it, it's too late. The money scatters across the floor between us.

I look up from the notes strewn about the floor, a scathing comment on the tip of my tongue, only to see that Dario is already across the garage. I watch helplessly, seething with indignation, as the elevator doors slide closed, sealing him out of view.

I stand there, fists clenched, staring at his car. For a fleeting moment, I consider doing something crazy like denting it, but I decide against it. I'm not that suicidal, and besides, I refuse to prove Dario right by acting immature.

Taking a deep breath, I try to calm the storm of emotions swirling inside me.

"What a jerk," I mutter, heading back to my car. I feel like such a fool, and I'm grateful no one was around to witness that.

I slip back into my car and find a new parking spot, and as I start maneuvering into my dress, one thought dominates my mind. Is Dario headed to the same event as I am? Will I run into him again?

I shake my head to clear the thought.

I may not know what caused the rift between Dario and my brother, but I do know that the teenage boy who used to lift me up so I could reach the Lucky Charms from the top shelf is long gone. In his place is the most gorgeous but infuriating man I've ever met.

Well, as far as I'm concerned, this entire encounter never happened. We don't run in the same circles. I'm sure I'll never see him again.

I won't let him ruin my night; I remind myself. Not at this event. Not ever.

Good riddance.

(Click Here to get Dark Mafia Vows)

Printed in Great Britain
by Amazon